HONEY IN THE MEAD

Dorothy Macnab Ramsay

First published in Great Britain 1991 by

Pittenhope Publishing, 72 Marmion Drive, Glenrothes, Fife.

ISBN 0 9519704 1 0 (2nd Revised Edition)

Printed and bound in Great Britain by

Atprint Ltd ., Glenrothes, Fife, Scotland.

To Jim, who inspired

For Laurie, June,
Lisa, Scott and Lauren.

This is the first novel in a Trilogy of Celtic Queens
by the same author

The Flame Within
The Harps are Hushed

Dorothy Macnab Ramsay was born in Rothesay, Isle of Bute, and lived for thirty years in Glasgow. Married with a son she now lives in Fife where she discovered the Picts. She had always believed she was descended from the Scots who came to Dal Riata from Ireland around 500 AD. Now she proudly claims that the name 'Mac N' Ab' means that she is descended from the Pictish clerics who were called Abs.

The Flame Within won the Constable Trophy in 1989

CHARACTERS
*Named in written records

PRETANI

Caterin	Princess of Pretani, daughter of King Bridei
*Bridei	King of Pretani, Overlord of Alba, son of Maelgwn
Devana	Caterin's aunt
*Cennalath	Devana's husband, Mormaer of Enegus cum Moerne
*Broichan	Chief Drui
Nechtan	Caterin's bodyguard
Iogena	Caterin's Dal Riatan slave
Artcois	Commander of the Pretani fleet
Maelchon	son of Artcois
Talorc	" " "
Drust	friend of Caterin
Prent	" " "
Fortrei	" " "
Wise Cau	the Law-Giver
Aeron	Guardian of the People's Treasure
Amis	his wife
Uurad	Officer in the King's Guard
Forgan	Deputy Drui
Uedo	a Drui
Nemone	a Drui
Leone	student Drui
Derelei	" "
Veleda	a Wise Woman
Eildon	a bard
Delys	Clan Mother of Pitmuies community
Aortan	her brother
Monikie	her daughter
Tomas	her son
Uuen	" "
Tarain	Uuen's wife
Gwair	Monikie's lover

DAL RIATANS

*Aedan	King of Dal Riata
*Dolmech	his wife
*Artur	his son
*Myrddin	(or Merlin) Artur's companion

NORSE FOLK

Gustav	leader of Norse community
Ingrid	his wife
Hild	a girl
Haral Smooth-Tongue	a Northman
Sigurd, the Stout	" "
Einar Belly-Shaker	" "

EIREANS

*Colum Cille	known as St. Columba
*Diarmait	High King of Tara
*Finnian	Bishop of Moville
Conaing	a goldsmith
*Ciaran	Abbot of Durrow
*Brendan	(the Navigator) Bishop of Clonfert
*Lasrian	Bishop of Devenish

OTHERS

Gort Mac Dafydd	Prince of Gwynedd
*Rhun	King of Gwynedd, brother to Gort
Hunnid	Chief of the Mountain People
*Mynyddog	King of Dun Eidyn
*Cynon	Prince of Eidyn
*Aneirin	bard of the Gododdin

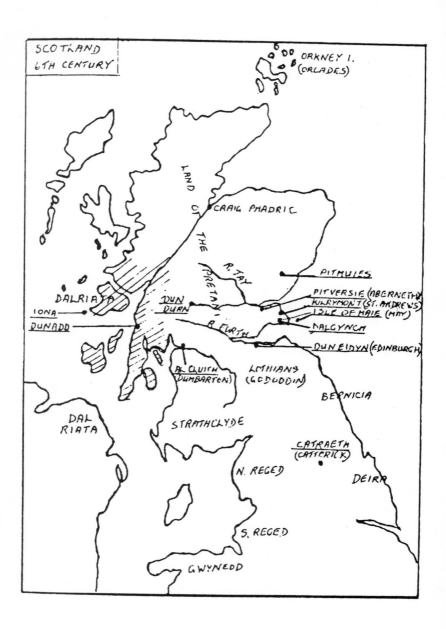

SCOTLAND
6TH CENTURY

ORKNEY I.
(ORCADES)

LAND OF THE PICTS

CRAIG PHADRIC

R. TAY

PITMUIES

PITVERSIE (ABERNETHY)
KILRYMONT (ST. ANDREWS)
ISLE OF MAIE (MAY)

DALRIATA

DUN DURN

IONA

DUNADD

R. FIRTH

DALGYNCH

DUN EIDYN (EDINBURGH)

AL CLUITH
(DUMBARTON)

LOTHIANS
(GODODDIN)

BERNICIA

DAL RIATA

STRATHCLYDE

CATRAETH
(CATTERICK)

N. REGED

DEIRA

S. REGED

GWYNEDD

IRELAND

UI NEILL LANDS

DERRY

DAL RIATH

DEVENISH

ULSTER

MEATH

CONNAUGHT

TARA

DUBLIN (DUIBHLINHE)

CLONFERT

VIKING SETTLEMENT

LEINSTER

MUNSTER

CHAPTER ONE

If Caterin had known there was Marriage talk in the air and a Prince on his way, she would never have gone on the boar-hunt. It had been the first warm day after the passing of the snow-winds. Her body had ached with the need to breathe in the damp clammy smell of the Royal forest. Her spirit had longed to feel the surge as the Earth Mother roused herself from her sleep.

A new and rigorous training schedule had deprived her of her usual comrades. Still she ought to have known better than to ride out with a parcel of raw youths, fresh from fostering. But her father had been adamant. 'Go with a retinue or not at all!'

A skirl of song whirled about her in three different keys.

"In the oak-mast of the forest we routed the fierce-tusked boar.
Silent as deer, we stalked him. Swift and sure were our spears.
Skilled we are as the hunting wolf."

Caterin's long honey-gold plait swung as she urged her mare forward.

"A plague on your empty bragging and clumsy verse-making!"

She turned relieved green eyes towards the Citadel that dominated the skyline, its sandstone walls warm and mellow in the afternoon sun.

And so she missed the shadow that slid behind the tree-trunk, the shaft of sunlight that dappled a head, the flutter of a hand that lifted a bow. She did not know of the arrow that came from inside a tunic, next to the heat of a heart. Nor of eyes that sighted along the shaft. She did not hear the crack of the breaking arrow. Nor the wail of anguish that burst from the cold damp pit that was someone's heart. She only knew that the wind had shifted bringing a streaming coldness from the sea.

She nudged her mare to a trot, eager to exchange her sweaty leather trousers and blood-stained cloak for a herb-scented robe and a scatter of jewels. For her father had hinted at an interesting visitor in the Banqueting Hall that night.

So it happened that she was the first to emerge from behind the birchwood that kept pace with the road, a road that began as a track among the white mountains and northern forests and led straight as an arrow to the Royal Capital at Dalgynch. And she was the first to sight in the distance a troop of horsemen with pack-horses approaching along the road from the south.

Her interest quickened. Their leader rode a handsome bay with negligent ease. Dark-clad legs in stirrups proclaimed him a foreigner. The heat of the late afternoon sun had caused him to throw back his riding cloak, showing a shirt open over a broad chest. He displayed his body with pride, as well he might, since it was lithe and graceful.

Her eyes lingered on the thrusting of leather thighs against the flanks of the horse. A current of excitement flickered from her breast to her groin, leaving a trail of disturbing warmth. Not for the first time she cursed the Pretani Law of Queenship that kept her a virgin at the ripe age of fourteen. Oh, it was irksome, when her blood sang a lusty song as it raced through her veins. And the warm moist air of this new Budding Season tasted like honeydew on her lips.

The Prince checked his mount in front of the carved gateway, tilting his head to study the skulls and antlers that decorated it. Her lips curved in a grin, guessing he was looking for the long-haired heads of her father's enemies. But only the Druad knew where these trophies were lodged. King Bridei had no need to boast of his conquests. They were sung by every bard from the Orcades to the Forth and beyond.

The nobleman's trumpeter cantered forward lifting his horn. At the same moment, the ragged voices behind her rose in another impromptu verse, drawing the indifferent gaze of the horseman. She gave him a brilliant smile with just the right amount of condescension. His bored gaze passed her by.

"Back for the feasting and the brain-swirling brew in the bowl."

Caterin silenced them with an angry gesture, anxious to hear the proclamation.

"Gort Mac Dafydd, Prince of Gwynedd sends greetings to Bridei, King of the Pretani, Overlord of Alba."

He was a Cymry, one of her father's kin. And there were no women in his train. That might mean a short stay. Or a summons from Bridei with a Royal Marriage at the heart of it! Oh, Anu of the Winding Stream, let it not be that! She had other plans for herself when the time was ripe.

Her lips tightened. Why had her father not told her that this Prince was coming? She ought to be standing at his side to greet the guest. Slowly she had come to accept that, although Bridei had been King in this land for over twenty years, he still thought like the foreigner he was, that daughters were used as pawns in politics. That realisation had come early to the motherless child and still hurt.

She swept back the damp tendrils of honey-coloured hair from her forehead.

It was time she reminded her father that she was a Princess of the Pretani. That the Pretani had different traditions and were proud of them. That the Royal Line descended through the Queens. That the Queen was Chieftain of the Clan Mothers. That the Clan Mothers were the real power in the land. And this time she would dare him to laugh and pinch her cheek.

The gates creaked and began to trundle open. The Prince set spurs to his horse and forged his way through the entrance to meet the King and Council. And how they would admire the promise that was in him to cleave his way through his enemies like an axe-head.

His retinue grouped themselves and followed in long lines. Why so many? Bridei had no need of more men. The land-hungry Scots and Angles were quiet this weather. Bridei had the nine clans and the Orcadians to call on to deal with any threat. Why this sudden appearance of a warrior with a force at his back? The hairs on the back of her neck quivered as though someone's gaze had settled there.

But who would answer her questions about this hidden menace? The Council of Elders with their long beards and short tempers? The Arch-Drui who talked with the All-Powerful Ones and knew everything? Though much of it wasn't worth knowing. Or the serving-women who knew everything that was worth knowing?

The mare slowed, spying a patch of fresh green grass. Caterin let the reins dangle. Why should she hurry back to a Citadel that was becoming increasingly like a prison, ruled by old men? While beyond the palisade there was laughter in the meadows, a place by the hearth and the peat-smoke had a tang of freedom.

Was it not time she stopped running wild, hunting, chariot-racing, seeking new thrills and adventures and all for the fun of it? Time she took her place among the Kings and Queens and Princes. Time these foreigners learned that a Pretani Queen was a

3

power to be reckoned with.

Filled with a burst of energy and new purpose she clicked her tongue at the mare. The Arch-Drui taught that every unborn spirit chose its own destiny in this earthly life so as to learn through experience. But she would not wait for her destiny to come riding on the wind. She would take her life into her own hands. And, by the Mother, it would not be the destiny her father had mapped out for her!

Her frustration exploded in a wild yell. Whipping the mare she galloped straight at the Gate. Within the wall, a caravan of traders newly arrived, had set up their stalls while the strangers amongst them recited their credentials. The wind lifted her cloak till it streamed out behind her. Men and boys ran from under her mare, pack-ponies reared, saddle-straps burst, leather gloves bounced in the dust, bundles of metal-ware unrolled across the stones. A plume of coloured ribbons arced into the air and her arm shot out to grasp it. Speeding past, she waved her prize at the upraised fists and planted it squarely on the head of a cursing pedlar. And looked to see if the proud Prince had noticed. He had gone.

Her high spirits spent, she led her companions towards the King's stables, the hooves of their horses sending up little spurts of dust from the earthen passageways. A groom, currying a stallion, eyed the single carcase slung between the ponies and sniggered. A soldier, perched on a mounting block, spat his contempt on his leathers and polished them, whistling.

Through the entrance to the stable-yard, Caterin saw the steaming bay being walked into the interior. Let others crowd in to admire the sleek animal. She was concerned with meeting its rider. And so she missed one pair of eyes that turned from the shining trappings, eyes that were black with hate and intent.

Caterin slid off her mare, slinging the reins at a passing slave who leapt in fright and let them slide through his oil-slippery fingers.

"Fumbling fool!" she hissed through her teeth. "I'll have you whipped!"

Tears spurted from the boy's eyes, confusing her with an unfamiliar feeling of pity. She tossed her head, trying to dismiss the thought of his pinched scared face and that foolish prank at the gate. From babyhood her rank had set her apart from others. It was a lonely thing to be Royal. Too often lately her restlessness and frustration erupted in wildness.

The nudges and glances of the Cymry retinue excited her. Sadly, her blue tunic of soft lambs' wool was a trifle grimy. But it was girdled to show off the vigorous swelling of her breasts. Her riding trousers were cross-strapped round shapely calves and thighs. Throwing back her cloak she strode with confidence between the houses towards the Great Courtyard.

At the corner of the Banqueting Hall and the Council Chamber she paused. Beyond the throng of curious citizens rose the King-House, rain-washed and sparkling after a soft shower during the day.

The entrance gave onto a cozy maze of passages, hallways, rooms and staircases. Some rooms nestled into depressions in the land. Some were set on a higher or lower level than others. Their ridged roofs, too, were at various heights. Yet there was a curious unity and fitness about the rambling King-House, lending it both dignity and homeliness. For the planks of each roof were painted red and each outer wall was faced with white quartz stones. As each new wing had been added, the stone-masons had raided the beaches and shaped the stones until they fitted together perfectly. In the noon-day sun, the quartz gleamed white but, when the sun was setting, the veins of rose and amber in the quartz glowed with an inner beauty. It was the only home Caterin had known and she loved it almost as much as she loved her handsome, indulgent father.

And there he was, on the steps, greeting his guest. His easy relaxed stance and informal clothing could not hide the fact that he was born to command. His simple brown tunic only accentuated the impression of quiet strength. The sun, slanting along his jaw and cheekbone gave his skin the glow of oiled wood. His dark-brown hair curling over his powerful neck and vigorous torso had always reminded Caterin of the Black Bull on the Royal Pennant. How manly he is, she thought. And felt a stab of pain at her heart. For she could only become Queen if a new King was elected. And that meant her father would leave for his own lands. She fervently wanted the Queenship. But how could she bear life without his tender smiles, his loving endearments. She would be alone. The thought frighened her. For who else in the world would love her as he did?

Her fear gave way to disbelief as she saw him usher the Prince into the King-House. It seemed that this warrior with the fine body of men was more than a mere candidate for the Kingship.

The guards at the entrance dropped the points of their swords as she swung past. In the empty Receiving Hall she turned over the bundles of guest gifts disdainfully with her toe. Nothing new here! Sealskins and silver goblets! By the Mother, his generosity was overwhelming!

Unfastening the kin-brooch at her shoulder, she threw her cloak at a servant and ran upstairs to the room where Bridei spent his leisure. He would be waiting there until the Prince had settled into his quarters.

This was a room in which Caterin always felt at home. As a child she had been brought here each time Bridei arrived back from his forays around Pettaland. This was where she boasted her prowess on the athlete's field or in the hunting forests. Here he listened to her stumbling harp-playing or hid a smile at her crooked embroidery. In return he told her about disputes he had settled, quarrelsome chieftains he had quelled and the strongholds he had visited. She had been an avid listener, with an aching need to grow up to be like him, bold and valiant, to earn her mead like a real champion. Or better still to marry someone like him, to have a real family around her. To be loved. For she had so much love to give in return.

Yet for a heart-stopping moment it seemed to be an old man who sat there, hunched over gnarled twisting fingers. Then it was her father who turned, straightening abruptly. Always he hitched his chair to the window that looked on to the garden where the women sewed and flirted at him with their eyes. Now Caterin strode forward, confronting him, restricting his view. Let the women signal in vain today.

"Who is this new arrival? Why didn't you tell me he was coming?"

CHAPTER TWO

Abruptly Bridei turned to pour two cups of wine, hiding his face.

"A surprise is like a dip in the gravy. It adds flavour to the bread." His voice was indulgent but there was a wariness in his movements.

"Why is he here? What does he want?"

Her eyes searched his face as she took the wine. New lines of worry puckered his brow and cut the corners of his mouth. Suddenly his face relaxed as he leant back, remembering.

"Well, long ago, Gort's father and I were fostered on the same lord." Bridei chuckled, glad to forget the pain in his fingers and the sadness at his heart. "By the White Arms of the Great Queen, we led him and his wife a merry dance! We shared every scrape and every beating. Until Dafydd left to take over his father's kingdom."

Caterin, waiting for the point he was surely going to make, began plucking out the long heavy braid of her hair.

Bridei held his winecup in both hands, musing over the rim.

"Dafydd was a wild reckless character. A true champion. When he was killed the bards sang how his deeds shone like sea-washed jet on a sandy shore."

The weight of Bridei's own years fell on him then and the duty that lay heavy within him.

"And now his son's here, a proven warrior at twenty. With an itch for power that I intend to scratch." A dark eyebrow quirked up at her. "Make him welcome, Kitten. Give him the same hospitality as you'd give to a kinsman." Her hair flew free from its braid, cascading down her back.

"And my bed? Is that included?" she asked sharply.

He inclined his head. He had always dreaded the time when he must part from his daughter, leaving her a Queen in her own land.

"A Royal Marriage with Gwynedd would be an excellent thing."

The clipped words fell like pebbles into her heart. And as if her heart was a pool, the ripples circled swiftly outwards towards the dark unknown. She wanted the Marriage, longed for it, but not with this Prince. For there was someone else, Maelchon, her dashing childhood hero. But he was taboo because the Law

7

demanded a foreign King and Maelchon was a Pretani.

Bridei saw her eyes darken in thought. He leaned forward eagerly.

"Listen, the land needs a new King and you're ripe for mating. It's high time I took my own name and went back to Powys. My homeland cries out for sons." She answered lightly, nudging the jut of his chin-beard, playfully.

"Sons? I thought you loved me best."

His battle-scarred hand caressed her arm.

"Of course I love you, my soft-breasted dove."

Fine words that sprang easily from his Celtic background! But Caterin was supremely confident she could win her father's approval. Her happiness had always come first with him. She tossed off her wine, screwing up her face at the sharp taste of it. Taking a deep breath she spoke the words that had to be said..

"I don't intend to marry this Prince."

Bridei's black brows puckered in disbelief. A flush of anger rose from his neck to suffuse his face. She had never disobeyed him before. And to stand against him, at this crucial moment when the Kingdom was on the brink of rebellion, was intolerable. He rose and came to her then, holding her chin between strong fingers so that she had to meet the full force of authority in his eyes.

"Then the Council will elect some coarse fighting man!" he thundered. "One who's learned his manners in an army tent or under the deck of a warship. I'm putting forward my candidate first. And, by the Mother, I'll see you accept him!"

Caterin's eyes darkened. Strongly into her mind came the memory of Maelchon, teasing her that one day he would come home from the sea and marry her. Thrusting Bridei's hand away she spoke, her eyes boring into his.

"Princess Onid didn't marry a foreigner. She chose a warrior King from the Taesali clan."

Maelchon had told her that and because she adored him she had vowed to make him her fine strong King.

"And look what happened! Onid's Marriage set the clans at one another's throats. Forget that idea!"

Bridei frowned. Diplomats and soldiers he could deal with. But this daughter with her mother's brilliant green eyes and vivid face was the one chink in his armour. He lifted his cup, pausing to control his wrath.

"I've studied your history, too, my girl, don't forget. And had a hand in making it."

Without thinking, Bridei poured the soldier's libation of wine on the mat before emptying his cup.

"Who burned the forts of the Scots, hey? Who stood on their frontier and cried 'This far and no further!', hey?"

She caught the glitter of his excitement. But the bards told it better when they sang of the long bloody furrow he had ploughed through the blackened stubble of dark heads.

"This time it's different. The clans are united now. They'll remain loyal to the Queen and the Kingship."

The idea of a King from one of the clans had made sense as she grew older. A native King, born and bred in the tradition, who would acknowledge her right to rule as Queen and Chief Clan Mother.

Bridei's hand slashed the air.

"That shows how little you know! There's been no election in twenty-five years. There's a new breed of Chiefs and Mormaers with new ambitions rising in their breasts! Someone has to teach them a lesson!"

The Chiefs and their sons had been like uncles and cousins to Caterin. Maelchon, son of the Chief of the Veniconie, had been like an elder brother. None of them would rise against the Law of the land. That was impossible! Or was it!

She began to pace the floor, beating her riding crop against her thigh to control her anger and marshall her thoughts.

In the cold season, it was cosy here with a beechwood fire and high, wide tapestries of hunting scenes lining the walls. It was homely and familiar. Even when her father had been away she had hidden her loneliness here, sensing his presence and gaining comfort from it.

Now that the weather was warmer, the tapestries had been taken down to be cleaned and repaired. The lime-washed walls were decorated with shields, each as tall as a man, banded with bronze and studded with precious stones, reminding her of her clear cold destiny. This room belonged to a warrior, a stranger. And she had deluded herself that he would listen and understand.

She paused at the window leaning out to see where pink puffs of cloud formed and reformed endlessly over the red roof-ridges.

At her back Bridei's blunt fingers tapped a tattoo on the table.

His mind floundered, confused by unfamiliar emotions, and caught hold of one thought. When she met Gort and saw how handsome he was, she would think differently. He took refuge in the world he knew, where he could manipulate people and ideas to his will.

"You must understand!" He cleared his throat loudly to sweep the impatience from his voice. "That's why the Law of descent through the Queens came into being. It does away with clan rivalries and the jealousies that rend other Kingdoms apart. An elected King who acts against the will of the people can be forced to abdicate. And there's no chance of a child-King to tempt the chieftains to gain control. That Law has a lot of merit, Kitten."

The childhood nickname grated on her nerves.

"Oh, I understand all right. I don't need a dissertation on the Law." Her voice was cold and bitter.

If only Dana had lived, Bridei was thinking. She would have handled this better. The memory of his Queen still hurt. Ach, he was growing soft in his mid-years!

"Don't forget that your mother married me under that same Law and our marriage was good."

Caterin caught a whiff, clean and dry, of the heather perfume worn by a woman in the Courtyard. And it was sweet as honey to her senses. She closed her eyes letting a silence fall with only the sound of her father's cat-like tread as he padded to and fro in his soft hide shoes.

Her mother had died when she was seven. She remembered eyes, green and deep like water on sand, the blue vein that pulsed at her throat and the ringlet of gold hair that curled over her white breast as she fed the new bairns that came and never stayed.

And the day her tender mother had shrieked once, twice, curdling Caterin's blood. And she had peered between the servants' skirts. To see a glistening snaking thing tied with dockens and cattle dung and her mother's white legs before they had pulled the bloody sheets over her face. And a few days later the baby had died too, gasping and foaming, his tiny pale limbs convulsing.

Since then she had been handed back and forth among serving women like a shuttle in a loom. With no one to kiss and hug her. No one to love her except her handsome indulgent father and he was seldom there.

Only Maelchon, son of the Commander of the Fleet, who came home from the hosting, bringing her silver earrings or a budding rose and went, singing, to the barley-fields with the older girls. How could a foreign Prince replace Maelchon in her heart?

"You're the one who doesn't understand! You never have, have you?"

Her voice was icy with disdain. "You've had no Queen to share your reign. But according to the Law the Queen is the real force in the land. Now you and the Council intend to give us another foreign King, another warrior, with no insight into our way of thinking."

"Oh, come on, Kitten. He'll learn as I did." Irritation sharpened his tone. "Look, it's time you behaved like a good little champion and did your duty."

A sort of icy anger fell on her then. How dare he talk to her as though she was a child? She felt humiliated, betrayed by her own father. Now she knew she must face the world alone. Hurt and disappointment surged through her voice.

"I'll refuse this marriage! I'll have a King who understands the importance of kinship through the mother." Her voice took on more power as she warmed to her theme. "Kings are only for fighting and fathering."

There was a surprised silence. His sudden burst of delighted laughter held more than a hint of condescension.

"A nice try, lass. But way off the mark. Listen here! Gort's brother Rhun rules Gwynedd. Think what a force these two could muster against the Scots and Angles." He caught his breath, leaned on the sill, and gazed out over the roof-ridges, one shoulder drooping. She hardly caught his whisper. "Or against an ambitious chieftain."

There it was again, this hint of menace, close and quivering in the air. She shook his arm furiously.

"For once will you speak the plain truth! There's far more to this visit than you're telling me! I've seen this Prince's retinue! Why has he come with such a large body of men."

Bridei kneaded his hands together, wishing he could spare her this knowledge.

"There are rumours of plots," he began.

"There are always rumours of plots!" she broke in. "But you don't send for foreign mercenaries!"

"They're here for our protection. Yours and mine."

"Protection?" Caterin stood back aghast. "I don't need protection from my people. Neither do you. They adore you. And if you abdicate they'll need me to marry the new King."

He spat a soldier's oath.

"Don't be so cocksure!" He wagged a finger in her face. "If a Mormaer wants to set up a new dynasty he'll overturn the Law without a qualm."

Caterin clutched the sill, trying to still the fear that trembled in her heart.

"That's treason," she said slowly. "The clans would rebel against him."

"Oh, I grant you, some clans might. But they'd be too late to save our skins."

Caterin's mind was in chaos. The familiar red roofs danced before her eyes, mocking her. Was it possible they might be sheltering traitors and spies? "I can't believe all this! It's the duty of your retinue to protect us."

The sadness in Bridei's eyes sent her heart plummetting. He shook his great black bull's head.

"My retinue was recruited a long time ago from my own countrymen. Now they're like me, too old. Look at these hands!" He held them in front of her face. "I can hardly hold a sword any more."

Caterin hid his twisted hands with her own, almost weeping.

"One after another my fine Cymry lads have died or been pensioned off. Oh, my new retinue is bold and valiant. But it is made up entirely of young Pretani men."

"Who have sworn to die defending us!" She cried out the words and was amazed at how little they quelled the turmoil in her heart.

"Ah, my dear, if the word goes out there's to be a new King, we couldn't trust one of them." Gently he freed his hands and patted her cheek. "For my retinue was drawn from the very Clan that I most distrust. The Clan that farms in the most fertile part of Alba. The Clan that surrounds our Capital here in the Bow of Fif."

"The Veniconie!"

It couldn't be true! Maelchon was a Veniconie! He and his father would never stoop to treason! How could Bridei distrust them?

"So you see, my dear, Gort's here to protect you when I leave."

There was mead in a flagon. It poured in a golden stream into the cup. Honey and wax, the taste on her tongue, sweetness and light. Yet bitter the after-taste.

There was a rustle and a footstep at the door and her hands leapt together with fright.

"Ah, Gort." Bridei's leather-smooth voice oozed with relief and satisfaction. "Come and meet the Princess."

CHAPTER THREE

There was a pause. And she felt, coming from the shadows of the doorway, a growing sense of menace. Menace? No one menaced the Princess Caterin! He came at her from the dimness, moving into the slanting sunlight so that it highlighted the tall, dark figure, poised as if to strike.

Fleeting impressions exploded in her brain. It was an arresting face, as hard as an axe-head. His height accentuated his lean frame. Hard muscles had been honed by long hours of training. He had fastened on a black leather jacket to match boots whose shine was barely dimmed by the dust of his journey. Even her handsome father paled into insignificance beside him. She shivered. This man had not emerged from the warmth of a womb! He had been carved from a block of crystalline granite!

"My daughter, Caterin."

As she met the full impact of his cold grey eyes, a shock jolted down her spine. Then true to her training she lifted her chin and met his gaze with a challenge. There was not a man alive who could over-awe the future Queen. The Blood Royal flowed in her veins. And no Prince born of woman could claim that with confidence.

Tapping her toe, she waited. Now was the moment for the courtly compliment on her beauty. Would he have an original turn of phrase? With maddening deliberation he folded his arms.

Gort's father had spoken warmly of this foster-brother who now ruled the northern Picts. A fierce and skilful warrior yet with a hard core of loyalty to friends and causes alike. Gort had liked the man with the shrewd eyes on sight. Yet his hopes of meeting a daughter of some refinement sank as he saw her. This woman was the embodiment of all the wild barbarian Queens in the bawdy songs of his boyhood. His nose wrinkled at the thought of having to mate with this blood-spattered hoyden. He gave an exaggerated bow.

"Your pardon, Princess." His Celtic language was near enough her own to allow him fluency. "When we met at the Gate I didn't recognise the jewel in the Pretani Royal Line among that pack of rowdy coxcombs."

Her cheeks flamed. Never before had she been humiliated like this. And by a guest! She rounded on Bridei, fully expecting him to avenge the insult to his daughter's honour. Bridei's face was purple. He was laughing!

"Serves you right! Go and pretty yourself up. Show Gort there's a beauty under all that dirt."

The Prince turned a half-shoulder, dismissing her.

"Now, why did you send for me?"

"I need a warrior."

"You? The man who united the clans? The man who rules from the Orcades down to the remains of that contemptible Roman turf-wall?"

"And is now past his prime." Bridei warmed to this praise from a younger man. He poured ale into beakers and lowered his voice. "I need a man I can trust."

Caterin watched them retreat towards seats in an alcove. The admiration in Gort's voice and the glow of pride on Bridei's face merged in her mind. Her heart ached at her father's betrayal. He had tried to be clever, hoping that history would repeat itself, that she had merely to look on the new King and be content to share her life with him. But he had made a mistake when he chose this warrior with the ice-cold eyes and the coarse turn of phrase.

Bridei would never believe she was adult enough to make up her own mind. She still loved him. But never again would she trust him. For he had spurned her, becoming obsessed with this son of a foster-brother and his flattering tongue. She turned once to stare at the two dark heads, absorbed in their talk and pressed her hand to her heart as if to soothe a pain. Then she left, walking slowly, her back erect and climbed the steps to her rooms.

A pine-scented bath was waiting. The green water slid smoothly over her skin. He was leaving for ever, her father, telling her in the same breath that her life was in danger.

"Oh, my mother, why did you have to go?" So intense was her longing for a woman to talk to that she crushed the floating rose-petals fiercely to her breasts.

The body-slave stood quietly, ready with warm cloths, lost in her own thoughts.

Down through the long passage-way of time Caterin saw the sweet sad face of her mother.

"The moment will come to you too, Cat, my girl," she had

said, "when you wait to meet your King. As I did. I didn't care that he was Cynwyd, Prince of Powys, son of Maelgwn, the Dragon of the West. Not once I saw his peat-brown eyes kindle at the sight of me!"

Caterin could still hear the low voice with the gurgle of laughter in it.

"It was a solemn thing to have to lie with a man that first night after they'd given him the time-honoured name of Bridei. But he was tender and joyful and we clung together and were glad." The rapture on her gentle face turned to blazing pride. "And then he raised his arms and swept the clans under the cloak of his leadership and defeated the Dal Riatans. For ever, some think. Ah, how lucky I am."

The slave-girl had forgotten her mistress. She was bathing once more in the loch, sliding on the dewy grass, wanting to soar with the larks till her heart nearly burst with the joy of it all. And at the doorway, the merry dark eyes of her mother, her floury arms and the smell of bannocks. And she felt again the lips that brushed her cheek and heard the warning not to stray or the Pictie would get her. With one finger the slave-girl flicked away the tear that threatened to drip into the scented oil.

Caterin stretched her shining wet legs, glad that they were long and slim. Too good for the likes of a Cymry prince. But the long smooth lines of them would tempt a certain tawny-haired rascal.

The slave dreamed of a soldier on the Citadel palisade, bright against the sky, who had taken off his helmet to mop his brow and caught sight of her, passing with dried herbs for the bath. And how time had stopped for a heart-beat for both of them. And Iogena had started out of her daze and hurried on. For she was a slave and only a death-sentence could come from that dream.

How many women, Caterin wondered, would sing praise-songs to Gort? Bridei's love-children were prized among their mothers' kin for they were healthy and vital and beautiful and clever. Like herself. Or so the bards said. But then they sang for a praise-gift.

She cupped her breasts in her hands and wondered if Maelchon would think them too boyish. No matter. One day she would be Queen and he would be the warrior King she needed to keep her frontiers strong. And if she was so minded she could be like the fiery Queen Scathach who taught the arts of war by day and the arts of love by night to the heroes of the legends. Laughing, she sprang from her bath, sending the slave scuttling into the corner for shelter. Indeed she might flirt with Gort this evening. Just enough to find out if the granite would crack. And if her father had spoken the truth and death came early to her, she would meet it blythe and bonny.

Her reflection looked back at her, mouth a trifle wide but full-blooded and tempting, honey-gold hair rippling with shadows like mead in a serving-bowl. What if she didn't have the alabaster skin that her kinswomen prized? She had the Cymry skin that bronzed at a glance from the sun. Tonight she would wear a robe that matched her eyes.

"Find me something green to wear, girl."

The slave rummaged in a chest, and straightened, shaking out a dress. And there it was in the girl's hands, as fresh and virginal as a newborn leaf, as fine as a cobweb spun in the night, tipped with a pearly sheen that sparkled like dew. A lovely dress she had forgotten about.

It was too tight. And too childish with its high neckline. Impatiently she ripped the bodice. The body-slave appeared wih a handful of gold chains. Cunningly knotted they drew the gaze downwards from the noble rise of her neck to the valley between her breasts. Here, against her skin, glowed her birth-gift, a carnelian, aflame with a magic orange fire. By the Mother, she would dazzle the man if there was any hot blood in him at all. And hide enough to whet his imagination.

She turned to study this wench, newly promoted from the kitchen.

"Where did you pick up tricks like this?"

Silence was expected of Iogena. Her dark head stayed bent as she fastened gold armlets on her mistress, too near to Caterin's snapping fingers to trust them.

"Speak up? I've heard you chatter well enough in that outlandish Celtic of yours. Don't pretend you're dumb!"

For a split second, Iogena's smudged blue eyes flashed directly at her mistress before she hid them again behind a curtain of dark lashes. Unwillingly, she spoke, her mouth sullen.

"I was the daughter of a chieftain before I was captured, Qurincess." She could not pronounce a P for there was no such sound in her Goidelic tongue.

"Then your father should have kept to his own pit of land instead of grazing his cows in sight of the Pretani."

As Iogena began to coil long strands of pearls into Caterin's braids, a sob escaped from her tightly pressed lips.

"Oh, get out of here!" What good was a slave if she pined and wept every time her mistress relieved her pent-up emotions? "I'll leave my hair loose tonight."

"Oh no, you won't! You're not a bride yet!"

That happy voice could belong to none but her mother's sister, Devana. Into the room she breezed, swirling off her cloak and causing the wall-hangings to eddy as she passed. She took a moment to slide an arm round the slave-girl and waft her through the curtain in the rear before hugging Caterin where she sat. Caterin's fingers clung to her aunt's arm. The Gracious Ones had heard her plea for the warmth of a woman's understanding. But Devana caught up the sheaf of her hair and the moment passed, leaving Caterin forlorn.

"Now hold still. If we lift these braids on either side, that will show off your high cheekbones. Hand me a few more pins. There! How's that?"

Devana had an inspired touch with anyone else's hair but no patience with her own. Once, it had been the same colour as Caterin's but now it was paler with an underglow of topaz. Today, she had piled it high on the top of her head where it perched like a loosely baked bun, tied precariously by a broken necklace of red and blue faience beads. Her amber eyes were merry. Her mouth was wide and mobile and quick to smile. There was a radiance about her that lit her whole personality. At last, she gave a final pat to Caterin's hair and came to take a long measuring look at her.

"Now, is it true that a Prince has come out of the south, riding on a bay?" Her voice was resonant, like a deep note sounded on a harp.

"You knew?"

"Of course. We've been summoned by the Council." If Devana had noticed the accusation in Caterin's voice she dismissed it briskly. It still rankled with Devana that Bridei had kept Caterin in the Citadel when she should have been brought up by her mother's kin and trained for the Queenship. But since her own husband stood in the King's place during his absences from court, she had let it pass.

She saw the stubborn set to Caterin's mouth and smiled grimly. Well, if his daughter was tempted to rebel Bridei had brought it on his won head.

"Oh, I'm famished. My Lord the King will have to put up with me at his table as I am. I'm not stopping to unpack." Devana opened a pouch and covered her travelling dress with a generous helping of gold brooches and dangling chains that would have swamped a less vibrant person.

"I'll see you in the Hall." A bright bead flew from her top-knot as she left. Caterin snapped her jewel-box shut.

"You just can't compete for attention when Devana's around," she told her reflection. Devana had more than grace and beauty. She had a warmth in her heart for everyone. Except for her own niece, it seemed. Caterin rose and looked for the weeping slave among the women in the outer room but found she had disappeared.

Making a shrewd guess, Caterin discovered Devana in the huge reeking kitchen. Spits groaned. Knives gleamed. Cauldrons muttered and steamed. Devana, muffled to the tips of her ears in a cook's smock several sizes too large, waved a wooden spoon. The Master Steward, cap askew, beamed at her side.

"We've just concocted a delicious stuffing for the caper-caillie." Devana licked her spoon and looked ecstatic.

"Stop keeping the scullions off their work."

The Steward muttered under his breath. Caterin thrust aside the hanging sides of meat. A startled cook scattered his armful of vegetables.

"You're eating too much anyway. You're getting fat, Devana."

"I know and I don't care." Devana's plump cheeks dimpled. "It's the sign of a contented woman." Her rumpled head emerged from the smock. "But you're as tight as a harp-string tonight. Never mind, we'll chat later. I want to see this brave gallant of yours." She led the way, smoothing her skirt over ample hips.

CHAPTER FOUR

As they entered the Banqueting Hall by one door, Prince Gort was coming in by another. Caterin's brows lifted at his short saffron tunic, its border stitched in dark-blue to match his leggings! And matching his dark good looks as well. His only ornament was a gold neck-chain with a stone of black obsidian lying on his chest, carved in the shape of a dragon with wings.

Devana gave a delighted gasp when she saw him. But Bridei's arms had opened in welcome and he must be greeted first.

"Welcome, sister." His finger-tips lingered on the white skin of her forearms.

"Tame your hot blood, Bridei." Devana's laugh was low and rich with a whisper of an indrawn breath to finish it off. She smiled at Bridei, the easy smile of a happy woman who can flirt and be outrageous without being taken seriously. "I'm only here to meet your visitor."

"Then here's Gort, a Prince from Gwynedd, a land in the Roman-loving south."

"Oh, I've heard of Gwynedd's snow-capped mountains and wild harp music."

Another bead flew as Devana sent Gort a swift glance, appraising his broad chest and manly thighs. And obviously finding both pleasing.

"As for Roman-loving, dear brother-in-law, even down your way, it was the fashion to lengthen your tunic into a toga and build a villa with a mosaic in the floor, wasn't it?"

She raised her voice.

"Only the folk in the north sent the legions scurrying back to lick their wounds behind their Wall."

Grunts of approval rose from the throats of men and women gathering around the tables. Devana's charm drew all eyes and she was hardly aware of it.

Bridei's grin swept the throng in the Hall.

"But think what your painted and skull-thirsty forebears might have gained. Good roads, for one thing?"

"Ah, you have the sword-edge on me there." Dimples flashed in her plump cheeks. She rubbed her wide hips. "Cenn, ask the wrights to look at that wagon-wheel tomorrow."

Cennalath, the Mormaer of Enegus cum Moerne, had joined them.

"And, since there's eider duck for dinner, I'll have some extra down for my cushions as well."

Cennelath, a tawny lion of a man, proud of the curling mane that frothed like spindrift from brow to chin, was blatantly in love with his little bed-mate.

"Welcome, Prince," he said. "Pay no heed to these two. They're long-time sparring partners."

Gort's stern features suddenly fell apart. He smiled broadly at Cennalath and crinkled his eyes at Devana.

Now is my moment, thought Caterin. Her skirts swishing, she made her entrance and crossed to stand in front of Gort.

"That's an unusual amulet," she said, smiling invitingly. "Why did you chose a flying dragon for your sign."

He gave her a slight bow, half-mocking, half-salutation.

"Because a dragon is the only animal that has wings and can mount into the sky."

Caterin spoke softly, for his ears alone.

"And do you mean to use me as the springboard for your soaring ambition?"

A spark flickered in Gort's eyes and was stilled. She had meant it as a joke. But it had come out awkwardly. Devana could have teased him better. She had gained his attention but his eyes were indifferent. Neither her appearance nor her pointed remark had made any impact at all. She was furious at herself. Yet she had a sudden feeling she had hit on the hidden truth.

At least, Gort was thinking, she has washed. And she was quite comely. Even elegant in that fine wool dress with the gold discs hanging from her ears. But he was wary of the haughty look in those green eyes and the arrogant tilt of her chin. With a slight inclination of his head he went to the guest-place at the end of the table.

Gort had rejected her once again. Clearly, Caterin thought, she would need to sharpen other weapons to dent his air of superiority. She stayed cool as ice. No one must guess at the humiliation she was hiding. One sharp glance in the Banqueting Hall could grow into the stab of a dagger in the space of an evening's drinking time. Eyes lowered, she took her seat.

Tall, branching wrought-iron stands held hundreds of cruisie lamps, flooding the Hall with light and sending wisps of smoke floating upwards to find the hidden outlets in the roof-tree. Benches scraped as women, bright as forest flowers, took their places. Greetings swung from table to table as men shouldered their way to seats.

Once Caterin had played and sported with the younger ones, glad to be allowed into their cosy group. But no longer. Even then the girls had been setting up their own hearths and the boys had been competing for places at their sides. Now they held posts in the Court while the girls were the new generation of Clan Mothers. And many of them belonged to the Veniconie clan. Her father must be growing old, his mind wandering.

Caterin sat surrounded by a wall of loneliness at the High Table among the Court officials with the gold torques on their arms. The Master of the Hunt guffawed at one of his own jokes, nudging the outraged Guardian of the People's Treasure. The Chief Law Adviser, a man of austere calm and ivory skin, lowered his eyes and pretended he had not heard. Deep in the body of the Hall, craftsmen, bards, scouts, messengers and traders appeared like ghostly shadows in the wavering haze of heat from the long-fire.

The hum and rumble of talk bubbled like soup in a cauldron. A woman nearby laughed deep-throated, glancing up at her man. Gold flashed as the King snapped his fingers to the Chief Steward.

At once, a great platter, heaped with haunches of venison, baked in honey, and surrounded by fat breasts of caper-caillie was borne in and laid before him. Giving his whole attention to the task, Bridei selected the choicest pieces, arranged them on a silver plate and dispatched them down the table to Gort.

"M-m-m, he's a dream, that Gort. With a nice taste in Celtic dress too." Devana's tongue strayed along the edge of her teeth. Whether it was in appreciation of Gort's looks or her steaming portion Caterin could not tell.

"Delicious," Devana murmured, tasting. The Master Steward bobbed at her back, as thrilled as if a bard had made a verse in his honour. The cup-bearer bounded forward to fill her glass with mead.

"I envy you, Devana." sighed Caterin, randomly spearing at the meat with her dagger. "You could charm the heart of a hungry wolf if you tried."

"But I don't try, dear." Devana leaned across Cennelath to speak. "If you like people it's ten to one they'll like you. Remember that!"

"I do try!" Bride, the Kindly One, knew how hard she tried to imitate Devana's easy way with people.

Hearing the flatness in her voice Devana swivelled to search Caterin's face.

"By the Sacred Fire, I'm such a dolt! I spoiled your entrance, didn't I? And there you are, girdled like a swan to fire the loins of the new King." Caterin had to laugh with Cennelath. What else was there to do when Devana was around?

"Come to my room later," she whispered. "I've no one of my own rank to talk to. If I put my thoughts into words they'll be shouted across the Pettaland Firth to the Orcades before daybreak."

There was no answer. Devana was absorbed in her plate and the air in the Hall was now heavy with the names of Kings. The gusty voice of a horse-trader newly arrived from the west was telling about the King-Choosing in Dal Riata.

"When his father died, everyone thought Aedan would succeed. Instead his uncle, Conall, became King. And now Conall's dead."

"And Aedan's King." Bridei oozed satisfaction. "With our kinswoman Dolmech as wife. I've been working for that."

"But Aedan wasn't the first choice for the Kingship." The trader faltered as he became aware of the sudden hush in the Hall. He had not thought that his gossip would rate more than a meal and a corner by the hearth.

"Tell me more," said Bridei, leaning forward, his voice silky. "I thought Aedan had been consecrated by the Lord Bishop of Eirean on the island of Io."

"Ah, but Bishop Columba wanted Aedan's brother as King. So Aedan summoned forty-seven Druad to back him up."

The whole assembly stilled at the name of this Bishop who had challenged the Druad in Eirean and won.

"It seems then that the magic of the Druad is still more powerful than Columba's." It was Gort's voice, low as a whisper, but yet it vibrated to the ears of those farthest from the High Table.

"Aedan's Druad didn't change the Bishop's mind. It was an angelic spirit with a golden scroll of King-names and a scourge in his hand that came from the Bishop's own Christ-God."

"Don't tell us! The angel's whip was tipped with Eirean gold," growled a chieftain.

Gort's patient tones silenced the laughter.

"Gold wouldn't tempt the head of the wealthy Ui Neill clan. He counts his riches in the number of heads that bow to his White Christ."

Bridei's eyes narrowed as he gazed into the smokey rafters.

"I see we'll have to take more account of this Bishop in our dealings with the Scots."

The trader caught the ring that arced over the heads and mumbled his thanks into his beard to King Bridei, to Dis the Father and, for good measure, to the Christ-God of the Eireans.

"He sounds quite a man, this mysterious Bishop," said Devana.

Caterin listened with a growing feeling that her knowledge of the kingdoms beyond the border was abysmal. How could Bridei expect her to learn anything from an Arch-Drui whose life was spent meditating in a grove? Or from a giddy aunt who was obsessed with food? Or from another foreign King? She slid a glance towards Gort where he sat brooding darkly.

Bridei's hand came down suddenly like a club-head on the board.

"Ha! So Aedan rides the whirlwind now." Bridei seemed different, younger, his nostrils flaring as though he smelled a threat. "He'll have supped from the Cauldron of Covetousness. That's a heady brew that stirs the loins to war. Cennalath, you've had dealings with him. Will he bring peace or war to his wife's kin?"

Cennalath, too, seemed to be scenting danger.

"He's ambitious." He combed his beard with his fingers, restless as a squirrel. "He's inherited a good fleet, fourteen benchers every one. But his army-leaders are forever quarrelling about who's to lead and where. I grant you the Scots attack fiercely enough but let them smell defeat and they run like rabbits."

Bridei's fingers drummed on the table.

"Yet I think Aedan lacks the foresight of his father. Let's hope if he makes a move it's a rash one."

The assemby stirred back to life with a touch of a charm here and a sign of the crescent there. The women leant back wiping cream from their lips. Bones were tossed to the hounds skulking by the long-fire. Empty plates disappeared and cup-bearers ran with brimming horns of ale and mead. The King raised a finger encircled by gold and radiant with a ruby's sparkle.

A bard, keen to serve a generous King, stroked the smooth wood of his instrument and formed the words of a praise-song in his mind. He shook out a strange, shimmering banner of notes but, before they came circling down from the roof-tree to settle into a melody, there came raised voices at the door. The guard was thrust aside by a messenger, dishevelled, narrowing his night-wide eyes against the glare of the lamps. His blunt face was well-known as that of the brother of the Mormaer of the Miathie whose border advanced and retreated in a dance to the death with the Dal Riatans.

"My Lord King!" He swept past the staring faces down the length of the Hall towards the King. At once, Bridei was on his feet.

"What news?"

"Reports are coming in that Aedan is preparing to march against us! Even now his fleet is getting ready to sail!"

"Why was I not told of this?" Bridei snarled. "What's happened to my eyes and ears in Dun Add!"

It was Devana who saw the sweat that beaded the man's forehead and gave her own cup of wine into his hand.

"One pair of eyes in that quarter have been closed for ever."

"Dolmech!" Bridei's meat-dagger bit into the table. "By whose hand?"

The man drank and let his gaze flow slowly along the length of the High Table.

"Her son Artur was miles away, sitting on our borders at Dundurn." His voice was heavy with meaning.

The silver cup slipped from Caterin's nerveless fingers and rolled across the table to clang on the floor. No one moved to wipe the trail of red wine.

Dolmech was Artur's own mother! Had he deliberately rid himself and his brothers of the taint of Pretani kinship? Had he rid his father and his people of a Queen with the blood of their enemies in her veins?

"We'll have a praise-song made for her." Bridei took his time about sitting down, deliberately cooling the heated air. "You say Artur's at Dundurn. With how many men?"

"Does it matter? He's at our threshold! And Aedan can command all the men he needs from the Dal Riatans in Eirean!"

Bridei nodded, his brows meeting in a frown.

"And Aed of the branching lime-washed beard? Will he send an army?"

"If the Bishop Columba commands, he will."

"What would Columba gain?" asked the Chief Elder of the Council. "Is he shifting from piety to power?"

"He wants the Island of Io from Aedan," said the messenger, not without a certain satisfaction, knowing the stir that news would cause. "That's his price. He wants to establish a monastery on our Island of Io."

A low keening seemed to arise from the very timber of the walls and found an echo in the throat of every woman in the Hall.

'Io'. The name tolled like a bell in Caterin's heart. Iona, as the Scots called it, and the Bishop Columba! She felt herself hover quivering on the brink of some grim foreknowledge. Io and the Bishop Colum Cille! The scene around her shimmered and then sprang to clarity again as Wise Cau rose and his anger burst forth..

"It's an outrage!" The Law-Giver's hooded eyes were ablaze with fire. "Aedan has no right to give our sacred Island as a King-gift. It's the burying place of the Pretani Kings. Since time without mind! Their mounds lie on the hill beside a tree hung with their shields. The Scots have no right to it. It's only with our permission that they consecrate their Kings there." He looked straight at Bridei, the foreigner, willing him to understand the deep-rooted feelings of the Pretani.

Impatiently the messenger spurned the plate of food that was offered.

"My toiseach awaits an answer."

"Sit and eat, man. Your commander has always had our support."

"Before I eat, may I remind you that only the Miathie stand between you and Aedan."

Bridei leaned back, seemingly at ease, an amethyst twinkling from the hand that lay along the arm of the chair.

"That's true enough. Artur may make the Strath of Clyde his stepping stone towards us."

Cennelath spoke drily.

"The Strathclyde Kings on Al Cluith have always favoured the Dal Riatans against the Pretani."

It had been a long time since there had been talk of war in the

Banqueting Hall. Caterin, immersed in the drama, came to understand why the chieftains trusted Bridei. Behind these intelligent eyes, he was already assessing his enemies, planning strategies, counting his assets.

"You see, Gort," Bridei leaned forward to talk down the table, "it's the shape of this land that both divides and unites us. Now Aedan may sail north, for if he captures the Orcades he can control Catness and blaze his way south. Unless my fortress at Craig Phadric is strongly held. Or he may invade from the west by sailing up the Lochs of the Great Glen. Again Craig Phadric blocks his way at the top of Loch Ness. One thing I'm sure of. The Mormaers of Mur and Ros are strong and will stand."

"Will the liegemen of Catness and the Orcades repel Aedan? Or join him?" asked Gort.

Wary faces loomed through the steamy air, the weather-beaten faces of large-boned young men, the seamed faces of hawk-nosed old men, the pale faces of wives and mothers, sharpened by fear.

"The time has come to find out," answered Bridei rising. "Cennalath, summon my chieftains. Can we expect any support from the Gododdin across the Forth, do you think?"

The messenger spat his contempt.

"Not with the Angles nipping their backsides!"

"Then go and tell your toiseach to assemble his men and leave the women to finish sowing the seed. He'll have one half of my army at his back before long."

The messenger emptied his cup and left.

"And the Isle of Io?" Wise Cau was still on his feet.

"I promise you," said Bridei. "Never again will the Scots consecrate a King on that sacred Isle."

The bard struck a chord and launched himself into a verse that told of Bridei's skill with the arrow-storm that beats on the breasts of the enemy, the spear-shower that blackens the sky, the sword that scatters sparks and the silver ring that greets the praise-song. Bridei, summoning his nobles and Gort, turned to seek a smaller room for his council.

'The Isle of Io'. The whisper still sighed and moaned through the dark corners of Caterin's mind.

CHAPTER FIVE

In Caterin's room, the fire had burned low, almost to ash. The glow of torches outside drew her to the window. Sparks from the hooves of horses on cobbles, servants clinging to reins. Messengers hurrying, leaping, clattering off into the night. And a rumble of voices from the Hall where traders mopped up the last of the ale. She had just been a bairn when the army had last gone to war.

Devana padded in and a flurry of beads lost themselves in the fleece on the floor.

"I wanted to send to Aberlemno for the boys. But Cenn won't let me. It's just to let them see their father before he marches." She paused to still the quiver in her voice. "War again! Oh, it was a bad day for us when the Scots set foot on Alba." Her voice broke again. Fiercely she punched the cushions on the fireside chair and sat down. "Let's talk about you. When are you going to let the Prince into your bed?"

The crimson silk window-hanging whispered back into place as Caterin turned.

"Never! Have you seen the way he looks at me? As though I was a blow-fly in his stew?"

Devana's own heart was heavy or she would have sensed Caterin's inner turmoil.

"Oh, don't be so stubborn!" Devana attacked the fire viciously with a poker, hanging onto her slipping top-knot with the other hand. "You can't refuse! Whatever happens, it's time for an Election. Bridei's had a long reign as Kings go."

"He won't abdicate now with war in the air."

"Why not? With Gort ready for service in battle and bed?" Devana pulled a small half-sewn tunic from her pouch. "I guessed Bridei would spoil you," she grumbled. "It was my duty as kin to raise you in Aberlemno. This is what he gets for ignoring the custom."

Now Caterin came and knelt, resting her hand on Devana's knee, appealing for understanding.

"He ignored the custom because he's a foreigner and doesn't understand our ways. I've tried to tell him that but he won't listen."

"What nonsense is this?"

Devana's fingers were making a mess of threading her needle.

Caterin rubbed her forehead, trying to put her thoughts into words.

"I want to make things happen when I'm Queen. I want to learn about the things the Clan Mothers do. Help them to do it better. The trading, the farming, the healing. Especially the healing."

Devana gazed in amazement at the rapt face of her niece. She sensed a new determination there, a quiet resolution that was already setting her apart from other women. Still, if this new independence brought her into open rebellion with the Law when war was looming, Devana would have no patience with it.

"Where do plagues come from, Devana? And sickness? Why do so many babies die? And mothers? Like mine. I want to find out what the Wise Women think about it."

Devana was taken aback by her vehemence. The deep green eyes shone with fervour. The green eyes of all the royal women. A wave of tenderness swept over her. If Caterin went on in this way she would be hurt. Nothing surer.

"These things are sent by the gods as trials," she said gently. "Why should we seek to understand them?"

"Devana, you're a Clan Mother. You know how important healing is. Together you and I could work to do some good in the land. Set up Centres to teach healing."

Devana thought of the clamour and the grind of the Sowing Season and the big farmhouse up north, empty without Cennelath.

"You can talk to Gort about it once you're married."

Caterin gave a strangled snort.

"He'll want a Queen to bed and breed from. I want the Queen and Clan Mothers to have real power as they had before."

Devana stitched thoughtfully.

"It's true Bridei has angered the Mothers. Did you know he's handed out parcels of land to his retiring retainers? That's not allowed by law. We hold the land in the name of the community. Only a foreigner would grant land to men."

Caterin jumped to her feet and threw her arms wide. At last she had found someone who understood! She hugged Devana, her heart overflowing with love and thanks.

"You'll talk to Bridei, won't you? Tell him ... tell him I want to marry one of our own warriors."

The needle jumped.

"What?

A bright spot of blood stained the yellow tunic.

"Girl, do you know what you're saying? Who do you have in mind?"

"No one." Caterin's was not practised at lying and her voice came out three tones too high.

"You can't do it! It's going too far!"

Caterin stilled, looking at her aunt and seeing her clearly for the first time.

"Bed, board and bairns are all that matter to you, Devana. I'm not like that."

It was the commitment that dismayed her. For she had a strong suspicion that once she had shared in love-making and child-making with a man she would be swamped by her urgent need to love and to be loved and might never be independent again.

Devana ignored Caterin's taunt. It was true and she could see no need to defend herself.

"If you flout the Law of succession, my girl, every Mother's brother's going to wonder what profit he can make if he overturns a few Laws himself."

Devana stopped for breath, her breasts heaving. Caterin stood firm under the storm of words.

"Bridei must have the loyalty of every clan while Aedan's on the loose! You'll marry Gort, Caterin if I've to take a birch-broom to you! Then you can bend him to your will any way you like!" Devana's explosion of anger sent Caterin sweeping outside to the little courtyard, her high hopes of a friend and ally in ruins.

Yet it was the truth that Devana spoke. In peace-time she might have had a chance of putting her case forward. But not now. With shaking hands she brushed back the tendrils of her hair.

Devana's voice nagged at her from behind.

"You'd think he was some misbegotten lump of a man. And even if he was, you must take him. Of course, you could back out of the Royal Line. Except that Royal female cousins are sparse on the ground in this generation."

Caterin licked her lips, welcoming the cool salt-tanged breeze that sighed over the low wall straight from the sand-dunes.

"But then, you don't want to give up your fine jewels and sleek hunters, do you?"

Caterin's elation had drained away leaving her with a strange emptiness in her limbs. She felt betrayed again.

The plaintive call of a sea-bird rose and fell. And what did he have to complain about, up there, riding the wind? He could mate as he liked and had no other debt to pay to the Earth-Mother than a healthy brood of chicks.

And then it came to Caterin in a bright and shining thought that an election and a marriage could not be arranged before the army marched.

She would be free to go to the Druad at Pitversie to study. The thought exhilerated her. Someone had made the right libation at the right time. The Great Ones had favoured her.

And when Bridei defeated Aedan and came home in a few turns of the moon, he would find that the Druad would not release her until she had completed her training. For her need to learn was overpowering. It might never return with such a white-hot intensity.

And more joy! The fleet would be summoned home for orders and she would see Maelchon. Oh, he might have changed, might not be all she hoped for. She was realist enough to know that. Yet she could not remember a time when she had not loved him.

"You'll be a luckily-matched woman if you mate with Gort."

There was an edge in Devana's voice that was not entirely caused by worry over her soldier husband.

"You make me wonder if you once hoped for Bridei and the Queenship yourself." Unseen by Caterin, Devana's needle stilled. How long ago that had been. As a young girl she had adored Bridei with all her heart. When her sister had died she had been bitterly hurt that he had turned to other women for comfort. And she had been wildly jealous of the child, Caterin, too.

And then one starlit night Cenn had caught her hands and carried her into the dance. And the froth of his beard swept the satin of her skin and from then on there was no one else in the land for her but this big broad cheiftain. And Devana caught her lip to stifle a shuddering sob.

"Being Queen didn't appeal to me. And my sons are too young to be King, the Guardians be thanked. But there's no escape for you, Caterin."

She suspected Caterin was not even listening, would not understand, would not care that her aunt longed to be away, wanting every moment of Cenn's time before he left. But she made one last try.

"I grant you that champions are as thick as brambles in the Clans. But it needs a warrior like Gort with allies and authority to follow the charismatic Bridei."

Caterin tossed her head. Maelchon was an experienced leader. If only he would come home. Then they would all see what a fine King he would make. And she would not have to battle alone.

A sentry on the palisade hawked and spat. The star-light cast a sheen on the tiled roofs, wet from a recent shower.

Yet even on her own she would continue the fight for she had right on her side, and determination.

A remnant of cloud drifted and the Moon Maiden sailed forth on her path. The door of the Banqueting Hall opened, letting out a gust of male laughter and casting a long triangle of light across the cobbles. A tall lean figure emerged, his black hair and saffron tunic backlighted by the glow.

Gort made his way through the passageways almost furtively, stopping once, his head angled as if listening for stealthy footsteps behind him. Satisfied, he climbed the wooden ladder leading to the palisade.

"If you've no more to say I'm going to bed." Devana began gathering her bits and pieces, feeling she had done her duty.

"Wait, Devana." Caterin said over her shoulder. "Why should Gort be visiting the palisade secretly at night?"

"You're sure it's the Prince?"

"I saw him clearly before he hid himself in the shadows like a thief."

"We've more than enough enemies on our borders without you creating a monster out of a milk-brother." Devana's deep voice was crackling with impatience.

The Maiden highlighted Gort's head and shoulders as he stood, brooding and silent.

"And why is he staring out to sea as if he's expecting a signal?" Caterin's hands tightened on tha wall. "There's more than one way of invading and plundering a land. With a dose of cunning and a dash of treachery not a blow needs to be struck."

"Treachery! Gort? By the Shining One, that's going too far!"

Devana's splutter of light laughter
goaded Caterin into bitterness.

"You might be paying tribute to the King of Gwynedd if Prince

Gort makes himself overlord here."

"Leave it to Wise Cau. He's the best ferret in the land for flushing out secrets. Use your pretty eyes to ensnare Gort, not to spy on him. By the way, our Shaman saw your Marriage to Gort in the twigs."

Caterin tossed her head.

"I don't believe it. My fate's not sealed in a fruit-tree bough."

Yet she shivered. She turned to ask more.

But Devana had gone, leaving Caterin alone with suspicions that were like a dark shadow without substance. From now on she would watch Gort. It would suit her very nicely if Gort was found to be a spy and sent home with his pride in tatters.

But oh, what a fool she had been to trust anyone with her innermost thoughts. Now she was filled with a terrible awareness of how alone she was. Yet she would not waste her time with regrets. She would be a greater fool to let this hold her back. It had been a shock but she was resolute now. She vowed she would speak to Maelchon, clear up this misunderstanding about the threat of the Veniconie, talk about the Kingship.

She guessed that Bridei had cunningly planted suspicion of the Veniconie in her mind so that she would marry Gort for protection. Now she had a few suspicions of Gort himself and she'd make use of them.

Caterin awoke next morning with a sense of urgency hearing the swish of brooms and the slap of sandals. The slant of the sun told her she had slept late. Outside, the jingle of harness and the staccato beat of hooves told her that some of Bridei's commanders were arriving already.

The King's Council Room was full of Chieftains and Mormaers and smelled of sweat and horses. Bridei stood studying a vellum map on the table, its edges held down by discarded plates and cups. Lines of strain furrowed his face as though he had not slept. Gort in his riding garb, scored the map with a probing finger, his deep voice with its foreign intonation questioning, searching, calculating. Newcomers, freshly summoned in the night, crunched bread and listened.

Sauntering to the sideboard, Caterin heaped a plate with meat, bread and cheese. Legs apart, she leaned against a wall, observing everything.

"And the fleet?" Gort was asking.

"Based here and here and here." Bridei's finger travelled up the coast-line. "Under three leaders, each with his own section of the coast to patrol."

"And how far under your command?" Gort's tone was relentless.

"My overall Commander is Artcois of the Veniconie. He's here." The King raised his hand to signal to Artcois, bluff and roistering Commander of his Fleet, newly arrived back from the first patrol since the ice-melt. Caterin's heart rose in her breast, fluttering like a dove in a cage.

"You old sea-wolf!" Bridei cried. "You smell danger threatening before the torches are put to the beacons."

She had been right! If Bridei thought Artcois was plotting against him he would never have greeted him in such a friendly manner.

The Chief of the Veniconie was a square-built and powerful man, his features half-hidden in a thick growth of dark-red hair and beard, powdered with grey as if the sea-maidens he courted had brushed them with salt. Moving like a mariner on a storm-tossed deck, he strove against the tide of men who leaned to thump his shoulder.

But Cennalath, all urgent talk and punching gestures had caught the King's ear. Artcois side-stepped and stopped beside Caterin.

"No greeting for your grizzly old Uncle?"

She gave him the fond smile he was looking for. The dove folded its wings, nestling softly to rest.

There was always a stir in the Citadel when Artcois put in on one of his rare visits with his Veniconie sailors, his foreign mercenaries, his hostages, his stolen gold and his outlandish stories. Many a time she had sat on his knee as a child, shivering against his salt-ingrained jacket as he told of monstrous sea-serpents and water-kelpies.

"What's new?" she asked, wondering where Maelchon was.

"Coasted north first." His wind-burnished nose, jutting like a hawk's beak, impaled her attention. "Quiet as a sleeping babe when we were there. Not a pirate to blunt our swords on. This weather raiders aren't out for a good fight. All they want is to snap up unsuspecting travellers and pillage outlying farms. Yet the winds were fresh and the bows sang through the waves."

A ripe chuckle erupted from his massive chest.

"So we spent a week in a host-farm in Catness, feasting and cock-fighting, keeping an ear and an eye open for anything that was the King's business. But north and south it was as dull as flat ale. Yet, now I hear that war-birds are screaming in the west." Grinning he rubbed his hands together briskly.

How could Bridei have thought the Veniconie would be disloyal?

"You'll have your chance for glory now, old Sea-giant. You used to tell me how you paced the heaving billows and ploughed up the sea-plain with your spraying prow," teased Caterin.

"Is it a gold-ingrained praise-gift you'll be wanting?" His eyebrow rose, three-cornered.

"Except that I didn't believe the fine bardic phrases that rolled off your tongue."

But his eyes were roving and his fingers drummed an impatient tattoo on the wall.

"Aye, lass, I'll be glad to spread my sails to the breath of the war-winds. All we achieved this trip was a howling of corbies in the Frisian lands across the Narrow Sea. Fired a few thatches, though, picked up a bit silver, not much, the coins they use for trading. A couple of flaxen-haired maidens, too, that kept me warm in my wet cloak on the way home. I'll barter them for a jar of wine tonight." His throaty laughter rumbled like the distant thunder of rollers on the beach. "Had both my sons with me this time. You remember them." A note of pride had crept into his rough voice.

The dove in her breast fluttered once more and was still, waiting. She remembered that Maelchon had a younger brother, Talorcan. Both had springing russet thatches just a shade lighter than their father's bristling mane.

"Aye, they'll bring glory to their mother's kin yet." Like a look-out in a sea-mist his eyes were ranging over the war-lords. "Maelchon's not a born sailor though. His legs were made to wrap round a horse. I don't think the sea-spray will soak his skin-coat again."

Caterin smiled at him, hoping her excitement wasn't too apparent.

"Now, Talorc, he'll be like me, riding the painted sea-stallion till the wooden stays snap and the anchor-line gives. Fill my cup, boy!" As the ale gurgled down his throat, his eyes, bright and sapphire blue, once more roved and settled on Gort. "And what do you think of the candidate for Kingship, eh?"

Taken aback by his direct question, Caterin tried to frame words that would walk a tight-rope between truth and discretion. And failed.

"I've found out he prowls our defences at night, looking out towards the sea."

Artcois quirked an amused eyebrow.

"Good man! Then he's just the leader we need after Bridei. But you've not much time for him, hey?" His glance was sharp, missing nothing.

"He's like a cow-tick under my skin, itching at me day and night."

"No need to fuss, lass. You'll have your pick of men after you've married a King and brought foreign Blood to the Royal Line. Mind you, we don't want the strain to get too weak and watery, do we?"

His elbow nudged her and she staggered. But more at this new line of thought. Already she was plotting how she could use it as an argument.

"You don't have to marry a foreigner, you know. It's been known for the Council to elect a Pretani as King."

Her eyes brightened with a soft radiance. Artcois blew into his beard. Rugged sailor as he was, he was not immune to the impact of these exquisite green eyes.

"Aye, your grandmother's mother, I believe. The Princess Onid who married a Mormaer from the Taezalie."

She began to remind him that the clans had rebelled when he deftly fielded a new ball into the game.

"She won the Council over by arguing that there were dangers in our system. And she was right! How can we assess the worth of a man when we've known him for less than a year?" He gave a smothered grunt. "But the Council say the tradition must be upheld."

"And you've a son that might fit the King's Chain of Office?" She tilted her head as if she was considering it. His eyes twinkled.

"What I say is this, lass. We've Eireans creeping in from the west. The Angles are welcomed in by the southern Britons to shield them from our raids. Some day we're going to be caught in the middle, like a nut in pincers." A hand as big as a bear's paw grasped the air in front of her nose. "Soon we'll have no pits of land left to protect and what good will our ancient customs do us then?"

She folded her hands on her throat. It felt as though the dove had moved there. Her eyes searched the throng for Maelchon's rusty thatch. Artcois followed her gaze.

"First day ashore, lass," he chuckled. "They might be in the stables." His hand tightened on her wrist so that she could not leave to look for them. "Or they might have gone where you can't follow."

Abruptly, his attention steadied.

"Is that Eildon there? Hey, Eildon, you wandering harp-twanger, you've been avoiding me. Do you time your visits for whenever I leave harbour?"

Eildon was perched on a cross-beam in the rafters. A long, thin, brown man from the slender length of his body to the lean fingers that stroked the golden flank of his harp and the silky hair that spread on his shoulders. He had the kind of looks that would merge with the grain in wood or the bark of a tree. One yellow-clad leg swung negligently in time to the quiet rhythm he was picking out on his favourite harp with its seven strings set into the swooping curve of willow bough. Head on one side, eyes lowered, he did not hear Artcois' roar.

"Strange fellow that," Artcois muttered still holding her wrist. "Disappearing up corries for moons on end and then - whoof! he's back with a new set of heart-stirring tunes. There's not a bard in my fleet can match him. But Bridei's a fool to keep him so near. I don't trust harpers with a reputation for spying. I've used them myself too often."

"Ah, but you need a good bard. He's your immortality."

Artcois nodded. "I'll ask my Lord King to lend me his favourite verse-maker in exchange for that ale-drenched Arnod. It's time my name was told in a song that'll last."

"If Eildon hears you he'll be gone in a flutter of a moth's wing," Caterin told him. "He belongs to no man. He loves the lone corries and the mysteries of the spirit. He's not one for a crowded deck in a heaving ship."

"Artcois! Your orders, man."

Artcois' grip on her arm fell away.

"By the Seven Spirits of the Sea, Bridei, it'll be good to see the planks stream with the enemy's blood again."

Caterin's half-nibbled crust arced out of the window to be snapped up by a passing seagull.

CHAPTER SIX

For days Caterin searched the Citadel for a glimpse of Maelchon's rusty thatch. After her seventh pointless visit to the stables she had to admit that she had not been his first priority. And it was obvious that Artcois had not shared his wenches with his sons on board ship.

On her way past the kitchens, she called for meat scraps and sent a boy scurrying for a cloak. In the yard beneath her windows, prowled her two hunting hounds. While they slavered and gobbled and crunched the bones, another sound brought her head arching up.

Outside the massive protecting walls of the Citadel, she could sense a great disturbance of sea and sky. High and clear on the air came the whine of a rising wind. Always the wild tumult of wind and sky excited her. And today with Maelchon near and challenges in the air she could not keep still. On an impulse, she loosed the chains of the dogs.

"Here, Dagger! Here, Hawker!" The hounds leapt to follow.

The guard at the gate scratched his head as she sprinted past. Who in their right mind would go beyond the walls when rain was on the wind and they had no guard-duty to do? Only a wild-spirited Princess and her two ill-tempered hounds that bared their fangs at him when he shouted a warning. "Rout out her bodyguard!" he told a messenger. "Nechtan's his name. Lazy good-for-nothing!"

It so happened that Nechtan had thought his mistress safely tucked away in the Council Room. Recently, he had found a snug corner near the oven which he hoped to share with a plump cook, a bit past her prime, like himself. Now he was offering to comfort her tonight in the night-lapped kitchen when the fire-spirits scattered sparks to light their dance and chimed the bronze hanging-pots for their music.

The squally wind caught Caterin as she left the shelter of the walls. The sniffing hounds dragged her to the top of a grassy knoll. Laughing aloud, she let the gale swirl her cloak and sport with her hair. The wind caught her laughter and threw it away.

The frenzy of movement delighted her. Long strands of grass streamed flat in abject submission to the elements, only to bob up, waving frantically, pleading for mercy. A low quivering moan sounded from the trees. Their newly-burst leaves fluttered in futile delirium. And booming out of the sea-mist, came the dull, rhythmic roar of the North Sea breakers. Salt laced her lips, as she faced into the teeth of the gale. She felt cleansed and exhilerated beyond measure. If only she had wings she would soar to freedom on the gale.

Suddenly, she saw a movement that did not fit in with the sweep of the wind. Away to her left lay a bank of gorse, brilliant-yellow when the sun was up but still palely shining. Enough to show up a dark shadow that climbed steadily and purposefully around it.

At a word, the hounds stilled, muzzles pointing. Swiftly, the trio began to glide forward, bodies crouched, heads raised, stalking their quarry.

There had been something fearfully familiar about that furtive figure. Caterin's suspicions of Gort flared again. Leaning into the gale the man made his way towards the round sloping tower of the broch that crowned the cliff, its crumbling stonework a constant reminder of raiders that came from the sea. And a grand place for sending out a signal, unseen by the Citadel.

The full force of the elements caught her after she skirted the bank of gorse and met ground that rose steeply. Now the gale became her enemy, seeking to sweep her off her feet. Twice she was caught off balance. In the end, it was the pull of the hounds that got her to the top. Once there, she realised the danger she was in, here on the exposed top of the cliff. Far below, mighty rollers pounded into the great black columns of stone that had been vented from fiery mountains in ancient times. Rollers that smashed themselves against the rocks and hurled furious plumes of spray high in the air. Foam formed into grasping fingers seeking for a weakness in the land to claw it back into the dark depths from which it had risen.

What fisherman had gone the wrong way out of harbour and angered Llyr, the King of the Sea? The unearthly scream of the wind was like the spirit of a drowned sailor in torment, begging to be cast ashore and burned to release his spirit.

A hot, meaty breath and dribbling tongue scoured her cheek, steadying her. Why should the sea-spirits seek to harm her? They had showered her with gifts. All the goodness of life, wealth and rank. Was she going to spurn their gifts and hide herself in a wool-basket for the rest of her life?

Danger was a challenge. The Mighty Ones loved those who took their fate in both hands. This was her chance to discover if Gort was false and confront the greybeards in the Council with the proof.

"Kill, Dagger! Kill, Hawker!" she commanded and went forward into the tumult.

At once, the wind whipped the breath from her mouth. It flung back her hood and lashed her long hair across her eyes. The biting chains of the dogs became her lifeline. Blinded by hair and sea-spray, she was like a rag doll with wind and dogs fighting over her body.

Loose stones began to roll under her feet. Her toes dug in, seeking a foothold but she was slipping, slithering downwards, the sky swinging about her. There came a burst of savage snarling and a snapping of teeth above her head, a shouted curse and then her arms were wrenched almost out of their sockets. She thudded, breathless, against a hard body that started to move, carrying her along with it so that her feet barely touched the ground.

Hammer still lunged and snarled. The edges of a wall bruised her without mercy. Then suddenly, unbelievably, the battle with the elements was over.

They were inside the broch, its sloping walls shielding them. The shrieking of the wind receded. The constant buffeting ceased. The relief was so great she leaned thankfully back against the stone. He, too, leaned against the wall, catching his breath. And, as the grey light caught the planes of his face, saw that it was, indeed, Gort. Before she could thank him, he spoke.

"Why did you set your wolf-hounds on me?" He ducked his head to suck the tooth-marks on his wrist.

"I didn't! But what can you expect? They're trained to attack strangers."

"Even one who's a guest?"

"You're a foreigner lurking on our shores where you could signal to an enemy!"

Gort bit back a stinging retort. She was right, of course. He would have been suspicious himself. But her intrusion on his privacy irritated him. He needed time to be alone to reflect on this unexpected war. And how it would affect the strange kingdom he had been called upon to govern.

41

Before he could find an answer, rain slanted down through the roofless building in wind-lanced gusts, and drove them tumbling into a narrow dark chamber set into the wall. Hawker and Dagger shook their shaggy pelts and squeezed in to huddle damply against Caterin's legs pressing her against the leather-clad body at her back.

His warm breath fanned her cheek, blowing a tendril of hair across her face. She became aware of the whole virile length of him, infinitely tantalising, mellowing her feelings, bringing an unexpected shyness. She wanted to distance herself from him. Perhaps then they could talk together easily and intimately, and come to some understanding of each other while the rain lasted. But as she eased herself away the hounds pressed closer.

"What in the name of the Woman of the Winds are you doing out on a day like this?"

His softly spoken words, cold as the lancing rain, chilled her heated senses in an instant.

"I could ask the same of you, my lord, a guest in our Citadel." She was cool now, and very formal, completely in command of herself. He would find he was dealing with a true Princess.

"Are you spying on me?"

"Have you something to hide?"

Gort paused, remembering how his elder brother, Rhun, had laughed with delight and rubbed his hands at the invitation from Bridei. 'Great stuff! Now we'll find out if the Picti are still a force to be reckoned with!' he'd shouted in his great voice. Gort had grown tired of being over-shadowed by his famous father and brother. Now he had the chance to carve out a name for himself. And if he chose to unite Gwynedd with Pettaland, he would be Overlord, not Rhun. First he had to deal with this young hoyden.

"I think you set out to follow me. Why?" Relentlessly he barked the question again.

The hounds shifted uneasily, growling a threat, ears pricked for a command.

He had seen her from the wall of the broch striding upwards with her great hounds, bright hair and cloak flowing in the gale. Something magnificent in her bearing had called to him. There had been something elemental about her as though she was at one with the gods of wind and sea and revelled in their fury. That climb had taken courage. But it had been done for a purpose.

"Now, why would a Princess follow me, unattended, into the jaws of the storm?" Mockery ran like a tight thread through his voice. "My guess is that I threaten your freedom to run wild. And you intend to discredit me in the eyes of the Council. Am I right?"

His accusation hit so precisely on the mark that she was surprised. But not at all put out. She sensed a deep rage working within him and was intrigued.

"Or did you think you could entice me into your bed so that you could prise out my secrets with a pint of wine and teasing fingers?"

A wild laugh exploded in her throat. That was not such a bad idea! Now she knew she had guessed aright. His inbred foreign ideas were all wrong for a Pretani King. At last the truth was emerging.

"Perhaps you came to meet a lover, is that it?" His lips were no more than a breath away from her ear. "But on a day like this? I've heard that the blood of the Picti women runs hot for men. Yet, to brave the elements on such a day needs hotter blood than most."

He could have searched for years and not found a more wounding insult. 'Picti' was the name the Romans had invented to ridicule the only race that they had been unable to dominate. It meant 'Painted Savages'. The words imprinted themselves on her memory. An icy hatred formed round her heart. She shrank back from contact with him.

"Play your wanton games if you wish, little swan. But if you pit your wits against the Prince of Gwynedd, you'll find your fine feathers decorating his cap."

"Spare me your empty threats, my lord Prince. And your foul insults." Her voice came low and sleek as a cat's pelt. She wanted to spit in his face but she could not bring herself to sink so low.

"You Picti women like a romp in bed with any passing stranger, don't you?" His mocking whisper finally brought her whirling round to face him in a fury.

"When we love we choose men with healthy minds and bodies. Mating's a natural thing. There's no shame in it, no secret lusting and lechery and debauchery. Only pleasure and loving."

He was confounded by the eloquence of her answer. Everyone knew they were barbarians, these Picts. Even in the dim light inside the broch the raindrops in her hair sparkled with a queer savage intensity that brought to his mind all the stories Gort had heard as a boy round the soldiers' camp-fire.

"Even the Romans sneered at your ancestors living in tents, naked and unshod, always half-in, half-out of swamps."

"In this climate?" Her voice mocked him, gurgling round the enclosed space. "You heard disgruntled enemies speaking."

Gort paused, ackowledging by his silence that there might be some truth in that. A man like Bridei would not have stayed so long unless he'd respected the people. Cennalath was a man he could work with. His wife was not what he had expected in a Pictish woman. Devana was brave and beautiful, not unlike the kind of woman he was seeking for himself. But this half-tamed girl! She was a throwback to barbarian times. In this small cell, their faces almost touching, it seemed as though the very air crackled and exploded around her. He would have none of her. Yet he could not remain indifferent. He felt a need in him to probe, to cut, to hurt. And he did not stop to wonder why.

"As for your men." His voice swelled with contempt. "Your men are known by the name of their mother's kin. The father's lineage is like chaff in the wind. What champion worth his mead allows his sons to be reared by a gaggle of women?"

"What about your women? You force them to marry elderly landowners and give birth to sickly heirs. While you give clever, healthy children the taint of bastardy. What kind of society is that?"

Gort found himself at a loss for words. The soldiers' tales had not led him to expect quick wits. But if he wanted the Kingship he had to mate with this Pictish girl. To father a child in her. And all his inbred feelings revolted against it.

"It's a society where chastity in women is honoured along with the blood of the sire."

"And where a man's worth is assessed by the amount of land he owns. It's ownership that keeps women in bondage and children starving."

Suddenly she was realising how strongly she felt about her own tradition. It was not just a Law that governed Royal Marriages. It permeated every aspect of living.

"Maybe some day, you foreigners will learn that the land is the body of All-Mother. You can't parcel out the substance of a Deity for one man and his heirs to grow fat on. The day will come when the All-Mother will turn against you and your kind for her own survival." "Pah!" He spat his disgust on the wet stones. "Your primitive customs are outdated! They'll be forced to give way in time, you'll see. If this land is to be defended it needs strong men who own it!"

"I knew I was right to distrust you." Caterin found herself trembling with the force of her hatred and contempt. "You don't intend to accept our ways if you become King, do you? You're steeped in a tradition where the leader is the warrior who can carve out the largest slice of the countryside and levy taxes on folk till they starve or rebel."

The deep prejudices that Gort would bring to the Kingship tormented her. He would never overcome them. Great Goddess Bride, there must be thousands like him in the Kingdoms of the earth!

"Very soon you'll be in command of men who'll fight and die for a land we all share. And you'll be a fool if you under-estimate the valour of our women, too."

Suddenly, her arms were caught in a biting grip that swung her round to face him. The hounds muttered in their throats at the sudden movement. Her head arched backwards to escape the intoxicating male smell of him.

"Under-estimate the Pretani women? Oh no, I'll never do that. In my own time I'll sample all they have to offer."

Gort glared at her, confused by her ready answers, angry that they made sense, troubled by an uncharacteristic tenderness that threatened to unman him.

No one had ever touched her with such vehemence. She tensed to resist him curling her fingers into claws. Suddenly a cruel hand angled her head and his lips came down on hers, strong and demanding. The hard outline of his mouth crushed against hers, forcing it open. All at once her senses were clamouring with an urgent response.

Roughly, he pushed her from him, wiping his mouth with the back of his hand.

"So, the bards were right! You're ready and willing to lie with me in the mud and boast about it when you spawn!"

Her sinewy palm, lean and hard, cracked across his face.

"That'll teach you not to violate a 'Picti' woman's mouth! Lips are for loving! For pleasuring the skin and for feeding babies. Take your degrading habits somewhere else!"

She knew with satisfaction that she had hurt his pride by the

45

savagery of his reply.

"Heed this, Princess! I didn't come to this land by choice. I didn't crawl here in shame like an outlaw with my crimes fresh upon me. I came with honour, invited by your Council. And I came with pride, to pay the debt of my father who owes his life to yours. Before he died, my father said,'Neither gold nor protestations of love can thank Bridei for my life. So if he ever calls upon you, my son, give him your service and your own life if the need arises.'"

He caught her chin in two powerful fingers and a vicious jerk sent a shaft of pain tingling down her spine. Yet she waited, yielding to his superior strength, knowing she would learn more about him, knowledge she would use to destroy him one day.

"It seems the need has arisen and the time is now. But I hold to my own beliefs. If I'm elected King, you'll get the seed of the Royal Gwynedd Line to freshen the Succession since that's expected of me. But neither I nor my kin will acknowledge any offspring. I wouldn't sully my family tree with the tainted blood of your Royal Line."

Neatly she swung up her arm in a blow that struck his hand from her chin.

"Calm your fears, Prince! It's the mother's right to name the father of her child. Neither you nor your people will be allowed to claim that honour."

With a grunt that was intended for a laugh he turned and propelled her out into the storm. Cleaving his way through the angry air, he drove her forcibly back to the Capital, leaving the hounds to follow at will, dragging their chains.

CHAPTER SEVEN

"That's a fine herring you've caught in your creel," called the sentry as they passed.

Within the high walls of the Citadel, the violence of sea and sky was muted. Gort deposited her on the Palace step like a bundle of dirty washing. While the Guard held open the door with practised patience, she watched Gort cross the Courtyard, not hurrying, yet covering the ground with ease. The Guards noted her red cheeks and drew their own conclusions. They thought the smouldering look in her eyes was the after-math of love-making. The rain on her face they took for tears.

Instead, Caterin was filled with a hatred so intense that it frightened her. He had poured contempt on her people and their customs. How could they trust him with their most precious gift, the Kingship?

"By the Royal Bull, he'll breed no child in me!" she hissed and was through the door before the startled Guard could stand to attention.

The following day it was as though the tempest of yesterday had never been. Caterin lay along the lower limb of a tree, her tunic dappled by sun and rippling shadows. From her hiding-place, she could see the broch, a serene, grey sentinel, silhouetted against the blue sky. Tiny innocent waves tumbled round the base of the cliff.

Silent and unmoving she thought about her confrontation with Gort. She had been shocked to discover that foreigners still thought that the Pretani were savages, the women promiscuous and their customs primitive. When she was Queen she would visit foreign courts with her warriors and ladies and nail those lies to the wall. The Arch-Drui had hinted there was a task the gods had prepared for her. Perhaps this was it. Yet she had a vague feeling that power-hungry Kings and wealthy land-owners would neither understand nor care.

She had spent her life setting goals in the sportsfield and sweating blood till she achieved them. Now she must enter a new arena, the politics of Kingdoms, although she knew so little about the issues involved. Her vehement defence of the tradition to Gort had surprised her. Her hours with Broichan had not been wasted after all. Nor had her morning in the broch with a man blinded by ignorance! Viciously, she swatted at a nosy, bumbling bee.

With a heart-stopping swish, an arrow thudded into the tree-trunk beside her cheek. Rock-still, her eyes ranged the wood for the hunter. Infinitely slowly she lifted her hand and pulled the arrow out. Nothing stirred in the forest. Without moving her head she glanced down at the colour and design of the feathers.

"Fortrei, you squint-eyed cur!" she shouted. "When are you going to learn to shoot straight?"

A twig cracked. She waited until a leaf fluttered, raised her bow and fired.

"Cub of a wildcat, you nicked me!"

Caterin sprang out of her hiding-place, hauling two arrows from her belt and brandishing them.

"Two of yours to my four." At the sight of fair-haired Fortrei impaled onto a beech tree by his sleeve, she crowed. "You've got to be smart to play 'Hide and Hunt' with me!"

Fortrei's pale skin flushed as he freed himself. With hands puckered by burn scars from his father's forge, he drew the rest of her arrows from his belt and threw the bunch at Caterin's feet.

"My head would be a trophy above the Citadel Gate if I winged the Princess," he said sulkily.

Caterin's eyes flashed green fire.

"Don't use my rank as an excuse. I take as many risks as you do. It's your own shooting that needs sharpening."

"Leave it be. It's only a game." Drust and Prent had crept up on silent hunters' feet.

"Caterin's beaten us all at one time or another. There's no shame in it." Prent cheerfully gathered up Caterin's arrows. "I wish I had her quick eye and the hand that goes with it. It's more than just practice, you know. It's a finely balanced judgment some are born with. More new arrows, Princess?"

Caterin smiled fondly at Prent. His round moon-face, red with exertion and shy adoration, broke into a wide, crescent-shaped grin.

"Nechtan may be a thundering nuisance as a bodyguard but he makes a fine flighting arrow."

Prent's eyes protruded from a clownish face with a rosy, bulbous nose in the centre. It was difficult to take him seriously, this self-effacing yet incredibly wise young man who had been born with a face that belonged above the red and yellow rags of the King's Joker. Yet, he had been fostered from babyhood by Wise Cau, the Law-Giver. And Cau had announced that it was Prent, young as he was, who should step into his vacant place when the Peaceful Ones took him. She took back her arrows.

"Oh, Prent. It's a comforting thought to know that you'll be at my side to advise me when I'm Queen."

And while she intended to use his innocent looks to fool others, she would never under-estimate his intellect.

Prent's hopeless love for Caterin shone in his eyes.

"Law-Givers don't give advice," scoffed Drust, cuffing his friend's ear. "Their brains are only storehouses. Start them off with the right word and the Law comes tripping out. Always the same law, the same tradition. They're like blinkered horses. Advice? You'd do better to scatter sand and read the claw-marks of a hen."

Prent's eyes protruded further and his grin widened. Yet, Caterin noticed a tension about his body as though his face had become a painted mask to cover his thoughts. He leaned on a branch and looked out over the fields beyond.

"Cornstalks must sway before the breeze or they break," he said quietly. His chubby face had not the contours to express the gravity of his words. "And so our laws must bend in the wind of change. It is the young stalks that are the most flexible, for in them the sap runs moist and milky."

It was a strange thing for a Law-Giver to say. It seemed to tie in with Gort's talk of primitive customs that must wither in time. My, but she needed away from this place, to talk with the Druad in Pitversie perhaps, or with the Wise Ones in the quietness of a grove. She sprang to her feet.

"The sap in my veins is clamouring for activity. Who'll come hawking?"

"I'm for the butts," said Prent. "I'm going to follow Bridei when he marches. I'll never have the chance again."

A crashing in the undergrowth sent bows springing into hands, to lower as Nechtan erupted through the bushes, glaring indignantly.

"There you are," he gasped, pointing a crooked finger at Caterin. "If the King only knew the dance you lead me."

"He'd give your post to a younger man," Caterin finished for him, removing a straw that dangled comically from his cap.

Nechtan swallowed his wrath, sensing dimly that his slow wits were a bonus for his mistress.

"You were asking about the sons of Artcois. Well, they're saddling their horses this minute in the stables."

Before he had finished speaking, Caterin was away, leaping over the young fern-fronds like a roe-deer.

"What hare-brained nonsense is she up to now?" Nechtan rolled his eyes at the sky. "They're ruffians, these two! Oh, Great Ones, don't let me be a horse between their thighs in my next life."

"It could be worse! You might be a Saxon filly," Drust grinned at his back.

Caterin could just make out Maelchon mounted on a chestnut stallion whose gleaming hide exactly matched the colour of his own thick hair. He was no longer the gangling youth who could climb the giant oak faster than anyone else. He had grown tall with the broad muscular build of his father and the handsome fleshy features of his mother. And a thick drooping moustache that made him look deliciously fierce.

"Greetings!" she called, waving both arms high in the air.

Resting his fists on his hips, he watched her come, tilting his head in that arrogant way she knew so well.

"It's not that scrawny wild-cat cub I used to wrestle with?"

She arrived panting at his knee, screwing her eyes against the glare of the sun that highlighted his head and shoulders with gold. He was her Shining One, back from the sea.

"Why didn't you come to visit me?"

"A rough sea-dog like me?" His roguish eyes scanned the fresh eager face and ripe body. "I can't compete with a black-browed Prince."

My, she had grown into a beauty. Her body curved and swelled in all the right places. Yet she was slim and lithe and far more tempting than a plump wench under the kitchen table.

"He means less than nothing to me! You know that."

"Do I?" His eyes devoured her, taunting, teasing, glinting. "Anyway, I knew you'd come looking for me."

"Still as conceited as ever!" She tossed her head. Only Maelchon had ever had the temerity to speak to her like this.

"I've not met the woman yet who could resist me!"

She smiled slowly, provocatively.

"I can. You'll find I'm different from other women."

Maelchon felt an unfamiliar tightness in his chest. For a moment he could not trust himself to answer her. Then he surprised himself by speaking quietly, dropping his bantering tone.

"Yes, you are."

What a weak-kneed fool he was! It was just a throwback to the days when he enjoyed having the Princess trail around after him with adoring eyes. There was adoration still in those green eyes but there was also a challenge. A challenge that excited him. He had not expected her to turn into such a raving beauty. It was maybe just as well he had his brother with him for his senses threatened to flare out of control.

"Where are you off to?" She laid a hand on his knee.

He and his brother had intended going to Pitshelt where a travelling family of horse-traders were camping with their covey of raven-haired daughters. But abruptly he changed his mind. The girls would be there tomorrow. His wide mouth lifted in a bold grin. His hand clamped on hers as if to hold her there.

"Hey, Talorc, we found nothing like this on the high seas."

His younger brother swung out of the stable on a grey gelding, stooping low to clear the lintel. He straightened on a long, whistling breath, raking her boldly with his eyes.

"By the two-headed Monster of the Lochan!" he gasped.

"Now why, Talorc?" said Maelchon, a husky chuckle in his voice, "Why were we wasting our time in the sweaty bowels of a ship when there was a dainty doe ready for sporting at home?"

"I'm not going to be the prey of two out-of-practise hunters," cried Caterin, laughing. "And I can match you two any day on a horse. Try me!"

"Oh I will, litle Wildcat, I will." Again that throaty voice, sending fire along her veins.

"A challenge!" Talorc cracked his whip. "Saddle a horse for the Princess." He threw a meaningful look at Maelchon over his shoulder.

The impatient, prancing horses and the reckless eyes of the brothers exhilerated her. She leapt on her mare, Crystal, russet-brown with straw-coloured mane and tail. It was the sparkle in her eye that had inspired Caterin to call her Crystal as a foal. Fully-grown now, she matched her mistress's skittish moods with an equal inclination to play tricks.

The trio set their horses at a gallop as they passed through the gate. Nechtan, mouthing curses, struggled to keep pace with them on his rough-maned garron. He had heard of her escapade yesterday from the Guard and his ears still burned at his language.

Flying along the roadway, they vied with each other. If Maelchon leapt to stand on his horse's haunches, Caterin copied him, waving her cap. If Talorc hung upside down below his saddle, Caterin's face, too, caught the spurting dust from flying hooves.

"Ay-ee! Slow down, Princess!" cried Maelchon at last. "Let's cool off."

They slowed their horses to a trot. Nechtan tucked his mount in behind Caterin.

"By the Silver-maned Mares!" Talorc edged alongside her. "Come next year you and I will sail north and wreak havoc up the fiords, shall we?"

"Steady, brother," warned Maelchon. "We can get away with a blaze in a cornfield. And a child in the belly can be paid for in cattle. But Queens don't go on the rampage among their own people if they want to stay skin-whole."

She warmed to Maelchon. He was still looking after her. It was fine, slipping into the old easy relationship. Yet having her old playmates for company made her feel as reckless as a moth at a flame. Only now and again as they rode north she drew back into herself, quiet and cool, watching him, liking the teasing that held a promise of caring, comparing him with the dark stiff foreigner, Gort.

No wonder Artcois had boasted that they were fine specimens of manhood. There was only a year between their ages but Maelchon, with his easy air of authority, looked years older than the callow Talorc. Their faces had the red-brown tinge that a pale skin develops at sea. Both had eyes of a pale metal colour as though they had absorbed the tones of billows and clouds. Being Veniconie their hair was lime-hardened from front to back in imitation of the bristles along the spine of their totem, the Boar.

"Hey, look at this?" Maelchon drew his horse up sharply at a rough stone at the road-side. "Do you think it's aiming to be a standing stone when it grows up."

"They're sprouting up all over," Caterin told him lightly. "The clans are setting them up at their borders with their totems cut on them and calling them Ancestor Stones."

"Then we've slipped over into your kin-land, Princess. That's the Vacomagie Deer. And the sign of the Striking Axe." Maelchon rubbed his open palm over the head of the stone and then over the column of his horse's neck. "Tell me, will the Vacomagie Ones grant me the fleetness of their Deer?"

"You'll do better with the brute-strength of our Boar," said Talorc. "You can't expect the Vacomagie Ones to share their spells with the Veniconie, can you?"

"It's worth a try." He lowered his voice, speaking to Caterin alone. "We could share more than spells between us, you know."

His voice had a husky growl in it. She turned her head away, half-liking, half-annoyed at what he'd said. Had he forgotten that Pretani women made the first move? And that she was royal? Then she shook herself, laughing, and steered the talk away from deep waters.

"See, here at the top. The broken arrow and Crescent Moon. That's powerful magic these days. It's a symbol of broken war weapons. And peace among the clans."

Maelchon took the hint. He let the other three ride ahead. He had been with too many foreign girls who liked a man to be forceful. He enjoyed the feeling of power it gave him. But this girl was no giggling wench to be taken in a hayloft. He would have to remember she was no longer his adoring slave.

"Isn't there a Wise Woman lives near here," he asked as he came up with them again.

"At the Cave of the Seven Maidens," Caterin agreed.

"Let's see if the old harpy's still alive," cried Talorc, bored and ready for mischief. "Come on! We'll dowse her in her own Well unless she tells us our fate."

Enormous clouds were building up powerfully from the horizon as they set off again with Nechtan plodding, grumbling, in the rear.

"Do you always have a shadow?" queried Maelchon, jerking his head back over his shoulder.

She looked over at him and some of the shine went out of the day. What a stupid question! Why would he ask it? Of course Nechtan was a thorn in her flesh. Once when she had escaped his constant vigilance Bridei had found out. Even now she could hear him shouting at her.

"That man was forced into the service of the Royal Line as a half-starved orphan. Since then he's given us that unswerving loyalty that others give to their kin. Can't you see? Any day danger could sweep in from the sea in the form of dark-skinned raiders. And they'd wax fat on the gold exchanged for a high-born Alban girl." But Bridei could never be angry with her for long. "Especially one with a honey-yellow sheen on her hair and a cherry-blossom skin."

Maelchon's hurt voice cut into her thoughts.

"But I've always looked after you well enough, haven't I?"

It was true. And she used to love him for it. Why did she find it irritating now? As though she belonged to him. As though she needed protection. Impatient with herself for these critical thoughts, she clicked her tongue at Crystal, urging her forward, game for any adventure.

And glanced over her shoulder to make sure that Nechtan had tucked himself in behind.

CHAPTER EIGHT

In the distance the high blue uplands rose to meet them. Beyond, towering thunderheads, tinged with copper, were massing. A storm would spoil their sport.

They topped a low hill and saw a brooding, barren valley, a desolate place, floored by stunted grass, broken by the flat pewter surface of a loch and swatches of iris and bog cotton flags, warning of marshland. A cold air, welling up from below, shivered across Caterin's skin.

Reeds growing in a perfect circle showed where a ditch had been dug once and a great earthen wall had been thrown up. Inside the ditch reared a circle of standing stones, grey and silent.

Caterin thought of the wild people, long since dead and burned, how they quarried these great sandstone slabs and carried them here and levered them upright and packed them into holes. Centuries of wind and rain had eroded the carefully dressed surfaces, a few had cracked, one had broken in half and another had fallen. Within the circle, overgrown kerb-stones lay on their sides. Here the Little Hairy People had sung their songs and danced by the light of the Moon Maiden. And still did, some said.

The long shadow-shapes of the stones crept across the grass, pointing accusing fingers at the feet of the motionless riders. A cloud moved with incredible slowness over the sun. The shadows vanished. Nechtan made the sign of the crescent in the air, his tight white lips muttering 'Mighty Ones protect us', over and over.

"On the night of the winter solstice, some say, the stones heave out of their holes and dance," whispered Caterin, half-afraid that her voice would be stolen out of her mouth by some nameless ghosting thing.

"And some say the spirits of dead Druad meet here." Talorc's voice rasped out of the stillness.

"This is the haunt of the Wise Woman," Maelchon taunted. "Are you both turning tail already?"

"Never!" Stung into action, Talorc kicked his horse and went swooping down the slope.

Crystal shied wildly at something only she could see.

"Race you round the ditch!" cried Maelchon.

"Don't ride into that accursed place." Nechtan leaned over to grasp Crystal's flying reins.

"I'm not afraid of ghost stories." Caterin soothed the neck of the sweating mare. "Mothers tell them just to keep their bairns at the knee. There's nothing to ..."

Out of the far distance came the howl of a wolf, eerie and echoing, chilling the blood. Caterin, clutching her amulet, went after the brothers. Nechtan followed, holding well back as if to prove to the Nameless Ones that he had no part in this madness.

He caught up with the trio at the far side. They had been forced to stop on the bank of meandering stream that had nibbled underneath at the earth-work. Yesterday's deluge had sent more soil tumbling down. Flat coffin slabs and pale bones protruded from the crumbling soil.

Caterin sat rigid, pressing her knees against Crystal's warm flanks, conscious of a silence as though unseen watchers held their breath.

"Old graves!" Talorc was full of glee.

"I'll bet you're afraid to have a dig around." Maelchon was up to his old trick of goading his younger brother into boyish escapades. He winked over at Caterin. "If you're lucky you might find a silver cup."

Talorc's reins arced over into Nechtan's hand as he slid from his horse and began gouging into the earth with his knife.

"This is all wrong!" Caterin cried. "You're desecrating a sacred place!"

"What's happened to the Wildcat Princess then?" Maelchon mocked her. "Once you were game for any bit of fun." He would not admit even to himself that the eerie silence was unnerving him.

"Stop it! These are our ancestors!"

"The wee Peskies?" Maelchon spat on the ground. "Our future Queen and you're scared witless by the wee Hairy Men?"

"These stones are our heritage! These people made us what we are today! Don't you care about that?"

"No! Why should I?"

Maelchon's flippant tone dismayed her.

"Are you moonstruck?" Nechtan quavered. "The dead will come to drink your blood." His mount fidgeted, catching the smell of his fear.

Maelchon's contemptuous laugh strangled in his throat as a

rumble of thunder growled and threatened, rolling across the sky from horizon to horizon.

"Ach! I've broken my dagger!"

As Talorc sprang up, a bleached skull rolled from under his feet to lie rocking and grinning up at them.

"Hey, I've always wanted one of these."

"Take the old warrior home and drink in his strength with your ale."

Maelchon glanced at Caterin expecting her approval. A lusty youth, his aggressive sexuality always wakened a response in women.

"Enough!" cried Caterin. "Up on your horse! We're getting out of here!"

Bones cleansed of flesh and spirit mattered little to Caterin. It was the awareness in every nerve in her body that the Earth Mother was awake and listening.

At the sudden note of authority in her voice Talorc's lip curled. He turned his back and hid the skull in his tunic.

Maelchon felt confused. He was seeing a new Caterin here. A grown woman with an aloof quality, an unconscious regality. But his pride could not let him be. He laughed and leaned over to tug her braid. His arrogant presumption infuriated Caterin. She struck out at him, her nails clawing his face and drawing blood.

Maelchon threw back his head and laughed.

"Why, the Wildcat's back! And I thought the granite Prince had tamed you."

Suddenly a blue flash leapt from stone to stone. Caterin's scream split the air.

"Sheet lightning." Maelchon's lips twisted.

Caterin's skin prickled. She was filled with a nameless dread. She felt, rather than saw, movement all around them.

"Anyway, I'm going to leave my mark to show I've been here." Talorc straddled one of the slabs and began to scratch out a three-pronged shape with the broken edge of his dagger. The grate of metal on stone rasped in the still air. "I swear within a year my trident will be known in every land that borders the ocean."

A whisper of uncanny laughter writhed round the silent stones. Wondering, Caterin raised her head to listen. The high, blue hills seemed to have moved a step nearer. On the skyline leaned the black skeleton of an oak, blasted by a lightning stroke. On one bare branch sat two ravens, still and ominous.

At the edge of her vision a dark form took shape, suddenly, without warning. When she looked, a figure stood, half-in, half-out of the shadow of the largest stone. Tall and commanding, shrouded in a cloak, it had to be one of the avenging spirits of the lower earth. Yet, the voice, when it came, was entirely human, a woman's voice, melodious and surprisingly youthful.

"So you want to know whom the Great Ones will favour or you'll dowse me in my Well." The echo of words spoken uncaring in the warmth of the sun brought Maelchon swinging round. Talorc's jaw dropped and he barely suppressed a high-pitched giggle.

"If you can speak with the All-Seeing Ones then tell us our fortune!" The curtness of Maelchon's demand sickened Caterin. Yet she found she was searching her memory. The Woman's voice had struck an echo that vibrated from somewhere in her past. Or was it her future?

The Woman stepped away from the stone. Her cloak was cunningly woven in strands of greens and browns and yellows and purples, the colours of the countryside in all seasons. It was made of fine stuff with a creamy sheen. Caring hands had woven it, showing she was respected amongst her own people. She leaned on a stout oak branch that still sprouted buds.

"I have the gift to see further through than most," the Woman acknowledged. Her hood hung low, shadowing her face. "Yet, the Power comes only when the Wise Ones send it. And only when good may come of it." Caterin felt, rather than saw, the hidden eyes rest on each one of them in turn.

Questions came to Caterin's tongue welling from some deep desperate need inside her. And she could not ask them. For there were no words in her mind, only a cloud that grew and burgeoned and then burst asunder. And beyond was a garden in a haze of sunlight and flowers. And she wanted to walk forward to reach it but the image darkened and vanished and she was aware of Maelchon at her side fumbling in his purse.

"Here, woman, if you've nothing better to tell us, take an offering to your spirits and be gone."

The golden coin, stolen from the saddle-bag of a murdered Saxon pedlar, lay glinting in the dust where Maelchon had tossed it. Caterin gaped at him stupefied. What right had he to insult a Wise Woman? A feeling of repugnance rose in her throat.

Then far away the mournful cry of the lone wolf, hunting for prey, tolled again and again like a burial-bell in the heavy air. Suddenly, as if startled, the ravens launched themselves from their dead branch on ragged wings.

"You attract ominous signs about you. The grey wolf and the black raven. Both scavengers of the battlefield." Disdain dripped slowly from the voice like honey from a comb. "The Great Ones have answered you. Take your unclean gold with you when you leave."

"You dare to foretell our death in battle, Woman?" cried Maelchon. He raised his whip to strike her.

"Ah, no." The sigh came like a whisper on the breeze. Maelchon's arm dropped suddenly as though invisibly struck down.

"Many roads lie before each one of you. Your spirit will choose the way it wishes to go. For it has lived before and knows the lessons it needs to learn."

Talorc stood, scratching a pimple on his chin, ensnared by his terror.

"Already each one of you has set your foot on the path you will follow. But beware! The Wise Ones are testing you." She paused. They waited, silent. "And it is certain you will live with the deeds of this day for ever!"

Haunting vibrations reached out from the stones casting tentacles of fear around them. The skull fell from Talorc's tunic and he kicked it, bouncing it along the turf. The horses milled round on anxious feet as he leapt to mount. When they turned to question the Woman again, she had disappeared. Only Caterin saw that, behind where she had stood, the grass was misted with bluebells where none had been before. And far off on the marsh, lights danced. They walked their mounts round the circle, thinking to surprise her hiding behind a stone but there was no sign that she had ever been there at all.

"Someone should tell that old mystic a few home-truths. That a champion doesn't earn his mead by cowering under a fleece." Maelchon's spirits had brightened as a freshening wind blew the rain-clouds away across the ocean.

Caterin's eye followed the direction of her mare's pricked ears and let her pick her way over to the stream to drink, her hooves hidden in a carpet of blue lady's smock. She felt infinitely sad. As if she had held something precious in her hand and lost it. It was to do with the Woman. She had not spoken directly to her. Yet she felt as if she had been called and, deep down, her spirit had answered.

One precious thing she had lost that day. Her first love!

"What's happened to you?" she asked Maelchon. "You've become crude and coarse. A lot you care about the tradition!" And she had thought she might marry him and make him King!

"Look! Fairy rings!"

Talorc had dismounted and was staring at thick rings of mushrooms snuggling round his feet. Kneeling, he picked a smooth head and bit into it.

Maelchon seemed strangely withdrawn, his eyes reflecting the grey of the sky. "Well, Maelchon?" she asked.

"I'm sorry, Princess," he said, his breezy charm returning. "I should have known better. Have a mushroom!"

His admission of guilt did not soften her feelings towards him.

"They're good. Here, try one."

Half-joking he forced a handful into her mouth. They felt silky against her tongue and had a faint musty taste that made her hold out her hand for more.

"Don't eat these pesky things!" Nechtan rode up, his arm flung wide in warning. "The Little People will take your wits from you."

"By the Crescent, Nechtan, you're always trying to spoil our sport." Maelchon's mouth was full. He pulled Talorc to his feet. Flecks of mushroom sprayed as he mumbled in Talorc's ear.

"Will you come away before the Little People spell you?" Nechtan's voice rose to a squeak in his panic. He urged his horse forward, meaning to trample the mushrooms underfoot. A shout from Talorc caused him to swing round.

"Hey, Nechtan, there's a boar in those bushes." Talorc leapt on his mount. "Come on! I'll show you how we Veniconie spit a boar."

"You'll show me, will you?" Nechtan drew his small-sword. "Just you follow me! I'll show you how it's done!" Splashing through the stream he plunged into the undergrowth.

To Caterin's horror Talorc winked at her over his shoulder and rode off laughing. Why did she feel alarmed? She was being silly. This was harmless fun. Like the old days. And little enough fun she had had lately.

"Have some more, Princess." Maelchon was growling softly

again and his voice was strangely possessive. "Happy mushrooms make you feel good."

As she ate she noticed that his eyes were queer and glittering. She was a rabbit in front of a snake. No, she was a thistledown seed floating in a world of dazzling sun and luminous flowers.

A wild, sweet longing possessed her. She danced around the man, her arms stretching and sinking. The earth was soft as the breast of a dove. Little eyes winked and nodded in the grass and sent up puffs of heady perfume as she crushed them under her body.

Maelchon's hand, delicate as a feather, caressed her face and arms, sending strange sensations to every part of the pink cloud that was her body. Joyfully, she dissolved into his embrace. And Maelchon's kiss was sweeter than anything she could ever have imagined.

Until his wet tongue invaded her mouth bringing a flavour that reminded her of an unclean drain. Her throat gagged and her stomach heaved.

Then he was tearing at the neck of her tunic, bruising her flesh.

And she became an animal, all snapping teeth and raking claws and bunching legs, punching and thrusting at the hard body above her, her senses screaming, her throat working, her fingers groping for her dagger and feeling it wrenched from her girdle.

Maelchon shifted to kneel astride her, imprisoning her legs, he knew all the tricks. One part of his mind warned him,'Too soon! Too soon!' Then in the heat of his desire he found himself shouting, 'You'll be mine someday!' 'The sooner the better!' 'I'll make my mark in you now!' And then he slowed down, began to take his time, a low sobbing growl in his throat.

His moist mouth with its long moustache slid over Caterin's face leaving a slimy trail. She dragged her face aside, drawing breath to scream but again his mouth clamped down. His hands moved up her legs, throwing back the thick folds of her skirt. His urgent body pressed, his thick knee forcing her legs apart. Slowly. But surely.

Above the grunting of the man and the sobbing in her throat, sounded a cry of rage and despair, echoing through the clearing. Maelchon's weight lifted suddenly. Rolling onto her side, she gathered her limbs into a tight protective ball.

Then as she lay, gasping, heaving, another cry rose in the air and went on and on. An animal cry, a cry of bewilderment and grief. It mounted to a shriek of anguish, vibrating through her head, piercing her spirit. Till it faded to a gurgling whimper and died. And there was a long pulsating silence, full of wonder that such a sound could have been.

Caterin opened her eyes. Maelchon lay dazed on the ground where Nechtan had heaved him. Nechtan had fallen, face down, an arrow sticking out of his back. In the shelter of the trees Talorc stood, smirking, lowering his bow.

It was a dream. The kind she had when she knew she were dreaming and squeezed her eyes shut and pleaded over and over to waken up. Hammers pounded in her brain. She hid her face in the cool moist grass.

"You stupid oaf! Why did you have to kill him?"

Caterin sat up, swaying, and put her hand to her head.

Maelchon thrust Nechtan's body aside as he staggered to his feet. The haft of the arrow stuck into the ground and Nechtan's body hung impaled on it. His loose limbs and head wobbled once and fell slack, all lop-sided like a cast-away rag-doll.

"I saved your life, you fool?" Talorc's voice was high and cracking with hysteria. "He'd have struck your head off!"

She knew she had to go to Nechtan. It was a long long way. His lifeless eyes accused her. Through his hanging jaw, his spirit was calling her to account. They were accursed, all three of them! Clenching her fists, she rounded on the brothers.

"Filth! Foul misbegotten pigs!" she screamed. "You've killed Nechtan! Murdered him!"

Talorc stepped forward sniggering.

"I told you I was a good shot."

"You mushroom-happy fool!" Maelchon's face was distorted with rage. "All you had to do was keep him away until I'd had her."

"Easier said than done. He thrashed around and then guesed there was no boar. Could you have done better?"

"You've landed us in the privy sewer now!"

"It was your idea!" Talorc kicked moodily at a tuft of grass. "You can set your own traps after this."

Maelchon stopped his brother's mouth with a swinging backhander.

"So you planned it between you!" Caterin spat the words, sickness rising in her throat. "By the Blood of the Bull, what did you hope to gain from raping me? Nechtan swore the Little People would turn their spells on you. Well, he was right!" It was hard to stay upright but she fought for dignity.

"You've killed a King's man between you. I'll see you both pay the full penalty for that!"

"And what price will you pay?" snarled Maelchon, thrusting his face at her. His eyes were white-hot, evil and baleful. "You were on heat for it. His blood's on your head too!"

The memory of her moment of mushroom madness was more than she could bear. Her happy euphoria had been replaced by a dull throbbing in her head. What had she been thinking of? She had actually loved Maelchon once, thought about him for the Kingship. Too late now she recalled the talk around the Capital, that the Veniconie men who divided their time between raids and rape, had become brutalised. Oh, Bride what had she done? Nothing would ever be the same again. She tore off a rag that fluttered from her bodice and bound up Nechtan's jaw.

"An old servant past his best," jeered Talorc. "I'll get you a better one on my next raid."

"The Thundering Ones take you! He was a better man than you!"

It was the suddenness of it that stupefied her. She had never seen violent death before.

Maelchon had come to his senses. By the Gods of the Storm, why had he forced the pace? He'd have her anyway once his father's rebellion succeeded. Where had the idea come from, that if he got her pregnant Bridei would relinquish the Kingship to him? From that cursed mushroom juice, of course! And the that old fool that blundered into it! And that dolt Talorc had pole-axed the whole scheme.

With eyes that were bleak as the grey sea-wastes, he turned to gather his reins and spoke across his horse's back to Talorc.

"No kin-fee will bury this deed. We're outlaws for this."

"You were only supposed to persuade her, not to force her," Talorc whined.

Maelchon's voice cut in low and urgent.

"I heard of a ship leaving the Firth for the Low Countries at the turn of the tide. We can just catch it!"

"And what do we do about her?" Talorc jerked his thumb in the direction of Caterin. "Do we let her carry tales to the King?"

He fitted another arrow into his bow.

"Leave her be!" Maelchon's command cut sharply across the clearing. "Our kin will pay the blood-fine. But if we kill the Royal Brood-Mare we'll have Bridei after us for evermore." His eyes burned into Caterin's.

"But I'll be back, my Lady. I'll use you as a stepping-stone to the Kingship yet. We'll cool our heels across the Narrow Sea until either Bridei or Aedan has set his seal on Alba."

Talorc's arrow still pointed straight at Caterin's breast.

"Come on, man!" shouted Maelchon, mounting his wheeling horse. "That one's trouble dead or alive."

Caterin saw Talorc's finger tighten on the bow-string and threw up her head. His mad, light eyes flickered dangerously. The arrow flew. And sank harmlessly in the ground at her feet. Swinging his bow round his body he threw a leg over his horse and his mocking laugh faded into the distance.

With her knife, Caterin sawed at the arrow that impaled Nechtan until his body could sink back and rest. She laid two flat pebbles from the stream on his eyes. She buried another pebble at the foot of a rowan tree in payment for a twig to ward off the beings who would try to steal his spirit for their own. Standing beside his body, she made the sign of the crescent.

There should have been words to say over him but all she could find in her heart was a burning shame.

Maelchon was right. She was accursed by blood-guilt. If Nechtan had fallen by the hand of an attacker, that would have been in the line of duty. Instead, he had died because she craved for excitement. She was not fit to be Queen, to set herself up as Chief of the Clan Mothers. The women would turn their eyes away and smile at the fool she was, a furrow in a field, ready to be ploughed by any drunken farmer.

Caterin mounted Crystal and gathered the reins of Nechtan's horse. Who would set the price the Princess must pay? The King must exact retribution for the sake of the community. For the law said that any violent action reverberated unto four generations. Even the death of a lowly servant without kin would spread ever-widening circles like a pebble thrown into a pond.

As soon as she saw that an unwonted number of lamps had been lit in the Citadel and the Guard on the Gate had been trebled, she knew that the pebble had been thrown and the ripples were expanding into an uneasy future.

Men summoned from field and workshop seethed in the warren of streets, jostled around the stables, diced in groups or kicked their heels on barrels. They were caught and suspended in time, hovering between the safety of the hearth and the thrill of the piper-led march. There was not a man of them that had not pulled on the caracalla that would act as both armour and bed-mat without a quickening of his blood at the thought of the home-coming, plunder-rich and glory-drenched, his reputation as high as his shield-rim. Or so the bards would have it.

And what of her reputation? It would serve to wrap round the withered corpse of her childhood fancies.

CHAPTER NINE

King Bridei was in the armoury, that enormous building with the extra high doors to give passage to the tall machines that would throw flaming fire-balls into the forts of the Dal Riatans. Inside, the shriek of blade-grinders assaulted her ears. Bridei stood examining spears that leant on storage racks. In the fading daylight Caterin swung past the lads examining chain-mail for rust, past rows of boxes filled with quivers of arrows lying open for the King's inspection.

Bridei made to wave her away. Then, seeing her drawn face and grass-stained skirts, he mouthed above the din, "What's wrong?" and bent his ear for her answer.

"Nechtan's been murdered!"

Bridei stared aghast. He beckoned Gort and Cennalath over to a corner where the fletchers were working and the noise was less ear-splitting. Gort's diamond-sharp eyes took in every detail of her dishevilled appearance.

"Maelchon tried to rape me. Nechtan drew his sword and Talorc killed him." Caterin gave back a flat, brief answer to Bridei's question, trying to control the tremor in her voice, the hot tears pricking behind her eyes.

Everyone heard clearly the voice that roared above the tumult.

"By the Great Black Balls of the Royal Bull! Are you hurt?"

She shook her head.

"Murder of a King's servant! The young idiots!" Cennalath drew a long exasperated breath. "Where are they now?"

"Fled to join a ship in the Firth making for the Low Lands."

"I commissioned it myself to bring back Saxon axes," said Bridei grimly. A fletcher pushed a fistful of arrows under his nose and was thrust aside.

"Where's the body?"

"On the Inch."

The crash of the King's clenched fists shattered a box-lid and set her teeth chattering.

"What were you doing with those gutter-rats anyway?" Bridei barked. He drummed a fist on a beam, trying to keep himself from striking her. "I hope you realise what you've done! On the eve of the march, there's been a spilling of blood and I'm forced to outlaw two of my sea-lords!"

The noisy preparations for war that grated around them highlighted the enormity of her crime.

"And you were right!" She could not help rubbing salt into her own wound. "Maelchon vowed he'd come back and take the Kingship!"

Bridei's great fists were working as though there had never been a pain in them. He knew now he should have banned Caterin from leaving the Citadel.

"I told you they were a threat! Had you not enough sense to leave them alone? And you think you're capable of taking power as Queen!"

Eyes narrowed, Gort flexed a bow of yew tipped with goat's horn. He approved of the way she had come to face them, bravely, her pride in tatters.

"She's not the first Queen to dice with the destiny of her people," he said.

His show of indifference brought Caterin's raw nerves to the surface.

"Who gave you authority over me?" she asked icily.

"I did!" Bridei flashed back. "I've made him Commander of my southern army. That post makes him my Heir. By the Crescent, I don't envy him the task of becoming your lord and master."

"I'll break her in when the time comes." The mocking lilt in Gort's voice froze the blood in her veins.

"What's done is done!" Abruptly, Gort dismissed the matter. "Shall I send a party to bring in the corpse before dark?"

"Leave it for a couple of days for the crows. I can't risk a fever in this over-crowded Citadel. We've no time for full burial rites and burning's too messy."

"The Ceremony of Retribution is going to be even messier." Cennelath glanced at Gort. "The two men to be outlawed are the sons of the Commander of the Fleet."

The screeching of iron on iron ebbed and flowed around them.

Bridei felt a stab of panic rise in his gut and knew he was getting old.

"Right!" he barked. "If we've to fit in a Retribution and get on our way before noon, the Leave-Taking Ceremony will have to come forward a full hour. Have the horns blown and announce it."

He turned to order his daughter out of his sight but something in her face made him pause. It was not hard to see how deeply shocked she was. He noticed the tiny nervous movements of her hands and the tension in the line of her mouth. Yet her chin tilted, not with belligerence, but bravely. He had deliberately heaped humiliation on her head in public and she had accepted it. Perhaps there were the makings of a Queen in the girl, after all.

"I'm sorry. I'm bitterly sorry for what's happened. Nechtan paid the price for my foolishness. And I must make retribution too." She paused and swallowed. "What's my punishment to be?"

"Your decision, Gort." Bridei stumped away, more moved than he cared to show.

Bitter shame burned in her heart at that. A spark of protest flared before she turned obediently towards Gort and waited, eyes downcast.

For a long moment Gort was tempted to be kindly. After all she was but a child, her crime confessed, her shame clear. The momentary flash of defiance decided him. It was time she learned that life was a brier bush growing in a compst heap. He arched an eyebrow, deliberately lending an impish twist to his expression.

"Your punishment is to marry a man who can read you as he reads the weather-signs in the sky."

Bridei was pretending to examine a ballisti, a machine first captured from the Romans but refined in design by the carpenters as they repaired it. He heard Gort's words and fingered his beard, speculation in his eye.

That night Caterin found she could not bear to appear in the Banqueting Hall.

Next day she lay on her couch, her emotions still numb, staring at nothing, at her belts and pouches that hung on the wall, at the way the sun shining through the slats sent stripes moving across them, slowly, slowly. Like the bars of a cage.

Devana stepped in as lightly as a kitten and began fidgeting through Caterin's bead-box. And Caterin saw by her trembling mouth she was not going to crow and say 'I told you so'.

"Have you heard? The army marches tomorrow. Cennalath and Gort are going to besiege Dundurn." A necklace of sea-polished agates slid through Devana's fingers and rolled with her tears to the floor. "And I go home to a land worked by women with one eye permanently cocked on the horizon."

Caterin closed her mind on the image of Nechtan's empty eyes and rose, opening her arms to her aunt. But Devana brushed her cheeks with her hand and waved her away and the moment for loving was gone.

"And Gort's been named Heir. You'll have to lie with him now."

There was a jug of mead on a table. Caterin put it to her mouth and drank, ignoring the cup.

"This is my cauldron of stew, Devana! Don't dip your fingers in it!" She slammed down the flagon. "Tonight Gort can relieve himself in a serving wench! And tomorrow I'm leaving, too. I'm going to the Druad at Pitversie."

"You're a fool!" snapped Devana. "Every lass will be with her lad tonight."

"I won't lie with a man till he's proved he's loyal. I've been a dice on the gambling board long enough!"

"That attitude, I imagine, is going to upset a lot of people." Devana's robes swished as she flounced out.

"Foreign Princes in particular, I hope!" Caterin called after her.

And she stood for a while, sorry she had spoken sharply, making herself an island in this sea of war. And the face that looked back from the mirror was still her own. Except for the shadows in the eyes and the firm set on the wide mobile mouth that had come with her new resolve. For she had thought she had known it all. And knew nothing! Surely the Druad, the wisest of all, must know the answers, straight from the Wise Ones.

There in the outer room wooden chests and leather bundles were heaped against the wall ready for her journey. Lifting the topmost lid, she saw that everything had been folded neatly. She had no cause for complaint. But Devana had been right. Iogena had worked quickly and made herself scarce. She would have to dress herself for the Banqueting Hall. Bridiei would never forgive her if she did not appear for the Feast on the eve of the march.

That evening, the Master of the Household had squeezed in even more tables, a feat that amazed everyone. Lords and Mormaers had gathered from all over South Pettaland to meet the rising threat.

The Master of the Insignia recited their names and ancestry in proud rolling syllables. The Mormaer of Muref had sent Fergus, Toiseach of Burghead and his underlords of Nigg and Cadboll. The three chiefs of Marr cum Buchen had sent their foster-sons as pledges. From the Province of Enegus had come the Princes of Brechin and Aberlemno. From Adtheodle where the great pyramid of Schiehallion presided above Glen Lyon had come the Mormaers of Dun Keld and Scone.

The very resonance of the ancient names was like a trumpet call that filled the heart with pride and resolution. It was a fitting homage to a worthy company. It was a glorious praise-song to preface a memorable battle-feast.

Yet from Fif had come only the Chiefs from Abernethie, Kilrymont and the Mark of Inch. For Fif was Veniconie country, the clan of Artcois.

On the eve of the march, the cooks had excelled themselves. There were a hundred swans roasted whole in their feathers; herons, baked in clay, garnished with leeks and chervil; succulent lamb, peat-smoked; followed by baked sweetmeats until even the roundest belly was full. The wine was spiced with cloves, but not enough to deaden the senses. The ale and mead would do that.

The talk round the High Table in crisp low tones was about the two expeditions, north and west. Gort was no longer the honoured guest but sat among forty chiefs who all received the rituals of hospitality. Taciturn and aloof, Gort sat, drinking little, his granite eyes moving restlessly around the Hall. Once Caterin caught his speculative gaze upon herself. Mercifully, she would be free of his presence after tomorrow. It had all started with his arrival, catapulting her into a whirlpool of emotions, emotions which she neither the experience nor the will to control. Could the Druad teach her how to do that?

The bones were chewed clean, the cups emptied and refilled and emptied again. A thumping of beakers and a riot of voices, blurred by ale, called for a livelier beat from the pipers in the corner. But it was Eildon who answered their call, a transformed Eildon. He strode into their midst carrying his sturdy travelling harp and sprang onto a table. Tonight he wore the colours of the Kingship, red and white. Planting his legs astride, he struck a series of strident chords that shivered up to the rafters and quelled the throng into panting silence.

His hooded eyes swept the Hall, gathering all eyes. Then he gave them what they wanted. The beat he set up with his stamping heel stirred the blood. Beakers and boots thumped in time. Louder and louder. Just when it seemed the beat would break the walls of heart and hall, his fingers took to the strings, forked and flying. His voice rang out in the first line of a verse and the men around him burst into song. It was a song sung by warriors since the time when weapons were made of stone and horn. Names had been changed and battles rendered bloodier but the age-old fierceness of the song was there. And it was reassuring.

They sang of the march through the clean air of the mountains with hearts high to the skirl of the pipes, of the shrill war-thunder and the crimson blood, how the foe ate dust and the war-bird screamed. With only a breath taken, they launched into the song of the slim-blade, humming and spilling blood, of the red, quick points of the spear-lunge, of rivers sobbing with the sap of the enemy. Then came the songs of Bridei's last campaign and, if there had been space in the Hall the men would have danced, arms crooked in elbows.

"Young the commander who created that Monday-combat.
Shattered were the Eirean settlements on that fear-day.
Thatch smoked and fire flared over fields.
The true prince took payment for treachery thrice in one moon-month."

Caterin sat perfectly still, letting the words trickle over her, hearing them with a terrible awareness. Her mind seemed to have been stretched in the past few days, almost beyond her capacity to bear it. She stood alone on the rocky pinnacle that was her heritage. Both Bridei and Devana cared little for the true meaning of the tradition. And her sweet first love had been rotten at the core. Treachery, as the song said, must be paid for in the end.

"The Scots will ever remember this edge-storm.
No greater ring-giver ever roamed with the war-guard.
Against the Angles, he has raised his war-banners.
Often his war-band bloodied the hawk-beak,
Fire shrank the walls, flame ravaged, smoke reared,
From the forts in the north to the those in the south,
Bridei went fearless through the dark fight-throng,
Many a horn howling, but high held his banner."

Fearless through the dark fight-throng she must go. But high held her banner. Yet who was she to despise the traitors? For she had betrayed herself and her people.

"Nothing weakened the warriors of the Black Bull Lord.
War reigned, steel dazzled, wolves dined on the dead."

And as she gently swirled the honey-heavy mead in her cup, she made a vow that hardened every fibre of her being. That she would pursue the Veniconie until wolves dined on their flesh. That never again would she be persuaded from her course. That she would become the greatest Pretani Queen that ever lived.

For she would seek knowledge. Knowledge was the pathway to power. Power over Kings to save the Pretani tradition. Power over her emotions, so that she would be invulnerable to love. She would be utterly single-minded in her bid for power. Nothing would weaken the resolve of the Black Bull Queen. She pledged her vow in the last of her mead.

As Caterin left, the ululating war-cry of the Pretani reverberated round the Hall.

CHAPTER TEN

At the entrance to her rooms, Caterin paused. One solitary lamp flickered in the draught from the door.

"Iogena?"

The snap of tension in the air of the Citadel sent a flash-fire of fear prickling along Caterin's nerves. With a slow finger, she moved the curtain and surveyed the inner room with one eye. All was dark and silent. Her waiting-women had their own secrets tonight. She stepped forward and her feet were caught up in a heavy mesh. Her breath strangled in her throat. The dim glow from the doorway fell on a tumble of her discarded day-clothes on the floor.

The outer door creaked. The light, through the curtain, brightened. Lamps were being lit one by one. Caterin's pent-up discontent and loneliness erupted in anger.

"Iogena, where have you been?" She held the curtain high above her head, confronting her servant.

The cruisie under Iogena's taper flared into flame and lit the girl's flushed cheeks and wind-blown hair.

"I knew it! You slut! You've been lying behind the cooking pots with the dirt of the army!"

Iogena whirled like an animal at bay. Gone was the sullen slave. Something or someone had roused her to a point where she had either to challenge or sink in defeat.

"I'm no slut! I'm as highborn as you are!" She faced Caterin, head high, lips pale and bitter. "I'd no more let that lot handle me than you would!"

"Don't put yourself on a level with me, slave. You could lose your life for it."

"My blood's as good as yours. My father's kin to the Kings of the Dal n'Araide." Iogena's voice crackled but her eyes were beyond caring.

"Scottie blood?" Caterin spoke slowly withering her with the word that meant 'scavengers' in any language.

"I can trade names too. Back home we call you 'Cruithne', the corn-eaters!"

"Take care when you tangle with the Royal Blood Line, Scottie slave."

"But it's Scottie blood that runs your veins!" Iogena laughed as Caterin drew back stunned. "When your Cruithne men came to settle in Alba, they asked the Eireans for wives. And they had to promise that the blood line would descend through the Mothers. That's how your customs arose. To safeguard the Eirean women. But you Cruithne forget that!" She wet her finger and thumb and nipped the smoking taper.

Caterin had heard a whisper of it from a pedlar and had laughed him to scorn.

"That's a lie!" Her hand swept up, her fingers curled round a riding-whip on its hook. Then she was looking into smoky blue eyes on a level with her own. Eyes that flickered with fear before turning deep and dark and wary.

Caterin lowered her empty hand and studied it. Those fingers had lately closed the eyes of a servant. One who had sacrificed his life for her. One she had teased and taunted unmercifully, treating him as less than a man.

Bridei's voice filled her mind.

"My bodyguards would die for me knowing I would die for them. Duty works both ways. Remember that!"

The words must have lodged somewhere in her head, waiting for the moment of truth, when she would understand them for herself.

Would she have given her life for Nechtan? Yet she had accepted his sacrifice.

Iogena could hardly believe she was not going to be beaten. Oh, holy St. Brigit, what devilish plot was this spoilt mistress thinking up now? She distrusted the way the Princess was staring at her palm as though her fate was pictured there. Sliding her hand behind her back she dropped the posy of wild flowers that had dried in her hand and ground her heel on it.

Caterin thought of the vow she had made in the Hall, to suppress all weakening emotion, to be single-minded in her bid to become the most powerful Pretani Queen ever. Or the most ruthless and most hated?

Devana, now. Servants fell over themselves trying to please her. Because she liked and respected them. She supped their sauces and was kind to a slave in a dowdy homespun tunic whose mistress abused her.

Caterin swung off the cloak that slung to her shoulders and threw it aside. The slave made no move to hang it up. Deep in her heart Caterin knew she did not want power that excluded all warmth and love. Devana had a different power, the power to draw people towards her. And if Caterin wanted to be liked she must start now, start by giving something first. Lost in her thoughts she picked up the cloak and hung it neatly on a hook.

She would gladly have wiped out these last few minutes with Iogena if she could. Somehow she would have to make a bridge over the past and start afresh. Maybe there was a way. Princess or slave, they were both women.

"Where were you then if you weren't lifting your skirts for a soldier?" she asked.

Iogena eyes widened in fright. She retreated backwards until she bumped against the wall.

"I swear by the gods of my people ..."

"What sort of a sidelong oath is that?" Caterin's voice quivered with the effort she was making to control her impatience.

At first, the girl would not answer.

"In our tuath," she said at last, "we don't name our gods for fear of calling down their wrath. But it's a binding oath for all that."

Caterin faltered. She tried to smile and failed. She was doing it all wrong. She sensed by the downcast eyes and crossed fingers that the girl had not told the whole story. How could she blame her? If she was a slave, Bride forbid it, she would be looking for comfort too.

Suddenly there were no more words. Only feelings that came bubbling to the surface. The bridge lay open and the crossing was easy.

"Iogena, I'm sorry. Don't you understand. I'd give my best brooch to be with a lover tonight."

Still suspicion lingered in the blue-dark eyes.

Iogena had suffered too much at the hands of this woman already. Yet, less than an hour ago, under an apple-tree, heavy with blossom, she had known wonder and ecstacy. She had grasped at the love that was offered because it might never come again. The future held no hope for her. So what did it matter now if the Princess had her put to death?

"I wasn't with any common soldier like you said." She spoke carefully, trying to justify her oath. "I was with the man I love." Her husky whisper changed to a defiant cry. "He wants to marry me! But he can't because I'm a slave!"

She threw a frightened glance at Caterin's face, ready for the outburst of anger. Instead she saw, was it possible, a certain sympathy. If there was the remotest chance that the Princess might listen, she must try again. She threw herself at Caterin's feet.

"It's the Master of the Household! He's going to give me to Donal, a blacksmith, a huge hairy man, with big feet and red hands." Tears sparkled under her lashes and began to slip down her face. She turned her shoulder and scrubbed her hand impatiently across her eyes.

"So we have a lot in common. We're both being forced into marriage."

Caterin pictured Prince Gort and Hairy Donald together and could have laughed but for the sob in her throat. Below her the girl's face glowed with hope like a pale lantern.

Iogena rose and stepped backwards, still cautious, for she knew, who better, that Caterin could fly into a temper at the swish of an arrow. But the woman in her was overcoming her fears as a slave. And this chance might never come her way again.

Caterin desperately wanted to help. But the impulse was buried under years of conviction that no slave deserved the luxury of emotions. She smiled grimly. In fine fancy phrases she had told Gort that the All-Mother gave to everyone, no matter what their rank. Not realising how she used her title to dominate people.

In a flash she recognised the cause of her loneliness. But not how to overcome it. What would the warm-hearted Devana say to Iogena now? One thing, for sure, she would not be thinking that kindness might be mistaken for weakness. The answer came, bright and shining as the face that Caterin turned to her servant. She took her the girl's hand and drew her to her feet.

"This man! Are you sure you love him?"

Iogena's misty eyes searched the Princess's face. There was a shimmer in the eyes that warmed Iogena. It seemed to tell of a woman-bond, of kinship, of compassion. She tried to choose her words carefully but her love was so strong that the lyricism of her forebears broke through.

"Every time he looks at me, I leap up and dance with the stars. When I'm with him, he fills me with his embrace. My hand rests in his hand and an hour goes on for ever. When I leave him, his love lies at my heart, warm as a candle."

The strings of Caterin's own heart quivered with longing but she dare not admit that music to her mind.

"How do you know it's not a boy's lust?"

"Because he says..." Iogena caught her breath. The words her soldier had used dared not be spoken here. "Because he means to buy me and have me in marriage."

"So, he's not penniless." It was also blindingly obvious to Caterin that Iogena's lover had thrown a few harsh words at her mistress's head. Caterin was elated at the idea that was growing in her mind. She hugged it to herself, tempted to keep the lovers in suspense for just a little longer. "I want to meet this man with the sharp tongue. Where can we find him?"

Iogena's hand flew to her mouth. Oh, this was not what she had hoped for. Had she really been so foolish as to sign her lover's death-warrant? It was too late to back out now. Her smudged blue eyes pleaded with Caterin.

"Please, I can't say..."

"Come on. Your gods have been good to you. If I was in love I'd want to show him off to somebody."

Hope blossomed like a flower in Iogena's smile. And it was as though the sun had melted an icicle at Caterin's heart.

"He's on duty. In charge of the sentries at the Gate."

"Bring two dark cloaks then."

Outside, the evening was warm and balmy but their hoods hid them from prying eyes as they slipped between the houses and round groups of drinking, dicing men. Since it was the onset of the warm season, pots holding herbs and plants had appeared on ledges and sills to catch the rays of the sun. Although the colours of the flowers had faded with the darkening light, their perfume hung heavy in the air.

This year, a special effort had been made to cheer the army on its way. Householders had filled bowls with seal-fat and set them out on every nook and wall to send a signal of cheer to the waiting men. So the whole Citadel was ablaze with long angling lines of flickering flames. Tiny pinpoints of light danced on the helmets of the guard at the Gate.

"Uurad's the handsome one," whispered Iogena.

"You only look at one. They're all good-looking." A new current of friendly teasing flowed easily between them now.

77

"True." Iogena was not to be outdone. "But Uurad has the merriest eyes."

The Officer in Charge strode forward to bar their way, his bronze helmet outlined by the light from the great cruisies that hung above the Gate on smoke-blackened chains. On duty, this stern-faced soldier with the military bearing did not in the least fit Iogena's description. But when Iogena pushed back her hood to let the light fall on her face, Caterin saw how his eyes flashed, brilliant as a falling star. And how his wild admiring gaze hardened to flint as he recognised the Princess and sprang to attention.

Caterin looked him up and down with candid curiosity. He was in his late teens with a certain erect assurance that sat well with his air of authority despite the fact that he was confronting his King's daughter. His honest, ruddy features were far too expressive to hide the secrets of his heart. He was not old nor experienced enough to dissemble his suspicion at the sudden appearance of the Princess. It was there to be read in the sudden guarding of his eyes and the tightening of his mouth. Yet, he was the kind of thick-set, up-standing fellow that Caterin would trust with her life in a crisis.

"So! I've to light my own lamps while you dally with my servant," she said with a trace of haughtiness, testing him. "Don't you know the law about consorting with a slave?"

He stiffened and a faint colour spread over his square features. It was written plainly in his expression that he was hostile and on the defensive.

"Lady, I don't dally! When I return, I'll purchase her. Name any slave-gift you want and I'll pay it." There was a hot sincerity in his words that pleased her but she persevered with her little game.

"For the loss of my trained maid-servant, let me see. No, I doubt the asking-price is beyond your means."

Uurad tried to mask his contempt that a woman of wealth should set such a high price on a slave. But the Princess held the power of life and death over them both. He and Iogena had known it all along. It was a cruel blow from the Great Ones that she had found out about their love on this night of all nights.

"Yet, I'll pay it no matter how long it takes."

Caterin smiled at that. Something in his background had set him apart from the usual reckless youths who joined the King's army for plunder and glory. Plunder he would use to buy Iogena and the glory he sought to lay at her feet.

"You'll spend your life paying it! For my slave-price is her happiness!" said Caterin. "And I hope the Guardians might send me a lover so willing to buy my freedom."

Iogena's long indrawn yelp of delight cut across Caterin's words. It took longer for Uurad to grasp her meaning for he had had no warning of a sudden change in their fortunes. Then he gave a quick open smile and sank on one knee. Quickly Caterin motioned him to his feet.

"Your authority will never be the same again if your men see you moonstruck over a woman," she said. "Come for Iogena when your spell of duty's over."

Back at the Palace she set Iogena to choose scented oils and trinkets for herself. She shared the girl's happiness for a little before a restless longing took her out to her Courtyard, slinging a fur over her shoulders.

Long ago, Barban, a Queen of her kin, had planted shrubs around the walls. They had thrived in the shelter. Even from the first of the snow-thaw, flowers blossomed until red and purple berries supplanted them. She breathed in the heady tang of a broom that billowed in a creamy cloud in the dusk.

The disappearing day had left a broad swathe of turquoise striated with grey wisps of cloud along the horizon. This day that was ending had brought her a taste of the power that came with privilege. At the time it had been stimulating. Now it frightened her. For she had played with the feelings of Iogena and Uurad, making them wait to satisfy some mulish bit of pride in her, pride in the power she had over servants. A thimbleful of power compared to the power she would have one day.

She sat on the bench and leaned back, settling her back against the hard stones of the wall. And for a moment knew them as a segment of the Body of the Mother, whose bounty she was sharing for her voyage on the Earth. Then she would be gone as her mother had gone. And another woman would come. And another. While the stones would stay, each snug in its allotted place in the wall, for ever. And how great was a Queen's power when a stone could outlast it?

What was it the Arch-Drui taught in his dry sing-song voice that did not belong in this swaggering gallop that was life. That within every being was a flame that was spirit. A part of the Great Infinite Spirit. And each person was not just a body with a spirit but a spirit that had clothed itself in a body for a tiny fraction of Eternity.

And when she thought about that it made her look at things differently. For after the grieving for the loss of a bairn or a mother or a lover came the comfort of knowing they were safe.

Caterin hugged her knees to her chin, a tiny pulsating particle in the unknown night. While above her the mantle of darkness spread over the sky and the Moon Maiden hung, indifferent, as lone and chaste as a Princess.

And Broichan told how people were tested. And it was how a person met the dreaded coughing sickness and the grief of parting and the knife of a raider in the night that made the flame shine brighter or dimmer. It made her feel braver just to know that. It made her feel brave enough to shake her fist at the sky and shout a dare at the Wise Ones. 'Right! What's next!'

Except that she was thinking how she had been tested. How she had been proud and arrogant. And humbled by a comic old bodyguard and a slave with a dream much like her own.

Caterin rose, stretching, waiting, leaning on the wall, watching the pale stars begin to show.

Power! It felt good to have power to make people happy. And it had cost her nothing. To make Iogena's dream come true, all she needed to do was to tell the Law-Giver in the morning. Vaguely, the thought stirred that Wise Cau might not be overjoyed to set a precedent that would anger other slave-owners. What else could a man do to make a profit from his prisoners? But she vowed to the stars she would never again own another human being as a slave.

'Slave'. The word sent a trickle of ice down her spine as though the cold fingers of the Moon Maiden had brushed her in warning.

CHAPTER ELEVEN

A cluster of petals had scented her fingers with honey. A thin, sad melody played on a flute pondered on the promise of the morning. A gust of laughter swamped it, a peal that plainly asserted,'Tomorrow we march, tonight we drink'.

"I guessed you'd be out here." The voice drawled from the open doorway at her back. Her fingers flew apart, scattering the crushed petals in the air as she turned.

"You're late," she said. "I thought you'd be sooner."

"You expected me?"

"I saw the look in Bridei's eye. He's sent you to claim me. To prove your virility." The unhappiness and longing that had drawn her into the cool night air had evaporated. Somehow nothing mattered except that she would not be alone.

"Not my virility. It's your fertility that's in doubt. This time it's not the mother's blood that counts. The chieftains want the blood of Bridei and Gwynedd to mingle in the Royal Line. So, you see, the seed of the father matters after all."

She felt light and carefree. Virginity was such a little thing to make a fuss about. Tonight she would be free of it once and for all. He had come seeking her and her fate was sealed. Her laughter pealed out joyously.

"I've never denied it! That's why we select our mates with care."

Her words jarred in Gort's ears. He had come hoping that she might be a virgin after all. Surely Bridei would have insisted. This uninhibited merriment convinced him that she was as promiscuous as the bard-songs insisted. At her ears hung great gold discs with long strings of gold balls falling to her breasts. They clashed like tiny cymbals as she passed him and entered into the yellow lamplight of her sitting-room. Barbaric, he thought, as was the swathe of red material flaring from each shoulder brooch to the ground. Suited to the inviting face that she tilted up at him. And to the striped wildcat pelt slung on her shoulders.

After their meeting in the broch it was not difficult for Caterin to read his thoughts in his eyes. Barbarian Queen, he thought her! And so, perversely, she had dressed like one. She was going to enjoy this night of her Initiation. Let the Moon Maiden fall and the

Earth Mother shake! Iogena's stars would also dance in Caterin's sky.

He followed her inside, filling the room, his head within striking distance of the beams.

Gort felt ungainly in this strange feminine room. It was his duty to breed in her. Easy enough! Throw her on the bed and get on with it. Then why did he hesitate, drawing away from her, to study the pieces laid out on her gaming table? Someone had carved them with infinite skill and a sense of humour. The white Queen had the Royal Bull in black and gold emblazoned across her ivory breast. The black King's chest-plate lay bare, empty of insignia.

Following his gaze, Caterin swept the little ivory Queen across the board to stand in front of her army of pieces, challenging the jet-black King, tempting him with her flowing robes and high-dressed hair. A half-empty goblet lay on a table. She toasted Gort over the rim with eyes that sparkled. The honey in the golden mead masked the herb that would stop her conceiving.

The last thing she wanted was a bairn, growing inside her, close, lapping at her breast and needing all the love and care that was in her to give. Maybe someday. Not now. Not even for Bridei.

"No, she's not the Queen for this King." Taking down her favourite whip from its place on the wall, Gort used the silver tip to slide the jet King to the forefront of his troops. "He's seeking a woman, tall and lovely, a star brilliant in her hair, her breast perfumed with passion, her jewels the wealth of love she has to offer. A woman who has earned her mead like the champion of a King."

The words came from deep in his throat as sincere as any she had heard him speak. Yet she could not believe him. His blank eyes spoke of a desert of emotion in his heart.

But Gort had been sincere. He genuinely sought his perfumed woman with a longing that sometimes astonished him. For how could he leave the arms of such a woman to go to war? Take Llywarch Hen in Rheged now. He had laid by his sword to dream and write poetry and father children on his Queen. Now he bowed his knee happily to Gwynedd in return for peace. But Gort hoped he was made of different metal. Love should inspire him to greater feats knowing he was protecting his woman. Or her land.

"How nice for him." Caterin felt a fleeting stab of jealousy and stifled it. She was using him as he was using her. As Maelchon would have used her. Never again would she indulge in a love that would turn her from her purpose.

"But what if this star-bright beauty offers her wealth of love too generously while you're away at war."

Gort admitted a certain disappointment at the mockery in her tone. He had hoped he was mistaken about her. She had answered him point for point in the broch with a surprising intelligence and honesty. She bore herself with grace and breeding. A woman like this could have fired his blood. Yet the customs of her race disgusted him and hedged him round with taboos.

"My King will bind his Queen with the fine silver chains of love."

Smiling a mysterious smile, Caterin made a series of quick, darting moves probing her spear-throwers forward from the left flank. Steadily the King inched his whole front line forward.

Gort had widened the gap between them by describing his ideal woman and Caterin was glad. Tonight she wanted to be awakened to the pleasures of love-making without the commitment of loving. It was the right of every woman in the land to summon the Initiator, especially at times when rape by the Scots was common. His experienced and gentle arts freed virgins from their maidenhood and opened them to pleasure. Instead, to Caterin, pain was appropriate at this moment. For she would never again lose her Self in the love of a man. Not even this enigmatic exciting one.

"How will he know when he's found his starry woman?" she asked, her excitement rising.

"Because her mouth will smile a welcome and her eyes will be gentle." Gort beat the whip nonchalantly against his leather-clad thigh. Then the black King retreated, summoning his army to gather round him.

"Does the Kingdom he'll win not excite him?" she flashed back, gaining confidence. She sent a single horseman forward to tempt the King into a rash attack.

Gort was not tempted. He looked up and caught a glimpse of the clever brain behind the green eyes.

"The Kingship of a land carries certain responsibilities."

That was the obvious reply, thought Caterin, well designed to disguise his true intentions.

"And the Queenship?"

He made no answer, preferring to surround her horseman with his pieces and throw him into 'Dead Man's Ditch'. This time Caterin urged her Queen forward to draw the King out from his strong defensive position. This time she would deal him the death-blow. It was time to stop playing with words.

"You're playing a power-game with me and my people," she told him, watching the steady stream of his foot-soldiers creeping up the side of the board to cut off the Queen from her reinforcements on the right.

"We'll let the Council reach their own conclusions, shall we? I don't play careless games with lives and loyalties as you do."

Half of the warrior Queen's host were penned in a corner. Now the King was advancing steadily on her with his troops.

"One day, you'll make one move too many. And then I'll have you!"

Gort saw her sacrifice the rest of her army, one by one, until the Queen stood alone, surrounded by jet soldiers. No matter where she turned, the Black King could block her escape. The only move left would result in capture and that was a move he guessed this defiant Princess would not make.

Laughing, Gort leaned down and picked up the little Queen. Triumphantly, he threw her up in the air and caught her firmly as she fell.

"You've sacrificed your whole army to keep your precious Queen intact. It would have been wiser to let her be captured and to promote one of your war-lords instead."

Her arm-rings jangled as she gestured to a Guardsman, his arrow pointing straight at the breast of the King.

"But I've won! I have the King at my mercy."

"That paltry little archer? We don't play the game that way in Gwynedd!"

"I'm aware of that! But you'll be playing the game our way from now on."

The flagon she poured mead from was alive with curling claws and tongues of beasts with fiery garnet eyes. She sipped, celebrating her quiet triumph, hearing the swish of his leather-clad thighs and the soft clank of the gold belt as he came to take the proferred cup.

"I'm not a piece on a gaming board to be used to gain a Kingdom," she said.

The heat of his body enveloped her as he paused at her side, almost touching her.

"Princess, we've finished playing out our battle of wits. The moves we make now belong to no trivial game. We dice with lives at stake."

Cup in hand he took a turn round the room. He thought of all the women he had lain with, from giggling slave-girls in the grain-fields in his youth to mature and elegant ladies whose husbands had been at war for far too long. By now, he knew how to read them, to know when they needed to be courted and when they were ready to be roughly handled. He had only taken a woman by force once and it had given him so little pleasure that he had no wish to try again. It had been an act of youthful relief, after his first raid. By now, he had learned to handle women so that they became eager under his hands, giving him back more pleasure and bringing him to greater heights of intensity than most men ever felt. Since he had arrived here he had been told more than once that his loving could match that of any Pretani man. Laying his cup aside he turned.

Whether by accident or design she was standing against a dark green curtain that highlighted her glorious hair. She had unfastened her brooches and her robes hung loosely from her shoulders. At a touch from him they would fall at her feet. Only a shift, delicate as gossamer, veiled her body. The curves of her breasts and thighs, honey-coloured by the lamp-light, brought an unexpected surge in his loins. The impact of her beauty stunned him bringing an urgent need to taste and touch her soft throat and the swell of her breast.

In other lands women flirted and teased. She used none of these tricks. Instead with a commanding gesture of her arms she threw off her robes. That was the Pretani way, he had discovered. When a woman had chosen a man, she let him know it. Her eyes looked straight into his, glowing with a desire as strong as his own. He found he wanted her more than he would have thought possible.

CHAPTER TWELVE

Gort loosened the laces at his throat. It was warm in this room, nothing to do with the firm, lithe body that lay open to his gaze. Yet he feasted his eyes on each rounded curve, each magnificent long line of her. Until the thought that she might have been enjoyed by all the riff-raff of the Capital filled his mouth with disgust. And his mind with a tinge of regret. What a waste of a magnificent woman!

Caterin saw the unwilling admiration in his face cloud suddenly. She had no means of knowing the thoughts that churned in his mind and could not fathom his reluctance. This was a moment to enjoy, to revel in the tingling flesh and the singing blood. This body she offered him was part of the All-Mother and ought to be used for pleasure and fulfilment like all of Her gifts. Yet she felt a kind of shame. Suddenly she needed to hide herself from his eyes. She stooped and lifted the red cloth letting it hang in graceful folds hiding her breasts and the golden triangle of hair at the join of her legs.

Gort sensed that her gesture was not meant to titillate. Yet it had excited him. He lifted his hand to draw the cloth away. The green eyes widened and he saw fear lurking there. If she was experienced it could not be fear of love-making. Was she afraid of him? He felt a surge of tenderness. Perhaps she had never known true pleasure. Perhaps he should court her a little, prove to her that foreigners were not merely seeking sons but treasured their women.

No! This was stupid! He was making excuses. That vulnerability he had discovered in her had roused his desire. With as much patience as he could muster, he unclenched the cloth from her fingers. And felt them tremble beneath his touch.

His gaze slid to her lips. He had tasted them before and they were sweet. She had responded with enough passion to fuel his suspicions. Yet, now her face turned to him like a white open flower. She stretched her arm behind his head and drew his mouth down. Her lips parted and tempted him. They were cool and soft but unresponsive, until they warmed to his gentle persuasion and began to cling. After a mellow moment, he withdrew, confused by this mixture of responses.

"You are learning," she said smiling. "In my country, the woman leads the way to show when she is ready."

He felt a surge of anger. What had she expected? Rape? Yet when he had first met her he had felt angry enough to force her and plunder her body. Yet her flesh was soft and alluring and drew his hand to explore.

She was aware of her breast moulding itself to the rough hand that cupped and caressed it, answering her need. The male smell of him filled her nostrils, intoxicating her senses. As his hands explored her further, she wanted to hold each moment for ever. Surely this pleasuring was more than just a duty to his host?

Gort was asking himself the same question. He had intended to take her without involvement. Yet, in spite of himself, with movements that had become sure and easy with practice, he was wooing her, exploring every hollow and curve, finding a need in himself to know every line and column of her body. His mouth savoured the scented softness of her skin and the clean silk of her hair. She leaned in his arms, an infinitely desirable woman. He looked in her eyes and saw the shadow of her insecurity. The faintest colour stole across her cheeks under his gaze. This proof of her shyness set a pulse throbbing in his body. For a heart-beat he waited. Then his manhood cried out for relief. He picked her up in his arms and shouldered aside the curtain of her bedroom. A tiny flame floating in perfumed oil showed him the way to the fleecy white bed.

Caterin watched as he drew off his clothes, as his shadowy body was lit by an occasional gleam on muscle or flesh. Then he came and stretched himself on the bed beside her. As his skilful hands fondled her, she moaned deep in her throat, partly from pleasure and partly as a plea to release her from a tension she could endure no longer. She yearned for him to enter her but when he did pierce her, the pain was as sharp as a knife-thrust. Her body arced with the pain of it and arced again with the rapture that followed and went on, throbbing inside her, slowly at first, and then thrusting deeply, urgently until the whole world exploded in a fountain of droplets that tingled through every fibre of her flesh. And when the ecstacy passed she lay still and calm, revelling in the joy of fulfillment.

The man watching her quiet face saw her mouth curve at the

corners in a secret smile and wondered. Had it been the best yet? Did she think she had tamed him to her will at last? Then she rolled on her side, cradling her head on her arm, and the red blood on the white linen blazed up at him. He scratched the scar of an old dagger-wound on his jaw.

She felt the movement and turned back. Her eyes opened on him, full of wonderment. He found he was shaken. Not by finding her a virgin in a society where that status was not greatly prized. But by an unfamiliar emotion that had jolted him and that he could not understand. And would not waste time trying to.

Quickly he dressed himself with his back to her. He did not feel the need nor the desire to say anything. He had done his duty. After he left the Citadel in the morning, the future was in the hands of the Capricious Ones. Those disturbing eyes had closed again and she seemed to be sleeping. In a rare gesture of tenderness, he drew the cover over her and glided out.

Caterin was glad he had gone. If they had been true lovers, they would have slept, fulfilled, in one another's arms, happy to be sharing not only a bed but a life together. But although their bodies had sung in rhythm that night, he would forget her as soon as he rode out tomorrow. And he would never know that, if he had stayed and talked and made love again, he might have bound her to him with a spell as fine as gossamer and as strong as bands of iron. Instead she could now go forward unfettered and with gladness to Pitversie.

The smell of hot barley cakes invaded Caterin's dreams and roused her from sleep next morning. She opened one sticky eye and was astounded to see a white-robed Drui at the foot of her bed. A longer look revealed that it was Amis, wife to the Guardian of the King's Treasure. And what in the world was she holding against her skinny chest? It was a robe that might once have been attractive. Now it hung limp and uninviting. Suddenly the magic of the night before vanished. She sat up and cried out in protest.

"I'm not wearing that ragged old duster! It looks more like a shroud than a ceremonial robe."

Amis, red-necked and scrawny, gobbled like a wild turkey at this affront to the tradition.

"It's the Queen's Robe for wearing at the King Choosing."

Amis's long nose quivered, searching up and down the bed for a sign of a man. Caterin felt sorry for her with no bairns and no joy from that dry stick of a husband. Just a bee in her bonnet that things had to be done right. And a deafening dreary sniff when folk did things their own way. And an eye ever alert for a couple together in the lea of a bush.

"All right!" Caterin cried. "I'll tell you! He came and was fast and furious! And I enjoyed it!"

She kicked her cover off and rose. Amis let out a squawk that a laying hen would have been proud of when her eyes homed in on the stain on the sheet. Iogena began to fold it neatly ready for the washing-women.

"Leave it!" Caterin told her. "I'll rinse it myself. A maiden's blood is a special libation to the Earth-Mother." Iogena slid her a long speculative look. They smiled at one another as women do when they have no need of words. Caterin guessed that Iogena was also looking for an assurance that her mistress would not forget her promise.

"There are scribes at Pitversie, Iogena," she said. "You'll have a proper statement of your freedom to show before the day's over."

At that Amis let her jaw fall open. Then snapped it tight shut and sniffed.

Caterin swung the gown about from back to front. At least, the fine linen was freshly washed and scented and the hem was nicely embroidered in gold but no amount of laundering could hide the fact that the cloth was ageing and showed signs of yellowing.

"I'll have to wear the red cloak to hide it," she decided. "But see that a new robe is woven for the next Princess. No daughter of mine is going to appear in a garment that's as faded as the pennant of a defeated army."

Today Iogena had a glow about her and moved with an assurance that became her. She braided Caterin's hair with fingers that were deft and gentle and she moved around the room with an unconscious grace. Truly Bridei had chosen wisely when he had picked this girl for her from the slave-band, Caterin thought. Everything about her suggested that she had been brought up in a household where comfort and beauty were appreciated. Why had her mistress been blind to this obvious fact?

Then she was moving outside, with a calm regal air that hid her emotions and resplendent with jewels that hid the faded finery. Caterin paused on the steps of the Palace. She looked above the Hall of Audience to where the pink pearly light of dawn surrounded a long, low wing of cloud, making it appear like a mysterious island in a sea of changing colour. The air was cool and dewy with the freshness of an awakening breeze. It was a time to go walking barefoot through wet grass, to clamber among gnarled green branches and shake down apple blossom and to make love among primroses and red campion. At the last moment, Iogena ran forward to fold back her hood so that the cobweb-soft white fur framed her face.

With Amis, strutting with self-importance at her side, and two stalwart Guards at her back, the Princess sailed across the paved Courtyard. Processions of Lords and Mormaers, great Chiefs and lesser Chiefs, all shining in war-array, drew back to give her precedence. Elderly Advisers and Historians, their high-domed heads filled with ancient lore, ready to be recited at the snap of the King's fingers, pulled up their pointed hoods to screen their watering eyes from the morning chill. Bards and musicians in motley colours, craftsmen and stone-masons in leather and hide, scurried along, eager to hear if the spiralling rumours were true, mouthing behind their hands the odd phrase that spoke of blood-fines.

Caterin desperately wanted to turn and run, anywhere, to hide her shame and humiliation. It took every particle of courage to keep placing one foot in front of the other. Only her firm resolve to make Nechtan's sacrifice worth while held her head high.

The huge doors of the Hall of Audience stood wide open. On either side were stacked the spears and swords of the army with a bevy of boys to guard them. Caterin stepped from the grey light of dawn into the brilliance of hundreds of lamps in candelabra.

They shone on pennants that hung from roof-tree to floor, displaying the crests of all the ancient tribes that were now collectively known as the Pretani. On one side, as she moved across the floor, on banner after banner, hung the brilliantly coloured discs and crescents and swirling designs that were the emblems of the lineages of the main tribes. Dedicated by music and ritual and dance, they had become traditions expressed, not in words, but in images and spoke eloquently to Caterin of time-honoured truths.

On her other side were the proud woven pennants showing the eagle, the wolf, the stallion and other signs that denoted branches of the great clans, birds and beasts that loaned their magic to the families who had chosen to emulate them. The Vacomagi deer was there, startled, fleeing on dainty feet. And the bristling Veniconie boar, head down, charging.

One day, Caterin promised herself, these same clans would know the power that lay in the hand of the daughter of Bridei.

The men channelling into the hall, row after row, furrow upon furrow, were as colourful as the pennants, for each flaunted their embroidered emblem on their chest, and a sprig of flowers or a bunch of jaunty feathers in their caps.

Straight ahead, dwarfing the humans who gathered below was an embroidery sewn by Caterin's grandmother. It showed the enormous shapes of fantastic beasts never seen in the natural world but revealed by the Wise Ones, to a chosen few of the Druad. Funny cuddly little beasts Caterin had thought them and loved to draw them in the sand as a child. Today, even the Blue Water Kelpie, had taken on an aura of mystic power.

Caterin took her allotted place at the side of a raised platform. Beside her was Devana's empty chair. Amis squirmed into a sliver of bench as near as possible to Caterin and sent a pointed sniff at the rest of the women. And Caterin knew that Bridei had appointed a new kind of bodyguard for her.

Before her stood the High Chair, its massive legs and straight back carved with intertwining serpents. The red robe of Kingship was draped across its back and emblazoned on it, in black and silver, was the virile Royal Bull, embroidered by Caterin's mother when she was still a girl for her future Consort. The robe was of wool as dense as velvet and as soft as silk, dyed to a glowing crimson tinged with purple, pure as the red of a dark rose.

Oh, how many weary hours Caterin had spent, scattering tears and drops of blood over a new robe for her King. Even now, she supposed, it would have been unwrapped from its coverings and be airing in the bleaching-field.

Flushed and breathless, Devana erupted out of the throng like a bung from a barrel. With emotions that always bubbled on the surface of her living, it was difficult for her to hide the unshed tears that glazed her eyes or to drag her yearning gaze from the face of her husband. One quick glance round at the other women told Devana that they, too, were grimly hiding their tears. She rallied quickly.

"What a splendid sight," she remarked gaily. "All in their ceremonial best. I wish my boys could see this. And look, there's

Artcois with the shame of his sons on him."

He stood among his chiefs, grim and steady as a rock in the shifting tide of men. Death would have been his fate if he had not attended the Retribution as Chief of the Veniconie. Caterin had had a genuine affection for this man. Yet he had been plotting to use her to carve out a dynasty for himself and his sons, a long-term project that had now been laid bare. How could you know whom to trust? Even her own father ...

At that the King in his battle-dress came in at the head of the Elders of the Council. Seating himself in the High Chair he surveyed the throng, restlessly fingering the massive silver chain that hung round his neck and was his badge of Kingship. Behind him, Caterin picked out Prent's round, red face shining out from among the wispy grey heads of his masters like a harvest moon wreathed in clouds.

Beside the High Chair, Gort had placed himself, standing relaxed, arms folded. Over his battle-dress he wore a ceremonial dark-blue tunic bordered in white and emblazoned with a silver dragon with red outstretched wings. The women's eyes measured Gort with pleasure and Caterin with speculation. Caterin indulged in a small glow of triumph.

When Gort inclined his head to hear a remark from Cennalath, the lights glanced along the strong line of his jaw. Her fingers had stroked that rough scar, had combed through the springing thick hair while he had filled her senses with delight. It would have been easy last night to fool herself that she cared for him.

His roving eyes suddenly locked in collision with hers, jolting her. Recognition flashed in his grey eyes to be followed immediately by a flicker of an emotion she could not identify before he looked quickly away. That turn of his head, she was sure, was his final rejection of her and the barbaric customs of her people. At that moment, the doors of the Hall closed with a decisive, hollow thud. Funny how it echoed and re-echoed in her heart.

There came a glitter and a clash of cymbals from six blue-robed boys, hushing the muttering and chattering, stilling every scrape of shoe-leather and jingle of mail. From a curtained doorway at the back of the platform, surrounded by his pupils, so close that they seemed to be supporting as well as protecting him, came Broichan, the Arch-Drui, the only man who ranked higher than the King.

Six feet tall he was and ramrod erect, fragile and brittle as glass. His long, austere face whose wasting flesh had shrunk over narrow bones, was framed by long, silvery hair. Straight lines etched by blue bramble dye accentuated the bonework of his face and the severity of his countenance.

Emaciated hands gripped a staff topped by a gilded eagle holding the emblems of fire and water suspended from each outspread wing. His white robes, flowing in long stiff lines from a gold neck-ring, completed the elongated effect, disturbed only by a necklace of tiny animal skulls that dangled to his knees. The faded lofty-lidded eyes looked out, appraising the company, seeing through and beyond them with the chill indifference of the very old and the very wise. Everything about him told that this was a man who understood portents and conversed with the Radiant Ones.

His voice when it came was purposeful, deep-sounding and terrifying. He announced the death of the King's servant, Nechtan, and called upon the people to listen that they be reminded, once more, of the ancient laws that bound them together. He closed his eyes and searched his prodigious memory. And Caterin moaned within herself. This recitation of the law regarding a killing on the eve of battle was not going to be left to the King's Remembrancer. It had become a matter of ritual and propitiation so that the Mighty Ones were not angered by an ill-starred spilling of blood.

And Caterin wondered why it was such a fateful omen when the soldiers were straining at the leash to spill the blood of the Scots. But it was. And she was vexed at herself for questioning it. And made the sign of the crescent to the Water Kelpie in case he had read the thought in her mind.

Now Broichan changed to the language of the Attecottie, that ancient people who had lived in Alba since the beginning of time even before the coming of Cruithne, the great Ancestor who fostered the well-being of the land. And Cruithne must have respected these people. For it was Cruithne who had infused the power into the Attecottie language so that the spoken word held all the magic of the ritual. And the great Hero had ordained that the language must never be written on vellum with oak-gall ink nor incised on stone or it would lose its power to reach the ears of the Noble Ones.

A blush of shame tinged Caterin's cheeks. Within the sacred

circle of stones they had been called the Hairy Ones, the wee Peskies. And she had allowed it.

Broichan spoke in the solemn teaching voice of the Druad with the sing-song rhythm that aided the memory. And Caterin listened, awed by a new insight into that tradition she had vowed so lightly to defend.

"And it is the fourth law of our Ancestors," he intoned, "that the kindred shall stand or fall together. That, if there is plenty, all shall be fed; if there is war, all shall serve; if there is killing, all shall be guilty. For it is the duty of the kindred to so govern their kith that the law of the land is upheld."

Caterin saw that a subtle distancing by the crowd had left Artcois and his stern-faced clan in a space apart.

"And if the kindred shall fail to maintain the peace, retribution shall be exacted lasting unto four generations. For a guilty act reverberates in the community until four generations have passed away. And an honour price shall be paid to the kindred of the injured party."

As the echoing vibrations of Broichan's voice died away, everyone heard the nervous rasp of Artcois' rough finger-nails on the bristles of his cheek.

"A blood-fine of one hundred milking cows with calves at heel shall be paid each year for Nechtan, son of..." For the duration of an indrawn breath, the Shaman hesitated for no one knew the kin of Nechtan's mother, far less who had sired him. "...son of the Pretani," he finished smoothly.

The Shaman turned his heavy staff sideways and slowly raised it aloft in two delicate hands, signifying that the most dreaded sentence of all was about to be pronounced.

CHAPTER THIRTEEN

"Furthermore." Broichan's voice had taken on a new resonance, thundering into the far corners of the Hall so that all might hear and remember. "From this day forward Maelchon and Talorc, sons of Gala of the Veniconie, are outlawed from their kin. Being polluted by the blood of Nechtan, they are excluded from participation in all rites and ceremonies. They may not appeal to the Law-Givers of the Land to protect nor to defend them. Within these boundaries, no person may allow them hearth, bed nor bread. The guardianship of the Powerful Ones is withdrawn. Let this be made known."

The company stirred like the billows of the sea when a southeaster falls on them from a lowering sky and sets the great waves on the move.

And the women looked at Caterin, thinking it was shameful the way she held her head so high and mighty, hardly blinking an eye. And her as guilty as the young men, no doubt. Not knowing how the Shaman's words hammered like nails into her heart.

"So be it." The brother of Gala, mother of the two men raised his palm in acceptance. As soon as news of the killing had come, the Veniconie had known that the penalty would be heavy.

The eyes of Artcois muddied like a pool stirred by a shadow in its dark depths. He turned his furious gaze on the King.

"My sons are outlawed!" he bellowed. "But your daughter goes free! A she-goat who lay with my sons and shouted 'Rape'?" His outflung hand jerked in Caterin's direction in a plain accusation that hit her like a blow. She drew in a breath, wondering if her father would order his immediate execution.

Bridei's hands gripped the arm of his chair as he tried to control his fury at this old friend who had betrayed him. But for the moment Artcois held the whip-hand. It had been a bonus for Artcois that the Capital lay within the land of the Veniconie. He and his men had not slept till they had dug out every lowly brother of every Clan Mother to stand at his back. Now his retinue stood four-square and menacing in the centre of the Hall.

Quickly Caterin grasped the fact that Bridei could not afford the loss of the whole Veniconie clan. She had forced this situation and must face up to it.

She sprang to her feet.

"You plotted treason!" she accused him. "You cannot lay the blame of that on me!"

She saw the sly smiles of the women and the frozen contempt on Gort's face. Before them all she must acknowledge her part in it. She arched her neck proudly and spoke to the company.

"I was foolish I admit! But I learned one lesson. That the Law of the Land rises from a sea of wisdom. I am going to Pitversie to seek knowledge and enlightenment. And on this day I make a vow to those of you who go to defend our land. That I will return, fit and able to stand before you as Bridei's daughter and your Queen." She let her gaze fall on Artcois. "May the Learned Ones send enlightenment to you and your sons also."

She sat, trembling with the effort it had cost her. Someone started a muted drumming of knuckles on a shield. Caterin looked wildly round. The sound grew louder. Devana nudged her.

"They approve, you little idiot! You were fine. They like fighting words."

"Whore!" Artcois spat on the boards at her feet. Stoney-faced, he and the men of the Veniconie turned on their heels and marched out of the Hall in a body. The tension eased, cramped limbs stretched, feet shuffled.

Broichan still stood, attenuated and brooding, holding the gathering together by his authority. Morgand, the Historian, stepped forward, a man of medium height and inordinate dryness whose lofty-domed skull ended in dark brows and eyes burdened with learning. His voice was low, pleasantly pitched, so that the company had to hold their breath to hear the pronouncement that came in their everyday tongue again.

"As the Season of Sowing ends, as the Season of Growing begins, as the clouds of battle gather, so the stars demand a King Choosing. As one planet wanes, so another must rise and no one can delay its rising."

There was a sound like a murmuring sea. This was an unforeseen turn of events, although a breath of suspicion had blown round the Citadel when Gort had taken his place among Bridei's War Chiefs.

Yet, wait! A King Choosing was a matter that required long nights of bandying words across the hearth. It was not to be settled with the flip of a disc on the morning of a battle-march. Still, Bridei knew how to value a man's worth better than most and had laid his hand on Gort's shoulder. The Historian gathered the threads of confusion that filtered from his audience and prepared to speak in plain words.

"According to custom, the Council of Elders proposes an Election to grant the seal of War Leader and Heirship to the Kingdom on Gort, Prince of Gwynedd, son of Dafydd, Dragon of the Island, destroyer of the Saesons and scourge of the Eireans. The Council asks for your support."

One chief after another voiced his opinion loudly and without fear. Times were uncertain and an elected Heir was a safeguard for the Kingdom. Better the Pretani rule of succession that attracted mighty Kings like Bridei than to have impatient sons slaying their fathers and brothers for power. Gort's antecedents were impressive and stood high in his favour.

Sea-rounded pebbles for the voting were brought forward in trays and placed in the centre of the floor, one containing white, the other black pebbles. Each chief had to take two pebbles and thrust his hand deep into the bag held aloft between Wise Cau and Prent. If the chief's vote was for the candidate, he dropped in a white pebble; if against, a black pebble. The unused pebble was kept hidden in his palm until the votes were counted. It was Cennalath who stepped forward first and selected a white pebble. Deliberately, he raised his hand so that all could see.

"My vote will not be made in secret. I'm the man who will stand at Gort's shoulder on this campaign and I'll be proud to serve under him. Now, get your bandy legs moving and let's get at the throat of our real enemy, Aedan Mac Gabrain!"

A rumble of laughter swept the assembly and a rippling movement started like deep corn bowing its ears to the onslaught of the wild West Wind. The men eddied round the trays of pebbles and flowed passed the Law-Giver, clinking their pebbles into the bag as a stream deposits its stones on its way to the sea.

Caterin saw that Gort's supercilious eyes maintained an affectation of aloofness without missing a move. A muscle twitched in his cheek. She guessed he was awaiting the outcome of the count in a fever of ambition. Was it the land or the glory or even the Treasure that tempted him? Forget those suspicions for now! Forget also that he had deep thrusting hips and fingers that roused a woman to ecstacy. Whatever motivated him, she would thwart it. If he ever became King!

Gort could only feel contempt at this primitive method of choosing a King. No, he would only be Heir as yet, he reminded himself. They would wait until he had proved himself. And he would! Yet his heart pounded. This war was a glorious chance to be as great a King as Bridei, as his own father and brother, Rhun.

The slow-paced file of men came to a halt. Prent cleared a space in the centre of the floor. The Guard made a circle around him as he emptied the bag onto oak planks scored by boot-nails over the years. A stream of white pebbles scattered free at his feet with the odd black one here and there that told how some chiefs had had doubts.

Caterin remained icy cool. So Gort was Heir. And she had not even the right to place a pebble on the pile. Not a man among them looked in her direction for her approval. A young woman stifled a giggle. Only the women were thinking how this vote would concern the Princess. And cared as little as the men.

Her hatred for all these men who thought they ruled the land, flared up in her like a living force. 'Wait,' she warmed them in her mind. 'Wait until I have the knowledge and the experience. No matter who is King. No matter what threats are thrown at me. I will survive. And I shall be more powerful than all of you who think you can advise and manipulate me.'

At that moment, the doors burst open and every head slewed round. Artcois strode back into the Hall, brushing aside the guards, the long-tusked boar on his chest swelling as he came. Behind him advanced the chieftains of the Veniconie. Cau's dismissive geature indicated that they were too late to vote but Artcois and his threatening group continued to charge through the crowd.

"You'll not deprive me and my kindred of our right to vote!" he challenged. "We waive our right to secrecy." Gone was the rollicking sailor-uncle. He was all cunning pirate and ruthless sea-dog now.

He strode through the ring of Guards to the trays and held up a black pebble to show to the crowd before dropping it with a contemptuous flourish onto the pile on the floor. The rest of his clan came forward in a rush to follow his example. At the Shaman's quiet nod the Guards stood back. Now the Veniconie took their time, making the most of their protest. By the time they had finished, black pebbles wholly covered the top of the pile.

"Begin the count!" thundered Broichan. Prent knelt to the task, picking up one pebble of each colour and placing them to one side.

Every eye was glued to each pair of pebbles. Hardly a breath was taken as the count wore on. At the end, only a few white pebbles remained in a pathetic little pile but the number was enough. Grins broke out on weather-beaten faces. The women smiled and nodded. The old men of the Council heaved a collective sigh of relief. Prent, beaming, although he came from Veniconie stock himself, lifted the trays of pebbles from under the very feet of Artcois.

Broichan motioned Gort forward to show himself to the people. As Bridei sprang from the High Chair to clap him on the back, the clamour of daggers on shields broke out with a metallic beating that settled into a rhythmic peal of acclaim. The Boar on the chest of Artcois expanded like a sail swelling full in the wind. Everyone heard clearly the voice that trumpeted over the din.

"I tell you now that carrion crows will feast on the results of this ill-judged deed and the Ever-living Ones will weep as they watch." His baleful eyes turned on Gort. "As long as the Boar of the Veniconie stands high, this dragon-spawn shall not wear the King-chain. Meat's not meat, comrade, till it's in the pot."

With this warning ringing in the air, Artcois and his clan shouldered their way out of the Hall. A low, sighing groan followed them through the doorway. The clamour of metal on metal grew louder, but it had the sound of defiant despair in its beat for this was the Commander of the King's Fleet who had mouthed rebellious threats and split the King's command wide open. Bridei's upraised palms brought an instant hush.

"The defection of the Veniconie was ... unexpected," he said quietly and paused again for effect. Bridei had not led men into battle for all these years without knowing how to lift their hearts with skilful oratory. Now, he let his voice go in a shout of triumph. "But not unforeseen! This morning I ordered the main body of the Fleet to sail for the Firth of Moray under Bili of the Taezalie. Artcois is left with nothing but his own three ships to command. If he doesn't see sense and join with us again, we'll deal with him after we have brought Aedan to his knees." A great, united cheer rose to the rafters.

A quiet glow of pride warmed Caterin's heart and a tear came sliding, at the sight of her father, vital and vigorous again.

King Bridei looked every inch a War Commander as his gaze swept the Hall. Each clan was grouped around its own leader and stood ready to defend its territory to the death. Bridei's courage was legendary and he had succeeded in uniting them in a common cause. He was also a past master at infecting them with his own great spirit and sweeping them off to victory. He began quietly but his deep voice carried to every ear and reverberated on every heartstring.

"We, of the Pretani, have always been a free people." A breath of a sigh rippled among the throng. Although an Heir had been elected, Bridei still belonged to them, heart and spirit. "Never forget that! When the whole might of the Roman Empire descended on this land, we were the only race who would not let a conqueror's foot stamp on our necks. Later, in the south, the mighty Vortigern, blinded by his fear of Pretani fleets, invited in, as a shield, the enemy they feared worse than death, the vile, the unspeakable Saesons. Now, from out of the sunset, the Scottie, the plunderers, come creeping. Shall we who spurned the Romans crawl on our bellies to our neighbours for aid? Shall we invite yellow-haired scavengers from across the sea to defend our territory? Never!"

The yell of approval, the dagger-beat on shield, the clash of six pairs of excited cymbals rang to the roof-trees. Fierce pride flooded Caterin's breast. She rose and the women with her, cheering and clapping. This was Bridei at his best, in the full vigour of manhood and with all the experience of a seasoned campaigner behind him. And this was her father! And she was the Daughter of the great Bridei!

"Now, some of you young men, not yet blooded, may wonder - how can this man, a foreigner, say, in truth, 'We, the Pretani'. I'll tell you." Rapt and silent, they hung on every word. "When first I came to your land, my ears had been filled with tales of the wild barbarian tribes I would rule. And would you believe it, every tale was true!"

With one light stride, Bridei had an arm resting on Gort's shoulders.

"Yet, I say to my Heir in the hearing of every man in this Hall, that few tales were told of your great spirit, of your clear-sighted wisdom, of your fierce courage. Few understood that your ancient tradition is your greatest strength!" He grasped at the air above his head as if plucking the tradition out of nothing. And he held his fist high and tight before them and shook it at them in tribute.

Caterin, hands clasped in front of her, was borne away by his oratory.

"People of Pettaland, I salute you! You took me to your hearts to live with you, to share with you, to fight with you." His fist dropped. Every heart beat to the rhythm of his next five words. "And now, fight we must."

Bridei had a fine sense of audience, a gift of oratory, a way of using a finger to point, to beckon, to challenge. It had enabled him to rally all classes of people to his cause, from warring tribal lords and foreign envoys, to ship-builders and architects. Some day, Caterin was thinking, she must learn how to crack open the heart of a person and point the way forward.

"The time has come when thoughts must be harder, hearts braver. There are those who revile us, the Saeson, the Scot, aye, and others that would put a slave-ring round our necks. If we give them half a chance they'll grind our children into the dust and our children's children will weep and curse us as they starve and shiver. These, our enemies, are the ones who call us barbarians! Then we'll fight like barbarians! They call us savages! Then we'll kill like savages in defence of our land! Fellow-Pretani! Take up arms and follow me and we'll make a legend in our lifetime!"

His sword hissed from its sheath and rose, whetted and gleaming above his head. The clamour that arose seemed as though it would never abate as voices, trained in the piercing war-cry of charging chariot, roared their approval. Bridei swung the red cloak to his shoulder. It streamed behind him as he strode towards Caterin and caught her hand. His eyes looked deep into hers and then he was gone, leaving her clasping a leather pouch.

The tide-race of chiefs narrowed, jostling, at the doorway and spread outside to find the lads with the horses and the lines of waiting foot-soldiers. The women waited till the Shaman had disposed himself in his litter, ready to lead the host to the sacred grove at Pitbirnie where the powerful spirits of towering oak trees were waiting for the ritual and the libation of blood. Then the women streamed out, to join the townsfolk gathering on the palisade.

Caterin plucked Iogena from a bevy of slaves, so far away that she would have seen nothing of her lover and took her to stand above the Great Gate of the Citadel.

The Arch-Drui's litter passed beneath them at the head of the procession. Wise Cau, too, had the privilege of a litter and Prent with his perpetual grin walked beside him.

The birds to be sacrificed followed, carried in wicker cages, squawking their empty threats - black ravens, brown skuas, and white gannets, the colours that would ensure victory. In a line behind them came three Druad, carrying the gold ceremonial dagger for the killings, the torch of fire and the golden cauldron filled with water drawn from the well of Bride. Last came a Drui holding aloft on a pole the billowing banner of the Royal Bull.

Seven times the army would circle the grove in the same direction as the path of the Moon, pausing on the last round at the Blue Stone to touch it with sword or dagger or axe so that each weapon would receive into itself the magic virtues of the indwelling spirit. By that time, the sun would have dispelled the mist that now washed the pastures and the dew that sheened every grass-blade.

Trumpets sounded, brassy and cheerful. The King emerged on horseback from the Gateway, flanked by Gort and Cennalath who would take a westward route after the ceremony. All wore helmets now and chain-coats under their cloaks but only Gort had his feet in stirrups. There was a long moment when the King twisted in his saddle and looked steadily back at his Capital, before raising his arm in a salute that Caterin hoped was meant for her. Cennalath's eyes searched for Devana and held hers in a long love-filled look. Gort sat his horse as though he was moulded onto it, his head turned westward where his duty lay.

At first the women were silent, watching, fingering amulets, beyond wailing or beating their breasts. But when the pipes struck up a jaunty tune that swung along with the steps of the foot-soldiers, they began to cheer. It was the only thing to do to keep their hearts high and hoping.

Next came the charioteers in their light, fast chariots, reining in the eager prancing of their dainty fleet horses. The physicians, bards, metal-workers, cooks, fletchers, farriers and sundry servants went in ragged bunches, mounted, perched on carts or on foot according to their status. Bringing up the rear, in splendid order and array came the King's Guard with Uurad, erect and manly, leading his company and turning to salute Iogena who gripped the shafts of the palisade till her knuckles showed white.

The rosy promise of the dawn had been overcome by a dank mist that had crept in from the sea. Yet still the women watched, silent now, until they could see only the tops of the pennants hanging limp and dejected from their poles in the damp air.

Caterin briskly told her women to wait indoors in the warmth. She had a task to perform alone. The area behind the palisade was strangely silent since the army had marched leaving only a scatter of broken thongs, rusty nails and horse-droppings. And lonely under a drizzle of rain lay a fine ceremonial wagon, all gold and silver, holding Nechtan's bones, cleaned and washed and wrapped in his soldier's cloak. Even in the haste of his departure, Bridei had remembered.

Then a long ribbon of elderly court officials came snaking from shelter to obey the King's command. And a cook with a withered leg and a glisten on her pocked cheeks hirpled from a doorway back into the kitchen.

Two dappled grey mares, too old for dancing to the drum, drooped in their traces as dejected as their plumes. At a crack of the whip they strained at the traces and moved off to Pitcairn where the Ancestors brooded on a hill that faced the sea.

Yet as Caterin walked the puddle-wet track, she felt Nechtan was there, chuckling and beckoning to the clustering spirits to see the honour that was done to him. Chuckling again as his bones were laid in a stone coffin lying north and south as was right, with the skull of a hound that he had preserved to guard his corpse in death as well as it had done in life.

"That beastie saved my life, once, when I was felled by a tree," Nechtan would be telling the oft-repeated story to his familiars.

For his journey, they laid a small pot, half-full of mead, on its side and a handful of quartz pebbles for currency ready at his hand. Last of all, Caterin took the last sheaf of arrows that Nechtan had made for her. One by one, she broke them in two, as a sign that the warrior would shoot no more. And the arrow-spirits she had released would wing him on his way.

His chuckles faded a little as the quartz stones were laid in place. Caterin poured the libation and the rain washed the stones clean again, taking the wine down into the living Earth. May

Nechtan and the Noble Ones forgive her foolhardy act. May the Kindly Ones grant that it would not bring defeat to the army and grief to bairns yet to be born. May Maelchon and Talorc live forever with their deed as the Wise Woman had prophecied.

It was one of the lesser Drui who lit the fire and he had difficulty with the damp wood. As they ate the funeral flesh, dense smoke from the twigs wreathed round them in the moisture-laden air, till they appeared to each other like ghostly figures in limbo. At last a little breeze came, as if Nechtan's unknown Ancestor had heaved a sigh. It spiralled the smoke upwards and westwards to where the rags and tatters of clouds hung around the hill-tops. It sped Nechtan's spirit still chuckling on its journey to the Home of the Guardians and they were free to take their leave.

But Caterin waited, damp tendrils of rabbit fur straggling into her eyes, while her hatred of Maelchon and his brother, consumed her.

"Some day I'll avenge you, Nechtan. Just you wait around and see."

CHAPTER FOURTEEN

In contrast to the rain-drenched burial rites of Nechtan, the journey north to Pitversie on the following day was a delight to the senses. Caterin chose to ride in front with the bodyguard and pack-horses. Devana, Amis, Iogena and the others rode in a wagon with its rain-cover pulled back and placed upwind from the cart carrying the lambs, the fowls and the casks of mellow mead, the guest-gifts for the Druad.

The wind freshening from the west, cleared the sky to an egg-shell blue. The last grey skeins of rain-clouds straggled across it. On the mellow plain sweeping banks of broom and hawthorns heavy with blossom perfumed the rain-washed air. The Paps of the Lomonds lay, smooth and clear-breasted against the sky with the ramparts of once-great fortresses encircling their tops. The Loch of Leven, brimming over into the meadows, quiet and peaceful now since the pink-footed geese had arrowed their way north in garrulous V-strands.

The tree-smothered Glen of Farg, was an explosion of colour, backlighted by sunlight. Birch, beech and mountain ash unfurled fresh, yellow-green flags, standing proudly, root-deep in anemones and bluebells. Everywhere a carolling of birds and a flashing of white mating feathers.

Here and there, a stream cascaded to the river, a rainbow-tinted spray clinging like teardrops to clusters of primroses and violets, red campion and king-cups.

It was a time when the All-Mother was displaying her pleasure that the Beltane fires had been kindled, the Carlin had leapt through the flames, the caudle had been spilled and She could give birth once more.

Yet, with their senses feasting on the countryside, every heart in the little procession beat with the drums of the army. It was one thing for the Druad to say that the spirit of a dead warrior lived on and came back in another guise. That was little comfort to the woman who wanted her own man back, the man that grumbled at his dinner, fondled his bairns, set the kingdoms to rights over his ale and waxed lusty under the blanket.

At every homestead they passed, the bustle of the morning was absent. An old woman carried water with a proud, easy bearing back to a house empty of sons. The chant of the milkmaids at the churns mourned in the air. An old man, huddled like a sad crow on a mule loaded with kindling, mouthed a sad greeting from under his hood.

They were following in the path of Bridei's army, seeing the signs of its passing in trampled ground and broken branches. When they emerged from the Glen onto the flood-plain of the Earn, they paused to let the animals drink before turning east. And their eyes followed the track where the army had branched off to go inland at the watersmeet.

The King's host would have forded the Tay high up where there were sand-banks before winding round the Mounth till the mountains reached the sea at the mouths of the twin rivers, Deva and Devana. At this point they would turn westwards, swelling their ranks with men from the Vacomagie and the Taezalie until they reached Craig Phadric on the Ness where the men of the Caledonie clan would be waiting.

Sitting among the willow-herb bordering the stream, Caterin untied the drawstring of the pouch her father had given her. She shook a silver brooch onto her palm, in the shape of two discs, the breasts of the All-Mother. The arrow, ornamented and broken in three, lay across them. And she held it against her cheek, aware now how much he loved her.

For the symbol was so ancient it had gained a powerful aura of magic. And even Bridei, the foreigner, must have known of its overtones of potency, gained from silver from the heart of the Earth, from water from the Well of Bride and from the seven nights it lay buried under an oak tree absorbing the benediction of the Life-Spirit. He must have had special permission from the Master of the Symbols. For this symbol was a link with the Ancestral Ones expressed in an image.

The company were making ready to move. She pinned the brooch in her cloak on the other side from the great carnelian brooch incised with the Royal Bull that was her birth-right.

Later they paused at the Earn, so that Devana could take leave of them and make for her home at Aberlemno. While her servants sorted out the baggage, Devana gazed up the River Earn as far as the eye could reach. In her mind's eye she saw them, Cennalath and Gort, following the river, riding through a valley covered in red clover until they reached the flood-plain and the Loch. There they would set up their seige engine that would hurl great balls of oil-soaked hemp to create havoc in Dun Durn. Who would win the victory? How many would never return? Caterin, seeing her own questions mirrored in Devana's eyes, folded her arms round her aunt but could offer no comfort. Leaving them, Devana, named for one river goddess, travelled on to pay tribute to another, Tatha of the Tay.

And after riding for a while Caterin rounded a hill and looked on Pitversie, still and quiet in the afternoon sun, waiting. And she paused to wait herself, full of wonder, and then went forward as if through an open door to a new life, new days and new ways.

Pitversie was no guarded Citadel, no huddle of homesteads, no straggle of hermits' cells. Behind rose the Hill of Law capped by a stronghold with eyes that watched for ships in the Tay or beacons from the Brown and White Caterthuns and a whole line of hill-forts in the north. Caterin's practised eye saw at once that they were well defended, the Druad.

No wonder then that they had planned something different, a community that would proclaim Pitversie as a place of learning and power. The tall honey-coloured buildings were set in an orderly pattern. The timbers of the sloping roofs carried on upwards, appealing to the spirits who inhabited the arc of the sky. Their foundations were sunk deep into post-holes in the soil of the All-Mother. So the powers of the Mighty Ones above and below were channeled into the very air inside the buildings.

No sounds carried to her ear from worksheds or stores, no smells of beasts, no smoke. To the east lay the village of Abernethie that supplied all the needs of the Druad. So the air blew pure and clean and peaceful along the paths.

On either side, as she rode the pathway, were yellow-grained doors carved with stories of great Ones of the past. Hastily she drew her eyes away from the flowing grace of them. To admire them was taboo. The pictures were for remembering the courage and wisdom of the Ancestors. Their skulls looking down from niches and ledges spoke to the inner ear. 'This is the place of communion between the Druad and the Powerful Ones, between the living and the dead'.

And look, above each door a sign showing the function of each building, Room of Writs, Refectory, but mostly Lodging-Houses, for these pupils studied for twenty-one years. What would it be like to study for so long and become a fully-fledged Drui? But she had no time for that. She had a goal to pursue. And quickly.

A handful of students in red, blue or yellow robes stood to watch them pass. The colours were something to do with the Fire and the Water and the Light, Caterin thought. But the real Druad in their pure white robes would live and teach in a cave or a humble hut in a grove.

Even Forgan, a Drui second only to Broichan, who now stepped from a doorway, would slip quietly away once his duty was done. It was a long-winded and tedious greeting he chanted, the same for everyone. For she was no longer Royal but a servant of the Ones. This was the door she had passed through.

Their lodge was a long-house, warmed by a central hearth where a spit turned and a piglet crackled. The women began opening bundles and laying out bedding in the stalls that lined the walls. They heated cauldrons of water and sorted clothes, hurriedly packed, for these women had devoted all their energies towards the needs of their men-folk before they left.

Caterin knelt by the fire, letting her newly-washed hair fall as a curtain over her face, unused to living elbow to elbow with others. No escaping to the sportsground though even the pupils of the Druad were not above the Law and would be fined if they did not keep themselves fit. Yet, strangely, the playing-field held no attraction for her now.

Her familiar world was retreating step by step into the background. She was safe from the Veniconie, safe from Gort. A new purpose in life was being presented to her. The aura of contemplation and learning that pervaded this place had roused a yearning in her. The very pillar of wood at her side, rough-grained to her hand, seemed to hold within its structure the sum of knowledge of all the students who had passed this way before. All seeking a wisdom that, once acquired, would stay in the memory, a box of delights that would never fail. A tower of knowledge that would always support her.

She was hungry for learning, hungry as a new-born kitten blindly seeking the teat. The fate of her father and her country lay in the hands of the Renowned Ones. Here she could serve them both and satisfy her own inner need. Surely the Ones must have a purpose for her, not just to be the Vessel that carried the Blood of the Royal Line.

At dawn she opened her eyes on the face of a girl of her own age. Her long straight hair was brown with a glint here and there as though a pollen-laden bee had brushed it in passing.

"I'm Leona. I've brought your robe."

Peat-stained eyes looked out from a face like a still brown pool.

"You'll be wearing blue. The blue of the sky mirrored in water. The blue of healing. The blue of innocence. We all wear blue for the first seven years."

The sing-song voice, trained by years of rhythmic learning by rote, had a melody of its own.

The soft woollen robe fell in folds to Caterin's feet. She lifted her belt.

"No girdle. You've no need of spoons or daggers."

Caterin laid her girdle aside with regret. Tomorrow she would hide it under her robe. And pin her birth-brooches inside her cloak.

"You're one of the children now. You must begin at the beginning with the young ones. What you'll learn in this short visit is very simple. History and poetry-speaking. That's all."

And that very subtly puts me in my place, thought Caterin.

As she followed Leona out, two of the guards hurried half-dressed to walk at her back.

"I'm one of the children here," she told them, her eyes twinkling. "Go back to bed." They would watch from afar, she knew, and then learn to leave her alone.

In the Refectory, Leona ate and spoke proudly between mouthfuls of oats and cream.

"Next season I'll be wearing the red robe. For seven years I'll study the wheeling of the stars and the healing of the body and I'll do service in the community. Today I serve by teaching you."

"I'm grateful."

Leona nodded complacently.

"Then I'll learn the secrets of communing with the gods and how to interpret the signs."

Astronomy and medecine! Incantations! How to plumb the secrets of the gods! It sounded just what Caterin needed to know. She felt offended at being classed with the children in blue. She knew the history well enough. Tomorrow she would apply to learn astronomy. But this was the first woman Drui she had met and she was fascinated by her.

"Are you happy?" she asked her suddenly. Leona's eyes widened in blank surprise.

"Happiness is not important. I was chosen by the Great Ones. I've known nothing else since I was seven. And I don't want to lead any other life." She spooned up the last of her porridge, eager to be away.

And why not? Nice and safe to know your route was mapped out for you. And, Caterin supposed, a student Drui had to be long-winded and a trifle pompous.

"Come along now." Leona's clear voice had already taken on the tone of the Wise Ones who must be obeyed. "You're going to be a student of Uedo. As an offering, take a white lamb for the Moon Maiden and a black lamb for the Earth-Mother and a pebble for the spirit of the Pool."

Caterin withdrew two lambs from the pen as she was bid. They joined more blue-robed youngsters, yawning and sleepy-eyed, and took a path upwards beside the uneven banks of a brook where Caterin found a white pebble. When the ground started to rise steeply they left behind them the soft gossip of the wood-pigeons and the flurry of disturbed rabbits.

At last, the ground evened out onto a gentle meadow and Caterin paused for breath. In its centre was a reedy pool which was the source of the stream. On their right, a precipice rose to the fort of Law. To their left, a semi-circle of massive oak trees brooded, spreading their branches in wide sweeping arcs. White rags on their trunks fluttered in the wind, sun-bleached remnants that had bound sores, pinned now to the bark by bronze or silver to replace the healing virtue that had been withdrawn.

The ground descended in folds to the tree-lined valley of the Tay and beyond to the land of Caterin's clan of the Vacomagie where the early light shimmered through a veil of mist blurring the ridged, mauve hills.

They ranged themselves on rocks and humps near where a willow hung weeping into the pool. It was sad and yet it was fine, to see them, sons and daughters of the greatest lineages in the land. Solemn and quiet, the children were, it sat strangely on chubby cheeks and rounded limbs. Grave and beautiful, the youths and maidens, hair of amber and bronze, graceful and shapely. What did they see, deep in the pool? Did they look on the face of the gods? Caterin holding her pebble over the water recited the spell. Smiles in the eyes that watched her drop it. The ripples spread and little pond-insects skated over them.

Half-hidden by the willow stood a hut with an out-house and a lean-to for a horse. Caterin tied her two offerings to the close-leafed canopy of ivy that framed the doorway and sat with her back against a boulder gleaned with purple lichen.

As a white-robed figure appeared in the doorway there was a stir of pleasure and a murmur of greetings. His name, Uedo, meant the Knowing One. He was not so old as the great Broichan nor so tall. He did not have the bearing that struck fear into the heart by his presence. His face looked strangely discoloured in patches from the dyes he used to pleasure the Ones he served.

It was a very mediocre face for a Drui, Caterin decided. Once seen, it would have been immediately forgotten if it had not been for his eyes. They did not gaze over and above the heads of his audience with the look of a seer but blazed with the fervour of a born teacher. Here was a man who loved his chosen profession and could not wait to impart the beauty of its history and traditions.

Uedo studied the upraised faces before him, bestowing on each a special little smile or nod of recognition, making his contact with his listeners. Caterin and two others received a salutation with an upraised finger as though noting the fact that they were new to the company. He took his place on a rock that looked as though it had been hollowed out by a spirit over a millennia of years to make a superb, high-backed seat. Resting one hand on his knee, he leaned forward to speak.

"To hear and to keep. That is our heritage. Listen again to the tale of our beginnings for all history begins with this song. And all people, whether they know it or not are touched by history for they are living the effects of it."

Not for nothing was he known as the Master of the honeyed word. He inclined his head and a boy struck a chord on a lyre. Uedo caught the note and began his chant.

"Far back in the early mists of time, Dagda, the Shining One, the Good One, the Lord of Perfect Knowledge, looked upon the beautiful maiden, Eartha, sleeping under the Ice. And he loved her."

The listeners relaxed, smiling, mouthing with their Shaman the well-loved story that they had picked up at the hearth. It was a time to test that they were word-perfect in the mellifluous long-sounding vowels of the ancient Attecottie.

"And Dagda took a flame, fashioned it into a fiery ball, breathed a portion of his spirit into it and hurled the ball into the blue dome of the sky. That night, when the ball descended, he caught it, breathed into it and threw it again. With patience and gentleness, for Dagda is All-Good, he continued to catch and breathe and throw."

A gentle breeze, floating from the mouth of the river, breathed life into Uedo's fine, mouse-coloured hair.

"And the heat of the Sun-Disc warmed the body of the maiden, Eartha. The ice that gripped her melted, forming rivers that flowed into the sea. At last, she awakened from her long cold sleep and beckoned to Dagda. And they mated with such joy and passion that mountains thrust through her surface and deep glens scored her body. Then her rolling breasts filled with fruits and herbs in abundance. Her swelling belly filled with life. Till with a loud exultant cry she brought forth all living things. And in the midst of the birds and the beasts, came springing from between her thighs, a man and a woman. It was Cruithne, fully-formed and glorious in his manhood. And, striding at his side, Cruithna, beautiful and golden."

With uncanny timing, the sun emerged from behind the cliff and bestowed an arc of light like a benison on each still head.

"In a ship of agate bound with silver and sporting a sail of pearl, Cruithne and his woman travelled the seas, meeting many races and learning their wisdom. In the fullness of time, Dagda guided them here to this land where the Attecottie dwelt. They beached their ship just a half-day's journey from here at the riversmeet of the Deva and Devana. They saw the golden birch-trees and the red mountain ash, the yellow oaks and the tawny bracken, the purple berries and the juice-laden nuts, the flaring golden sunsets and the creamy orb of the Moon Maiden. And Dagda showed them the twin breasts of Eartha, the All-Mother, rising from where she slept now that her labour was over. And they looked at the Paps of the Mother of the Top and called them Bennachie."

"Bennachie," echoed the rosy lips, lengthening the word in a long, voluptuous sigh at the smooth feel of the syllables on the tongue.

"And Dagda warned them that his strength was failing, that

each dawn the Sun-Disc would arc lower and lower. But Dagda would send a sleep upon Cruithne. In his trance he would see the symbols and would hear the words that would revive Dagda's strength after the snow-melt. Cruithne must make the signs and repeat the words in the same order. And Dagda would regain his vigour and awaken his Beloved again with the heat from his ball of fire. And the All-Mother would give birth in abundance once more."

Eudo's voice ceased, knowing the value of a pause and a change of tone to throw a noose round the wandering attention of his listeners. But his audience was alert and only too eager to show off their own aptitude.

"Now, the Attecottie were wanderers, hunters and fisher-folk," the youngsters breathed in unison and hushed again, aghast at their own temerity. Uedo sighed. Tomorrow he would have to explain to them the effect of a dramatic pause in story-telling. Smoothly he took up the rest of the story.

CHAPTER FIFTEEN

"The Wee Folk knew the couple had come from Dagda by their white skins and fire-gold hair. So they gave the sign of welcome and pushed the ship out on its journey back to the All-Father in the sunset. The Attecottie shared the wisdom of the ancients with the newcomers. From mouth to ear and mouth to ear it has come down through the generations. And this is now the wisdom of the Druad."

Nearby a blackbird burst into a frenzy of flute-like notes. Uedo paused for a moment to listen and went on.

"And the couple shared with the Attecottie all the skills they had learned. The choosing of seeds, the storing of grain; the breeding of beasts; the healing with herbs. Each year, Cruithne and Cruithna said the ritual words, made the signs and acted out the dance. Each year, Dagda and the All-Mother fulfilled their promise."

Caterin guessed he had chosen the story of the Creation especially for her, so that she would begin at the beginning. But she fidgeted, impatient to extend her knowledge.

"Each year, also, for seven years, Cruithna was fruitful and gave birth to a son. Then the Attecottie made Cruithne their Leader and they took the seven sons with the Blood of the Woman as was their custom. They made the sons to be chiefs over seven districts in the land. And they named the seven provinces after the sons. And these were Circinn, Athfotla, Fortrenn, Fib, Ce, Fidach and Caitt."

A chorus of voices had taken up the chant at the end. On the last word, there was a stirring and stretching of limbs. Uedo's servant handed round honey cakes and beakers to dip in the spring that fed the sacred pool.

"A blackbird cannot warble without a raindrop in his throat," said Uedo, flexing a stiff knee and trying to recall a potion that might ease the joint.

"It's a fine story that, and easy to remember," remarked one lad, the first downy hair of manhood soft on his cheeks. "Not like some."

Uedo shook his head.

"Nothing is easy to remember. You must be sure you have every word correct and in its right order. Each word was chosen for its fitness as well as for the music it makes as it trips off the tongue. You may think it doesn't matter if you change a word now and again. But you are the keeper of words for future generations. If you recite a wrong word to a boy it will stay in his memory and he will recite the wrong word to a younger boy and the song will wither and die. A good song deserves remembrance. You drive a stake at its heart if you distort the truth that lies there."

"Is there no easy way to remember?" asked a ten-year-old boy, heavy with the labour of it.

"Practice, that's the thing, practice." Uedo heaved a sigh, knowing that next year there would be another one asking the same question. "There's a rhythm in the swing of it that begins to sing with the heart-beat. Remembering comes when you stop relying on words as crutches and begin to hear with the heart as well as the ear."

They sat still as mice, respecting his wisdom. But the smell of smoked lamb wafted up from the Refectory. Stomachs rumbled and mouth-juices flowed. Smiling Uedo released them and they ran, laughing and leaping down the hillside.

After the meal Nemone, Daughter of the Waterfall, a woman, lean and vigorous as a mountain pine in spite of her many years, brought an air of briskness to the circle of students who waited outside the Room of Writs. There were no children this time and only a dozen students. Caterin wondered if she had ben given promotion.

Leona had told her to dress for riding and both girls wore trousers under their robes but Nemone had made no such concessions. She had hitched up her robe with a cord and a knot and that was that. Her long sleeves were rolled back from sinewy arms and capable hands as nut-brown as her seamed face. Her outflung arm swept round the group and they bent as one, like saplings before the gale, to sit on the ground in front of her.

"The Spirit of the Mountain is in every cliff, every rock, every sea-washed pebble, every grain of sand," she barked, fixing each one with a stare that dared them to question her. With a satisfied grunt, she unbent enough to sit on a boulder, knees apart and hands resting on them. She spoke in a rapid tattoo that kept ears cocked and she hammered her words into their minds. "And it's in the stones that we read our history, not in dusty sheets of vellum in the Room of Writs."

"Have you been in the Room of Writs?" asked the red-robed young man who sprawled next to Caterin. Turning, she met the liveliest blue eyes she had ever encountered and, what was more, they were looking her over with a most un-Drui-like interest. He laid a warning hand on top of hers.

"Tomorrow I'll take you in there. But Nemone's worth going with today, after she's recited her piece."

"The Attecottie! The Hill People! The wee Peskie Folk! I don't care what you call them! But don't call them stupid! We never see them. We never hear them. But in their time, they were a great race of people."

There was a smothered scream and a stifled giggle as a girl swatted a probing horse-fly on her arm. Nemone's gruff teaching voice did not falter. Only her eyes swivelled to the culprit, pinpointing her like a butterfly on a point of a dagger.

"In the last year of my Drui learning, I was sent to lands that border that sea they call the Middle of the Earth. There, scholars wandered round the walls of ancient cities. They stood open-mouthed gazing up at temples and tombs. I told them then that the Attecottie, in ancient times, knew more about mathematics and astronomy and architecture, than all these dark-skinned races put together. The fools laughed at me! But I tell you that the Attecottie were erecting great temples and tombs and Moon observatories long before their Pyramids rose from the sand. And you know better than to laugh at that, don't you?"

No one dared to move a muscle. Caterin was impressed. She had heard it all before but not with such vehemence. There was just one thing worried her. Would she have to learn to squint along a line of stones to tell which star was which? That was a talent she thought she could do without. Besides, she was distracted by the awareness of brown, blunt fingers still lying on the back of her hand and the feeling was not unpleasant.

"Yet, the Attecottie for all their wisdom, made one fatal mistake. Their accuracy with alignments probed the paths of the Sun, Moon and Stars, and into the very dwellings of the Renowned Ones. And they grew greedy to learn more. But the gods were jealous of their celestial secrets. Dagda sent a veil of cloud so that the land became a bog and the wind blew cold. Then the people could no longer see the stars and had to turn their eyes to the earth below. For now they needed all their great skills just to survive. Their punishment lasted for countless generations until Dagda relented and sent the Cruithne to save them."

"I didn't know the wee Hairy Folk, I mean the Attecottie, had been so clever," whispered Caterin. "I thought the bards were making it up."

She did not dare to turn for fear of Nemone's piercing eye but she glimpsed a cap of auburn hair, sleek as a fox's pelt with a tawny twist that sprang above his forehead and fell over one eye. The young man's grip on her hand tightened.

"Sh! She's sounding off again."

"I can take you to valleys where the sky-line is humped with more cairns than you can take in at one viewing. Some are as tall as a two-storey house with massive pillars, oversailing roofs and wide curving horns."

Stone tombs sounded incredibly boring to Caterin despite Nemone's enthusiasm and the flutter of excitement that she sensed in those around her.

"Leona, what Day is it today?"

"It's the Day of Dagda's longest throw."

"And this Night, Derelei?" Nemone had directed her question at the youth whose hand still lay on Caterin's. He paused before answering, then the tremor in his clear voice sent a thrill through every heart for this was a night of magic.

"It's the Night that never darkens. The Night when the Light never fails."

"Then let us go."

Nemone led the way with her long, swinging stride to the waiting horses.

"No guards!" Nemone spoke to Caterin's bodyguard. "We're protected by our powers."

The men averted their eyes and went to saddle their horses behind the stable intending to follow a couple of miles behind.

"My kin are stone-masons," Derelei told Caterin. "For generations they've studied the skills of the Attecottie. I want to see their workmanship for myself."

Caterin found herself caught up in his excitement and rode near him, as they followed the valley of the Tay. The expectation in their hearts was echoed by the buoyancy in the feet of their mounts. At each homestead, smelling delightfully of woodsmoke, honeysuckle or rabbit stew, Nemone's greeting was impeccably lengthened or shortened depending on the status of that community.

Yet, the elders who listened and responded, eyed the sky and jibbed like ponies scenting danger for they, too, were aware it was the Night of the Solstice. Kilted women cutting peat shaded their eyes from the band of Druad and muttered a spell till they were past. Giggling girls, bare legs flashing, straightened from their weeding and fell silent. The riders sensed other eyes, boring into their backs, following their progress, watchful eyes from strongholds on exposed headlands among the wind-tortured scrub on the skyline.

They kept their own eyes and ears on the alert, for this was dangerously near Scots country and, though they carried nothing worth plundering, a young Drui with some learning might make a useful slave.

Caterin exchanged glances wih Derelei that quivered with awareness. There was something thrilling about this man and the night that was to come. Something that shone in his face and crackled between them and hung in the heavy afternoon air.

The Loch of Tatha, the Lady of Tay, lay calm and elongated like a long, pewter shield, studded haphazardly by crannogs, for the Caledonie still clung to the custom of building round wooden houses on islands of sunken stone. There they dwelt among the most beautiful scenery in the land. And were not plagued by midges!

"May the morning smile on you."

Nemone called a greeting across the water to a woman standing at the edge of a causeway, spinning with a whorled spindle and drawing out its thread. The woman bunched the combed wool under her armpit and pretended not to hear.

And as they rode Derelei spoke of the ancient mysteries. How they challenged his thoughts and intoxicated his spirit. And all around was the grandeur of snow-pocketed mountains and swift-tumbling, rock-strewn rivers. And all that wild and lavish beauty set up a clamour in her blood.

When the party dismounted to water their horses, Caterin and Derelei stood between a pair of standing stones. The male was a thrusting rounded shaft of granite, the female, tapered to a lop-sided point. They looked into one another's eyes, wondering that their thoughts could flow together in such a happy communion that they had no need of words.

And she saw that one of his eyes was blue. But the other was half-blue, half-brown. And it was queer and nice and she wanted to laugh and did not. For there was a feeling inside her that was as old as the ground they trod and as overpowering as the stones that hid them.

Derelei's lips were as cool as the kiss of a petal at dawn as they touched Caterin's cheek. She knew it was fitting. For the joy to come that Solstice Night was to be a wonder of the spirit and not of the passions.

On the other side of the Loch, standing out boldly, half-way up a brown mountain, lay a massive round cairn. The sunlight glanced off the quartz stones, hit the burnished surface of the water, to angle back into the wide dome of the sky. Looking westward, to the rose-tinted mist on the horizon, it was easy to imagine Dagda at his strongest and most virile, waiting to field his fire-ball and breathe one immense breath so that its pearly light would not fade from the sky before it was launched upwards again.

They rode round the head of the Loch, through fields pink with a glow like a maiden's blush. Tethering their horses, they began to climb to the cairn. The evening air was full of the piercingly sweet song of a single thrush. When they saw the black opening in the stones, the students stopped, uncertain.

As Nemone lit a taper, they sighed with relief and crawled in after her through the low entrance.

Caterin found it an eerie journey along the long low passage. Her head, elbows and knees bumped and grazed on the stone slabs that walled and roofed and floored it. The flickering light ahead showed, fitfully, the spirals and circles that decorated the walls. At last she could stand upright in a round chamber where Nemone had lit more tapers.

Four lofty columns of stone held the flags of the domed roof. There had been a loving skill, a delight in craftsmanship, in the making of this building. Flagstones divided the area into stalls in which the bones of long-dead people lay in careless heaps on shelves and on the floor. Above and around her, Caterin could feel the tremendous solidity of the ancient tomb with its walls and roof of native stone.

"Buildings speak in strange tongues, in a language few can

understand. Listen..." Nemone nipped her tapers out, one by one. A silence as heavy as the roof above their heads pressed down on them. Then the darkness was filled with a whispering of ghostly haunting things and a rustle of spirits that did not rest. They waited, hardly drawing breath.

Startling in its dramatic suddenness, the last shaft of sunlight pierced the long tunnel that had been perfectly orientated centuries before for this annual marvel. The sunset flowered on a massive slab before their eyes, on a smooth face of sandstone that glowed ever brighter and dispersed its mellow golden reflection throughout the chamber. It lit the wondering, young faces with an unearthly radiance. There was a communal feeling of being at one with the Life Forces flowing from the past, swirling round the present and streaming straight on into the future. There was a vivid glimpse, a tantalising insight into the very core of truth.

Then the light vanished. Darkness hit them like a blow. In silence, they stood, feeling their spirits reach out after the moment that had gone and would never return. But they had seen the glory of the Magnificent Ones, channelled into stone by ancient man and their hearts were uplifted.

They came out backwards, crouching, bowing in humility.

"It's the only way to leave the presence of those who envisaged such splendour and made it a reality." Derelei dusted his hands.

Above, the sky was dark-blue. In the north-west, the sun had disappeared into a carmine mist. In the north-east, the promised dawn cast a salmon-tinted radiance on a swathe of purple. The students rode with upraised faces and cleansed spirits through the long-drawn-out twilight till they came to a plain that stretched like a dark ribbon between two lochs, silvered by the stars. One by one, they came slowly back to themselves as their horses picked their way across the moor.

"This night we'll see another great wonder. If you're lucky." The very simplicity of Nemone's words gave them added weight. "I've only seen it once myself. And it was cloudy that night. But it only happens once every eighteen and a half years."

Nemone reined in her horse in the shadow of one of the massive slabs always found outside a stone circle.

"This is the Night of the Caress when the Moon Maiden kisses the Mountain wherein her lover is imprisoned for ever."

The stone reared into the sky, dwarfing the riders, making

Caterin aware of a kinship with the small, scurrying animals and the waving grass in the empty landscape around them. Trees leant from shadowy undergrowth that was full of small sounds and rustlings.

"The Ancestors of the Mountain People set up this stone as a marker. From here they studied the mysteries of the Moon Maiden. But such knowledge was forbidden. Its magic was too powerful for mortals. So the Moon Maiden drew a veil over the memories of those who violated her privacy with their Measuring Stones. Yet, generations later, still they come in stealth on this special Night to see the Moon Maiden caress the Mountain."

Gradually, Caterin became aware that the countryside was moving like an eddying pool. Small, dusky figures began to emerge from behind hillocks and along sheep paths. Cloaked, hooded, secretive and burdened with bundles, the misty forms converged on the group of riders, still and silent beside the stone. These were the Attecottie, who had retreated up to the high corries on the edge of the tree-line and who sniffed the air for strangers like the deer.

"Take warning, you Druad, who watch with me tonight," cried Nemone. "The mysteries of the Great Ones cannot be measured by Stones. The Druad path to knowledge is through meditation. Only by the reading of the signs will you gain insight and wisdom."

By this time, the stone towered over a dark, moving sea of people. Now and again, a silvered eye flashed up at them from the depths of a fiercely pointed hood, acknowledging and accepting their presence. The people turned to face south and stood silent, waiting. Following their gaze, Caterin made out a ring of stones on the thin neck of land between the two waters. Twenty-eight slim pillars in a flattened circle, elegant and poised against the pale background, set like jewels within the confines of a ringed ditch and earthwork. In the centre, a single slender post floated in a swirl of ground-mist.

"Lift your eyes up and beyond the central post." Nemone's voice was hushed. "Now can you see the Mountain where the Maiden's lover lies?"

In the distance, against the pearly sky Caterin saw the grey shape of the Mountain as perfectly formed and rounded as a half-circle. Earth, air and humans breathed with one breath. Their hearts beat with one pulse. The Moon Maiden began to lift herself over the rim of the world at one side of the Mountain. Slowly, majestically, the milk-white Moon sailed upwards, pale and sad. A veil of mist drifted across as if to screen her chaste love from the world. When the cloud passed, the Moon Maiden was poised delicately on the horizon. Serenely she skimmed the curve of the Mountain. Shyly, graceful as a wood-nymph, she rolled in a dainty arc up over the top and downwards.

There was a hissing of breath at the wonder of it. When the Moon Maiden coyly slipped beneath the horizon again, Caterin felt bereft. It was as though She would never again sail in her orbit in the midnight sky.

So Caterin were unprepared for the triumphant yells that broke from hundreds of throats. Her horse reared and plunged. Only when he quietened and stood, quivering, white-eyed, did she see the man in the skull of a stag, fleshed out with clay and still carrying a magnificent spread of points. He led and the dark forms followed to a low crooning chant that soothed and excited at one and the same time. One by one, the shapes came up to the outlying stone and passed their bundles through a well-worn, knee-high hole.

Caterin caught odd phrases - 'May the Great One remember Bran', 'Shining One, free the spirit of Cinie' and she knew the bundles contained the bones of loved ones, cleaned and washed and freed from flesh. The words muttered by the Little People, had twisted away from the purity of the Old Tongue that the Druad used in ritual. Living apart as they did, the accent had blurred and the inflections had mellowed but the meaning was clear.

Still the procession of people moved round the stone like the ripple on the dark surface of a river when the salmon are on the move. Occasionally, a figure would detach itself from the mainstream, darting forward to put his own arm or leg through the hole or to press against the stone. 'Anu, Anu, heal my sore'. Once a crying baby was passed right through. Seven times the stream whirled and eddied moon-wise round the stone, chanting. The dawn cast a fine sheen on soft leather cloaks, patterned with the symbols of moon and sun, life and death. Then the dark river took a new course, meandering after the stag-head who was heading towards the stone circle.

Caterin following behind Nemone, saw that the movement of people had become a dance. As they passed through the entrance in the earth-work, they fragmented to form groups and began to observe age-old patterns that mimed the lives of those whose spirits had been accepted by the Spiritual Ones. Scenes were being enacted of things that had been or as they might have been. Coloured masks, specially made from clay and cobwebs, with trailing leaves for hair and beards, flourished and withdrew, advanced and retreated, threatened and submitted in the never-failing dramas of every-day life. Here and there, mock battles were acted out portraying the striving of a man or woman for the prosperity of the family and ending by being vanquished by death. Two men fought a daring duel with flaming torches. Exotic headdresses of flowers, seeds and shells cavorted and pranced around them like ponies decorated for a festival. The dancing went on and on, figures fusing together and exploding apart, throwing up fragments of waving arms.

Caterin and Derelei dismounted and stood in awe at the necks of their horses. Deep from a throat came a new chant with a pulsing beat that plucked at Caterin's heart-strings and ravished her senses. Without a word she took Derelei's hand and ran with him into the dance, fitting her steps to the fluting, sparkling notes of the reed-pipes. Her eager face flared in the light of the torches that were springing to life. The merry black eyes of a woman flashed a look of shared enjoyment with her. Her dancing feet crushed the herbs planted secretly within the henge, spicing the air with perfume.

There was a roll of thunder or it may have been a drum. The pattern of the dance changed into a formal weaving around the pillars. The threads of life were being braided together with gossamer strands spun by the Celebrated Ones. And the tempo quickened and Derelei drew her close with an arm round her waist. They moved together in harmony, the strands of their lives fusing to become part of the great pattern. Faster and faster until Caterin was brushing the stars with her hair.

This was in truth the Dance of the Lights around the Stones that Caterin had always thought was a fairy-tale.

CHAPTER SIXTEEN

Nemone and her pupils ate by a burn that made music in the dawn-light of a new day while the guards lurked in shadow of a hill.

"They're a shy people." Nemone drank long and deep from a goatskin bottle. "Now that we've gone they'll throw off their cloaks and enjoy themselves. The've celebrated dying. Now they'll celebrate living."

"And the bones?"

"They'll be put in the cairn tomorrow or maybe even the day after. But if the weather holds they'll feast for days."

Leona tossed her head.

"I think they're primitive. They might as well throw the bones to the hounds as leave them in untidy piles like sticks in a hearth."

"What does it matter if a father's arm-bone goes with a daughter's thigh-bone? The ceremony's over. Their spirits are safely on their way. The masks and headdresses will clothe the bones. It would be bad magic if they were used again. Then the passage will be blocked and the cairn will never be opened again."

Caterin and Derelei sat close on the spangled grass, smelling the moist peat and watching the dew-drops fall, one by one, from the pointed leaves of the tree above their heads.

It was too much to take in, all in one night, Caterin was thinking. Stones and cairns, boring old dusty things, she had thought them. And they had come alive and she had lived in the legends and been stirred beyond measure.

And the Dark Folk. A primitive race, she would have described them, as Leona had. Now she saw that Leona with all her knowledge had little insight into the heart of a person. She also would need more than knowledge when she was Queen. Instead of swallowing everything she was taught like a hungry nestling. And listening to opinions of the ignorant. And it came to Caterin as she leaned against Derelei's shoulder that knowledge was nothing without insight. For insight brought understanding. Uedo must know the Attecottie for he spoke of them with respect. The gap between herself and the Attecottie woman with the merry eyes had narrowed a fraction tonight. Nothing in her life had prepared her for the kinship she now felt for the woman who ate and slept and made love and danced to celebrate life. They were different, maybe, with their lone way of life and their mystical rites. Not primitive. Never again would she call them primitive. Like foreigners who miscalled the Picts. And did not understand. Like Gort.

She turned her head needing to be aware of the warm breathing man that was under the robe. And remembered how they had danced, exhilerated, aflame with the beat. Was he sharing her thoughts while sharing her silence?

But Derelei was marvelling at the skill of the cairn-builders, how they had balanced the weight of the great slabs, one with another, till the cap-stone had been placed and the weight shifted from the sides to the centre.

The hair of the girl at his side blew across his mouth and he was glad she was here in the crook of his arm. And glad she was royal and unwed and taboo. For today he had run his fingers along stone and the in-dwelling spirit had called to him. And he had answered 'no' to the call for he was a red-robed Drui and not a sculptor. Nor would he be tempted by a petal-soft skin and eyes as green as a leaf.

The next day, true to his promise, Derelei took Caterin to the Room of Writs. Taut parchment stretched over the windows let in a diffused daylight that showed a deserted room.

On a rickety table beside a pot of elderberry ink lay the Calendar of Events, dusty and worn as though it had been brought out from the back of a shelf ready to enter in the name of the new King. The last entries in it, Caterin saw, were lists of Bridei's battles, bald statements that told nothing of his valour and skill.

"What you're missing is the cadence of a voice," Derelei told her. "Stark words on vellum are dead things and always will be. I thought you might be disappointed in this place."

"There's nothing here about the latest campaign," she protested.

"They say news of the outside world would distract us from our learning."

"But what if my father was killed, or Cennalath ... or Gort?"

"Any real news and they'll tell us."

Caterin had to be content with Derelei's assurance. In any case she had faith in Bridei's power backed by Broichan's magic. She forgot her fears in the days that followed. Though it may well be that half of her delight came from Derelei's company. And why not?

In their free time, she walked and talked and laughed with him, bubbling with happiness, knowing he found joy in her company, too. He lived life in a constant source of wonder at his surroundings and he could not rest until he had found out all its secrets. He was a mine of information on the everyday landscape, urging her to look at it with new eyes. Like when he took her to the shore to study the stones and the beauty that was within each one. Until after a while she could home in on the precious ones, sea-polished agates and carnelians, for a luck-charm for Iogena's baby.

Yet day after day, the rote learning with Uedo went on.

"There's not a bard-song he hasn't sung, not a law he hasn't explained, not an ancient site we haven't explored," she told Derelei.

And Derelei began to climb to Uedo's hut to be with her. Sometimes, when their hands touched, he would pause suddenly and look at her and the warmth in his eyes would stir with a kind of wonder.

"Kelpie's eyes," she would tease him.

Those eyes disturbed her when she lay in the long-house listening to the breathing of her sleeping women. Yet, a pair of grey indifferent eyes haunted her too. With Derelei, she shared in his every thought and feeling. All Gort would ever share would be her bed. Yet, he had awakened her to love and at times she hungered for him again.

Derelei remained an exasperating, bewildering yet lovable mixture of dreamer and realist. One day, they went with Nemone to visit a broch on a promontory that probed into the sea like the hook of a finger. From inside the high circular walls Caterin looked up and saw Derelei's fox-brush, sprouting like a flowering weed, above the sill of a gallery where the hollow wall began to taper inwards. A brown arm appeared and blunt fingers traced the clean-cut edge of the stones, following their setting as they curved upwards and inwards.

"Did your family build these giants?" Caterin shouted up to him.

"My grandfather boasts that they did. And after five hundred years there's no one can prove him wrong. Come up but mind the broken step." Together they climbed the rest of the staircase, past the holes where the timbers of the roof had been lodged, till they were out in the open, looking over the sea. Derelei leaned over to gaze down at the unbroken wall.

"The Roman army with its war machines was the only force that might have launched an attack on a structure like this," he commented. "But they never did."

"It was a good place to hide the youngsters from slave-traders," she said. "But I think my father had the way of it. When the chiefs were boasting over their ale, it was a fine thing to say, 'My broch's bigger than your broch'."

Derelei threw back his head and laughed. Caterin studied his tanned, square face with its strong chin and jawline. Not for the first time, she wondered what had attracted him to leave the building trade where he could work with his hands, to take up the rigid life of a Drui where mind and spirit were all that mattered.

"When I am a Drui I shall live in a cave of stone," he answered as if divining her thoughts. He laughed again, shyly, and ran his fingers through the swatch of rusty hair that rose and fell back over his eye. The half-brown one. "Maybe you can understand. When I take a stone into my hands it tells me something. Maybe it has the spirit of a hand-matching tool in it or, perhaps, a crystal is hidden at its heart. Or it might imprint in my mind the kind of building it would fit or a carving I could fashion on it."

"You don't talk like a Drui," Caterin accused him, smiling. "Are you not nearly finished your training?" He was older than she had thought at first, about twenty, she guessed. If the term of study lasted for twenty-one years, he had only a few more years to go. It may have been the reflection from his red robe that flamed across his fine, freckled skin but she thought not.

"There are many ways in which a Drui can serve the gods," was all he said. His fingers caressed the stone, passing lightly over the lacy pattern of lichen that had formed where the wall was sheltered from the wind. Caterin wondered if he had ever touched a woman in quite the same way or if his love was all for the inanimate rock. Was he capable only of a kinship of the mind or did he ever feel a wild pulsing of blood? He turned towards her and his hands fitted themselves round the curve of her waist.

"Don't think that I'm going to be like the Hill People, aligning monoliths to study the movement of the planets and having my knuckles rapped by the Great Ones." His laugh was infectious. "I go where the Great Ones lead me. I want to discover the mystery and beauty in the bedrock at the heart of the Mother. Some day, I'll carve monuments that will be worthy of our Ancestors and you'll believe in me then."

His hands had made only a brief contact with her waist but it had caused a fluttering response in her senses. Slowly, she turned into the curve of his arm. His bantering expression changed. One hand came up to caress the nape of her neck in a curiously intimate gesture. Then she was in his arms, locked against his body. His mouth captured hers and, for a long space of time, they were wrapped in the sweet bliss of a growing desire. Somewhere in the yard below, a girl laughed and a male voice spoke, teasing her. Caterin pivoted out of Derelei's arms.

Derelei let her go. He felt easy with her, this right royal girl. For they were both committed to other paths. If it had not been so, he would have been lost in the depth of love he had for her. He winked his half-brown eye as if he knew she had wondered about his manhood.

And that night, she wondered no more. Under a canopy of stars, they made love and romped in the river and made love again and fell asleep couched in the great roots of an oak, absurdly and deliriously happy.

So the following days and nights were filled for Caterin with a heady intoxication. She sprang up to meet each new day with delight.

"For the first time in my life I'm free to do as I like," she told Derelei. "No guards hovering at my back." She chuckled. "Everyone's taken up with Iogena's bairn. Amis is as thrilled as if it's her own. They're roaming the countryside collecting wool from the thorn-bushes before the plucking of the fleeces begins. When I leave in the morning, they're hard at it trampling seal-fat into the wool in a bucket, one pair of long, bony feet beside a chubby pair with rosy toes."

"So that's why the slope at the back of your lodge is always festooned with drying skeins."

"In the evening, they're busy spinning, spinning more tales than wool, I suspect. Back at Dalgynch, they'd have bargained for wool that was cleaned and dyed. But here they've little else to do and they're enjoying themselves. I've to gather meadow-sweet, flowers, stalks, leaves and all for the special yellow dye Iogena's set her heart on. Even the bodyguard has joined in. They're stripping branches to make a willow cradle. And that suits me just fine."

If Caterin had known, one warm, lazy morning, that it was the last time she would sit listening to Uedo, she might have paid more attention. He had the gift of the three-line verse used by the bards. Besides being loved by the Singing Ones, it imparted a rhythm of statement that heightened suspense. But all Uedo's skill that day could not compete with the drone of bees or the thrill of Derelei's finger caressing the tender skin in the crook of her arm as they sat where the honey-suckle had formed a quiet bower.

"When the feather of rumour swept through valley and glen,
It was time for the Clan-Gather and the Plan-Making.
When the far-off glitter of Roman armour dazzled the eyes of the scouts,
It was time to send the army swarming into the hills.
When a woman, knowingly, left a bait of a cow in the water-meadow,
It was time to swoop and slay the red-plumed Roman, caught muddy-thighed in the morass."

Drowsy with delight, Caterin contemplated the wide, wide sky with all its variations of shade from the pearly grey above her head to the smokey-blue near the horizon, streaked with wisps of grey that were infant rain-clouds. Each subtle difference of colour in the grey-toned scene washed over her like a balm.

"When the wild mountain pass narrowed and the Forest of Caledon grew close and dark,
It was time for the ambush, the cutting-down, the destroying of Legion upon Legion.
When the dripping heads hung at the saddles and horses and weapons found new masters,
It was time for the Emperors to scurry south and send their sons back, arrayed with fresh hope.
When the eyes behind the timber-laced walls saw the glow of fires from the Duns in the south,
It was time to send the beacon-beam to the crannogs on the lochs and the turf dwellings in the valley."

Until Pitversie, Caterin was thinking, the sky had been merely a place to find the weather-signs. Fields and forests had been merely a hunting-ground for her pleasure. Who would have thought, back in the Budding Season, that the 'Wildcat Princess' would be sitting here now, stirred by a landscape? It had been a fine Growing

Season for the land and, more so, for herself. Her widening horizons had opened up new pathways, making her yearn to know more, to understand more. And she was learning, about things, about people, about ideas. About herself.

"When the Romans built an camp down there by the Tay,

It was a time to marvel at the ships they had brought from the Rhine.

When they built their bridge of boats across the sandbank to the other side,

It was a time to find out if the Mighty Ones would keep faith with us.

When the Romans held the rest of the world in thrall,

It was a time to rejoice that the Pretani were still unvanquished."

It was not a movement that caused Caterin to focus on a clump of trees in the foreground. Nor was it a difference in the shape of the tall pines. It was a sense that there was someone there with a mind that was reaching out to hers.

Before her eyes, a tree-trunk resolved itself into a well-remembered figure in a mossy bark-brown cloak. No wonder the Wise Woman had seemed to vanish into thin air. It was a rare gift to become more invisible than the hunter on the bare hillside, a secret of patience and stillness. Yet, a prickle started at the hairs on the nape of Caterin's neck and rippled down her spine. She knew, before Uedo spoke, that she must rise and go. Slowly and lingeringly, she drew her fingers from Derelei's hand.

"Veleda, the Seeing One, calls you."

Caterin was already moving across the grass, hardly aware that Derelei had withdrawn back into himself. Although Uedo's songs had been fine blood-swirling stuff, she had had her fill of history. The Wise Woman was calling her into magic realms and she had to go. Liquid eyes filled with ineffable sorrow looked Caterin over and became suddenly transformed with a glow that bathed Caterin in warmth. Compelling eyes that drew her to follow.

The sun burst forth as they walked downhill and round the curve of the cliff until they were out of sight of the Drui. Caterin did not look back. She felt oddly removed now from the place and its people. They came to a wildwood, so thick with trees and bushes that it seemed impossible they could enter it. Gently, so as not to harm them, Veleda turned aside a barricade of saplings and they plunged into the cool dimness. As the light of the sky was shut off, the excitement of going forward to meet the unknown took hold of Caterin.

"I didn't know you were one of the Druad, Wise Woman?" she asked, stepping over a root. The trees began to thin now, allowing the sunlight to filter through. Then they were in a clearing where herbs grew in wild luxuriant clumps. Unmistakeably, it was a garden in the middle of the forest with each herb planted and tended.

"A Drui?" A merry chuckle came from under the hood. "No. I've no need to use rituals or drugs to communicate with the Ever-Living Ones."

Veleda's cloak swirled to the ground at her feet.

"The Essence of the Ancestors is in my flesh. Their Life-Force surges through my veins."

Caterin saw that she was old, at least, forty-five year-cycles. Yet, her silver hair had the gloss of youth and sprang thick and shining from her head into two plaited braids that rested on her breast. Her robe was of fine linen that had been tied and dipped in flower-dyes until it bloomed like her own garden. Her skin was supple and fresh, like rosy cream in a milkmaid's pail at dawn.

"At my core lies a portion of the Great White Spirit who is around and within us all."

Yet Caterin held back, fearful.

"If you're not a Drui you must be one of the Dark Ones!"

Yet she could not connect this vibrant being with one of the mysterious blood-soaked Dark Ones.

Veleda lifted her face to the sun. Her eyes had changed. They were clear blue and lively. She laughed in delight at Caterin's withdrawal.

"Aha! You mean the babies boiled in cauldrons and virgins stabbed for the blood-sacrifice."

Veleda began to move among her flowers, touching a leaf here, stroking a stem there, greeting a flower newly opened.

"Use your common-sense, lass. Those who oppose a practice always make it seem worse than it is."

Slowly Caterin's fears abated as she watched Veleda touch each plant with love.

"Is it not better, in a time of fire and pillage, for a bairn to have its eyes closed before it sees the light than to be spitted on a spear in the morning? Then its spirit can wait for a better time to breathe in life."

She came and laid her herb-scented fingers on Caterin's cheeks.

"I'll tell you a secret. It was your own Druad long ago who put the bodies of dead enemies in cauldrons." Her laugh trilled out like birdsong in the air. "As for the virgins, they competed for the honour of the sacrifice. They gave themselves for the community with laughter on their lips, as willingly as their brothers on the battle-field. They knew they would have honour in the after-life and would live again on this earth in glory."

Veleda began touching Caterin with light fingers on her arms and face just as she had touched her flowers. Caterin felt no surprise. Her touch was full of affection. It was a measure of greeting, a sign of contact, an acknowledgment of the Life Force that flowed within them both. A sense of peace stole over her as though she had always belonged in this garden. She felt a great longing to be loved and nurtured by this woman. In a little while she roused herself to speak.

"Who was I in my past life? Can your magic powers tell me?"

"Haiii! What a foolish question. Born of idle curiosity, nothing less."

Caterin's eyes snapped. Was this woman trying to insult her? She had come to learn, not to be mocked. But Veleda's eyes twinkled merrily down at her and laughter gurgled in her voice.

"What will it help you to know about your past? Learn to live through your body in the present as I do. My powers were not granted to satisfy whims. My knowledge has nothing to do with propitiation of the Mighty Ones and the murder of the innocent. Haiii! This sort of talk darkens the mind."

Veleda stretched her arms up towards the sky. The wind moulded her robe to a body as rounded as that of a young girl. Calf-hide pouches hung from a girdle round her waist. She stood on tiptoe and, as her robe lifted, Caterin saw that her feet were bare. Graceful as a slow-moving swan, she danced, humming, among her plants.

Surely Broichan cannot know about this, thought Caterin. He would never permit me to be here.

"Broichan and I have an understanding." Veleda stopped before Caterin, smiling into her eyes, answering her thoughts. "He knows you have need of every type of wisdom. The more knowledge you have, the better your chances of survival."

"Survival's not something I've had to worry about," said Caterin shortly.

"Not yet." Veleda let the words fall lightly from her lips and stroked Caterin's hair as if to take the ominous ring out of them. "Throw your sandals away and come."

CHAPTER SEVENTEEN

It was a pleasant walk they had then, swishing through the knee-high heather, feeling under their feet the spongy carpet of peat overlaid with pine-needles. Then into the green twilight of the trees among the tightly curled bracken fronds. Here they were heedful of the quiet, subdued life of the place. The only armies were the teeming, toiling legions of ants. The only Queens were the matriarchs of the bees in the hollow trunks.

Aware of the denizens of the forest only as a hunter, Caterin was used to tiny creatures slipping silently out of her path with a mere flutter of a leaf to denote their passing. Along with the Wise Woman now she was accepted as a friend. A soft-eyed doe, nibbling delicately, glanced up and stooped to feed again. A shrew turned from his burrowing, his whiskers twitching. The sleepy croaking of pheasants and the crooning of pigeons served only to intensify the calm hush of the forest. Caterin could have walked for ever between the solemn pillars of the trees, savouring the earthy tang of the place. But Veleda had not brought her here for pleasure.

"Like you, I enjoy the stillness of the dark pines, the peace of the birch groves. But you'll see that everything in the forest has its purpose." She walked with the long, tireless lope of a woman used to the country paths. "See the young leaves on the tall rods that will bloom golden in the Harvest Month. Distil them to help the joining of broken bones. There, these tiny deep-violet petals. Boiled in whey they allay fevers." With her thumb and forefinger she nipped off a few purple bells from the soaring spires of fox-gloves, translucent in the sun. "Just a snip here and there does not destroy the beauty nor harm the spirit within the flower but tomorrow I shall have a potion for the weak heart of Fergot."

They came to the edge of the forest where siskins lilted through the trees, tails fanned, uttering sad little cries. Wagtails alighted in front of them, saucily flirting white tail feathers. Pipits piped their tiny piercing note as they soared and swooped in their song-flight.

Then almost hidden under rambling honey-suckles and roses, they came upon a hut. As far as Caterin could see it was built of pine logs and its roof was thatched. At one side was a spring, bordered by plants who love water. Veleda went to bathe her feet before drying them on her robe and examining them for thorns.

"Now, come to see my treasures," she said, rising.

Veleda opened the door and they entered into the herb-scented dimness. It was a workshed typical of all Wise Women who were called upon whenever illness or injury had proved too much for the simple healing knowledge of the community. Bunches of roots and plants hung from the roof to dry. As Caterin passed they touched her hair and sent out puffs of dust-motes that danced in the air.

All the tools for grinding, mixing and distilling were laid out neatly on a rough-grained table. Jars and bottles, full of the pastes and powders that were her raw materials were arranged on shelves. Higher shelves held her finished salves and brews.

Caterin stepped round the hut, looking, touching, smelling and tasting, delighted by the orderliness and sense of purpose of the place. Veleda followed her progress with approving eyes, satisfied that she had aroused in this woman a sense of wonder that was more than ordinary.

"These salves will be needed if there's a battle," Veleda's spoke again. "It's my hope that Bride in her wisdom will keep the armies banging on their chariots, looking for a champion to uphold their honour. That way the farmers won't start slaughtering one another."

Caterin perched on a stool beside the unlit fire edged with stone. A tiny cauldron hung over it on a tripod.

"Here you'll find I keep more cures for the pain of childbirth than for the gouging out of arrows. My mission is to bring peace as well as healing."

Caterin sent a sly look inside the cauldron. To her surprise, it was dry and clean.

"You won't find bat's wings and snakes' tongues in my cauldron." Veleda had begun emptying her pouches onto the table and sorting them carefully into piles. "Tcha! It wasn't a good day for the plucking," she went on, sniffing a root and throwing it into a corner in disgust. A mouse crept out of a hole to pounce on it and scuttle back. "It's best to gather before the sun has risen. Then the dew is on the flowers and the sap is running."

Her voice lost its briskness.

"The hand of Bride, the Exalted One, is with me when I pluck a herb for healing. Give your libations to her, my dear. None of the

Ones is more skilled in learning and healing than the Daughter of Dagda. Weave her crescent into everything you do."

She began tying her leaves and plants together and hanging them up. Pieces of stem, bark or lichen she scraped into a jar or bottle.

"Crottle." She held up a tiny piece of lacy lichen. "I take only a very little because it takes so long to renew itself. But it has many uses from dyeing to reducing inflammation. Soldiers on the march powder it into dust and use it for the heat in their feet."

"Aha!" She pounced on a clump of moss and held it high. "Every woman should know about this." She thrust it at Caterin. "Carrageen, spagnum, any moss, make a sponge of it, tie it with a ribbon of wool and dip it in a vinegary wine. Easy, isn't it? Then you have some protection from unwanted childbirth." Vividly into Caterin's mind came the image of her last night with Gort at the Palace and the herb she had used, intruding for a moment before sliding back into limbo.

Veleda was sniffing at jars and emptying the contents into pouches.

"Now here are herbs that every woman should carry at her belt. Smell that one and remember the mark on the pouch. That's for pain. This one for dizziness. This for vomiting. And one for the Moon Maiden's Curse." She dusted her hands. "That's enough for today. If you want to know more, come back tomorrow before dawn."

Disappointment engulfed Caterin as she fastened the pouches to her girdle. Surely she was not going to be dismissed so abruptly. Was this all she was to learn of this new and fascinating knowledge? Unable to leave she paused at the door and turned back, her eyes full of appeal.

"So, you have been given a taste for healing, Princess." Veleda's voice purred. "Then you shall stay here with me for a time."

It was as simple as that.

What they ate during her stay, she had no means of knowing, for Veleda prepared all their meals; first thanking the spirits of the living things for their sacrifice. They slept on thick mats woven from leaves that were as soft as a fleece, sharing them with tiny spiders that fell from the thatch when the wind shook it. Every day before dawn, they went out into the countryside while Veleda instructed Caterin in the lore of healing. Each evening, Caterin would repeat Veleda's wisdom over and over to herself in the way of the Druad so that she would fix it in her memory.

"Why do you never tell me the names of the plants?" she asked Veleda once, as they lay resting in the sun after their noon meal.

"Why do the stone-masons never carve a leaf? Why do the embroiderers never sew a flower? It's because these are the gentlest of the spirits. They have none of the anger of the bull, none of the fierceness of the boar. They don't make war on each other like the armies of men. Their lives are spent in giving, healing, peace and the benison of beauty. When we name them, we draw from them a tiny portion of their power. Too often and their magic will begin to wither and die."

And Caterin thought how the part of herself that had been haughty and perverse had withered away. And in Pitversie, a new shoot had risen, piercing the dry dead leaves, to come to flower here in the timeless forest.

Time as she had known it had ceased to exist. She had taken to going barefoot like Veleda. The feel of the earth sent ripples through the soles of her feet into every fibre of her being, signals that she understood.

Words were becoming meaningless. Talking between herself and Veleda became more of a bodily sensation than an interchange of words. Yesterday and tomorrow had become a vague dream. Here only the present counted. The colours in the world around her began to transmit themselves to her as emotions. Some gave her strength, some joy, some sadness at the ugliness of mankind. And she was aware of the forest pulling her deeper and deeper into its dark caverns where there was no fear, only peace.

Sometimes, walking along trails bordered with tree-trunks that repeated themselves endlessly or by quiet lochans that reflected the sky, she wondered if she was imagining it, if some part of her was running away from her responsibilities. She had sworn she would be single-minded in her bid for power. Nothing would weaken her resolve. Or had Veleda cast a spell on her?

Yet, there was such joy in their companionship. There were so many subtle colours to discover, so many new scents to savour, so many tiny sounds of birds and trees, so many tastes to explore, so many things to touch and ponder on.

It was the touch of things that affected Caterin most. For as she touched, her senses filled with knowing. The vigour of the sap under the rough bark, the goodness in the crumble of brown earth, the sweetness in the core of a flower. And she drew in a feeling of belonging, of kinship with the All-Mother, the source of Life itself.

"See what you've missed by living behind the walls of a Palace all your life." Had Veleda spoken or had it been the Mother herself.

But when it came to passing on her lore of healing, Veleda always used words. She muttered all the time as she walked as though there would never be enough time to tell all that she knew. "Tell me again," Caterin would protest. "Sometimes I don't know if you're speaking to me or to the spirits in the trees."

Mulling over Veleda's ramblings, Caterin began to find that she was contradicting herself. The next day, she pounced on something Veleda said.

"That's not what you told me yesterday," she cried.

Veleda swung round and caught Caterin's hands between her own.

"And tomorrow I'll say something different." She threw her head back and laughed up at the canopy of trees, a full-blooded lusty laugh. "You've plumbed the secret of the healer. Every person is different. Every healing is different. All that matters is today and that the patient gets better. You'll see! You'll see!"

And on she went through the trees. Soon she stopped to raise her head, sensing something on the wind. She ran foward to push back a hanging spray. Underneath, a linnet pressed his rosy breast to the ground.

"Ah, your poor wing," she crooned. "Some wild cat nearly got you. Did it not know you're Bride's favourite bird?" He lay unafraid in her palm as she enclosed him with her two hands.

"Haiii! There's no merit in teaching and telling," she murmured as if to herself. "It's in the doing of it that the real knowledge comes. That's when you begin to feel within yourself what is the real need of the broken body in your hands."

She kissed the tiny pink head and threw the linnet high in the air. Without faltering, he spread his white-edged wings and flew, circling first and then away.

"Shall I be able to heal with my hands one day?" cried Caterin.

Veleda smiled.

"The gift comes with the desire," was all she said.

One morning Caterin awoke as usual with the soft rustle of Veleda's feet over the packed earth on the floor. She sensed something unusual and lay letting her senses tell her what they could. But it was indefinable, this feeling. It was as though there had been a Presence that had come and gone, taking their carefree happiness with it and leaving a mood that was sad and solemn.

Veleda had put on her cloak and with it her air of mystery. One tiny spear of flame in a bowl was all that lit the hut. Her movements were slow and stiff as she coaxed the embers of the fire into life.

"Have you never wondered why I'm passing on my learning to you?" She spoke with an odd intensity.

The question had lurked at the corners of Caterin's mind.

"Well, I'll never be asked to follow in your footsteps as a Wise Woman, that's for sure." Caterin sat up and began to dress, trying to dispel the
heaviness in the air.

"Ah, but you'll be Queen some day, our first since your mother." The laughter had vanished from Veleda's voice. Absently, she took up a mortar and pestle and began to grind down a few fragments of bark.

"This morning I dreamed I saw a white Dove coming out of the West."

Her mouth had crumpled like a petal trodden in the dust.

"What does it mean?"

"All I know is that the dove is the only bird that kills its own kind to maintain its pecking order. So I fear this White Bird, yet I've no power to stop it coming."

"A Drui could interpret your dream for you," suggested Caterin.

"Perhaps I'm afraid of the answer." It was a mere whisper as she bowed over her pounding.

Caterin had guessed that she obtained a virtue from her healing simples that constantly renewed her youth. But now, when her thoughts were dark, her age and weariness showed through.

"You, young Queen, are our hope for the future. In your smooth palm lies the fate of our people."

"But what can I do? Forgive me, I can't see that brewing up a healing potion will keep a killer bird from our land."

"I've had this vision for so long, I forget others can't see it." The bark was ground to nothing. Veleda pounded on at the image behind her dull eyes. "Between us, the Druad and I have given you a taste of the infinite Truth. In the past we taught only to a chosen few, perhaps wrongly, but holding the knowledge gave us a certain power. Yet since my dream, I feel the knowledge is in danger of withering and dying. Although the Druad won't admit it."

Gort's taunt had buzzed about in Caterin's head like an angry bee since she had come to Pitversie and it needed an airing.

"I've heard it said that our traditions are outdated and will be forced to give way in time."

"That's the fear I have."

The pounding stopped. Suddenly Veleda went to stand at the open door.

Caterin, following, looked where she was gazing. A shaft of sunlight, like a ray of hope, had pierced the cloud and lit up a clearing at the edge of the forest. A half-grown fawn stood there, spreading his shaky legs, his wide eyes filling themselves with the wonder of his surroundings. The gossamer leaves, the spangled grass, the dappled hide of the fawn were all backlighted in gold and caught in a moment of breath-taking loveliness.

"And yet, you know, customs show a surprising capacity for survival."

As Caterin spoke she heard a new note in her own voice. A note of authority as though all her training in Pitversie had blossomed into this moment.

"Kings and Queens come and go, conquerors rise and fall, old laws make way for new laws. But the people who live and love and work go on much as before. It's the way of things."

Veleda turned from the fawn to Caterin.

"When I look in the faces of the young I find myself hoping again." Her face was smooth and blooming again, her back erect, her smile joyful.

"I remember that Faiths may come and go but the Truth of the All-Mother remains, flowing underneath the surface of our living, waiting to be recalled so that she might give forth of her bounty."

Her touch lingered on Caterin's arm.

"Haiii! My time with you has been short. There's something more I must tell you." She drew Caterin out of doors to walk towards the clearing. The fawn, feeding daintily, unafraid as they strolled towards him, was a gold-speckled delight.

"In life, every one plays the part appointed by the Great Ones before the spirit sparked in the womb. In one life you are a man, in another, a woman. In one a seaman, in another a Queen, a soldier, a body-slave. You may die of war or hunger or flood or you may live in plenty and peace. But you are the one who chooses whether to live your life for good or ill. Whichever you choose, you'll learn something that your spirit has a need to understand." Veleda'a eyes were on the fawn again and the doe who had joined him. "Then when you've lived through all aspects of good and ill and have become wise beyond your dreams, you'll become as one with the Infinite Good."

Eyes like lamps turned on Caterin, burning into her mind, willing her to understand.

"More and more people must become aware of the Truth. We must save our heritage for the generations to come." "Houses of Learning. Places of Healing. You'll have the power to bring this about when you are Queen."

Questions tumbled over one another in Caterin's mind. She sensed that the forests were calling to Veleda and she could not bear to let her go.

"Wait, Veleda. You speak like the Druad and yet what you say is different. Stay with me and teach me more!"

"My time with you has ended." Veleda paused. "As your time with the Druad has also ended. Now the All-Mother will test you, maybe to the limit of your endurance. Do not fail her. Or yourself." Her eyes had taken on a curious blankness. "You must seek out this White Dove! Learn to understand him! But if you survive, Queen Caterin, the bard will not remember your name when he sings."

Veleda drew a veil over her face as a signal that it would be discourteous to press her any further. Watching her walk towards the forest, Caterin felt the air quicken and change about her. When Veleda had disappeared among the trees, Caterin took a last look at the hut with its lintel of honeysuckle. Suddenly it was time to go. There were people to see and things to do.

"She spoke of a strange White Bird in that shadowy way that seers have," she told Derelei as they lay comfortably, shoulder to shoulder, by the long-fire that night. "But my name will never be sung in bardsong."

"Now there's a shame for you," teased Derelei. "And you with hair as silky as a beechnut and eyes that shoot fire straight into my heart."

"Ah, it's a pity you work in stone and not in words," sighed Caterin.

"Now there's a thing." cried Derelei. "A praise song in stone! I'll have to think about that."

But, however strange and impossible, Veleda's words had sounded, the following days changed Caterin's life for ever.

CHAPTER EIGHTEEN

It looked like rain so the student Druad were warmly clad as they rode out with Nemone. For a change, they could venture westward, for Artur had flung wave after wave of Dal Riatans at Gort on the flood-plain of the Earn. And Gort had flung them back and was nearing Dun Durn to surround it.

So with the Scots pinned down, it would be Gort's scouts on the summits, watching the ambling unarmed group that believed themselves protected because folk feared their powers. Never thinking that their heavy cloaks hid the Drui robes. Or that there was a band of raiding Scots sidling round the battlefields, creeping through the beechwood.

Caterin, laughing at a sally from Derelei, saw his face change to horror. A swarm of dark heads came pouring from the wood. A hand and an axe rose above Nemone. Her cloak swirled and fell. Her head went flying, the great braids working like wings.

And the quiet gladness of the day was ripped apart. Yelling, neighing, screaming, curdling the blood. Dirks whirling, slashing, biting and the bright blood spurting. A white blur of faces, dark caves for mouths. Hooves knocking on the sky and the earth tilting. Huge teeth gnashing, spitting froth. Leona lying, skirts high, hairy hands on her legs twisting them apart. Flying gobbets of blood from the bowels of horses.

The earth hitting her and pain driving through her like a heated blade. Derelei leaping to shield her, a dirk soaring, his body falling limp across her face. And she curling in on herself in the darkness under his tumbled cloak, stifling a thin wail that rose in her throat. A scream spiralling, gasping and dying. Someone breathing and groaning, on and on, and falling silent. Grunting Goidelic voices coming and going. A searching for pouches and jewels and weapons. Then a strangled cry.

"Druad!"

A hush. Then.

"Kill them all!"

No one left alive to tell the tale. Derelei's weight leaving her chest. A dark face blotting out the sky. A cry of triumph that she was a woman. Only one weapon might save her life. Leaping up and a tumble of words.

"Stand back, you scum! I'm Bridei's daughter!"

And the white-hot pain of a thrown dagger cutting her shoulder open. And the rain lancing down.

"If you kill me he'll track you to the ends of the earth!"

Wild-eyed faces swimming into focus and the earth slowing down and a silence. The silence of death.

And the rain slashing down, cooling their fever to kill. A mumble that retribution for killing a Drui was awesome enough but Bridei's vengeance was real and very near.

Baleful eyes, wagging heads. A cruel fist grasping her wounded shoulder. Her own fist clenching and smashing into an unsuspecting jaw. A shrill fight breaking out at her back. Then a dirk slicing into her neck and forcing her forward. Her heel crashing into a shin-bone.

"Leave me alone!"

The Daughter of Bridei stood erect, taller than the men around her. Her cloak swung as she strode out, swinging her hips, feeling the blood run from her shoulder with the effort. They harried and cursed her up stoney paths, beside stagnant pools, through stinking bogs, where they would not meet travellers. Still she paced steadfastly, gripping the stuff of her cloak so as not to betray the pain that lanced at every step, her senses alert for any means of escape.

At first she could not see for a driving wall of rain and then it settled to a steady drizzle. Anyone who had business out of doors would put it off until a better day.

A loch appeared before them, grey and forbidding and speckled with rain. With the knife at her neck, she stood still as a stone. The boats they uncovered were little more than skin-covered coracles. Once aboard, they forced a paddle into her hand. And she brought it down on the nearest head. His return blow almost knocked her over the side. But time was passing and a coracle needed balanced handling and all their skills.

They left the Loch by a stream, following it to a river and another loch. By now Caterin was lost. She only knew they had rowed west, steep, dark mountains threatening on every side.

The paddling stopped only once when they saw in the direction of the Loch of Earn a glow that flickered on the cloud canopy above them. And then Caterin laughed aloud.

"That's your outpost at Dun Durn! The Pretani army is burning it!" A fierce fist pummelled her to the bottom of the coracle, half-swamping it.

Now she knew she was deep in enemy territory. Dun Add, the Capital of Dal Riata lay ahead. The long happy days of learning were over. Mother Earth was knocking her head against reality.

Spray stung her cheeks and salted her wounds but her mind was on fire with possibilities. Somehow she must survive and must avenge the slaughter of her friends.

She had saved herself from death by threatening them with Bridei's wrath. Back at their own hearth they would feel safer, remembering that Bridei was confronting Aedan in the north and could never trace her among these glens. Then these dagger-happy barbarians would want to get rid of her. She could persuade them that the folk at Dun Add would reward them and use her as a hostage. She must force the men to take her there. But how? She had no gold to bribe them. Only her wits were sharper than theirs. And her determination was stronger. She would get to Dun Add if she had to swim there.

The daylight was fast disappearing. Now and again, they splashed out of the boats to carry them on their heads over a neck of land by hidden, lonely tracks. Beetles marching from nowhere to nowhere, they seemed. At length, they were in a sea-loch travelling south. The paddles kept up a remorseless rhythm for it was almost dark. Even the random, winking lights of homesteads were hidden behind a curtain of rain.

Then the horror of that sorry day struck. Images swam in her mind, vivid, tearing into the darkness behind her closed eyelids. Of Nemone's dripping head, of Leona's twitching legs. Of Derelei, oh, Derelei, dying amid the entrails of a horse.

And she held herself tight within her cloak, rocking, and keening, quietly, softly, over and over, the same three thin notes. And she knew she would never be the same girl again. Yet she must go on. The memory of the twisted broken bodies would never go away until the Pretani army had avenged their death.

And through the nightmare of her thoughts she heard a shout and raised her head, startled. A bonfire on a beach lit up a cluster of huts and flickered on a girdle of trees behind. Gilded nets hung on poles. Suddenly with a practised twist and loud guffaws the men upended the coracle. In a flurry of skirts, Caterin found herself in the shallows. She stayed there, unaware of the chill, only her eyes rising above the shield of her cloak.

A stolid older man came and sat on a pile of net-weights. Straggling black hair and beard faded into grey. Tunic and trews of green and red tartan

covered his barrel-shaped figure. The men squatted, supping stew, boasting of burned thatches and paltry trinkets wrenched from the girdles of women.

Half-joking, half-jumpy, they told how they mistook some pathetic Druad for a company of rich travellers. How they silenced them ... except for one, there in the water, a woman. Well, she'd claimed she was a Picti Princess. That was a laugh! But they'd brought her back with them. Nervously they watched for the older man's reaction. And, if she wasn't royal, they didn't care, for she was a lusty piece.

She forced her bruised body out of the water and strode forward, her dripping cloak flying. Her eyes ranged each staring face, despising them all.

"You took the lives of my friends!" she shouted at them in her blind fury. "You killed folk who were good and kind! And you joke about it! It's a game to you, to take human life. A terrifying game! But some day I'll see you all hanged for it!"

They stared, uncomrehending. Her swollen mouth and stumbling Goidelic had mangled her words. She gritted her teeth so that she would say no more.

The leader gave her a long searching look. Then he sprang up, rounding on his bemused men, shrieking oaths, his swinging palms bouncing off their heads. "May you be damned to hell for imbeciles! If she's royal, and by the Lord, she looks it, we could lose our heads for this when Aidan returns!"

At once the men began to slink away, heads down, all but three raw youths.

"In the name of light what's all the fuss about?" yelled one. His mouth had a leering, lop-sided twist. "All we did was creep in at the back-door of the land. Aidan's done the same many a time." Wry-mouth leered across at Caterin. "And we sent a few pagan Druad into the next world. That should make the priests happy."

"Hey, if she's really Bridei's brat, Aidan should have a gold arm ring for us." A little ferret of a youth with a narrow pointed face, showed his sharp teeth at Caterin. "He'll enjoy a sprig off the Royal Tree for his bed when he comes back? Eh, Mailoc?"

"Ach, forget that!" cried Mailoc, pinching his bleeding nose. "He's had one Picti filly already."

"I'd sooner slit her throat than gift her to Aidan Mac Gabrain," the leader growled. "It was our turn for the Kingship. But the Cenel of Loarn was passed over!"

"We could give her to the priests once the rain passes," giggled Wry-Mouth.

"Fool! They'll reward us in prayers, not in gold."

Caterin wiped the fresh blood from her face with the back of her hand. Her voice cut across their blustering, speaking slowly and distinctly so that they would understand.

"Your only hope for a reward is to take me to Dun Add in the morning."

In a smooth, sliding movement that took Caterin completely by surprise, Mailoc leaned over and had a knife pressing against her throat.

"Come on, out with it! Who are you? Drui or royal?"

Caterin arched back from his foul-smelling breath and let loose a stream of garbled threats in a rough dialect of her own tongue.

"That's a spell!" yelled Wry-mouth. "She's a Drui right enough."

Mailoc's mean eyes roamed over her.

"There's some right fine weaving here." For the space of an indrawn breath, the knife eased from her throat to cut the lace at her neck. She slashed out with her arm. The cloak flew open. Ferret snatched at the pouches at her girdle and poured the powdered herbs on the ground.

"Medecines!" He spat in the fire. "I told you so!"

"But a Drui with Clan Brooches, eh? That's new!" Mailoc gloated. The knife was back at her throat.

Caterin bunched her cloak round her hand, ready to attack the knife.

"Give them here!" The chief's voice was dangerously low.

"I saw them first!"

The knife trembled as Mailoc faced up to his father. The brothers tensed, heads aslant, eyes darting between the two. A woman smothered a cry.

These butchers had the minds of children! One false move and the waters of the loch would close over her head.

Her terrible fear left her breathless. But she was determined that the old man should see her brooches. He would know what

147

the signs meant.

Quick as lightning, she swept the knife aside with her cloaked hand.

"Look!" She thrust the brooches at the chief's face.

He squinted at the carnelian.

"Aye." He grunted, huge fingers picking over them. "Two suns. That's a Drui sign right enough."

"Look at the other one!" demanded Caterin. Her voice was rough and her neck sore where the knife had cut her.

"That's the Royal Bull of the Pretani!" she cried. "And when Bridei hears of this he'll come storming down the passes after me."

They stared, began milling around taking quick glances up the loch, and stared at her again.

"She's Bridei's whelp, right enough!"

"Kill her!"

"Into the loch with her!"

"Wait! Riderch at Al Cluith might buy her."

"Not Riderch! He's too stingy with his rewards." Ferret hooked a sliver of meat from the small dark hole he used as a mouth. "And Kentigern's back from Rome. Riderch is keeping his nose as clean as the Abbot's surplice."

"If it's gold you're after," Caterin cried with contempt, "there's someone else, though, someone who'll pay through the nose for me. Someone who needs a hostage."

She had all their attention now.

"Aye, Artur Mac Aedan." The chief took up her theme. "He'll be at Dun Add by now."

"And needing to buy time till reinforcements come from Eirean. I'll keep my mouth shut! I'll tell him how you rescued me from raiders!"

She had to make it sound good. For she knew full well that Artur would not believe any story this scum told him.

"We could strike a pretty bargain, eh?" Ferret's eyes glinted.

Her heart almost burst with relief. She had won! She had played on their greed and stupidity and they had believed her.

"Leave the Clan Brooches alone! She'll need them to prove her worth to Artur." The chief barked an order over his shoulder at the women. "Take her inside. Dry her and feed her!"

The hut was a little more than a shelter, but a faint odour of cattle urine meant it was lice-free. From a straw mattress three children in patched woollen tunics stared at her through wild tangled hair. A resentful woman gave her a bowl of stew and bread.

"At first light tomorrow it is then." The chief entered and towered threateningly over his sons. "And not a leg to be thrown over her or I'll beat the lot of you to a pulp!"

Sullen-browed, the men rolled themselves in their cloaks, lying between Caterin and the doorway, blocking any means of escape. The women raked out the ashes of the fire. Soon all was dark.

And Caterin lay awake in the snorting, muttering silence, sorting out her thoughts. What would happen if Artur was in Dun Add and used her as a hostage? With mounting horror she envisaged the result. The price for her release would mean defeat for Bridei. The purpose of his war would change to become a rescue operation. Artur would demand time until his reinforcements arrived. Gort would be forced to call off his seige. Then Artur would be free to help Aedan defeat Bridei. Mother of Bride, there must be some other way!

Gort's scouts must have seen her capture. The Drui must have reported her missing. Her vision filled with the shining and marvellous sight of Gort battling his way to Dun Add to her rescue.

Or, once inside Dun Add she could claim she was a farmer's daughter and sink into anonymity among the crowd.

There would be bards and traders there, some of them spying for Bridei, perhaps. Together they could plot to throw open the gates when Gort's siege began. And change the pattern of the war. For it could be done, there on Dun Add. That thought was warmer than the wet cloak she hugged round herself.

No, her brain was playing tricks on her because she was suffering from loss of blood and exhaustion. And she was fighting against sleep.

Yet each plan she pictured ended with her return to Dalgynch. It was an even more wonderful thought that Dun Add might be her gateway to a wider world. Nothing was impossible. Why not leave the soldiers to fight their battles and to bathe in the glow of a bard-song?

For she had lingered long enough with the Wise Ones. It was time to act, to seek out this White Dove that would come to roost in her land. Time to assess the power of this enemy of her people and study how to vanquish him. He was coming to them from the west, Veleda had said. From Dal Riata? Or from Eirean?

149

But first she had to outwit Artur.

And Artur had strangled his own mother because she was a Pretani.

It was not a morning for sailing when the leader bullied the three yawning, scratching brothers into a fishing curragh.

"And you!" Hard fingers gripped her wounded shoulder. "Tell them we found you! Or your throat's cut!"

The waves were white-capped and angry. All the way across the Sea-Loch, she gripped the wet thwarts on either side till her hands hurt.

For this Artur in Dun Add was a man who had gathered legends about him with every swirl of his cloak. He had fought against the Saesons. Some said he had saved the north from invasion. Although the Saesons were still sweeping everything before them in the south and sending refugees tumbling off the edge of the land to sail for Eirean or Gaul.

There was a heart-stopping moment when the men began to bicker and grumble among themselves. The horror of dying in that cold dark loch after all made her scream at them to keep paddling.

Then they were beetles again, squelching through a marsh. Now Caterin's shoes held onto her feet more by caked mud than by thongs. At last, she saw the Dun on the Add, its twin peaks rising out of the mossy bog. The Capital of the Scots. And she would enter it before the warrior, Gort!

Their arrival at the harbour did not go unnoticed despite the bustle. Two ships from Gaul were being hurriedly unloaded for it was rumoured that they had brought the plague last year along with their glass and wine and rats.

The guards on the ramparts signalled to them to wait while a convoy of wounded was transported up the steep path to the gateway. They had to wait again in the courtyard beside the fires of the iron-smiths, among soldiers, reeling with exhaustion while Mailoc strove to convince the guards that he had property worth showing to the Commander.

Her mouth twisted in scorn. If this was the Capital of the Dal Riatans, it was a rough sort of place, a soldier's fortress and not much else. It had none of the grandeur of the Citadel at Dalgynch, although, to be fair, the Scots had been here for a mere two generations. Even the soldiers looked like ragged amateurs compared to the professionals in Bridei's Guard. Her eyes roamed everywhere trying to guess at their numbers and the state of their weaponry.

A creak above her head made her glance up. A blackened swaying body hung from a gibbet. She stared in horror! That was how an army treated its spies! Tomorrow she could be hanging there! She clenched her fists and swallowed her sickness, her blazing hatred of the enemy overcoming her fear. Desperately she tried to decide what to tell Artur. The more Mailoc gobbled and gestured, trying to make himself heard above the ringing anvils, the more the guards turned from suspicion to sly nods and winks. At last they were led into the presence of the Commander, and Caterin had her first sight of Aedan's son, Artur.

He stood in the centre of a small comfortless chamber. Long narrow windows were open to the chill, bleak air. Spears and bows leant in readiness against the wall. Judging by the powerful smell of burning that came from his clothes and those of his companions, they had recently escaped from Dundurn. They would be smarting under that defeat.

Unflinching, she met Artur's gaze, measuring him as he was measuring her, her curiosity overcoming her wariness. His was a warrior's face, beak-nosed, strong-chinned with vibrant black curling hair and eyes as grey and cold as a stormy sea. His leathers were faded by weather and scuffed by use. Only the thick gold torque about his neck proclaimed his leadership. Supreme confidence radiated from him and Caterin could well believe the tales that said he had some supernatural force at his command that bore him to success.

"What's this gabble about a Picti Princess?" he barked.

At first, he eyed Caterin with the detached interest of a soldier interrupted in the planning of his defences. And then, more slowly, with the lingering look of a man who has been deprived of women for far too long. He cut short the abject mumblings of the three fishermen and put the question directly to Caterin.

"Who are you then, ragtail?"

That fearful black corpse on the gibbet had brought home to her the quick harsh penalty for spying. And now that the moment of decision was here she found she could not form the words to deny her royal birth.

Proudly she faced him with a regal disregard that her cloak was stained with sea-water and her feet encased in mud. Her eyes blazed defiance at him.

"I am Caterin, daughter of King Bridei, first Princess in the Pretani Line," she announced.

"Prove it!" His answer came straight as an arrow. She flinched at his tone. It had never occurred to her that she would not be believed. Her hand over her brooches, she hesitated. This mother-murderer might see only the silver and not the power that was in them.

Artur caught the flash of incredulity in her eyes and needed no further proof. She was as she had said. Only a Princess would have expected to be believed implicitly, an imposter would have had half-a-dozen glib lies ready.

Meanwhile, he would have a little fun with her, despite the grim-faced warriors who waited for his commands.

"Sure now and 'tis a divil of a Princess with hair like a corbie's nest and her toes poking through her shoes." He chuckled, turning to his companions. "Shall we draw lots for her?"

The swarthy impatient men around him stretched and stamped.

"Let's get back to the business that knocks at our front gate!"

"There's plenty of women below in the tents."

Artur turned his sharp mocking eyes back on Caterin, pinning her where she stood.

"Yet, I think this moth-eaten garb hides a pot of gold. This hen-sparrow might save our lives until Aed's army arrives."

Bushy eyebrows rose, eyes cocked, leather creaked as they straightened from the maps on the table.

Only then, slowly, her heart near to bursting, Caterin drew back her cloak and showed the Royal Bull Brooch.

"Daughter of Bridei!" she repeated. "And kin to Queen Dolmech."

Her eyes searched among the bland faces of the servants. Somewhere there would be a friend to that gentle woman who had hoped to stand beside her husband in queenly robes.

"This is the one that Kings are made from." Artur's laugh was harsh. "The pivot of their contemptible custom of choosing Kings through the female line. And she's promised to the very war-leader who fired Dun Durn, Gort of Gwynedd. What shall we do with her, Myrddin?"

CHAPTER NINETEEN

Artur had spoken to a man on the outskirts of the group, an ordinary-looking man, tall, his dusty cloak faded with exposure to weather, his horseman's boots split in the creases. He spoke the Goidelic with a strange lisping accent that stole in on the ear.

"Use her as a hostage! Send a messenger to Gort of Gwynedd. She'll gain us time till Aed stops plotting against the High King of Eirean and sends our reinforcements." For all his shabbiness he had the authority of a Prince.

Artur had used the man's British name but this was the magician known as Merlin. Caterin's eyes raked over him.

He looked too ordinary to have the power to make the Standing Stones dance, to appear as the Shining One with a ring of wrens flying about his head. More likely he used that keen intellect that showed in his eyes to persuade people of his magic. Although she spoke to Artur, she knew that Merlin was the more dangerous of the two.

"Have you no spies at Dalgynch?" she cried. "They'll tell you that Gort won't redeem me. Nothing will stop his onslaught now."

"Why not?" Artur barked. "You're his pathway to the Kingship."

"He needs only the backing of his brother Rhun to change that Law!"

Artur's glinting eyes rested on her thoughtfully. And Caterin sensed he had ambitions beyond his father's Kingdom.

"Enough!" Merlin hissed. "Be sure that Bridei will call Gort's army off and pay the price!"

"Bridei is holed up in Craig Phadric where my father will deal with him!"

Caterin fought to stay calm. She seized on that gleam of interest in Artur's eye.

"Don't give away your greatest asset for a few day's grace. Send me to Eirean for safe-keeping." Her voice became more beguiling. "For when this war is won, I can make you King of all Alba."

Merlin's eyes grew opaque like water in a loch before a storm.

"Don't let your eyes stray eastwards," he warned Artur. "Your destiny lies in the west and south. You'll dissipate your strength if you spread your net too wide."

"But you need land for your Scots tribes." Caterin said. "And the land in the east is fertile and green. Like Eirean."

Artur was too wise a politician to show any real interest in her promise. There was enough jealousy among the Tuath without stirring up more with a ladle fashioned in the shape of a woman. He signalled to the servants.

"Give these blackguards to Baitan to rig them out for battle."

Mailoc and his brothers howled and protested all the way down the corridor. And Caterin closed her eyes and called on the Vengeful Ones to ensure thay met their just rewards.

When she opened them again she met Merlin's eyes, golden-brown with a dark rim to the pupil, beaming hostility at her from under heavy hooded lids. With his dark, thin hair receding to show a high thinker's forehead, his beaked nose and long sinewy hands there was something of the bird of prey about him. No wonder he was called after the hawk that hunts its prey close to the ground, she thought. And shivered.

"Then have this muddy object scrubbed and de-loused. Later I'll see what's under the dirt."

Caterin threw off the hands that fell on her and walked alone to the door.

"Now let's defend our Duns in the time-honoured way," Artur grunted at her back. She had won the first round.

In a room down the passage, a scared young slave whose yellow hair told of a dallying Norseman, brought water and wine and chicken broth to Caterin before he fled. A guard locked the door firmly after him.

It was a comfortable room. A brazier glowed between two gigantic firedogs. Their grotesque shadows danced on shields and cloaks lining the wall. She found a voluminous cloak to wear while she washed and brushed her clothes and hung them on hooks to dry.

As she combed her hair, her eyes roamed over chests, a carved chair, a table with a lamp on it, and homed in on a blanket-strewn couch in the corner. This was the room of no ordinary soldier! This was where Artur slept! And she was there for his enjoyment!

The thought of being violated by a Scot, Prince or not, revolted her. If he tried, she would have a greeting for him from the dagger that was strapped to the back of her leg. Yet a dagger was not the answer. She would need to find another way to persuade him to send her to Eirean.

A key grated in the lock and Artur stood there bandying words with the guard. And she knew by the leer on his face what he had come for. He had brought a bronze flagon of wine, probably plundered, for it was a lovely piece. Nothing she had seen in Dun Add had indicated that they valued objects for their beauty. As he poured, her eyes were drawn to the doe that stood high and long-legged on the lid and the reclining doe with coral eyes that was its handle.

"Drink!" he commanded, holding out a beaker. "And drop that cloak!"

Her chin rose.

"A modest Picti? I don't believe it." He emptied his beaker and belched explosively.

"Take care! I'm taboo to all but the King!"

It was a practised hand that wrenched the cloak from her grasp. He swung it carelessly, surveying her body, licking his fleshy lips. Beside herself with fury she cried out.

"You're forgetting I'm blood-kin to your mother!"

The sea-green eyes of his mother swam out from the pale face before Artur, fuelling his hatred.

"That'll add a new dimension to the trip, won't it?" He spat on the floor.

"Remember the fine sons she bore to your father!"

Contempt sparked in his eyes.

"Like Gartnait, my brother, with his a Picti name? Now there's a mystery for you."

He unhooked his belt, flexing it between his hands as if he would beat her. His mouth curled, as he waited for the response he knew she would make.

"Barbarian!"

His belt snaked into a corner. He was revelling in her fury. But she was more disgusted than angry. Close-up, he was uncouth and dirty. His mat of chest-hair was as unkempt as that curling on his shoulders. Picti women demanded that their men kept themselves clean, well-dressed and agile.

His eyes glowed like sea-coals as he emptied her untouched beaker. It spun it over his shoulder to clang beside the belt. He stepped closer, great hands outstretched to clasp her breasts.

"T'would give me great satisfaction to soil the Royal Vessel of the new King." His hands touching her skin, charging her with energy. She spoke straight into his lustful eyes.

"You won't wipe out the shame of your defeat by violating me!"

"Why not? It would be grand to roast him with the story at the very doors of his own Palace." He gave a great shout of laughter. "Come, tonight we'll make a new little Princess for the Pretani."

The thought of his invading juices was more than Caterin could bear. She caught up her dagger and faced him, challenging him to make a move. As soon as she heard the husky laughter deep in his throat, she knew it had been a mistake. He would enjoy hunting her down.

"I like a woman of spirit!" he cried and lunged at her. She slashed at his arm. As he drew back, she sprang on to a chest.

"I'll kill you if you touch me!"

He bellowed with laughter and pressed forward again, her words serving only to inflame his senses.

Her foot caught him on the chin. He came at her again, grinning and shaking his head till his long hair swung. She leapt from his grasping hands onto the table, sending the flagon spinning. Naked legs astride, body swaying, she watched for his next move.

"Listen to me! I can make you King of all Alba!"

He feinted towards her and, as her dagger arm sliced downwards, he caught her wrist, jerking her over his back. She hit the floor with a sickening thud and found she was trapped in a corner where his bulky figure cut off any escape.

"I can make myself King of all Alba!" he growled deep in his throat.

Opening his trews, he advanced towards her, desire in every glinting line of his body.

She searched her mind for words. Yet words seemed to bounce off him like blunt arrows. In a reflex action she drew up her knees. Just in time he saw that her bunched feet were aimed directly at his crotch. He lunged to one side out of the way of her strongly-muscled legs and rolled on the floor.

Springing up, Caterin snatched up her dagger and stood watching dispassionately while he lurched to his feet. She was under no illusions. If Artur had not been tired and under pressure she would not have escaped so easily.

"You tight-arsed little bitch," he muttered, scattering flecks of foam from his mouth. "I'd get more satisfaction from a kitchen-wench."

"Go then! You might get the pox, too. But you won't gain a Kingship."

With callous contempt, he caught her wrist, twisting it back until pain zig-zagged up her arm and the dagger clattered on the floor.

"Listen," she cried, her mouth close to his ear. "If Gort becomes King, Rhun of Gwynedd will become Overlord of my land!"

She felt his back stiffen and his hot eyes darkened. This was a possibility he had not foreseen. She hurried on, gasping at the pain in her arm.

"You'll be facing two leaders and two armies then!"

Slowly his desire faded. But the merciless grip on her arm increased, arcing her body backwards.

"I'll strike a bargain with you," she cried desperately. "Hide me in Eirean! And when Bridei abdicates, you'll step into the Kingship with me as your Queen"

"Will I now? And how can you guarantee this will happen, me darlin'?" Suddenly he released his grip and let her fall.

"Why are you dicing with the destiny of your people?"

She lay for a moment, catching her breath, knowing she had captured his interest at last! His voice was light and mocking again. She had fired the ambition that showed in every forceful line of his body. Just let the Magician keep away.

With a bound she retrieved the cloak and wound it round her body, leaving the dagger where it lay.

"Because I know my people! They won't accept Gort with Rhun at his back. Believe me! For if you wait for proof you might be too late!"

Hardly aware he was doing it, he fixed himself into his clothes again, his eyes thoughtful. She hurried on, trying to keep him thinking, trying to keep her hatred of him out of her voice. "Listen! This is your last chance to defeat Gort. Because most of the Pretani army is with Bridei!"

She saw that her words had hit home and knew why. Like Bridei, Aedan had divided his army. He had gone north, depending on Aed of Ainmire to send reinforcements to Artur. And now Artur's position was weak, having lost too many men at Dun Durn to defend Dun Add adequately.

157

"Send me to Aid. I can persuade him to send aid against Gort."

He turned and poured ale, his knuckles showing white with the fierceness of his grip on the flagon. He drank and threw himself on his couch, arms behind his head.

"And what's in this for you, Wildcat?" he said quietly, his shrewd eyes watching her.

"I shall refuse to be Queen under Gwynedd! But a foreign King is our Law. You'll be accepted because of your mother."

His fingers found a piece of straw poking from his mattress. He began to chew on it, thinking.

"And when I follow my father as King of Scots? What then?"

"Kingship of Alba! But only through marriage with me. Is it a bargain?"

As she waited for his answer she found herself looking at his long, bare dirt-encrusted feet. His toe-nails were thick and uncut and the nails on each little toe had grown round into the shape of a ram's horn. Her stomach heaved in disgust. This was proof that a malicious spirit held him in thrall. Artur saw her involuntary movement to make Bride's sign of the crescent and made up his mind. He rose and picked up his scattered clothes.

"Bargain with a Pretani? Never!"

He left the door ajar so that she heard his order to the guard.

"Hang her from the ramparts in the morning. That'll fix any other traitors in my camp."

The heavy door thudded behind him. She put her shaking hands to her face. She had failed! Had even signed her own death-warrant! It had all been for nothing! Artur had not believed a word of it! Would he send Merlin to silence her? Or a slave whose tongue would be cut out? A heavy pair of fire-tongs lay on the hearth. She would leave her mark on anyone who came. Quickly she dressed herself and sat by the fire.

Far away, muffled by the thick walls she heard the steady tramp of sentries and their gruff exchanges.

Veleda's words came into her mind. 'If you survive'. Only two days ago? During the long dark hours, Caterin gazed into the fading embers and railed against the Implacable Ones and inept Wise Women. Veleda had wrung her hands over the loss of the healing knowledge. What about the survival of those who were learning to use it? Fine, sensitive, laughing Derelei who loved life and all its beauty, whose warm, healthy flesh had been ripped and slashed, ending all his promise for the future.

And what would tomorrow bring for her? She rested her shoulder against the wall and shed bitter tears. But by the time her cheeks had dried, she was listening for sounds, knowing she had a fight for survival on her hands. And she would survive!

A trampling of hooves on cobbles and a flare of torches in the courtyard roused her to search the walls for a window. Among the shouts and commands that echoed round the outside walls she made out one cry.

"The bastards have turned north! They're surrounding the Dun at Ollaig!"

Then Artur's bellow sounded almost at the very door, over the blaring of horns and the clash of hastily-gathered weapons.

"Myrddin, send a messenger to Leinster to kick Aed into action. And get rid of that vixen's whelp! She's no use to us!"

At once she was behind the door, the fire-irons ready. The door began to open and she swung her weapon. A brawny hand grasped it. A great black-bearded head appeared.

"Wheesht!" it said. Only a Pretani-born would use that word! Her seed of thistledown thrown on the wind had borne fruit! He was a craggy giant of a man, still strong and handsome despite his middle years. Together they pushed the door shut and leant on it.

"Bridei's man?" she whispered.

"Dolmech's man!" Bleak grey eyes looked down on her. And Caterin guessed this was the father of Gartnait. And his Pretani name had been Dolmech's act of defiance! "But Bridei's man till I avenge her murder!"

When one door shuts another opens, she thought.

"I'll help you to escape! No one will spend an arrow after a brown cloak in a bog when the Pretani are in a burning mood!"

"No! I'm going to Eirean. Can you get me on the Messenger's ship?"

She had made up her mind in an instant. Better than going back to grey days without Derelei and the tedium of waiting for war-news.

He stared at her, not understanding. Angry voices came and went in the passage outside. He swiped the cloaks off the wall. One peg was a lever. He wrenched it down and a side-door slid open. Without hesitation she followed him through. They came out onto a rocky ledge and stopped, crushing themselves back against the wall. Far below the army was loading carts with tents and weapons.

"Why Eirean?" he hissed. "What about Bridei?"

"Let him win the war without the hindrance of a hostage!" she hissed back.

"Keep your head down!"

Beside her cheek, cut deep in the rock, she saw a footprint and bit back a startled cry. It was the legendary footprint of Fergus Mor, the first King of Dal Riata.

"The man whose foot fits that will be the next King," said her companion. "You can be sure Artur's tried it. That scrape at the heel is new. Now slide down to that next ledge."

But Caterin had seen something else in the rock that held her frozen with fear.

"What's this?"

"Haven't seen that before. It's a boar, isn't it? What's wrong now?"

The blood had left her face. There was no mistaking it. This was the Veniconie Boar!

She shook her head and slid before him, her thoughts in a turmoil. How could the Veniconie Boar have been cut into a rock in the midst of the Capital of the Scots?

"Veer left!" the giant prompted her.

Had Maelchon and his father sold themselves to the Scots as mercenaries? That made sense if they were planning vengeance on her father. Down a steep stony path and they were hurrying through the throng of milling soldiers, too busy to notice them. And only once as they crossed the Moss, did she cast a fearful glance backwards at the Capital.

At the Quay he questioned her again.

"Eirean? Is that what you want?"

She laid a grateful hand on the giant's arm.

"One thing more," she said. "Who's the White Dove?"

"Colum Cille, of course. The Bishop Columba."

There was no time for the Messenger to query the order that they said came from Artur. She was rammed down on a heap of damp fishing-nets beside some wooden chests in the belly of a rocking ten-bencher. A fight broke out. Two men of different cenels would not pull together. Until the Messenger used the flat of his sword on their backs. At last, the oarsmen grunted, the boat swayed sickeningly and began to pick up speed. The giant had

160

already gone. She was on her way to Eirean. Land of legend and springing new ideas!

The growing light showed up low scudding clouds and dark, looming islands. Somewhere out there was the Isle of Io, their Isle, the Isle that the White Dove wanted for his own!

Then the long, probing finger of Kintyre lay behind them and they were in a wide sea. And it was amazingly empty of ships.

The reason for their loneliness became a suspicion and then burst upon them with certainty. A longship with a billowing, striped sail was bearing down on them with the full power of the north wind behind it. Round shields lined the deck-sides and, by all that was marvellous, it had a prow at both ends!

Caterin's first thought was that they were slave-traders from Rome. Yet the heads that bobbed between the shields were not dark but golden-fair. It was useless to try to hide herself. She watched them come with a sort of fatalistic calm.

Panic broke out among the rowers. A few pitiful weapons appeared from under plaids. They jabbered among themselves as the stately ship rode the water swiftly and inevitably towards them. What were Northmen doing in their sea? This was their pathway to the Land of their Fathers! Northmen never came this far, did they? Only those seeking to settle, wasn't it? Wasn't it?

The fair-skinned faces laughed down on the rowers, mocking them. It took only a trio of swordsmen to leap into the small boat, swipe off the head of the Messenger, carelessly split open a few skulls and herd the remainder of the crew into the stern. Ropes grappled the two bucking ships together, crushing the planks of the small boat with every grinding crash. The nets were thrown aside and the cargo was manhandled over the thwarts.

The discovery of a proud-looking woman aroused shouts of glee. And she, too, was hauled over the shields. Horrified she watched as the oars were cracked in two and tossed into the sea. They floated away like broken twigs. The half-submerged boat was pushed off to drift or sink with its cargo of wounded and dead. The helmsman leaned on his massive steering paddle, the huge sail cracked and filled with wind and they were off again.

Someone on Dun Add must have known there was a raider in the vicinity. And cleaving its way into Caterin's mind came Merlin's face with his hostile hawk-like eyes.

Clinging to a shield Caterin swayed with the run of the ship.

These golden giants must come from the land that was called Northway because it was more of a sea-route than a country. And the lush, green and misty land that floated ever closer must be Eirean. Oh, it was easy to make the connection. The Northmen had come to settle. But, true to their nature, had been tempted to pirate a lonesome boat, less than half their size, just as a thief in a crowd cannot help cutting the pouch of a fat merchant in passing.

Dolmech's man was bound to have sent word to Gort or Bridei that she was sailing. But there was no one left to tell them that the ship had been attacked. The land of Eirean lay before her. But her hope of walking and talking with Kings and Bishops was gone. She smiled grimly. She thought had chosen her path forward. But had it been Merlin with his hooded Magician's eyes who had sent the Norseman's ship?

It was after noon when they put into an estuary. At an order from the Master, the sail rumbled down, thirty pairs of oars shot out and took up the beat from the horn-blower.

As they edged towards the land, ropes snaked over to the jetty and youths ran to haul the ship alongside for the promise of a jar of ale. Boxes, chests, and packages were unloaded and dumped ashore. Caterin jumped to the jetty from between two shields, ignoring the jeers and whistles.

Only half of the crew disembarked, about eighteen young men in all. It seemed that their arrival had been expected. An exact number of horses and a guide were waiting. She crushed a silver earring into a boy's palm and cried "Bridei's daughter!" in his ear. Delighted and uncomprehending, he grinned and waved as she was scooped bodily onto a groaning cart that was already dangerously full. The sailors lined the sides of the ship to cheer them on their way.

She shouted again as she passed the straggle of houses. Folk waved, thinking she had come from the Northway and was glad to be on land again. Her heart sank. As far as Bridei and Gort were concerned, she had disappeared.

The pace of the ox-cart was too slow for the exhuberance of men newly landed. As it ambled along paths they ranged far and wide over the gently rising hills on either side. Handsome lusty lads they were, setting out on a new adventure. When darkness fell and they stopped to make camp, Caterin waited for them to force her to the cooking hearth. She would see them rot first! Instead, in high good humour, they built a fire and had food cooking in a pot with the efficiency of men used to looking after themselves. The stew they shared with her had tasty chunks of meat and a variety of fat beans floating in the gravy.

As she ate she watched them warily, hardly able to believe that these cheery zestful men had so cruelly pirated the Scots ship. Their embroidered headbands were rather fine. And she had never seen anything like their long cloaks that touched the ground on either side in two long points. They fashioned them into hoods or threw them over their horses' rumps. Now, they tied knots in the points to form snug sleeping bags.

What had they wanted her for? Why had she escaped being killed? The fur they threw at her was so soft and silky to the touch that she could not believe its warmth when she rolled herself into it. She had meant to stay awake to try to steal away while they slept. The next thing she knew it was dawn. Horses stamped and jingled their bits. Food and drink were being taken standing up. In the cold light of dawn, escape into this unknown countryside did not seem such a good idea, after all.

But she had survived. And she was here where she had planned to be, in Eirean.

CHAPTER TWENTY

Twice during the journey, the cart sank into bog-land. Caterin sat regally, leaving the men to push and curse and get it moving.

A haze revealed enough of the sun to let her know it was just past midday when the procession topped a hill and she saw a wide plain before her. A good-sized settlement took up most of the foreground. Some derelict farmsteads in the distance spoke of the yellow plague, a shadow that lingered in this land. It had decimated the Celtic peoples. Yet it had spared the blonde sailor-races, the Angles, Saesons and Northmen. She could understand now why the High King of Tara welcomed in the settlers from the Northway to till his fields and keep the tribute flowing. Just as these sons of farmers whose lands were bounded by fjords and mountains were glad to settle on the wide plains of Eirean.

At least the settlement looked prosperous and well-kept. They would not need to barter her for gold. A wattle wall enclosed well-made timber houses. Drain-lines criss-crossed the countryside and a variety of crops ripened in the sun. Further afield, mares with spindly foals grazed knee-deep in lush buttercup-bright grass that almost hid a flock of ewes and lambs. Smoke from a dozen thatched rooftops swirled into the sky. A loom clacked loudly, punctuated by the squeaky rhythm of a windlass.

A herd-boy, saw them first. He waved his stick and yelled a warning. At once the space between the houses was filled with shrill dogs and shriller children. Men and women came, shading their eyes at first, then shouting a greeting and clustering round the riders. Gustav, the undoubted leader, tall and rangy, scarred with battle-wounds, stepped out of the crowd. A tooth that stuck out at the front sawed his words in half and garbled the pompous speech of welcome he embarked on.

Caterin sent up a plea to Bride before she jumped down. Hidden in hood and cloak, she stayed behind the cart, watching, listening intently.

As a toddler, she had had a Nordic nurse for a time. She had forgotten the woman's name, but certain words came easily to mind.

The lad who came to lead the oxen to the trough started when he saw her and gave a shout. The news-telling stopped. The back-slapping stopped. And she could feel the chill of the cruel sea in the air as the crowd began to converge on her, Saw-Tooth in the lead. She need not have worried. For they fell on the cart, ripping off the covering, pulling and pushing and grasping at the huge bales, slitting them open. Furs and fleeces, coloured cloth and fine-spun wool spilled on the ground. Caterin gasped in amazement.

Fine ivory and bronze rolled at her feet. Bowls and spoons, brooches and buckles, weapons and horse-ornaments, tools and cooking pots, carelessly piled in a heap that glittered with a hint of gold and silver here and there. Caterin's eyes rounded. Her quick brain told her that the fathers whose land-holdings were too small to support younger sons had not been poor. This store would be bartered for beasts and seeds to fill the extra bellies. And would she be included in the communal treasure and bartered?

A plump woman, like a new-baked bun with her fresh skin and fair braided hair, pushed her way forward. Even Saw-Tooth reluctantly fell back before her. Greedy glinting eyes roamed over the pile. And then she saw the chests from the Scots ship. Sharp questions flew over the heads of the crowd to the travellers sitting in the open-circle, juggling with plates of cold meat and beakers of ale. Answers flowed back hot and strong. The chatter stilled, and Caterin heard the woman clearly.

"You were fools to plunder a ship within sight of the coast!"

Now every eye turned on Caterin where she stood. And again she felt the menace of the cold grey sea, trickling in icy drops down her spine.

Braying with surprise Gustav sprang towards her. But the woman was before him, facing Caterin, their eyes on a level. Her baleful gaze took note of Caterin's healthy skin and strong body.

And Caterin saw written plainly on her face that, of all the things the new settlers had brought, this woman desired above all else, a body-slave.

Throwing back her hood Caterin threw out her challenge.

"I demand a guide and a horse. I am travelling to Tara!"

Despite her stumbling Nordic they understood her.

"Oh no!" The woman shook her head decisively. "The High King must never hear of this foolish act!"

And Caterin wondered if she had not made a ghastly mistake in coming to Eirean. In the following days, the only thing she had to be thankful for, was that the woman, Ingrid, did not put an iron slave-ring round her neck.

"I said scour the pots, not tickle them!"

Shrill-voiced and sharp-eyed, Ingrid followed her around until Caterin decided to make them so sick of her they would be glad to send her to Tara.

So one day she put too much salt in the stew. The men roared and spat it out. The women flew at her, beating her with their spirtles. The next day she let the heifers into the same pen as the bullocks. This time it was the men who beat her and that was worse. She tried to stay cool and calm. Not easy when her face was pushed in the mud and her body was black and blue. Next morning she stayed inside her cloak.

"Right!" cried Ingrid, infuriated by Caterin's silent contempt. "No work, no food."

By evening Caterin had given in. She had to stay healthy and strong to survive.

"You really messed it up this time," she told Bride in a fit of temper. "For Veleda's sake, get me out of here! I've got to find the White Dove!"

At least she could talk to the goats. "Come on, force yourself! That trickle wouldn't fill a thimble," she told the oldest nanny. "Good girl! Now do you think my silver earring would persuade a pedlar to send a sign to my father? No?"

Later when she was scouring the wooden milk pails with a brush of birch twigs, it dawned on her that no traders had visited. She sat back on her heels. These Northmen were self-sufficient. They had regular supplies from their own country. The Eireans, too, kept their distance. So she was cut off from any travellers who might carry a message!

Ingrid's cheesecloth whipped round her ears. And she began squeezing the birch-sap down into the crevices to cleanse them.

Now if she announced that she was royal would the Northmen return her to Alba? Without thinking she laughed out loud. Ingrid would become insufferable if she thought she was the mistress of a Royal Princess.

Grinding the meal was a task she hated! So that she would not be tempted to spit in it she carefully thought over their journey here from the coast. She had already worked out that the settlement must be inland from the Duibh Linhe, the Black Pool, a village on the east coast that was attracting a growing number of trading-ships.

Ingrid was nowhere to be seen. Rising on tip-toe she looked over the wattle wall. These birch-woods might hide the huts of charcoal burners. And there were strange swellings on the horizon that could be in-built houses with turf growing over their roofs for weather-protection. Someone out there might have a horse for hire that could take her north to Tara.

Don't think of it!" Ingrid had a hand like an axe when she let swing.

But if she was closely watched by day, by night she was a virtual prisoner.

Caterin had a warm corner to sleep in beside the iron firedogs with curling tongues and gnashing teeth that were a misery to clean. That the cauldron chain rattled in the wind was a bonus. The young men, thinking to reap some benefit from their captive, crept from their cabins in the night and tried to sidle in beside her. At the first creak of the cauldron in the draught from the door, Ingrid was out wielding a broom. Not on the back-sides of the men but on Caterin.

"Slut! Slut! Slut!" she would cry.

"Keep your filthy men off me then!" Caterin would cry.

She had already shown her dagger to Gustav who would jump on her behind the out-houses, pressing his body against hers, his saw-tooth bruising her mouth until her knees and elbows found their mark. One day she could bear his fumbling hands no longer. The next time he sprang on her, she curled her hand under his tunic and squeezed hard. He checked and rose on his toes. His mouth opened wide and let out a croaking whimper. Slowly, he sank to his knees, his face pale and glistening. After that she had no more trouble.

This was a scary new landscape she was in. With every breath in her body she wanted to fight it. But there was nowhere to go, no one to turn to for help. This was a world in which she had no contacts. So she was powerless to help herself. She would have to wait with what patience she could muster for some chance happening that she could use to escape. Now she understood the helplessness of people caught in the trap of slavery or poverty.

There was a sort of rough justice in her present state, Caterin supposed. The thump of the butter in the churn each time she turned the handle thudded into her heart. How rude and unfeeling she had been with her own slaves! She knew with certainty that was why she was here. A lesson to be learned. An obstacle to be surmounted. The proud Princess needed to have her face rubbed in the dust.

Yet her whole nature rebelled at the thought. Surely she had learned to be humble when she had freed Iogena. Must Bride go on repeating the lesson interminably? This was a time for action. She had to find that White Dove. If this slavery was a test it was testing her patience to the limit! If nothing happened soon she would be forced to take some drastic step.

That night with a bowl of water, she created in the hearth, the Drui symbols of fire and water. Before she slept she breathed in the fragrant wood-smell of the fire and the herb-scented water and withdrew into a quiet place deep inside herself. There she found such a feeling of space that the bonds of slavery loosened for a precious little while.

Yet in that quiet moment it came to her that there had been a huge gap in experience between Princess and slave. She had been utterly ignorant of Iogena's life. Freeing her had been all too easy. Although she had been genuinely sorry for the girl's plight, her feelings had been touched only on the surface. Now, she knew what it was like to be degraded and helpless. Some day she would look back on this time and be glad she had come through it, glad she had coped. When she was free she would remember this time and feel a kinship towards those who suffered.

But she had no feeling of kinship with these North-folk! She would never understand them no matter how long she lived among them! So fair and good-looking and yet so cruel and unfeeling!

Then the harvest was upon them. Long hours of training in the sportsground had hardened Caterin's muscles. She developed a rhythm to her work at the reaping and threshing that harboured her strength.

But the weaving of willow saplings to line the new storage-pits was another matter. The settlers had found that, in this wet climate, storage pits did not last long. To ease her skinned and blistered fingers, Caterin searched her memory and came up with a salve that Veleda had taught her.

The tips of the yarrow plants that she gathered in the meadows were past their best and the smell of the chicken fat she stole from the cooking pot turned her stomach. But the resulting mixture soothed the cracks in her skin and softened the callouses that were hardening on her palms.

And a strange feeling of self-satisfaction stole over her. A strong will to survive was helping her to bear the harshness of her existance. There was little else for it but to blunder on with dignity.

Yet as time went on, the incessant hard work and her meagre ration of food began to sap her energy and dull her mind. She found she was accepting this life of drudgery. Each day she had to force herself to rise to face another burden of work. She had no energy left for thoughts of escape. She would fall asleep over the butter churn and start awake thinking, 'I mustn't weaken!'

One day in the dairy she set down her pail of water and took out her tally-stick to count the marks. Yesterday had been the Festival of Lugnasad! And she had forgotten to say the spells for next year's harvest. And what sort of harvest was she going to reap if she did not escape from this drudgery? She wiped the sweat from her forehead with a straining cloth.

She began to wash down the table letting her thoughts wander to the merrymaking back home. Even though she had lived in the Capital she had gone out with the rest to bring in the Corn-Maiden with the last sheaf. Oh, the feasting, the leaping dance and the heart-joyous, pulsating music, the songs and stories that turned into images in the embers. And walking home in the soft, warm gloaming, she had heard the whispers of lovers, giving and taking love where the landscape swelled and curved like a woman's body.

And she laid her head on the rough wood and wept again. For here she was alone. Even Bride had deserted her. Instead of Lug of the Long Arm, the One of Many Skills, the Northmen had fearsome gods with cruel features that repelled her.

One morning Ingrid appeared, swaggering, in her best fur cloak.

"Walk at my back and hold the hem of my robe!" Ingrid told her.

It was to be some kind of Harvest Festival. Caterin joined the procession, dragging her tired legs, into the heart of the forest. The seat of their Godhead was in an area enclosed by slabs of stone carved with rough images. Thor swung his huge hammer. Odin raised his axe. A Priest-god in a helmet with great curving horns stood with his phallus erect.

Through a haze of exhaustion Caterin watched the tall, virile Haral Smooth-Tongue put on a similar helmet and wondered if his sexual organ would spring out of his robes. That would provide a bit of excitement. But his robes remained unruffled. And Caterin sank back into a half-stupor, haunted by the images on the stones around her of metal-working dwarfs, monstrous spawning serpents, the grisly Valkyrie and blood-thirsty giants that would one day destroy the earth.

Then they were all facing grotesque wooden images of the twin gods, Frey and Freya, fearful-looking with their enlarged sexual organs. Haral Smooth-Tongue scattered ears of corn in front of them calling for a nice blend of rain and sunshine. Unfortunately, this intercession brought a downpour that nobody wanted. And Ingrid skipped home fast and threw her dripping furs at Caterin.

As Caterin brushed the furs she found herself shuddering at the story the carvings told. Wanton destruction, implacable fate, a dark destiny for the world. How could they live with these beliefs? Yet they cast no blight over the high spirits of the Northfolk. An aching longing grew at her heart to be back with Veleda among the Gentle Ones. It almost seemed as though that idyllic time had never happened.

She spread the furs out to dry, running her hand over their silkiness, remembering the fox she had once brought down with a sling-stone. She had been ashamed of her nausea as her hounds had killed it. Only the bird feathers in his mouth had restored her common-sense. It was the way of the Mother. But now she would not kill for the sport of it.

That had been when she was a person of rank and privilege. Privilege? One thing she had learned. Privilege was not permanent. That was why it was privilege.

Surprisingly, Caterin found a friend in a young girl, just coming to puberty. Hild, eldest daughter of Greth who had a child regularly every year. Caterin came across Hild one day sitting beside an empty loom, making a mess of a cat's cradle between her fingers. She had a light oak sheen on her sun-flecked hair and would have been pretty if it had not been for the sullen set of her mouth.

"Here, let me show you." Caterin took the cast-aside strands of wool and showed her how to intertwine them. From then on, whenever Hild could snatch a moment, she followed Caterin around, pathetically eager to be friendly.

One morning Hild raced in and lunged at Ingrid, knocking Caterin aside and scattering the porridge bowls.

"Come! My mother's sick! She's burning with a fever! Come and see her!"

Ingrid went white and threw off Hild's clutching arms.

"Fever?" she screamed. "Keep away from me then!"

"I don't know what to do! Please, please come!"

"I don't want to catch it! Get out of here!"

She pushed Hild out of the door and barred it.

"I don't believe this!" Caterin exploded. "You're the chief's wife. How can you expect a child to cope?"

"She'll have to!"

"Then I'll go!"

Ingrid stood in front of the door, arms outstretched.

"Don't you dare! I don't want the plague brought back here!"

Plague? The word terrified Caterin. But it had never touched the fair races before.

"Gustav!" Ingrid shrieked. "Warn everybody to keep clear of that house!"

"You can't do that! They'll need food!"

"They can starve for all I care!"

"You heartless, callous woman!" Caterin, running to pull Ingrid from the door, met Gustav's swinging fist and darkness.

A bucket of icy water roused her.

"Think I don't know you're pretending?" sneered Ingrid.

Gustav coming back in at noon announced that three of Greth's children were down with the sickness.

Ingrid shrugged.

"The fever will have to work itself out. You, slave! See to the goats!"

Caterin almost ran outside. She heard the children moaning as she knocked on the window. Hild's thin tear-stained face appeared and Caterin pressed a jug of goats' milk into her hands.

"Water," a thin voice moaned. She cast around for a bucket and filled it from the rain-butt outside the nearest house and left it at Hild's door.

There was a kid missing when she counted the goats. She followed the faint pathetic bleat until she found it in a hollow where it had fallen from an overhang. It tried to run from her but

171

its back was broken. Its front legs dug frantically in the earth while its back legs lay helpless.

She turned her head, partly to avoid the pitiful eyes and partly to find a heavy stone. She tested one in her hand and chose another from under a bush, gay with red berries. Taking a deep breath, she brought the stone crashing down on the soft head. The head with the long ears fell limp. Caterin's head sank, too, amazed, remembering how many wild things she had killed for the sport of it, and that she should have found it so hard to put this little one out of its misery.

She dragged the body out of the hollow by its legs to take to Hild and paused because those red berries were revolving around in her mind. She went back down to look at them. Without knowing exactly what they were, she knew she had seen Veleda take flowers from a shrub with similar dark-green, pointed leaves saying that the berries were good for reducing a fever. She gathered them all and wrapped them in her head cloth.

That night, secretly, she pulped the berries in a pot and boiled them with water. When the liquid was cool, she stirred in a little honey and hid the pot under her bed-cover. Next day, the word went round that Greth and her children were dying and no cries came from the house. Caterin held the pot in her two hands and wondered. Maybe it was too late? She tested it with her tongue, sucking the sweetness and the bitter after-taste tentatively. This test gave her no clue as to whether it would work or not. Hild's haggard little face peered round the house-door in answer to Caterin's knock.

"Don't come in," cried Hild. "They're all dying! I don't know what to do!"

"Where's your father?"

"He hasn't come home!"

"I'm coming in!"

The smells of vomit and urine hit her and made her gag at first. With Hild helping she held up each child in the big filthy bed till they had drunk from the pot. Greth, dull-eyed and yellow, lay in a bed by herself. She focussed on the stranger and her face creased with horror.

"Take that muck away, you foreign slave!" she moaned.

"It'll do you good."

"Poison!" Greth's arm like a pealed twig shot out from under

172

the banket with surprising strength. She dashed the pot out of Caterin's hands. Caterin watched the potion sink into the earthern floor, knowing there were no more berries on the tree.

"I've left water," she told Hild. "Cool them with damp cloths. I'll be back in the morning to change the beds."

Before Caterin was properly awake next morning, a sheepish-looking man came to see Gustav. It was Hild's father. No mention that he had crept in fearfully at dawn. But he had found Greth lying yellow and drained of life while the children were awake, sweat-drenched. And Hild was feeding them broth and weeping because the slave had cured them.

"You're a witch!" screamed Ingrid the next day. "I always knew there was something evil about you."

"Evil?" Caterin screamed back. "You with your obscene gods and cruelty and greed. And you call me evil?"

"You'll be wanting to get rid of her then?" asked Gustav. "She might put the Evil Eye on you after the way you've bullied her."

Ingrid's eyes grew cunning.

"If she'd been going to curse me she'd have done it before now. I'll keep her as long as she's useful. Though if she starts dropping your brats I might think again."

Gustav left in a hurry.

"I'm going to help Hild," said Caterin and walking past the staring Ingrid.

From then on Ingrid and the women eyed her with some respect and not a little fear. And Caterin could spend time helping Hild with her motherless family.

It began to grow dark earlier in the evenings and for a few days the rain slanted down without stopping. The women brought out a tapestry that told the tale of Baldur and would be part instruction and part decoration in the Council Hall they would one day build. The women sat down one side of the hearth with the tapestry in their knees while their men sat opposite drinking.

One night, Caterin was listening to Hild complaining that her fingers were chapped when she caught a phrase in Gustav's garbled Norn that stilled her needle.

"It's near time to pay our tribute to the Ri at Tara," he said. The recent arrivals clamoured to hear more. "Every year the High King calls his chiefs and lesser kings to a meeting they call the Feis of Tara. That's when all disputes are judged and all new laws proclaimed. So tomorrow, rain or shine, we must look at the cows and wethers and decide which we'll take."

Sigurd the Stout produced a tablet on which he had been keeping a tally of the milk yield. There followed a hot debate about which cows looked healthy but gave the least milk and which ewes were most likely to drop dead lambs.

"We must seem to pay our tribute to the full," Sigurd explained.

"Yet it wouldn't do for the King to think we're wealthy or he might raise his tribute.

"I'll swear by Odin's runes that he'll raise it anyhow now that we have more men," Haral Smooth-Tongue reminded them.

174

"Can we trust this King?" The young men were full of questions. "I've heard the great Hall is lined with gold."

"Paid for by settlements like ours, eh?"

"That's why we were granted the land in the first place, dolt!"

"Do we have to keep bowing our heads until we're taxed out of existence?"

"Ah, cool your hot heads." Sigurd fitted his fat legs to the back of a sleeping hound. "We're comfortable enough and can afford the tribute. That way we keep the goodwill of the King."

Einer the Belly-Shaker's stomach rumbled with the beginnings of the laugh that had given him his name.

"If we're that anxious to please the King," he managed to bring out, "Why not throw in the slave-girl as an extra? She wanted to see the High King at Tara."

Caterin's needle jumped from her fingers.

"She's young. She could be made to look presentable. Better still, she cost us nothing." The man who spoke was one she had nicked with her dagger for catching her skirts in his filthy hands.

Ingrid kept her head bowed but Caterin could guess the thoughts that chased through her mind. The young men needed wives. They would be looked on with favour in neighbouring crofts with dark-haired daughters and too many mouths to feed. Soon there would be plenty of young working wives.

Anyway Ingrid had never been at ease with the slave since she had cured the children and all the pleasure of beating her had vanished out through the smoke-hole in the roof.

"The High King can have her if he's crazy enough to want her," she said finally.

Caterin hid her exultant face in the shadows as she groped for her needle among the reeds on the floor. At last the gods had stirred and touched Einar Belly-Shaker with brilliance. She had been right to wait. She would never have achieved entry to Tara on her own. And once she was inside, who could foretell? For she was every bit as Royal as the High King himself. Every bit as royal as the Bishop Colum Cille.

Ninety-one tallies counted the nights from one Festival to the next. The Feis of Tara was held at Samhain and that was only ten nights away. Then, oh joy, a New Year full of promise would begin. She would start reciting her spells and pouring libations to the Mother. What was more, she vowed she would not tell the

Northfolk about the rowan branches. Let the elfin armies come from their caves and mounds and wreak havoc on their unprotected settlement.

But good fortune depended on the angle of the notched tallies. Just before Samhain, three lines pointed straight up from the Line of Time instead of slanting downwards. The omens were good! With renewed hope she found her strength renewed. And she had one secret nugget of information that she would use against the Northmen.

"I'll need to dress as a boy for travelling," Caterin told Hild, entering into her role with zest. "And will you shear my hair for me?"

Hild wept over the bright silky strands. But Caterin laughing, ran her hands through her new crop and shook her head from side to side, revelling in its lightness and the feeling of freedom it gave her.

Pausing she took Hild's tear-washed face between her hands.

"Within a year you'll be a beautiful and intelligent woman. No, I'm telling you the truth. And soon you'll find one of these young men thinks so too. So lift your chin in the air. And believe in yourself."

The great day of freedom arrived at last. Caterin dressed in a tunic and trousers, wrapped salt meat and bannocks in leaves for the journey. To the accompaniment of Ingrid sullenly clattering her pots as though she was hammering out Siegfried's sword, they left.

Caterin pressed her silver thimble into Hild's hand and mounted a wise-eyed old mule. Her allotted place was behind the tribute herd where, as she rode, the warm, moist breeze carried the now-familiar smell of beasts into her face.

They followed paths bordering bogs and fields and beaten out by the patient feet of peasants and their herds. Once a covey of children, wild as gulls, broke out from the bramble bushes, their mouths stained black with juice. They raced alongside the riders, yelping and piping, and disappeared as quickly as they had come. A lone charcoal burner leaned on his axe and sent them a brooding stare. These were a strange breed of men who, in every land, lived apart from the communities but kept stoking the charcoal mounds on which the forgers and smelters depended. In the lower hills, miners' lodges clustered for convenience round the shafts that had supplied metals for generations.

Caterin was aware of a growing excitement. Few Pretani had visited the fabled seat of the High Kings at Tara. So many legends had grown up around that place that it hardly seemed possible that it existed. Bard songs always had an air of unreality about them. And what was more, come what may, she was not going back into drudgery with the Northfolk!

Sometime after the noon break, they rounded a low range of hills. Caterin drew in her breath. A rolling plain opened out before her with the proud and impregnable Hill of Tara dominating the countryside, its base firmly imbedded in its wealth, the lush meadows that fed vast herds of plump, contented cattle. Whether it was a memory of snatches sung by the bards or the effect of the thin sunlight, the slatted palisade round the crest of the hill glowed like the golden brow-band of an Eirean King. In the misty, diffused light, the citadel on the towering plateau shimmered as though it might vanish clean away in a trill of harp-notes. Then the illusion was shattered as it came sharply to life.

The spears of guards glinted on the palisade. Groups of travellers, like themselves, herding tribute cattle, converged on the Hill from all directions, making for the causeway that led to the Gate.

With Gustav leading, they approached and were waved through, the size of their herd being enough of a credential to gain entry. They crossed several wooden bridges that spanned a series of defensive ditches and entered a gate in the palisade.

Inside, the noise and size of the citadel hit her with an impact that confused her senses. Caterin's first thought was that it was a good breeding ground for the yellow fever that littered the streets of towns with corpses. Tall buildings were hemmed in by smaller dwelling houses, all elbowing for space. Soldiers were everywhere, mounted and on foot, directing chieftains and their retinues. Yet, as their party reined in to absorb the scene and await instructions, she saw that, although the streets were littered with debris, they were not foul nor dirty and there was a well-ordered purpose behind all the activity, brought about by long years of practice.

A squat soldier with horse-bowed legs and fiery red hair sprouting in all directions, came forward briskly. He asked the name of their settlement, counted their beasts and assessed their worth, making tally marks on his tablet. Servants drove the animals into a pen that already seemed full to overflowing with noise and dung and beasts. A guide materialised out of the crowd to show them their allotted lodging hall and the stable nearby.

Caterin carried her bundle into the long, wide building furnished to accommodate the King's visitors. Around the walls were alcoves, each just large enough to hold a man and his servant. Clean rushes were strewn on the floor and the King's hospitality even extended to sleeping benches with rugs on them. Already, many alcoves were occupied by travellers, divesting themselves of dusty garments and greeting old comrades with back-slapping and ribaldry.

"Right! Let's get ready for the Inauguration Banquet."

Gustav had found three neighbouring recesses. He and his retinue dressed in plain but finely-woven woollen tunics tied with girdles of soft kid-skin.

"No fancy brooches!" ordered Gustav. "We don't want to draw attention to ourselves."

Caterin eyed the gaudy colours and gold adornments of the men around them and privately thought the plain Norsemen would stick out like a sore thumb.

"You'll need a cup-bearer like all the other chiefs," she told Gustav. And stuck a cock's feather in her cap.

Gustav glared suspiciously around at the boys helping their masters to dress and grunted. Caterin hid a smile as she joined the throng of men winding through the streets of Tara to the Banqueting Hall.

The Norsemen did not know the bard-songs as she did. Tonight she would penetrate the Hall of her enemies. And a tradition would be smashed for ever. And because of that, everything she saw had a glimmer of excitement in it.

Tara was different in the twilight. A place of enchantment, wreathed in the pink mists of evening. Buildings and faces gilded by the flicker of a fire or a lamp. A hush on the Hill broken only at times by the note of a deep-toned bell.

And it seemed to Caterin as though the maidens and heroes of the past walked with her in the procession.

At every corner, with every whisper of a name, a legend sprang to mind. And the echoing of the bell had the resonance of a harp. Yet underneath the fairy magic, Caterin reminded herself, blades clashed, heads flew and hearts were full of murder and treachery.

"The Rath Laoghaire," a whisper in the air. "The House of the King." The richness of wood hung with banners.

"The Rath of the Princess Grainne." And, to Caterin, she was there in her gilded doorway, a transparent delight, shaking her twinkling hair till the golden balls and silver stars in it chimed.

A breath of a wind moaned across the grass-grown Crooked Mound as though the maiden sisters of Tara still keened over the fickle love of the King of Leinster.

The line of chieftains flowed to the west. The rich pastureland rolled away before Caterin's eyes, until it was brought up short by range upon range of misty blue hills. The evening sunlight slanted over the landscape, veiling the soft greens with touches of shell-pink and shadows of charcoal. Oh, it was easy to see why lesser kings and chieftains cast envious eyes on the lands of the Cattle Kings of Tara. Nearby, to the south, was the hill where lay the ruins of the Palace of Queen Maeve, floating like a dream in the gloaming, as shadowy and insubstantial as the stories of its fairy-like owner.

An immense grass-grown mound taller than a man! The Mound of the Hostages! A host of high-born youths! Their ransoms had been paid! Yet they had been murdered and their bodies thrown into this very mound. Thus the murderer, Niall of the Hostages, was remembered.

And it seemed to Caterin as though her feet touched the ground again. It was a gruesome reminder of the power of the High King. Good reason why the winding path lead the procession of chieftains past it. And Caterin's hands gripped together with fright at what she had vowed to do. And she cast her eyes down to the path at her feet.

But the path was over-shadowed by the Rath of the Synods. Built by the Bishops of the White Christ on a site which had been holy to the gods from the beginning of time. Battles of wit and magic had gone on for years between the Bishops and the King's Druad. The grandeur and elegance of this Rath proclaimed that the Princes of the new Faith had won.

Then the massive main door of the Great Banqueting Hall sent a brilliant shaft of light out into the night to welcome them in. And Caterin drew back, the enormity of her action suddenly overwhelming her. Fourteen doors it had, seven on each of its long sides, but, for the Feis, all must enter at the north between massive doorposts, intricately carved. 'The House of Mead Circling' it had been named by King Cormac when it was completed to his plan. It was the wonder of its age, hundreds of years before and it was still a noble sight. The white-washed walls were flushed rosy red by the setting sun. The thatchwork on the immense roof was elaborately coiled and plaited so that it seemed as though a sea of curling waves had been frozen into stillness.

Caterin's mind was already overpowered by places, names, stories familiar to her since childhood. Many long dark evenings she had spent in thrall as the travelling folk spun a magical web of words around ancient Tara. This wonderful evening, she had viewed it for herself. Now the greatest experience of all lay before her. She would see the King at his Banquet in all his glory. She must not falter!

As she stepped over the threshold behind Gustav, inconspicuous in her brown tunic, she was fiercely glad she had hugged her secret to herself. For it was taboo for any woman to enter the Banqueting Hall! And the Northmen did not know! And the penalty for the man or woman who broke the taboo was death!

CHAPTER TWENTY TWO

Light and colour dazzled Caterin's eyes. The Northmen paused to wonder and were jostled aside by those at their backs. Sigurd growled in his throat and was silenced by a warning punch from Gustav. He lead them to lowly places on benches, far from the splendour at the other end of the Hall. Caterin followed meekly like a good cup-bearer should.

Dwarfed by gigantic chieftains she could see little but the carved beams of the massive roof and the seven lamp-holders that hung from it, each one a blazing garland of light. Seven lofty, branching standards banked with torches stood along the central aisle. Walls lined with bronze, gilded, silvered and enamelled, dappled with reflections.

A trumpet blew and the whole assembly sat. Now Caterin had a view of the champions taking their places. Fifty men to each great couch up and down the length of the building, each man's shield hanging behind him. On the lesser couches, physicians and craftsmen, poets and wise men, musicians, builders, torcs on their forearms. Just when it seemed that breathing was going to become a problem in the press of bodies, a roll of drums and a blast of trumpets announced the arrival of the High King of Tara. And all movement ceased.

From the shadows at the back of the platform stepped a tall, graceful figure. At once, every beam of light seemed to flow towards him to be broken into a thousand fragments and reflected back into hundreds of dazzled eyes. A man in the prime of his youth and at the peak of his power. Yet, Caterin remembered, a man whom Brigid, the holy woman of Eirean, had foretold would be 'bloody, cursed by his birth'. Oh, it could not be, he was so beautiful!

Years of wielding supreme authority in his unruly kingdom had endowed him with a regal presence but there was an added force about Diarmait that he had been born with. This was the man who upheld the peace so strongly that no man dare strike another in anger, no robber could escape the death sentence. This man had executed his own son for stealing the cow of a nun. The four fierce Kings of Leinster, Munster, Connaught and Ulster so feared him that they would not enter into battle with him on their own. Or so it had been said.

Everything about him suggested the warrior king but the strength in him had been tempered with beauty. He was a river of rippling colour as he advanced with a flowing grace towards the High Table. Hair that gleamed with a brighter gold than the ceremonial crescent at his neck or the twisted torques on his bare, bronzed arms. His long white silken robe was embroidered with exotic birds, their brilliant plumage in shades of deep blue and emerald green, birds that took flight with each easy stride. A crimson cloak was fastened on his breast by a golden brooch set with rubies. It hung from his shoulders in wide descending folds and draped itself over his ornate couch as he sat.

With one elegant hand on the arm-rest and one resting on his knee, he surveyed his subjects, noting each face and its emblem, the tightening of his jaw telling that someone was missing. Behind, framing his head, hung a red buckler and painted on it silver stars for the tears of the moon and golden discs for the sweat of the sun. It was the most impressive display of majesty that Caterin had ever seen.

She stood and gazed, over-awed, gulping down her apprehension. How could the Northmen think to approach this god-like creature with their gift? How dare she face him in threadbare rags and claim that she equalled him in Royalty? And how could she demand to meet with the Bishop Columba who matched him in power?

The signal for the start of the Feast was given. The champions received a whole porker each, identical in size so that no dispute could arise. The Kings each had their traditional portion, a succulent thigh. The charioteers accepted their due of a boar's head.

The formalities over, long, meandering lines of servants came bearing platters, weaving in and out of the tables to turn at the bottom of the Hall and trundle back to the kitchens with dishes empty of all but the gravy.

"Cup-bearer!" cried Gustav. Caterin had no time now to stand and wonder for the Northmen had beakers to be filled.

Later, deafened by snarling wolf-hounds and the cymbals of acrobats, by coarse guffaws and loud belches, Caterin took time to pause and run an appraising eye over the others at the High Table.

Could any of these Kings of the Four Provinces be enlisted to her aid? She searched her memory for their ancestries but the Clannas and Cenels changed their dynasties as often as their alliances. Then there was the Head Olave who might send word to Bridei. The Olave sat oblivious to his neighbours, lost in contemplation of the philosophies for which he was famous. Or perhaps he was merely pondering on his depleted retinue. His retainers had begun to outnumber even those of the King and, for a time, he had been in grave danger of being banished. It seemed that even his Bardship had been stripped from him for, as the drinking began in earnest, the King signalled with a flash of emerald and sapphire to his own favourite harpers.

The nine harpers of the King were an enchanting sight, a legend in themselves. Nine young boys, trained to music and song from birth, sat on their own special couch. Misty grey mantles swirled about them, fastened with pins of gold. A thumb-ring of gold encircled each boy's thumb, an ear-tie of gold hung from each boy's ear. Around their arms were rings of crystal and around their necks were torques of silver. They laid aside their rods of white silver and drew golden harps from bags, as soft as dreams. Each harp was intricately carved and decorated. And, if Caterin had doubted their ability, she was soon enthralled.

A trickle of preoccupied tuning-notes rose and fell from the arching roof. A commanding chord from one, shivered the Hall into silence. Magic fingers began to play on the deepest emotions of the rough chieftains. The music danced on their heart-strings and sang through their blood. Colours turned into sounds and painted intricate patterns in the air. The harp-strings vibrated with the elation of battle, rang with the jubilation of victory and died away to the very essence of grief, a yearning for lost companions. This was music fit to resound through the fairy Palace of Queen Maeve, to resonate down through the centuries, to linger for ever on the breeze that sighed over the hill-top of Tara.

The rapture was almost too much to bear. It was a relief when the harpists bounded into a plucking rhythm that set fists pounding and heels thumping. Mead and ale replaced the fine foreign wines. Battle-songs shouted in chorus shook the rafters. Bawdy verses roared from one end of the Hall to be answered at the other. A chief beside Caterin rose unsteadily to his feet. He drew a ring of red Eirean gold off his finger and, staggering up to the harpers' table, laid it there for all to see.

"My gift is to Briun," he announced. At once, the bard who had been named for the praise-gift began a song, proclaiming the bravery of the chief, his kin and his ancestors, rolling the names off his tongue with practised ease for it was his stock-in-trade to have the antecedents of the humblest chief ready to be recited. One after another, the chiefs rose to lay a gift near a favoured bard and be rewarded by a song. It was then that Gustav made his fatal mistake. His normal hard-headedness had been sent reeling by the quantity of mead he had drunk. He saw only the right moment and the dramatic gesture that would flatter this majestic King in the same way as it would have propritiated his own gods. Amid good-natured jeers at his foreign appearance, he made his tipsy way up the centre of the Hall to the High Table.

"My gift is to the High King," he announced, his voice cracking with excitement, his saw-tooth flashing. He had just enough of the Goidelic to repeat the phrase the others had used. He waved his hand towards his countrymen, blissfully unaware that those nearest the King had grown still, their faces shocked. Who was this peasant who dared to place the High King on a level with a bard to receive a praise-gift?

A sudden hefty push from Sigurd at her back sent Caterin sprawling out onto the floor in front of the King.

"You drunken pig! You've spoilt everything!" she hissed, rising. She turned to the King to disclaim any kinship with these fools and was almost blinded by the light from the gem-encrusted gold circlet that lay on his brow, half-hidden in his fine hair. But that was as nothing to the shock of meeting his icy eyes. She cursed Gustav from the bottom of her heart. This was a travesty of the meeting she had intended between herself and Diarmait. The King slowly clenched his fist and Caterin felt as though it was closing round her throat.

"A slave for the King, extra to our tribute, to prove our loyalty." A flash of inspiration seemed to pierce Gustav's fuddled brain. "And a woman at that!"

Dimly aware that they did not understand him, he lurched forward. Catching Caterin's tunic at the neck he tore it open. Filled with shame and outrage Caterin found her arm pinned at her back so that her body arced towards the King.

No translation was needed now. Her breasts lay bare for all to see. The twitching finger of a frightened harpist drew a tremulous note on a string that sounded and died in a silence that pressed downwards from the roof. It touched the spark that released the High King's fury. He sprang to his feet, a tide of angry red flooded his face.

"Who brings a woman into the House of Mead?" he cried. "Who are these foreign barbarians who insult me at my own High Table? Take them out and hang them!" Before the guards could leap forward Caterin twisted her arm away and ran straight towards the King.

"Don't class me along with this filth for I'm as royal as you are!" she cried, the words tumbling out in a hotch-potch of languages.

The King's fist crashed on the table making the glasses sing.

"Get that cumel out of my Hall!"

Caterin waved the guards back with an upthrust arm.

"I'm no slave! I was captured at sea by these idiot Northmen! I am Caterin of the Pretani, daughter of Bridei. Here's my insignia!"

She uncovered the hidden brooches and thrust them before his eyes. The King turned his head away, rejecting both the brooches and the woman whose presence offended him. A Prince came forward to examine them. He drew a quick breath of surprise.

"This is the Bull of the Royal Family of the Pretani. And the sign of Bride, daughter of Dagda," he told the King. "Who did you steal these from, cumal?"

"I am Caterin, daughter of Bridei, and I demand the right to be treated as befits my rank."

It took a moment of consultation with those around him before the King was sure what she had said. The blood darkened under the fine skin of his face.

"Gods of my fathers, do I not have enough rivalries and feuds in my own country without becoming involved with those of Aedan and Bridei?"

"Wait!" Caterin cried. "Remember that tomorrow the whole of Tara and far beyond will know my name and rank!"

The King halted the quick movement of the soldiers. At first his hot Celtic blood had blazed with fire at the insult to his Kingship. But, where a lesser man might draw his weapons in haste, Diarmait was High King because he could direct the force of his anger to his own ends. Caterin saw his gesture and threw caution to the winds.

"I claim the right to lay my case before the Bishop Columba."

At the name of his mortal enemy, Columba, that royal Prince of the Ui Neill, Diarmait seated himself slowly, his back ramrod straight, both palms flat on the table, As high-born as himself, Columba would have rivalled Diarmait for his place as High King, if he had not been a monk. Yet Diarmait still found himself locked with Columba in a struggle for power. Already, he had had his fingers burnt by tangling with the Bishop. Now he was wary, measuring every move, trying to foresee whether Columba could use it against him.

And there was no doubt that the Bishop would use this woman, slave or Princess. The secret intrusion of a woman into the House of Mead was worthy only of a sly smile behind the King's back. But if she proved to be a royal Picti, Columba would send a belly-laugh echoing round Eirean and the lands beyond. And there was no more devastating weapon than ridicule to undermine the Royal Authority.

'Daughter of Bridei,' he thought. Some day he might need the pagan Picti as allies against the Church. Then, the reminder of a daughter, kept alive in her skin and returned, would mean a debt of honour to be repaid. And despite the bird-brains of these Northmen they might prove useful if tales of their seamanship were true.

"Since you insist on being generous, I shall not hang you. Yet." He did not attempt to hide his contempt. "But may I remind you that a load of ivory tusks and thick furs from the Ice Lands are a more fitting gift than a sluttish daughter of a barbarian King."

His eyes narrowed to slits and his voice had knife-blades in it as he spoke straight to Gustav.

"As for the girl."

Caterin's indrawn breath brought her whole body arching up defiantly.

"Since you brought her here, the honour of returning her to King Bridei falls to you when our Feis is over. Is that clear?"

Gustav gobbled and sawed. Caterin was utterly taken aback. This was not what she had planned. She threw up her arm, pointing at him, her torn sleeve billowing like a sail.

"You are famed in my land for your wisdom and justice, Dairmaid. But this is neither wise nor just!" The clear voice rang to the rafters like a bell. "We share Royal Blood, you and I! Yet you are condemning me to a bog with a sacrificial noose round my neck!"

A sighing harp-note came out of the hushed air. And a great fear fell on Caterin. His goodwill was crucial if she was going to escape with her life. Yet she had dared to question his judgment.

At last the King looked on her. And in his cold blue eyes she saw an empty wasteland of ice that froze her blood. He saw hair that crackled in the light, a lithe figure clothed in majesty and bright intelligent eyes that burned into his. Her appeal to their shared royalty had moved him powerfully. It was the mention of Columba that had irritated him and impaired his judgment. His finger moved. The guards hustled away the unhappy, bewildered group of Northmen. The King rose and the bright wings of the birds took flight once more as he beckoned her to follow him. In a bare anteroom he unfastened the ruby brooch on his breast and swung his cloak till it rested on her shoulders. As the cloak fell in fluid lines to the floor she nodded, grateful for the streak of sensitivity in him that had understood the indignity and terror she had suffered this evening.

"And what case is this you wish to lay before Columba, Caterin of the Pretani?" he asked.

His immense presence filled the room as it had filled the Hall. Yet she was not intimidated. Instead she felt only exhileration that the challenge had come and she could meet it unafraid.

"Would it make sense to you if I said he's the enemy of my people?"

The King's slight inclination of his head encouraged her.

"He's demanding our sacred Island of Io to use as a base to spread his teachings. And we can't allow it. It's my duty to keep the White Dove from setting foot in our land. I need to meet him, to negotiate with him, to assess his power. Unless I know what he's like, how can I stand against him when I'm Queen?"

Her innocence hit the King like a blow. He heard the resolution in her tone, an echo of his own youthful determination to bring peace through power. He began to pace, three steps one way, three steps back. Tall white candles lit his path.

"I can tell you where his power lies. It's in his enormous vitality. Disciples flock to him. Forty or more Abbeys in the land look to him as chief and ruler." A harsh bitter laugh erupted and died in his throat. "And he's my adversary too. For I inherited the resentment of the monks and the antagonism of the Ui Neill the day I became King."

"And I'll inherit a tradition when I become Queen. And I mean to uphold that tradition until the day I die."

He stopped then and looked down at the pale face and saw the shadow that formed there as her spirit awakened to the enormity of her task.

"If you tangle with Columba it will take all your strength, all your ingenuity, all your resolution. Can you do it?"

"I can't tell until the day comes when I'm tested."

"And you will be alone in your battle. That will be the biggest test of all."

She saw the darkness behind his tortured eyes. And knew it for the loneliness of the one who held the power.

"Tomorrow he'll come to the Council Chamber. Be there and you will see this enemy you have chosen to pit your strength against."

Suddenly Diarmait's fists crashed on a table, splinters of wood flew, wine spilled. And he clutched a tapestry and hid his face in it.

"Ah, Morrigan!" he cried. "Raven goddess of war! Harden my spirit for the task ahead!"

And he tore the tapestry from its nails and stood with his back to the wall, arms outstretched raising his tormented face to the roof.

Fear stabbed through her body, twisting and turning like the sword of an enemy. But when she sought for another path there was none that she could take and live with. There was no turning back for her now. She went from him, swirling off his cloak to let it lie like a river of blood on the floor.

She found Gustav and his men in a snoring huddle and took her cloak and bundle from under their noses. She curled herself into an angle of a wall where she could see the sky. The same stars shone here in Tara as in Dalgynch. The clouds that drifted across the face of the Moon Maiden were heading towards Pitversie. Veleda's White Dove would spread his wings and ride on the same north-easterly wind. What inspired folk to turn from the Truth of the Mother to kiss a Bishop's ring? She had to answer that question if she was to defend the tradition.

Yet she could not sleep. For the icy wasteland in the eyes of Diarmait kept coming back to haunt her. And she wondered if she could bear to be alone for ever, seeking to bring peace to her people, and never able to find it within herself.

And her body suddenly flowered with the need to love and be loved as though it had been waiting for this moment of decision. All through her slavery her mind and body had been concentrating on survival. Now that she was free, her heart ached to be back in her homeland among her own people.

Tomorrow she must find out what was happening there. From the way Diarmait had spoken the war between Aedan and Bridei was still unresolved. At least her father was still alive and safe. But what of Gort and Cennelath? As she allowed the name of Gort to enter her mind a flame of desire spread through her body. And she was horrified at the needs and longings that suddenly burgeoned through her, inflaming her with their urgency.

She wrapped her arms round her bundle, clutching it fiercely to her. She twisted and turned on the stone pavement, telling herself that it was Derelei she had loved, Derelei she was needing. Yet it was Gort who was caressing the secret places of her body, with his fingers, with his lips, until she was on fire, moaning, quivering, writhing, until she felt she was a flower blossoming under him and in a rush of heat and ecstacy she bit the strap of her bundle to stop her crying out. And as she relaxed and lay back to wonder at the contentment that flooded her, the tears came. She looked on the empty face of the days to come. And she knew then what loneliness was.

Next morning from the moment Gustav groaned himself awake, Caterin was at his side demanding to be taken to the Council Chamber. She followed him to the pump. As Gustav peered through a curtain of dripping hair, calling on Odin to send him a glimmer of an idea about how to get rid of her, a horn sounded, announcing the start of the Feis. Remembering with awful clarity that his life depended on her safety, Gustav took her with him, hemmed in on all sides by the husky Northmen. Heads bent, they sidled into a corner of the Chamber. A swift glance around the hall assured Caterin that there were no men of the Church present. Had the High King deceived her?

The business of the Feis had already started at the far end of the hall. The High King, resplendent in royal purple, erect in a high-backed chair, listened gravely to the chieftains who stood on the Disputants' Rugs to put their cases to him. Sullen brows, secret grins and bitter mouths told of swift, sure judgments. Yet although

189

the King gave each man his full attention, Caterin saw sweat gleam on his forehead and his fingers were tightly locked on the arms of his chair. He was waiting, as she was, taut as a tuned harp-string, for Colum Cille to appear.

When the last case had been dealt with there came a lull, a moment of waiting and tension ran crackling through the hall.

The Toiseach, General of the Royal Army in the Field, stepped towards the King and asked a question. At a nod he began to administer the Oath. Caterin knew that the Feis was over. Her chance to see the great Bishop had gone. At the end the chieftains rose from their bowed positions, creaking and shuffling, covering their bared heads. Now, they could break their fast.

As they turned to leave, they found the doorway blocked by a row of monks in brown habits with wooden crosses hanging from their girdle-cords and sandals on their bare feet. The line of clear-eyed young men broke at the centre and flowed like a pointed arrow-head into the Chamber, making a passage-way for their leader. Caterin pushed between the staring men until she was at the front. And the Bishop passed so close she could have touched him.

In stark contrast to the simplicity of his followers, their Bishop had chosen to display his royal lineage, his power and his wealth at this Feis of Tara.

CHAPTER TWENTY THREE

"Columba."

"Colum Cille."

Whispers winged round the hall.

His robe was as white as the Bull of the King-making dream and his over-mantle as purple as Diarmait's own robes. Over these, as if signifying his negation of his claim to the throne, lay a vestment of gold fabric, bordered with emeralds and stitched all over with pearls. The hand that held his spiral-headed crozier of gold, the symbol of his great power, blazed with jewelled rings.

Given the name Cremthan, the Fox, at birth, he had changed it to Columba. Since this was a common name in Eirean, his friends called him Colum Cille, the Pigeon of the Church. His lineage was impeccable. Son of Fedilmith, son of Fergus, son of Conall Gulban, son of Neill of the Nine Hostages, Neill of the Silver Arm.

But it was the man beneath the outward show that Caterin looked at. She was surprised at how young he seemed, not much over thirty, with wide shoulders and princely stride. Yet, it was not the face of an autocratic, arrogant intellectual that moved past her between his monks. It was the face of a man who had lived with nature, a peasant's face, round, with a flattened nose as though he had taken a hard punch there in boyhood. His expression was calm and his skin unlined, much like the Druad who also contemplated in small cells and disciplined themselves according to the seasons. His hair was a shade darker than the High King's but cut short as if it got in his way at times. His lively, blue eyes, keenly intelligent, were not those of a dreamer but of a worker.

"Io! Io!" the name moaned eerily through her mind. And Caterin felt the brooches of her ancestry burn beneath her tunic. He passed so close to her that she was tempted to put out her hand to touch him. But her hand flew to her throat instead to still the wild beating of her blood at the fear that rose in her.

"You have come to take the Oath, Columba? You are welcome." Diarmait's voice was smooth as silk. For answer, Colum Cille took up his position on the woven rug to the left of the King and it was clear there was a dispute to be judged.

A stir at the doorway heralded the advent of Finnian of Moville, son of a poor cartwright. His ancestry was of no account yet he had risen to be the Bishop of the King.

Like his followers he wore a simple, white habit, a trifle muddy at the hem after his journey. He had none of the presence of Colum Cille but his features were finer, thinner, nobler. Taking his stance on the opposite rug, Finnian could be seen, by the fury on his face, to be the accuser. He could barely wait for the King's signal before launching into a verbal torrent that needed all of Caterin's concentration to follow.

This Finnian, as everyone knew, had just returned from a visit to Pope Pelagius bringing back to Eirean the whole Godspell in one Book. This sly Bishop, Colum Cille, had borrowed the Book and, working day and night, had copied it in secret. Now, Finian insisted that the copy, too, was his by right for it was as though Colum Cille had reaped Finnian's corn without permission.

Diarmait raised a lazy eyebrow and one finger in Colum Cille's direction. And Caterin watched, knowing the darkness that lay in Diarmait's spirit, and how he controlled it with his iron will.

Speaking with little expression and even less emotion, Colum Cille admitted he had copied the Book but it was with his own labour and in his own time. It was right to transcribe the Word of God and to place it at the disposal of other men. Having finished what he had to say, he waited tranquilly, knowing full well that the King had a difficult decision to make. Finnian's laboured breathing was the only sound in an assembly where everyone else was holding theirs.

Diarmait dropped his veined eyelids to consider his judgment and the question in his mind was present in every other seething brain. Finnian's book was none the worse for being copied, Diarmait decided. But if he settled for Colum Cille, the Bishop and his ever-restless family would take this as a sign of the High King's weakness. He must throw down a challenge, warning the Ui Neill to curb their ambitions. Finnian, after all, was the Royal Bishop.

Only those nearest to the King, and that included the two Churchmen, saw the sudden tightening of his mouth. The Hall was still, waiting to see if the King would throw another ember on the fire that the Ui Neill had lit and that could blaze through the whole of Eirean. Then clear through the Chamber ran the King's judgment with a thread of contemptuous laughter woven into it.

"As the calf is to the cow, so is the copy to the Book. You shall return both to Finnian, Columba. And I have a gem of advice for you. Go back to fishing for salmon in the Boyne instead of guddling in the muddy waters of politics."

At the deliberate insult there rose a hum as if a hive of bees was busying itself to swarm. And Caterin thought, he is bound to win, this King. He is wise and in his heart he wants peace. His people will respect him for that and his gods will uphold him.

"So be it," answered Colum Cille, his voice serene, his eyes wide and blue and innocent.

To Caterin it was as though he had expected the judgment, perhaps even wished for it. And she gazed at him, trying to reach inside to the real man, the man she must persuade that Io was not for him. Yet beyond the calm face and the rich clothing there was nothing that spelled either good or evil, only a supreme and radiant confidence.

The High King rose, cool and implacable.

"I have made the country secure. I have established the rule of law in all places, so that the churches and peoples shall live in security and peace for another twelve cycles of the moon. I defend the right ... " It was the traditional ending to the Feis but it was fated never to be finished.

Someone at the door shouted. It was a cry so full of outrage and disbelief that no one stirred to stifle this interrupter of the King's closing speech. A warrior strode forward to make his salute to his King, his face livid, his jaw working.

"My lord, the peace has been broken! The Feis is defiled! There has been a slaying on the training-ground! A hasty word, a sword that went too far and then further. The son of your steward lies dying, his blood clotting on the grass."

A combined groan of horror swept through the crowd. This offence beat at the very heart of Kingship, at the time of its most rare and solemn festival. The High King's face became a mask of stone. Stiff lips formed the question.

"And who has dared to flout the convention at this solemn festival?"

"Curnan, son of Connaught. A hostage in your hands. But now fleeing north with a pack of my men at his heels."

The High King's eyes sliced round the Chamber. The Four Kings of the Northern Provinces, including the King of Connaught, had slipped quietly away during the dispute of the

Bishops, a circumstance not unusual once their Oath was taken.

Caterin's eyes flew towards the Bishop. He had pulled back his shoulders and tilted his head. To Caterin's eyes the White Dove was poised as if this was the moment he had been waiting for and he was barely holding in check the force of his tremendous energy.

Diarmait's voice thundered out.

"We shall pursue him in force! Muster your men! We shall march within the hour." His eyes were daggers pointing at Colum Cille. "The Lords of the North will render a sorry price for this offence."

Caterin side-stepped quickly behind a pillar covered with shaking embroideries as the tide-race of men with ferocious faces jostled to get outside to their weapons. And she heard Colum Cille's quiet words addressed to Diarmait's back.

"And the price is this, that your royal town of Tara, from whence the Kingdom of Eirean has been ruled these many years, shall be left empty and sighing in the wind."

And as Caterin stepped between his monks to confront him, his chest expanded. One great long-sleeved arm swept her out of his way and he soared out of the Hall.

Outside, a swift glance around Tara convinced Caterin that she did not want to remain here once the main performers had gone. The stage was about to be set elsewhere and she wanted to see this confrontation.

She retrieved her bundle, stood in line for rations and mounted the old mule standing unwanted at a tethering post. She let the chieftains with their seasoned soldiers go past and avoided the Northmen, sullen and growling quietly at having been caught up in the battle of the Eireans. When a large body of men went past with supply carts she joined a hotch-potch of craftsmen and went unnoticed past the guards at the Gate. When they made camp at dusk, she shared their fire, a mud-spattered youth, watching from under a hood and listening to the news that filtered from group to group.

"The word is that Prince Curnan took sanctuary!" The smith who spoke had his arm deep in his saddle-bag.

"Then the saints above help him. He'll be plucked out and have his head in a basket before the night's done. Diarmait's done it before!"

"And he's done it again, the King." The smith drew out a stray slice of salt pork and sniffed it suspiciously.

A man who had set out from home with no thought of soldiering, drew his finger along the edge of his sword and spat in disgust.

"What else can the King do? He must uphold his own laws or that pack in the north will be at his throat."

"Aye, but the sanctuary monastery was under the protection of Columba. Now the fat's in the fire!"

The bacon flew and Caterin drew back as the heart of the fire exploded and spluttered. The smith took the blunt sword.

"Aye, this'll need sharpened. With his Ui Neill kin and the four Meath Kings behind Columba will smash us."

And Caterin could smell the fear and the sweat come and go with the woodsmoke and the tang of the pork.

"And didn't he have a dream, the Ra, the High King, himself?" said a voice, tight and breathless, "that the great tree that cast its shadow over all Eirean was felled by the sharp axes of one hundred and fifty clerics?"

And Caterin closed her eyes against the flames. For it was the icy wasteland that was Dairmait's spirit that held her mind and the loneliness that must be hers some day.

For she knew there was bound to be a battle. The whole country was bubbling like a cauldron. And when it boiled over, she thought, Eirean would never be the same again.

The rest of the night was broken by hooves galloping to and from the King's pavilion. No one was surprised when at dawn the horns blasted a summons. Names went from mouth to mouth. Colum Cille, King Aed of Ainmere, the Ui Neill, the sons of MacErca, the grieving father, King of Connacht, even Munster, the father of Diarmait's wife were marching south. The High King intended to meet their united army at a place called Cul-drebene.

As soon as the fighting battalions had formed up and marched away Caterin scrounged round all the saddle-bags for food and saddled up a decent mare.

It was a wet dreary morning that crawled over the fields and dowsed the smoking ashes of the camp-fires. She followed the wasted scrub that was the path of the army, and the gathering crows that sensed a battle. Then she knew by the clang of armour and the shouts of command that the King's army was about a mile away, just beyond a low-lying hill. This was the place called Cul

Drebene.

Halfway up the hill, she tied the mare to a branch and climbed the rest on foot. As soon as her head topped the rise, she dropped to lie flat, peering between the woody stems of a shrub, and saw the banners flying bright against the dark rain-clouds. Of course, she was courting danger but if the battle came this way she had her means of escape. The outcome of this battle would influence her whole future and she would watch it, whichever way it went. For if the High King was defeated, the White Dove would be all-powerful. Not only the Isle of Io but her home-land would be in danger.

In later years it was written that the royal army dispersed in flight, losing three thousand men, their opponents losing only one man. A lie, Caterin knew, told for one reason or another by someone who was not there. But a lie that was potent and would live because it was written in words on vellum that lasted beyond the memories of bards.

Below her the High King's army ebbed and flowed, chieftains and farmers, thrown into battle-lines, fearful and confused, yet staunch, ready to defend their safe living under the King's peace. She picked out the King, outstanding in glinting mail and long purple cloak, in the fore-front, shouting commands. Bishop Finnian in the rear held his arms to the sky pleading for victory, his golden cross waving over the heads of the milling army. Far away, on the enemy hill-top came the flash of another crozier, sweeping over a glinting sea of men, disciplined, confident.

Then Diarmait raised his sword aloft. The horse-boys beat on the sides of the war-wagons, yelling, working up to a frenzy. The throats of the army swelled in a war-chant that carried them forward under a forest of glinting spearheads. And the army of the Church answered with a yell that rent the wide sky. They charged across broken, scrub-strewn ground towards the hill where Caterin lay. And she saw, leading the three main bodies of the charge, the pennants of three of the Kings who had sat at the feast at Tara. While the pennant of the fourth King could be seen away to the left, standing back in reserve, waiting among a host of helmets.

The two sides met with a resounding shock that sent waves of noise back and forth across the plain. The battle raged this way and that, one force pushing forward under swinging axes while another surged back under a hail of arching spears. Showers of arrows, bright as raindrops, winged and fell, at first, in perfect formation and then, as the day wore on, more indiscriminitely, more ragged, more desperate. Here and there, a fluttering pennant was surrounded, wavered and vanished.

The fighting was ferocious, taking place between small groups or, even, hand-to-hand. It was impossible to tell which way the battle was going since they were all Eirean-born men and the insignia of the clans meant nothing to Caterin. All she could tell was that the blood that spurted from open flesh was as red as that of a hunted animal and it had the same stench.

There came a cheer from the centre of the field that swelled to a great yell of 'Colum Cille! Colum Cille!' Not a man on the plain could fail to see what happened next. Colum Cille had found a bare crag and stood there outlined against the grey sky. Two rainclouds parted at that moment to allow a slanting ray of sunlight to turn his robe into shining gold. His face, raised to the heavens, was transfigured with faith. His arms were stretched wide, making himself into an emblem of the Cross he worshipped. A cheer went up from a thousand throats and the fourth King thundered forward.

From then on, there was little doubt of the outcome of the battle. Diarmait's soldiers, seeking for a sign from Finnian, found that the monk was kneeling, head bowed, paralysed with failure, hardly discernible to the men who were fighting for their lives. The High King's army, demoralised, broke into small groups and fled, only to be cut down by pursuers, elated with success.

Caterin did not wait. Refusing to be mown down by the advancing horde, she slithered down to the mare. With the cries from the battlefield growing steadily louder and more blood-thirsty, and the croak of the circling carrion crows in her ears, she mounted and dug her heels in. The mare, as desperate as Caterin to escape from the sound of screams and axe-blows, from the smell of blood and sweat, laid her ears back and shot forward, flying like the wind. But where to?

To the south lay the Hill of Tara, the goal of the victorious army. In the north, burial parties and looters would be at their busiest. On the east coast, ports would be watched for men with a price on their heads fleeing into exile. Caterin wheeled the mare round to face west and set it at a gallop, into the fading sun.

As if to hide her presence in the landscape, the Merciful Ones drew down a blanket of cloud and enveloped her in a fine mist of rain. The open moorland was treacherous underfoot with clumps of reeds and long soaking grass. It was impossible now to see far ahead for a curtain of grey linked earth and sky. Skeins of fog swirled and writhed at her passing and she became aware of a desolate stillness over the earth. The mare had slowed herself to a steadier pace, her breath making white plumes in the air. Her hoof-beats and the nervous jangling of her bit echoed back from the white wall that pressed more surely around them. Caterin searched in vain for lights that would mean human company of some sort. With no signs from sky or land to guide her she could be going round in circles till nightfall.

A low branch of a tree whipped out of the mist and almost caught her unawares. More branches swung at her. They were in a wood. The mare snorted with fear and blew through her nostrils, protesting at the sinuous, slippery roots clawing at her feet. Her ears pricked and she stopped abruptly. The mist ahead seemed to gather into one place, darkening into a ghostly, hooded horseman, trailing white tendrils of the mist that eddied about him. The mare backed her huge hind-quarters into a tangle of undergrowth, breaking twigs right and left in her panic. Wet leaves showered on Caterin from above. Silent and menacing as ravens walking a battlefield, more figures solidified from the smoking air and stood, barring her way.

All in one instant, a command barked, a sword sliced from its scabbard and the mare reared. Caterin had been ready as soon as she felt the tremor of fear in the horse-flesh between her knees. She leapt from the saddle, twisting out her dagger and was diving, weaving, plunging around and between the horses' legs. Swords barred her way until she was caught, panting, in the centre of an ever-decreasing circle.

The tallest man dismounted and came towards her. When he was near enough, she lashed out at him with her dagger, only to find herself laid gently but firmly on her back, gazing up into a lean, implacable face, her dagger-hand held in a powerful crab-like grasp.

"May all the spirits of the sky stand between me and my destroyer!" she choked out between clenched teeth, tensing her muscles to take him between the legs.

At the sound of her voice, the black-hooded figure gave a grunt of surprise. His fingers bit hard into her wrist until he could prise the dagger from her clutching fingers. He stood, towering above her, legs astride her body, his long cloak touching her legs.

"From Pettaland, are you?" He spoke in her own language with an accent that grated. "Then what are you doing here, bolting through an Eirean forest in front of an Eirean army? Whose side were you fighting on?"

"I belong to no army! I'm a slave."

Eyes as hard as oak-galls examined her from under the black hood, checking on her faded boy's tunic, her slave's hair-cut and her lack of fighting weapons.

"Where did you steal the mare then? Come on, the truth!"

"It belonged to my master! I was a cup-bearer to him at the Feis!" That placed her fairly and squarely on the King's side in the battle and was dangerous. She rushed on. "My master was summoned to fight with the King. When he was killed, I took his horse." She hoped she sounded like a frightened refugee, caught unwillingly between both sides. "I took no part in the battle. I just wanted to escape." Attempting to put a quaver of fear in her voice, she found it was easier than she thought. The black horses in the circle stamped and blew through their nostrils. There was still a hiss and whisper of unsheathed swords.

"We've no time to waste on a run-away slave." The harsh voice behind them spoke pure Goidelic. "It's almost nightfall. Let him go."

"Wait! Where were you making for, boy?" Caterin gave a gasp of relief. They were not going to kill her. Yet, if they left her to wander all night in this fog, they might as well slit her throat and be done with it.

"Anywhere! I don't know! Somewhere I can find shelter and a ship to take me home."

A short bark of laughter came from underneath the hood.

"A curragh on a river is all you'll find hereabouts. How old are you, boy?"

"Thirteen, Master. Don't leave me here, my Lords. I can pay for food."

She swallowed, hoping that the admission had not been a mistake. If they were robbers, they would search her anyway. Yet, the fine leather-work and bronze trappings on the horses did not belong with rascals who lived by thieving. The leader's hand bunched her cloak at the neck and hauled her to her feet.

"Come. Put up your dagger and mount." Caterin obeyed quickly before he changed his mind. The horsemen closed in around her, setting their horses at gaps in the trees until they met a well-worn track and quickened their pace.

Caterin pulled her cloak closer around her and shivered. Her eyes searched for a clue to the loyalties of her escort but no emblem or colour broke their over-all black garb. If they were the High King's men they would have been refugees trying to escape like herself. Besides they were riding deeper and deeper into Ui Maine country, ruled by the King of Connacht whose son had been beheaded by the High King and none of Diarmait's men would dare to venture there. She must be in the hands of the victors. Would they be sympathetic to the claims of a Pretani Princess?

After a while, she stopped thinking. Lack of food and sleep were taking their toll. At moments, she felt so light-headed that she had to grip with her knees to keep from sliding off the mare. Waves of faintness washed over her, sending her rocking. She bit at her lips to clear her senses. If she fainted, they would discover she was a woman and was fair game for after-battle lusts.

She was jerked into attention when a yellowish light beamed at them through the fog and the party clattered into a cobbled courtyard with stone buildings looming eerily out of the murky depths on every side. Doors opened and more light spilled out. Dismounting, the horsemen threw back their black hoods and she caught her breath as their tonsured heads gleamed forth.

Monks! Of course, she should have guessed! The Bishops and their followers would be involved in the aftermath of the battle, even if not fighting in it. And this was their monastery!

CHAPTER TWENTY FOUR

This monastery was no quiet retreat for contemplation, judging by the main hall. A troop of soldiers, battle-weary and blood-stained, ate at tables down one side of the building. Travellers and traders, caught on the road between fog and the aftermath of battle, heated their knees at the central hearth. Black-robed brothers moved on silent, sandalled feet serving food and tending wounds. All were too engrossed to note the arrival of another wayfarer, a young lad who sat in their midst, the warmth of the fire heavy on his eyelids. A white twig of an arm poking from a black sleeve handed her a bowl of hot broth, thick with vegetables. Hardly had she finished it when she slid to the floor and fell asleep, propped against her rolled blanket while her damp clothes steamed gently.

She was jerked back into the world again by a stealthy movement at her side and a puff from an onion-laden breath.

"Be Dagda, I didn't mean to waken ye, boy, but it's thankful I am for a bit of warmth and shelter on a night when the ghostlies are writhing round your mount's legs."

It was a voice with a chuckle in it. Under her cloak, Caterin's hand unfastened itself from the hilt of her dagger. The man who stretched his legs to the fire was round and rosy with shrewd eyes that missed nothing, not even Caterin's stealthy movement. His chins multiplied as he undid his heavy gold brooch and hid it in a pouch before removing his cloak. Not a poor man, this, nor a man afraid of being robbed.

His servant, young but with massive shoulders and black brows, set the fearsome weapons at his studded belt jangling as he folded the cloak. More of a body-guard than a slave.

"Me name's Conaing and this is Ulla." Conaing nodded round the huddled group. There was an answering greeting here and there but the fog had nipped their throats and dampened their spirits. "'Tis not a night to be crossing the moorland so me lad and meself thought we'd partake of the good brothers' hospitality till the weather clears." He winked at Caterin. "It looks as though the hospitality hasn't risen to a drop of ale yet judging by the long faces around us. But it will, it will. Would ye be sharin' a leg of chicken with me?" From somewhere Ulla had procured a platter of chicken and bannocks and Caterin ate hungrily. Conaing arched a bushy red-grey eyebrow at her and she realised he was waiting for the courtesy of a name from her. She grasped at the first name that came to mind.

"My name's Derelei," she told him. She would have to learn to fend off questions quicker than that. Better still, she could attack with questions of her own that would keep him talking in the queer mixture of Celtic tongues that showed he was a traveller and likely to be garrulous. "Have you travelled far?"

"From the Duibh Linhe, six nights out. Ah, but we lingered on the way because business was good. 'Tis usual for us to turn towards Tara now but that's a town that will be filled with the wailing of women this night. Will ye have a little draft from my flask now?" It was a strong spirit and her eyes watered. But a cup-bearer would be expected to be familiar with his master's dregs.

"Aye, it won't be such a golden treasury of a place after the Kings of the North have finished with it. I mind I was in Tara when they chose this Diarmait to rule over them. They were there to proclaim their vote, all those Kings and Princes that fought against him today, standing high on stones planted in the ground so that their deed would be as lasting as a circle of stones. Well, the deed didn't last. D'ye know why?" He pointed a leg of chicken at Caterin. She shook her head to encourage him.

"It was not the ancient power of the Kings that overcame Tara but the new power in the land, the Church. It'll be the end of Tara as we knew it. As sure as chickens come from eggs, they'll build a monastery on the Hill and the Nine Golden Harps will never sound through Tara's Halls again." He shook his head sadly. "Tara was the shining heart of Eirean but maybe also the curse of it. If all I hear is true there's a power greater than the dynasties of Kings rising in the land." He lowered his voice to a whisper that had a great deal of awe in it but a suspicion of a question at the end. "'Tis said that Colum Cille appeared flying across the sky like a great White Cross, calling down the wrath of his God on his enemies. That his God smote the King's army and destroyed it. The whole army killed, would ye believe it, except one, a young cup-bearer who fled?"

He guessed too much, this man. She would have to be careful. Chuckling, Conaing slapped his thick thigh.

"These stumps will have to stir themselves further north to find such rich pickings for next year's trading. Would ye like to see what I trade in, boy?" Ulla, crouched at his master's side, threw him a warning look. "This one's only a nestling, Ulla, and might never set eyes on such a sight again in his life. Well, we'll let Ulla have his way. We won't let the jackdaws on the other side of the fire in on the secret." He laid his finger on his bulbous nose and smiled at Caterin. "Ulla's right, you know, to chide me. He's the one who defends me from a quick thrust in the forest. Maybe I trust too much in the rule of the road that the trader's worth his weight in gold for the news he brings from clan to clan. Maybe that'll all change now that the stern justice of the High King is no more. Here, boy, draw that cloak round us."

In the shadow of his cloak, he fetched a roll of calf-hide from between his legs, undid the thongs and unrolled it. Inside, fastened onto the finest of kid-skin, glistened brooches, pins, buckles, necklets, belts and dress-fasteners.

A monk threw fresh logs on the fire and, as the sparking flames leapt higher, suddenly, the gold caught the light and came alive. There was a latchet with an ornament of spirals against a carmine background; a brooch with gilt-silver interlacing set with amethysts; a belt-buckle with scrolls and trumpet-spirals, washed with silver; a neck-ring set with coral, ringed with rock crystals and amber. Caterin's smile began in her eyes before it touched her mouth. Her fingers touched and traced the delicate gold filigree. Then her hand paused, sensing Conaing's intent gaze, and she raised her eyes to meet his.

"So! All is not what it would seem." He rolled up the bundle and tied it.

She knew she had given herself away as a woman. A man who sold jewellery thrived on reading the minds of his customers and noting their reactions. But would he betray her? To the soldiers? Or to the monks? If there was a profit to be gained by it, she supposed he might. A stout boot kicked aside a sleeping dog and a soldier stood casting his shadow over them.

"A blessing on you, lad," said Conaing to the soldier. "Come here beside us and heat your backside. Would ye be wanting a drink from my flask then?" With a steady hand he poured wine for the soldier and turned back to Caterin. "In my trade I need keen eyesight, not only for the working of the metals but for the little mannerisms that give away who can be tempted to buy and who is there to steal. But when it comes to someone young and defenceless, in disguise, I find me eyesight fails something terrible." He saw the faint film of sweat on Caterin's upper lip and chuckled. "If I thought that same person needed protection in these troublesome times, I might be persuaded to take on another servant for the next part of my journey. That is, if that person was travelling north."

"Travelling north, are you, pedlar?" The soldier handed back the cup and Conaing fitted it neatly onto the top of his flask. "Well, I'm thinking you'd be fools to risk it yet. This isn't a time to be on the road when the woods are full of hungry soldiers and the women in the cabins are keening for their lost ones. They won't be wanting laces and ribbons to dry their tears. The sweetest harvest this year has been in young men. Where are you making for, lad?"

"Just what I was asking the boy myself." Conaing came in smoothly before Caterin had time to reply. "For I've sore need of another servant." Ulla gave a sidelong look at his master and emitted a sullen grunt that boded no good to Caterin. "But, once the fog lifts, we'll be off home to the Duibh Linhe as fast as we can go since ye've been so kind as to give us such good advice."

"Ah, the good brothers are mulling ale at long last." Quickly the soldier lost interest in their conversation and moved away.

"Ulla," said Conaing. "It'll do you no harm if we give the lad a lift on his way, now will it? Let's tell him a bittie about our trade. It'll while away the time and the knowledge might come in useful to him if we're questioned on the way."

The atmosphere in the hall had relaxed. There was a good deal of laughter from the soldiers and some traders were dicing at the far end. A few more travellers had come in, shaking their cloaks and the brothers had come round with hot food again.

"Do you really go looking for flakes of gold in the watery gravel?" It was a trade that had always fascinated Caterin.

"Indeed I did that very thing in my youth." Conaing belched and patted his abdomen. "Now I can afford to buy ingots of gold that have been melted and hammered into bars or sheets or wires. I only need to cut it into shape before I begin work on it. Ulla, will ye be letting us miss our fair share of the mulled wine?" Again, Ulla shot a sulky look at Caterin and unhooked his long legs. He was back in a trice with three beakers, and sat at the other side of

Conaing, straining his ears.

"Would ye look at the boy, sure that I'm going to open my mouth and pass on all the secrets of my trade to a young whipper-snapper like yourself." Conaing reached for a beaker and drank heartily. "Never fear, Ulla, your ugly ears will be the only ones to hear all of my hard-won knowledge because I fear you're the only son I'm going to foster. It's the only way, to have a skill that the people in the towns and villages need and respect. Then you can travel in safety. Even the very charcoal burners are honoured for they've a better understanding of trees and wood-cutting than any farmer. But there's something more that's needed, Ulla, and that's a feeling for the work. That hasn't come to you yet."

"Have you no sons of your own?" asked Caterin.

Conaing's nose had suddenly become buried deep in his beaker. Ulla's resentment had faded enough for him to reply.

"His wife and family were killed in a Saeson raid while he was off trading. After that he bought me and promised me he'd teach me his trade. It's my only chance to make something of myself." The urgency in his voice was not lost on Caterin.

"Then may the Great Ones smile on you," said Caterin, "for truly, it's not a trade I'd be much good at."

"Aye, the Great Ones." Conaing took a quick look around and lowered his voice. "It's to the old gods you have to look if you want to work with the king of metals. 'Tis an awesome moment when you chance on the first gleams in a stream in a wild place and you know that the gods have chosen you. Later, when it glows white-hot in the heat, you see a radiance greater than that of the sun and you know that the gods have given their brilliance into your hands to fashion a beautiful object to their glory. That's how I look at it. When the gold has cooled and hardened, I ask the gods to work through my fingers. Together we look at the fragility of flowers and try to match it to a dainty piece that will deck a queen and maybe live in a bard-song. Then again, we may be struck by the brave deeds of a king and fashion a strong piece with bold lines like the sweep of a sword." He laughed a shade ruefully. "Most times I sell to a stout farmer or his good lady. But a little bit of myself goes with each piece and it lingers in my memory." Conaing eased himself against his bed-roll, clasping his hands across his thickening middle.

"Ah, 'tis a fine thing to let your tongue run away with itself now and again. When I shut up my workshop and take to the roads in summer, most of my wares are for lads to give to their lasses. But that roll I showed you was for the wealthy. I have another bundle with chalices and reliquaries for the Abbots. I'll be giving the Abbot here a guest-gift in the morning. If it pleases him I might earn an armed escort for the next stage of my journey."

The hall was quieter now. The monks had retired to their devotions in their cells. The soldiers had disappeared leaving their wounded comrades in a poppy-induced sleep. The torches that had burned throughout the long dark day had been replenished. At the fire, the travellers and traders had gathered closer and the talk was all of Tara.

"I'll miss my visit to Tara this year." The pale-eyed man who spoke showed by his leather clothes and dust-muffler that he was a stone-mason. "I wonder if the days of the High Kings are over. The greatest sight I ever saw as a boy was the High King Cormac. He passed through our village driving his chariot of gold showing himself to his people. 'Twas the flash and glimmer of his enamelled weapons that caught the eye of us boys until he threw a shower of coins for us to dive for. My father told me Cormac kept a fenced field where he set barrels of ale and food for people to help themselves. I fear we'll never see his like again."

"I was working in Tara when Diarmait was chosen." A carpenter idly tossed and caught his hammer as he talked. "Cormac had been killed at the very moment of victory in battle. A bitter blow, that! That night the men of his kin gathered in the grove of the oaks by the light of the moon. Some of the war booty had been gathered into the Cauldron of Sacrifice."

"Indeed, I remember that!" Conaing roused himself. "Some of me own fine brooches lay there. When it sank into the bog, I remember hoping that the gods would know that I'd had a small share in the offering."

They talked easily and familiarly about their deities. That they were in the house of the newest of these gods troubled them little for they had fitted this new one neatly into the hierarchy of their ancient beliefs. Caterin wondered if it would happen that way in her own country.

"I don't know why the old tradition of the bull-dream was brought back for the King-Choosing." The carpenter took back the telling of the story. "In my lifetime it was always the most powerful

of the lesser kings who had been chosen. It may be that the Druad
were seeking a more potent magic against the rise of the Bishops.
Who knows? But it was a fearful sight." He paused to whet the
appetite of his listeners for everyone in Eirean was a born story-
teller.

"And what happened?" A tall, lanky foreigner in shabby, rust-
brown clothes passed along a beaker of ale to moisten the throat of
the carpenter.

"It was a night of a thousand stars. We stood on a hill-top near
Tara where there was a great stone cairn wreathed with briar. The
names of the three goddesses, Maeve of Tara, Macha of Ulster and
Rhiannon, the Great Queen, sang in the soft-breasted air. Under
the dagger of the magician, the neck of the white bull flowered red
like a collar of rubies. In the white heat of the fire, the flesh curled
and spat. The Chief Seer ate the flesh and fell into a trance. We
waited there, Kings, nobles and the free people of the Tuath. Not a
breath of wind stirred, not a night-bird called."

His audience leant forward, enjoying the familiar tale and the
new touches of drama that the story had gathered since they had
last heard it.

"Slowly, the Drui came to himself, back from the world beyond
knowing. He paced round the circle of Kings and their kinsmen,
peering into their faces, looking for a sign. At last, he laid his
hands on the shoulders of Diarmait where he stood in his robe of
flame-coloured silk. We cheered and rattled our weapons. Then
the whole multitude of us raised the new High King on high and
took him to the Lia Fail Stone, the Stone that roars when the true
King steps upon it. Certainly, as the crown touched his head, a
mighty wind swept across the hill-top and moaned through a crack
in the stone. It whirled our cloaks and took the breath from our
mouths. The gods were in it right enough."

An old man on a bench, resting his hands on his staff, cleared
his throat. His grey hair fell on his shadowy cloak and the firelight
threw a ruddy glow on his weather-brown face. What urgent
business had taken him abroad that day in such weather?

"Yet, I would not be High King for all the gold in Eirean," he
said. "For all his riches and power, he's tied hand and foot by the
customs and taboos of the Tuath. The sun mustn't rise on the King
in his bed. He mustn't climb a mountain after sunset. He mustn't
travel the road to Duibh Linhe on a Monday."

"Is it true he can't banquet at night during harvest?" asked the foreigner.

"'Tis the very reason why the Feasting at the Feis is so lavish. He has to make up for lost time somehow."

"He's forbidden to attend the horse fair at Rath Line." This was the carpenter now. "Forbidden to listen to the fluttering of birds after sunset, to go in to Magh Cobha in the month of March, to go in a grey-speckled garment on a grey-speckled steed to the heath of Dal Chais. 'Twould be a brave man would defy these ancient taboos."

And hard work remembering them, thought Caterin, imagining Diarmait hastily reciting his taboos before he dared to set a foot out of bed in the morning. And banished the thought quickly, not daring to ask if the lonely blue eyes were closed for ever.

"Ah, give me my freedom to walk the roads and my heart singing with the joy of it." The carpenter drank deeply and smacked his lips.

A tentative arpeggio of notes floated in the air and all eyes turned to a youth who held a small harp on his knee. His eyes were full of dreams but his next chord was resonant with authority. He began to sing of how Eochaidh, a High King of Tara, came upon the beautiful Etain beside a clear spring and fell in love with her.

"A purple mantle fringed with silver swirled about her as she sat.

Her arms were white as the snow of a single night,

Her cheeks rosy as the foxglove,

Her eyes blue as the hyacinth,

Her eyebrows bluish-black as the wing of a beetle.

A maiden with a silver comb plaited her golden hair.

At the end of each strand, she tied a little ball of gold."

There was a pause while each man painted his own picture of Etain. Then the young bard struck a sad, plaintive chord that lingered shivering in the air.

"Last night I saw the Great High King in my dream.

He sat on a couch curtained round with silver cloth.

On his visage I saw the ardour of a sovereign and the wisdom of a historian, His cloak was like the mist of a May morning, ever-changing in colour.

A wheel-brooch of gold reached from his chin to his waist.

Like the sheen of burnished gold was the colour of his hair.

Then I dreamed of danger-crowding phantoms, a host of
creeping enemies,
A combat of men beside the Dodder and, early and alone,
The King of Tara was killed."

The song died away and the men sat silent, staring into the fire.
And an unutterable sadness came on Caterin. For these men
thought on the greatness of an era that was gone and none knew
for sure what lay ahead. Whereas one day she would sit in a High
Chair at the Banquet and know the fear and the loneliness of
Diarmait. And maybe watch the downfall of her hopes and dreams
and desolation would come to her land.

Abruptly, Conaing awoke from his reverie and clapped Caterin
on the shoulder.

"Well, 'tis time I relieved myself of this bladder-full of ale. Come
outside with me, boy."

Startled, Caterin found herself being propelled out through the
door and round behind one of the outhouses.

"Listen to me, girl," Conaing hissed. "'Tis in moments like these
that you're in danger of being found out. Your eyes betray you all
the time. I've no wish to pry but I hear a Picti twist in your speech.
'Tis my judgment you are making for your own land."

He hardly waited for Caterin's nod before hurrying on.

"Then you'll have to travel by boat where living conditions are
crowded. There will be no way that you can hide the fact that
you're a woman. I offered you my protection but, while the talk was
going on, I thought of a better way. Tomorrow you must speak to
the Bishop. Tell him your story and ask to be sent home."

As the door of the hall opened on men's voices, he drew her
further into the shadows.

"There's danger for you in Dal Riata since your countries are at
war. But the Church sends missionaries across to Alba and they can
cross borders safely. Throw yourself on their mercy and they'll
protect you for these monks are sworn to celibacy and revere
womanhood. Think on it. Come now, let's prepare ourselves to
sleep."

Later, lying snug by the fire, Caterin thought over Conaing's
suggestion. Although it seemed sensible enough on the surface,
royal hostages were valuable pawns in the political game.

Yet she would never again be inside a monastery, a learning
place of the New Faith. For Veleda's sake she must discover as

much as she could. It could be disastrous to attack the Faith without whetting her arrows with knowledge.

CHAPTER TWENTY FIVE

Conaing made it easy for her to meet the Abbot Ciaran next morning. In his baggage he had a particularly handsome chalice. By presenting it to the Church, it would procure for him the hospitality and protection of the forty or so related monasteries up and down the land. Caterin carried it into the Abbot's office. It was a bare, unheated room with a rough wood floor and plaster walls. It held only a darkwood table and a stiff-backed chair. A black oak cross was nailed on the wall behind him. Clearly, the Abbot's mind rose to higher things than his comfort.

Conaing made his speech and Caterin laid the chalice on the table. The Abbot's blue-veined hands remained still. His eyes merely glanced at the gold filigree work and the jewels round the rim. She hoped Conaing had not offended him. That would bode no good when it came to her turn. Still, Conaing appeared satisfied and went away, leaving the 'lad' to make his own request.

The hooded lids rose and the Abbot contemplated her in silence. She waited for him to speak while the air in the room grew steadily colder. Someone would have to start the conversation soon or she would be frozen to the spot.

"Your monks brought me here last night," she began. For a moment she thought he was deep in meditation and had not heard her.

"So, you are the Pretani boy who was fleeing from the battle." His small, thin-lipped mouth had hardly moved.

If she remained in the disguise of a runaway slave she might never be able to return home. She needed to be treated according to her rank to learn what had been happening in Alba and to assess whether it was necessary for her to return there.

"Except that I'm not a boy but the Princess of the Pretani, the daughter of King Bridei."

If she had expected a reaction she was disappointed. Stumbling a little in the Goidelic, she told her story. The pale eyes never left her face. But when she came to the part where she had been presented to Diarmait as a bard-gift, she was sure she caught a gleam of amusement in his eyes.

"So you're the daughter Bridei's been seeking like a man

demented?"

Caterin would have danced for joy if she had not been royal and half-frozen.

"Then can you return me to my father?" Deliberately she had stressed the family connection rather than the political one.

"Impossible!" The word fell like the drip from an icicle between them. "Bridei has wiped out Aedan's fleet in sea-battles around the Orcades. You can't expect the kin of the Dal Riatans to make a present of you to the very King who has annihilated their fleet." His voice was wafer-thin through lack of use and the complete absence of emotion. Yet, by his accent, the Abbot Ciaran was a Briton. Surely he might be inclined to a certain neutrality in the matter.

"And Bridei's southern army has caused even greater devastation. A new leader has emerged, a Prince Gort of Gwynedd, now Deputy King of your country."

Caterin drew in her breath at the mention of Gort's name.

"This man has brought fire and pillage and death to the sons of Aedan and to the very walls of the Duns of the Dal Riata."

Caterin thought of Artur and exulted before her heart sank like a stone. What hope of justice did she have now?

"But recently, I've had news from my brothers in Rheged." Ciaran leant forward with his elbows on desk. The atmosphere in the room seemed to have warmed a little.

"Prince Gort has joined forces with Urien of Rheged. They've turned their attention on a brood of Saeson cubs that had fixed their claws on the eastern coasts." Suddenly, Ciaran's watery tones had a tinge of poison in them. "The kingdoms of Bernicia and Deira have been toppling their neighbouring chiefs and taking over their lands. Even York lay undefended before them at one point." His voice had strengthened. His hands were tightly clasped till the knuckles whitened. Caterin was sure now that his heart was involved with Gort and Urien and the army of the Britons. Her hopes see-sawed upwards again.

"Urien and Gort marched to Catraeth where the road from York branches north-east to Bernicia and north-west to Rheged. They seized Caetreth, thus keeping Bernicia and Diera from joining together, a well-planned strategy and it worked for a time."

This was the kind of news she had longed to hear. None of it had filtered through to the settlement of the Northmen.

"Then, Aethelric, the Firebrand, from Bernicia invaded Rheged. He was beaten back. Riderch Hen of Clyde and Morcant of Lothian were called upon to forget their differences to help stem this Saeson tide. This was too much to expect from such jealous princes. So Urien and Gort had to put on a greater boldness than ever before. With the help of Rhun of Gwynedd they pursued the Saesons to the very Island of Metcaud that we in the Church now call Lindisfarne. There, the Saesons had to stand siege and were starved into surrender."

The Abbot stopped and seemed to sink back into his own thoughts.

Caterin's mind worked quickly. It seemed that Gort had used the Pretani army to further the power of his brother. Surely Bridei would have realised Gort's true intentions by now. If not, it was time for her to reappear to argue against Gort's ambition for the Kingship. A gift to the Church, Caterin thought. That might regain the Abbot's attention.

"I'll reward the Church handsomely if you'll return me to my motherland."

The Abbot touched the rim of the chalice in front of him with a finger like a bent, bleached twig.

"This chalice is wonderfully constructed. Yet, it would have been better for Conaing if he had given it with the glory of God in his heart."

Caterin could make nothing of this statement. Glory was something that was won on the battle-field and sung by the bards. Offerings were made to the gods when you wanted something in return. Ciaran's finger tapped decisively three times on the delicate rim of the bowl.

"You will stay here in Durrow for the present. I will have a room made ready in the guest-house and find a village woman to tend you."

"But will you send a message to King Bridei?"

The thin lips tightened. It could have been an attempt at a smile but Caterin suspected she had been too demanding.

"Many years ago I tutored two boys who became great Kings. Dafydd of Gwynedd is dead and the other, Cynwyd, is known as Bridei. Now the son of Dafydd is set to become greater than his father and to marry the daughter of the other. The Church has great hopes of that union." His speculative eyes rested on Caterin.

"Have patience. While you wait you will be tutored in the True Faith."

It was a most unsatisfactory solution, Caterin thought later, but one she would have to live with. She was lucky to have escaped with her life. It was obvious that Ciaran wanted to convert her so that when she returned she would allow his missionaries access to her land.

An elderly woman with a twisted foot was assigned to her, one who needed a refuge from the cold weather. Macha was useful in that she knew her way about the monastery to bring washing water and food and actually managed to obtain a skirt and shawl in return for a silver ring.

Caterin revelled in being dressed as a woman again. Even though the skirt was thick and shabby, it flared out as she walked. And she could bathe often. The water needed no oils nor perfumes for it was as soft as silk. She could attend to her own hair now that it was short and growing in a tumble of curls around her face.

The woman insisted that Caterin attended the ceremonies that the monks held three times daily in a special building that they called an Oratory. Caterin found it difficult to understand why, if their God lived in the sky, they did not speak to him in the open where the God could draw near. Like the Northmen, they had an image of their God, a man, thin and tortured and he, like Odin, had also sacrificed himself on the Tree of Knowledge. Although his face was more beautiful, neither of the sacrificed Gods tugged at her heart-strings. Neither did Bride, but then Bride was a part of her innermost being, ingrained for ever. She did not have to look in the sky for her.

She enjoyed the sonorous chanting that sounded like a whole choir of bards reciting their songs of praise. A monk came daily to tell her stories about saints and miracles, prophets and prophecies, good and evil. She thought of Colum Cille standing on a hill and how it had been told as a miracle before nightfall. She thought of Veleda who had foretold the coming of the White Dove. She thought of the simple Druad who owned no wealth but found riches in their communion with the spirits of Earth and Air.

Gone were the days when the monks accused the Druad of atrocities to win the people over to the new Faith. Now she learned how they had taken over the ancient festivals and called the age-old wells by new names.

There was a unity and a strength of purpose in this vast organisation that she feared. Their Books, their language, their laws came from Rome and their purpose was to convert. But if folk severed the strands that bound them to the Seasons of the All-Mother, what would come of it in the future? What would happen to the kith and kin? To the Earth-Mother?

And to kneel before the Son of the God? What about the Life-Giver, the Daughter?

The Druad did not need to refute the arguments of the Churchmen. Truth was inborn. Folk might make the new signs and name the new god and his saints. But they would still throw silver into ponds and celebrate round bonfires. Yet, how could the scattered communities of the Druad stand against the force of this organised Church? Veleda had been wise to fear the White Dove.

She longed to be home where the totems had presence and the Faith was as old as the Mountains. Daily she spilled her libations into the Courtyard Well. Nightly she invoked the Moon Maiden, remote Queen of the Splendid Ones. She said her spells to Wise Bride and the All-Mother. But still Bishop Ciaran sent no summons for her. They were all too busy with a festival they called the Christ-Mass.

Happily, the monks laid no restrictions about where she wandered within the rath of the monastery although she was warned not to linger near the wattle cells of the brothers where they fasted and entered into deep meditation. She would pace up and down the frosty grass sward in the cold clear air with Macha, passing and re-passing the monks who stood with their feet in the freezing water of pools for long hours of vigil. The bowed heads sported two kinds of tonsure. Those who had been to Rome had shaved the crown of their heads. But some still clung to the traditional tonsure of the Druad and shaved from ear to ear over the tops of their heads.

When the season became colder, she visited stables and byres where the air was warm with the breath of beasts. She fed the animals and asked about the remedies the monks used for ailments.

In the sheds where mead and ale were brewed, she turned her sleeves up and lent a hand. Even the huts where tools for the Sowing season were being repaired interested her. When she became Queen, the folk could say they had never had a Queen who had so much practical experience.

Another cycle of the Moon came and went as she waited in vain for the order to leave. None came. Regularly, she asked for interviews with Ciaran and was told that no arrangements had been made yet. Common sense told her she had missed her chance because of the weather. Bitter winds brought sleet and snow and few ships would be ploughing through the seas to Alba. She took refuge from the depressing cold and her even more depressing thoughts in some of the larger buildings and that was how she found the scriptorium.

It was full of light from many tall windows. The floor space was entirely taken up with desks and chairs. Tonsured and untonsured heads bent over pages of parchment. The only sounds were the subdued drone of the readers, the scratching of quills of the clerks and the odd cough. She guessed they were making copies of their holy books like the one Colum Cille and Finnian had wrangled over. Looking back on that dispute she remembered how Colum Cille had almost rubbed his hands with glee when the judgment went against him. Had he forseen Cul Drebene?

Intrigued, she hung over the nearest shoulder, watching a page being prepared. Faint lines had been ruled for the black script to sit on and ornamentation in the shape of intertwined flowers and birds had been drawn lightly in around the borders. The monk in front of her laid down his quill and leaned back, revealing a fat, cherubic countenance beaming with delight.

"You're interested in our work here, my daughter?"

"We've nothing like this in my country." Apart from her own fascination, she felt this was a craft that she might introduce at home.

"If it pleases you I'll show you round." He heaved himself out of his chair, smoothing down his robe over his ample frame. "You'll forgive the other brothers who must use every iota of daylight to advantage at this time of the year." And he almost winked. "But I'm in charge so I can take time off"

Caterin followed him down the length of the room, careful not to cast the least shadow on the work of the monks.

"My name is Dagaeus," he told her. "I used to be a teacher of reading, writing and manual skills in a small monastery school at Devenish. But the demand for books is growing steadily so now I have both pupils and apprentices. Here the younger craftsmen are practising their script-writing, copying rolls of instructions, laws, prayers and psalms." An odd eye quirked up curiously to look at her as they passed. The tip of a tongue appeared now and again following the line of a curving letter.

A row of absorbed men sat in pairs, one reciting the words, the other writing them.

"Here we copy the Godspels and decorate each page with pictures so that the reader may contemplate their beauty while absorbing the Holy Words." Never would the Pretani artists draw flowers or leaves as mere decoration. Since her time with Veleda she knew that the spirits within the growing plants would lose their potency if they were imitated merely because of their beauty. Yet the animal and bird-like figures had a familiar look about them.

"These are like the symbols of my own people." She studied them again. But where the Pretani weavers and embroiderers and stone masons managed to convey a sense of strength or daintiness or humour as they thought fit, here, the designs had been flattened, elongated, twisted, turned round on one another to form a new style designed to enhance the letters of the script. She looked up into the twinkling eyes of Dagaeus.

"Of course, you're right," agreed Dagaeus. "In times of peace, your craftsmen come to Eirean and ours visit your land. Like all artists, we get our heads together and learn from one another. We've merely modified some of your ideas to fit on a flat page."

The capital letters were curled into pictures so minute and intricate that Caterin marvelled. Other decorations flowed across the page, boldly and dramatically, irradiating it with jewelled colours. Yet, she thought that the Pretani designs had been twisted out of all recognition and their virility and realism had been lost. In her mind's eye she could see the great Ancestor Stones with their vigorous symbols standing out proud after a shower of rain. And she heard the snipe that sounded from the hill and the tang of the new-furrowed earth was in her nostrils and she could feel the rough grain of the stone on her palm. And she yearned to be home wondered why she was here in a foreign land and a kind of prisoner at that.

Then a white-haired monk unrolled a time-stained vellum and sneezed as the dust-motes danced in a shaft of weak sunlight. And she found herself wanting to know more about these strange things

217

called Books.

"The older clerics work in this corner. Their eyes may have grown weak but their wisdom has strengthened with age. They gather facts from the ancient Books to preserve the traditions for those who come after."

Dagaeus opened a door and the chatter of young voices within the room hushed abruptly.

"Boys! Boys!" One grinned up at them as he pounded his pestle into chips of green malachite in a mortar. "Remember to test it between your fingernails to see if it's truly powdered," warned Dageus.

Another raised a flushed face from a pot over a brazier which, by the smell of it, was glue made from boiled hooves. An older boy with a template drew a shape carefully onto a wafer-thin sheet of gold.

"When we're older, Dagaeus is going to let us do a marvellous cover for his Godspel in gold and silver and precious stones," he told Caterin with pride. Dagaeus ruffled the lad's hair smiling but was suddenly called to a crisis over the consistency of the glue and Caterin was left to wander alone among the monks, wondering at their skill.

When the Day of Bride, the Imbolc Festival, arrived it brought new hope to Caterin. At home the lambs and calves would be arriving, bringing an abundance of milk in place of the scarcity of the Dark Days. Surely there would be sailing weather soon. While the monks were all in the Oratory celebrating the Candle-Mass, she dropped her last silver trinket into the Well.

"Mother of healing and learning, patron of poetry and metal-work, Guardian of the hearth, hear me," she pleaded.

An insistent piping above her head made her look up. It was an oyster-catcher, a servant of Bride, winging his way across the sky. She opened her arms and danced for joy. It was the omen she needed!

Sure enough, not long after, she was summoned again by the Abbot Ciaran. Her heart leapt as she hurried to his room.

There were two other monks with him. One pounded the table in a forthright manner with a fist that was no stranger to hard work judging by the callouses and scars on it. Caterin waited beside the door, full of impatience, but nothing was going to stop his flow of words.

"It was when I returned from finding the Promised Land that I went to Connacht. I saw what was hatching then and I warned Diarmait that it needed just a spark to set it alight."

This must be Brendan, the Navigating Monk, who had sailed far across the sea through a bank of freezing fog to a land he called the Island of Delight. It had seemed like a fantasy when she had heard the story yet, here was the man, as large as life, and angry.

"I saw the signs before I left - that if the Church won a powerful victory over the High King, Columba might be asked to take the crown. And now it's happened and I want no part in a Church that also rules the state. We are monks. We founded monasteries to withdraw from the world of politics, not to become a force in them."

"No, no, Brendan, let your sails flap in the wind of rumour but not your ears." Ciaran's thin voice rustled from a still face.

"Rumour? I hope that's all it is." For a moment, Brendan seemed mollified, then he burst out again turning to the other man. "What is the truth of the matter, Bishop Lasrian?" Caterin had become aware that the third man of the trio had been covertly watching her from the shadows. Judging by the change in Brendan's manner from a blustering rage to a tone of respect, Bishop Lasrian was a senior and honoured man. His voice when it came was gentle and kindly but Caterin could see little of him for he sat with his back to the window where the light did not fall on his face.

"One man cannot become both Head of the Church and Master of the Kingdom. Columba knows this well. He went to Culdrebene to keep the Church independent from a pagan King who opposed it, that was all."

"But he was present, praying for his army of relatives in the battle. Out there in the countryside, people see him as Druid, as King, as Saint, even as God because his prayers can make one ruler victorious and vanquish another. Our movement was begun in protest against the continued warfare of kings and now the greatest monk of all has used prayer as a military weapon. Did you know that a synod of Diarmait's kin in Teiltiu have excommunicated him because of it?"

A breath of a sigh came from the shadow at the window.

"I know what you're going to say, Brendan. Now the Ui Neill will have a synod to condone Columba's action and every king in the land will want a priestly prayer-worker at their side in battle. But if we allow him to be excommunicated, the Church submits to the next dynasty of High Kings and Columba's fight to uphold the right of sanctuary in the Church will have been lost."

Caterin shifted her weight from one foot to the other as quietly as she could. This was powerful talk to take home in a corner of her mind to Broichan. It had no relevance to her own situation, yet she was aware with every tingling nerve-end that Bishop Lasrian's eyes returned again and again to scrutinize her.

"Yet, the monarchy fell, Bishop Lasrian," put in Ciaran. "God made a clear decision."

"But it is God's servants who must see that the decision is used to the benefit of the people and the glory of God," said Lasrian decisively. "Who are you, girl?"

Caterin was startled by the abrupt question but, before she could answer, Brendan had spoken.

"Ah! I've taken on the services of a goldsmith at Clonfert, a certain Comgaill, who insisted that this one was the missing Picti Princess there's been all the hullaballoo about."

So the shrewd Comgaill had guessed more than she had given him credit for.

"I am the daughter of Bridei." Caterin stepped forward confidently, determined to take a stance now that she had their full attention. "See, here is my insignia."

"The magic talisman of a pagan country!" Brendan snorted.

"And I would be grateful," Caterin ignored him, "if you could find your way to return me to my homeland."

"Has she been baptised into the True Faith?" barked Brendan.

Suddenly Caterin saw the danger she was in. They wanted a Christian Princess to return to Bridei. If she refused conversion they might never send her back.

"She has attended all our offices and has been tutored." Ciaran had risen to light a lamp that shone on the alabaster planes of a benevolent face at the window.

"And how much did you understand, my child?" There was a thread of laughter in Lasrian's quiet tones.

"Frankly, very little," she said and waited for their reaction. It took her by surprise.

Briskly, Lasrian rose to his feet. He took her hand with courtesy and smiled down into her eyes.

"I have heard well of your father, Princess Caterin. He is riding high on his victories over the impetuous Aedan but in peace-time, I believe he is a worthy King ruling a worthy people."

Pride rose and swelled inside Caterin's breast almost choking her. It had been a long time since she had been addressed by her title. Surely now, she could look forward to going home.

"As soon as there is sailing weather you will leave." Lasrain patted her hand. "You see, I have a use for a woman like yourself."

"You mean to open the door to the conversion of the pagan Picts?" asked Brendan. Caterin stiffened at the contempt in his voice.

"Well, maybe that too. Be assured, Princess, I shall send for you soon."

CHAPTER TWENTY SIX

From now on Ciaran himself tutored Caterin.

"Are you ready to be baptised, daughter?" he asked after each session, his eyes boring into hers.

"Is that the price I've to pay to go home?" she would ask in return.

And he would make his sign in the air and leave, muttering about the Devil and his works. And Caterin would go down to the pasture among cows heavy with calf who gazed at her with the sad gentle eyes of the Earth Mother and blew on her hands as she fed them grass.

"What do they mean when they talk about being baptised?" Caterin asked Macha, wondering if they would force her into it.

"You're dipped in the river by the Abbot. And the choir sings." Macha's head bobbed with delight. "And you feel right fine after it. Like you're important."

"But what oaths do you swear?"

"They say something in Latin." Macha shrugged her thin shoulders. "I just nodded. I eat better now."

But even if she pretended to be converted, the trumpets would blare the news of her conversion abroad and the shadow of the White Dove would darken the face of her land.

The waiting time might have been tedious, if Bishop Brendan had not stayed on in the monastery with his companions. And the sailor-monks had a fund of stories. To be sure they did their share of praying and fasting. They kept their vigils and they stood in contemplation in the freezing rain. Caterin saw them as she paced round the oak in the courtyard seven times moonwise, moaning to Bride about the lack of sailing weather. But round the evening fire, the monks stretched their rope-scarred hands to the blaze and their gaunt, weather-red faces lit up if a traveller knowingly mentioned the Other World.

"The Other World? Aye, so the bards call it."

"But we sailed in no magic chariot."

"And we found no beautiful maidens dwelling beneath the waves."

"But did you find the Land beyond the sunset?" Caterin knew

there was always a grain of truth at the heart of a poem.

"Abbot Finnbarr calls it the Promised Land. Promised to men of great virtue. Like us." Sea-green eyes twinkled but the monk was in deadly earnest.

"Seven years we searched for it." An energetic sprite of a man with leathery skin and large ears took up the thread. "We'd have reached it but God in his wisdom hid it behind a cloud. This year we'll pierce the fog."

"You're mighty sure." A lounging pedlar bit into an apple. "By my reckoning you'll fall off the edge of the world."

"Rubbish! The world is as round as your apple. Finnbarr has writings from Rome to prove it. And mathematical measurements too."

"Pah! There are no lands to the west." The pedlar spat his core into the fire. A barrel-shaped monk pulled up his sleeves and planted his hands on his knees, delighted to be drawn.

"Indeed there are," he said. "Islands where monks from Eirean live. What does an ignorant land-crawler like yourself know?"

"Enough! I know it's not possible to sail westward from the shores of Eirean because of the current and the westerly winds that work against a boat."

"So we let the wind take us north to the Iordoman Islands and the Orcades. Then, when the wind is right, we slant across the westerlies for about fifteen days until we come to islands with narrow stretches of water between them."

"We put in to the Island of Sheep for water." Another monk plunged in as soon as his brother drew breath. "You've never seen flocks like these. Sheep as big as cattle. Splendid white fleeces on them. The monks say it's because they're never milked. Next to that is an Island we call the Birds' Paradise. Thousands and thousands of them, pouring out from the cliffs after a storm."

"Aye, we caught the tide-race there last year." Another voice broke in. "The current drew us forward and a full southerly gale blew us backward. And all the time the cliffs loomed nearer. We were helpless. So we knelt and prayed in our little craft. And the wind began to veer and slowly we slid past the cliffs."

"Will you ever forget the Island of Smiths?" The monks were reminiscing among themselves now, their audience forgotten.

"Smiths! By the big toe of Abraham! There was nobody there! It was the Island itself that spat fire at us!"

"I'm telling you, I heard the roar of their furnaces and the clang of their hammers."

"Brendan kept trying to steer us away. And no wonder! But the wind blew us towards it."

"High cliffs, as black as coal and as straight as a wall."

The pedlar's mouth was a gaping hole in his face.

"I tell you, I saw wee dark gnomes come out of caves and hurl glowing coals at us. Lumps that left a trail of sparks and made the sea boil and steam. And what a stench!"

"Ach, you had your cowl over your head. What could you see? It was the mountain that flowed fire and the sea that exploded."

"Well, either way it was like sailing into the Gates of Hell. I wasn't the only one that was glad to win clear."

"And when we looked back the whole island was on fire!"

One evening, Caterin remembered Artcois and his sea-monsters that had brought her goose-bumps rising.

"Monsters ye're askin' about? Aye, great black ones." The monk's eyebrows were leaping all over his face.

"Riding the waves, rolling and wallowing and diving under us, day after day, keeping us company, watching us out of evil eyes."

"Blowing fountains of spray at us, Rubbing horny skins against us till we nearly overturned. Gnashing great pointed teeth."

"Whales," said Caterin. There was a sudden silence. "I've seen them stranded on the beach."

"Aye, maybe," admitted one monk grudgingly. "But you haven't seen them loom over you and yourself in a skimpy wee boat."

"I thought they were friendly, just curious to know what kind of animal we were."

"Monsters I still call them. One lash of a fluked tail and we were lost. What if one had come up underneath us, hey?."

Another evening they spoke of the enormous pillar of crystal they had seen.

"Shimmering in the sunlight, it was, blinding us."

"It seemed near enough and yet it took us three days to come up to it."

"Towering above us, brilliant white, covered with a silvery mesh. When we touched it, it was harder than marble."

"Below in the clear water we could see its foundations and it was as bright below as above. Brendan saw a gap and we sailed through it while he took measurements. On a ledge we found curiously shaped pieces that looked like chalices and church plates. That was a sign that God was with us."

"I mind the frozen sea with lumps of ice floating in it, like curds on top of milk."

"With a quality of light that took your breath away." Brendan had joined them. "The setting sun hides itself behind a small hill so that there's no darkness."

"A man could pick lice from his shirt in that light. And then in no time at all the sun's up again."

Each time Brendan appeared, Caterin hoped there would be word from Lasrain.

"Even in these cold lands we found monks who'd sailed from Eirean. They fed and sheltered us."

"Then God sent birds," said Brendan, "little birds, landing on our sails exhausted. And we knew, for sure, there was land to the south-west. Last year, almost at the limit of our endurance, we found the Island of Delights, a wide land full of fruit-bearing trees. Then the great fog swallowed us. This year, if God wills, we'll find the Promised Land."

And that was the night he turned abruptly to Caterin.

"Tomorrow we're taking the craft out on trials from Dingle to St Enda's Island for his blessing. We'll pick you up at Derry and take you to Alba."

A great bubble of happiness swelled in Caterin's breast. It was still there next day when she set off for Devenish with an escort of horsemen. And a warm black cloak gifted by the monks. She glanced back once at the monastery and chuckled. And thanked Bride she had escaped the bath in the bleak river.

It took them four days to cross the bedraggled countryside. There were three days of blustery showers and gusting winds that knifed through the warmest cloak, followed by a day when the air was mild and the warmth of the sun promised that buds could think about swelling and birds about gathering twigs.

A long path led up to the doorway of the monastery at Devenish, lined on either side with a hedge of fuchsia and honeysuckle, not yet in bloom. Through a break in the hedge she saw land sloping down towards a lake. A brown-clad figure stood on the edge, head bowed, hands clasped before him. Yet something about the broad shoulders struck her as familiar.

She was shown at once into Lasrian's chamber where he settled her beside a blazing brazier and talked while she ate.

"In two day's time, there's a ship leaving Derry for Alba." Lasrian paused. "Is this not good news?"

Suddenly, Caterin was unable to say a word. She put down the beaker of water because her throat had thickened and she could not swallow. Having waited so long, now, when the news came, it stunned her. She nodded and, finding that her cheeks were wet, brushed away the tears with her hand.

"There, there, my daughter. Don't mar a happy day with tears. Brendan will take you to the west end of the Great Glen." He caught the question in Caterin's eyes. "Then Bishop Columba himself will escort you to your father's stronghold at Craig Phadric."

Of course, she should have known him! It was Colum Cille she had seen standing like a humble sparrow by the lake.

"The Bishop?" she gasped. Great Princes of the Church who held most of Eirean in the palm of their hands did not make hazardous journeys merely to deliver lost Princesses. Like a blow between the eyes, the realisation hit her that she was being used as a pawn. They were setting a snare for Bridei with herself as bait. His hands would be tied when his daughter's freedom was at stake. "You're going to barter me! What do you hope to gain? I have a right to know."

Lasrain moved to his desk, absently arranging the tied rolls and pages of vellum. He surveyed the result with distaste and sorted them out again. At last he came to a decision and sat. Lacing his fingers neatly together on the polished surface, he raised deep intense eyes to her face.

"You have such a right, as you say. This story is known only to a few. After the Battle at Cul-drebene, the Bishop Colum Cille went walking over the battlefield, comforting the dying and succouring the wounded. For two nights and a day, without food or sleep, he laboured there. He looked on the dead faces of boys who had hardly tasted life. He held men, screaming in agony, to his breast until they died, calling on their children and their wives. He heard them pour out their grief for their loved ones as their life-blood spilled over. He entered that battle field a proud and haughty man. He came away from it, pale and sorrowing and humbled, straight to me, his vestments still stained with blood and vomit. In his agony, he cried out to me that he, not God, had set in motion this terrible massacre. By his prayers, he had maimed and killed just as surely as if he had held a weapon in his hand. He, and only he, had been the cause of this appalling loss of life."

There was a shocked silence between them as he paused, both hearts moved beyond words. Caterin's mind was filled with the memory of the golden, god-like figure blazoned across the skyline.

"Colum Cille feels the word of God within him, telling him that he must make penance for his grievous fault, that he must make remission for his sin, that he must free himself from the blood-guilt. I have advised him to exile himself from Eirean. As penance he must release as many living souls from eternal torment as those whose perdition he has caused."

Most of the words and ideas were unfamiliar to Caterin but she had grasped the significance of it and that stung her mind into alertness. If she had not heard the Bishop Brendan tell of the dilemma that faced the Church, she would not have been aware of all the implications behind this statement. Colum Cille's penance would remove him at just the right moment from all the turmoil between Church and State in Eirean. The sympathy she felt for the suffering Bishop remained but it was tempered by a feeling that this penance was more to do with politics than repentance.

As she undressed for the night in her lodging, another word used by Brendan rang in her ears. He had called her people 'pagans', a word that meant 'rustic folk'. But Brendan had used it to insult those who believed in the Time-honoured Ones. Pay no heed, she told herself, Bridei and Broichan could be as wily as Lasrain and Colum Cille any time of the night or day. The King and his Chief Drui would have been well warned by events in Eirean.

As the night wheeled to morning, sleep eluded her because of the creeping excitement in her veins. From now on, every rising of the Moon would bring her a step nearer her homeland. She was glad Gort would be absent, furthering his ambitions on the battlefield. Would Bridei have changed much? Oh, it would be good to feel the warmth of his arms round her again! And he would find a change in her. A silly innocent girl she had been when she had left Dalgynch. Now he and Broichan would want to know all she had learned. But how would they deal with this White Dove who was coming disguised as a hedge-sparrow?

The stirring of the monks for their early morning offices found her eager and alert and not heavy-eyed as she had expected. By starting before dawn and riding hard they reached the monastery at Derry before nightfall for the days were beginning to lengthen again.

Caterin paid little heed to the moody, silent figure shrouded in brown homespun who rode with them. It was not until they sat at table for food and she looked across into the sunken blue eyes of Colum Cille that she realised that Lasrian had not told half the story.

There was agony in the drowned depths of his eyes and despair in the lines etched on the youthful face. He spoke to no one and, at times, brushed a hand across his eyes as though trying to push away sights that would not leave him in peace. Only twice he roused himself from his inward-looking anguish. Once was when a monk read from a book called 'The Life of Finnian' to those who were sitting round the fire. Colum Cille heard the name of the man who had been his mentor and roused himself from his brooding to listen.

"With great tenderness, he healed the minds and bodies of those who came to him...From a pure heart he loved others...He never slept on a bed but on bare ground with a stone for a pillow...He was kind to others, austere and harsh to himself..." intoned the young monk. Columba nodded, and, as though he had taken the words into himself as good counsel, the lines of sorrow on his face eased and his eyes became calmer. Later, he took a harp from the hand of an unskilful boy and, plucking it, sent out a note that hung on the air with infinite sadness.

"The homeless land of my sojourn, of sadness and grief," Colum Cille sang,

"Alas the voyage that I am to make... For the fault that I went myself

To the battle of Cul Drebene."

His voice resounded in the bare wooden hall that threw back the echoes of his grief and longing.

"I have loved Erin's land,

Its waterfalls, all but its government....

Death is better in reproachless Erin Than everlasting life in Britain."

Caterin wept a little at that and the sighing lament haunted her all night. But the sight of Brendan's ship next morning drove everything else from her mind.

It rode high and proud in the water, bright against a finger of green moorland. It was long and slim with a tapering bow, its stern curving gently upward. It was so beautiful and yet it smelled so foul! Once she was on board she saw the reason. For the leather casing which was stretched over the wooden frame of the ship had been newly greased with sheep-fat!

Brown habits flapped and bare legs flashed. Caterin dodged the curragh that was swung aboard for the journey up the lochs into Alba. How did Brendan and his crew work and sleep and eat in such a cramped space? Colum Cille's twelve disciples lent a hand with the oars. Deep-laden and sluggish, the boat pushed against the swell. Beyond the river-mouth they all went mad again. Caterin was routed from her seat on a coil of rope. Bare brown arms hauled and tied flying ropes. But once the sails were up and billowing in the wind, a calm settled over the ship.

Caterin, sitting with Colum Cille near the bow, gazed up at the two sails, each emblazoned with a red ringed cross. The leather skin muffled the usual slap of wavelets against the hull giving a curious disembodied feeling of being part of the sea's motion. Even the stench of sheep wool grease was tempered now by the salt tang of the sea. The hides that had been sewn together to make the skin of the boat had been greased also to make them waterproof. She studied the fine bone-white strips of ash that curved to follow the line of the boat. They were bound together like a wicker basket and lashed by leather thongs at every joint.

"Heartwood of oak and barkwood of ash," Brendan was telling Colum Cille. "Oak seasoned for ten years is as hard as iron. Trunks of ash, straight in the grain and no boat is more flexible. Oxhides, tanned in a rich liquid of ground oak bark and stitched with patience and skill."

"And if the leather is pierced by a rock?"

"We stick on a patch. A man goes over the side and a needle is passed backwards and forwards through the skin. Sheepskins to sleep on and a fire-cauldron to cook in. A silver medallion under the mainmast and a bottle of St. Enda's holy water tucked in the gunwale at the bow. What more could we ask to do God's will? There's even a bucket wedged under the gunwale for use in rough weather. This journey it's for the Princess's need and the men can hang outboard at the stern and risk a cold slap on the buttocks from a wave."

Colum Cille seemed to have gained a new lease of life since the ship had sailed. He leaned forward at Caterin's side, scanning Alba in the misty distance, although he must have travelled this route many times to Dal Riata.

Caterin strained her eyes for the first clear sight of the coastline. Every screaming gull and diving gannet had taken on a new significance. Every wave sang to her of her kin.

"Princess Caterin," Colum Cille said, acknowledging her presence without removing his eyes from the land, "will your father welcome us monks or not?"

"He'll want to thank you for my return," Caterin told him. He could make of that what he wished. She was very wary of this great Churchman, sensing a piece of the mosaic that was still not yet in place.

"There, ahead of us are the twin peaks of Hinba," Colum Cille went on as though she had not spoken. "When Conal was alive, he gave the island of Hinba to me to found a monastic retreat. I've a longing to lead that simple life again. But not in Hinba. It's become over-populated. Now when I came to consecrate Aedan, we travelled to the Island of Iona. Do you know it?"

"Know it? The Kings of Alba have been buried there since time began. My father graciously allowed the Kings of Dal Riata to use it for their King-making since we've a carved Symbol-Stone at Scone for the purpose. But Io has always been our special place, sacred to our Ancestral Ones and our gods."

"And would the presence of one more God make any difference?"

"It's not the god we object to but the people!"

"Men of God?" It was still the same resonant voice that had rung out in the Council Hall of Tara but without the note of arrogance. He spoke humbly, as though confiding in her alone. "I want to retreat there to compose a hymn asking God for forgiveness. We'll see Iona soon. Before we sail through the Strait of Muile, Brendan is going to circle the island. They say it floats on top of the sea and that the light there is more pure and clear than anywhere else in the world."

It was Caterin's first sight of Io. As they approached it from the south she could just make it out, seemingly tucked in at the foot of the sloping mountains of Muile. Against the background of the dark, bare hillsides it began to stand out as a green, pleasant island with translucent, blue waves frothing gently on sand as white as the cockle-shells from which it had been ground. It had an aura of enchantment for Caterin. Come and be at peace, it seemed to say.

"An emerald, fringed in ivory, set in a turquoise sea. Remote and yet not too remote. That's where I wish to make my peace with God, dwelling apart from humanity and all its striving for wealth and power."

"Yet, not cut off entirely." Diormit, Colum Cille's attendant, had come to lean beside them. "It's just a shout across the water to Muile for supplies. We'll need of wattles for building and we'll need food in the beginning. Later I could build us a new curragh with a removable mast and a lug-sail. So, until we can grow our own food, we'll not starve. And see, there are seals on the south end. This Iona is better placed on the sea-route than Hinba for sending monks on missions, is it not?" The last piece of the mosaic fell into place for Caterin. Colum Cille was looking straight at her. Her heart pounded as she heard his next words.

"Will your father give me the holy island of Io in return for his beloved daughter?"

The joy of her homecoming vanished. She knew then that she had failed in all she had set out to do. She had forgotten that these Eireans were the same Scots who had killed the Druad and Derelei, the same Scots who had attacked her homeland, the same Scots who would come at the Pretani again and again for land and cattle. Even these Churchmen, like Lasrian who had seemed kindly, like Colum Cille who had wept for his folly, were not to be trusted. She had come to Eirean to learn how to keep the White Dove outside their borders. She had been beguiled by cunning and cruel men. And she had let them use her.

She had come seeking knowledge. And the knowledge she had won had saddened her. For Veleda's White Dove had wings of silver and feathers of burnished gold. And he hunted like a hawk.

She had learned too, that people, great and small, good and evil, would always seek to use her for their advantage. It was her destiny to have to look into every new face and wonder what each person hoped to gain.

"Bridei hasn't the power to grant your request," she said. "Only Broichan and he'll never allow it."

"Not even if I decree that it will remain a holy Island for ever?"

"For ever? But which of the Gods will inhabit it? Yours or ours? And which of our two Peoples will be remembered there? The Pretani or the Scots?"

She had persuaded herself that she was a tool of the Splendid Ones chosen to uphold the tradition. She had thought that the Truth of the Ancient Ones would stand firm against this upstart Faith.

Across the sea came the sweet sad song of the seals. And a great desolation filled her heart.

CHAPTER TWENTY SEVEN

Now, Brendan turned the ship up the Firth of Loarn and Io was hidden behind Muile. Brendan's own red Irish cross on his sails was enough of a signal to let them pass the fire-blackened Dun at Ollaig unchallenged.

A freshening wind brought them swiftly into Loch Linnhe. Used to the gentler hills of the east coast, Caterin found her eyes constantly drawn to the grandeur of the slopes on either side. The very height of the mountains wholly altered her perception of distance. Homesteads, trees, sheep in the narrow belt of farmland seemed surprisingly tiny, until she realised how far away they were and she had to blink and look at the scene with new eyes. Only then did she understand how deep were the tree-lined gorges that gouged the hillsides.

To the south over a ridge of mountains, the snowy plateau of Nevis towered, rosy in the early evening light against the pale blue sky. Its majesty sent such a shock of happiness through her that she almost wept. It was a fitting place for Bride to dwell during the Snow Season, awaiting her rescuer, Aengus of the Milk-White Steed, who would drift in on the silver tide of the Atlantic. As the sun sank, the nearer mountains lit up with an incandescant pink glow. In the distance, range after range of blue mountains looked like shapes cut out of cloth and laid one against the other. And then, straight in front of them, a huge segment was cut out of the sky-line that showed where the Great Glen lay.

Where the Loch narrowed, Brendan brought his craft into a sheltered inlet. The sails were furled and stowed before they paddled ashore. A young monk called Drostan carried Caterin ceremoniously over the splashing waves and deposited her gently on her feet on the sweet sand of Alba. It mattered little to her that the countryside was peopled by Scots. The borders had never been too clear in the north.

The women of the village lilted a song as they gutted and salted an unusually heavy catch of fish. The men swung their nets on poles between the houses to be dried and mended. The ringed cross had been sighted from afar and food and tents were ready.

It was no use trying to sleep. Between the gladness in her heart and the blue light that lingered in the dome of the sky, she succumbed to the temptation to sit on a rock in the cool air, drinking in peace. A hunting owl hooted. The scent of peat-smoke lingered in the air. And for a little while she longed for no other life than to live in a humble cell with a loch at her front door and a mountain at the back.

Where the sun had disappeared, the sky was rose-pink, changing to speedwell blue overhead, and deepening to violet where the Moon Maiden, at her fullest, cast her spell over the mountains and the pines.

During the night the weather changed and rain bounced off her shelter. In the morning tendrils of mist curled and floated across the summits leaving patches of blue sky.

Four monks crawled under the curragh and crouched. At a command, they straightened smartly and the curragh moved along the path like a shiny black beetle. They followed the trail along the river bank, Drostan and Rus carrying the paddles.

Every step on the springy turf was a joy to Caterin. Farming people, locked in the slow rhythm of the seasons, watched them pass and returned the radiant smile of the girl with the honey-gold hair. The very air seemed to taste differently on her tongue.

The wild and lavish beauty of the land stunned her senses. The dark, rugged outlines of the high rocky landscape stirred primitive emotions in the depths of her being. The beginning of the Budding Season was no time to look for colour on the mountains, yet each turn in their path revealed a vista that changed subtly in colour and contour. Streams, swollen by melting snow, tumbled across their path. Waterfalls had appeared overnight, cascading down the mountain-sides. Indomitable highlanders, as poor and rugged as the rocks around them, climbed the craggy slopes straight-backed and silent. And the interminable call of the cuckoo, resounding from the mountains, followed her all the way.

To her surprise, Caterin found Colum Cille an exhilerating companion who knew the name of every bird. When they ate he always sat apart. Once Caterin joined him and they watched for birds together. A wheat-ear streaked across in front of them flirting his white tail-feathers. With a flash of his long neck a heron speared a fish and lifted his huge body on splendidly marked wings. They heard the shrill twitter of a pair of sand-pipers but almost missed seeing them, so quick was their flight.

"I'm proud to be known as the Dove of Peace," said Columba softly. "I've loved watching birds since I was a boy. Look!"

A tiny tree-creeper, spiralling his way up a tree-trunk in fits and starts, had paused to eye them suspiciously, his beak crammed full of insects.

"See, I've birds carved on my reliquary."

He showed her the box he had carried with him all the way. It was shaped like an oratory and decorated with gold and silver birds.

"But I thought..." Caterin paused.

"You thought that birds were pagan symbols and that the Church would despise them. Yet we love all God's creatures."

"In Tara you were decked out in gorgeous vestments and jewels," Caterin began softly. "You say that your God lives in buildings and you furnish them with gold and silver. Who do you glorify? This God who delights in riches? Or yourselves?"

She saw that Columba was giving her all his attention and went on, pouring out all the thoughts she had had during her stay in Eirean.

"We've treasure in my land but it's for the benefit of the people and no one goes hungry. The Great Spirit who dwells within and around us all and whose power reaches far beyond the skies has created a House for itself to dwell in. And the House has more treasures in it than all your monasteries. And the treasure is more beautiful. That House is the Mother Earth. We share that House along with the Guardian Ones who guide and care for us. Now you must see why I can't allow you to come to my land. You with your royal power and your armed force. For I'm afraid that we'll lose all that's most precious to us."

Columba nodded and pulled at the lobe of his ear.

"Yet it's a simple faith that I would bring now." He took the plain wooden cross that hung at his girdle into his hands and showed it to her. "I haven't come here with gem-encrusted raiment. You see, I've no wish to destroy the ancient lore. It's part of the fabric of the race and its loss would render the people helpless in the face of evil."

There was a truth there that Caterin wanted to cling to. She had not expected him to have any insight into the needs of ordinary folk.

When he rose he raised his arms in a blessing on the land. But

Caterin could only remember him as the golden symbol that had heralded the downfall of the High King at Cul Drebene. And then the blessing became a muscle-wrenching stretch and a yawn and they were off on their journey again.

Where the river broadened into Loch Lochy, the monks made their way to a jetty. They lowered the boat, turned it right side up, waited for the next wave and then swirled it afloat.

"Take care not to put your foot through the skin," warned Rus. Once they had arranged themselves seven to a side, they dared not move for balance was critical. But once the rhythm of the paddles had been established, the curragh flew over the steady rolling eddies, feather-light, skimming the surface like a dragon-fly.

They spent the night where the stream ran into Loch Oich, in a shed used occasionally by fisher-folk and smelling, not unpleasantly, of cured fish. Across the stream the walls of houses rose among bare fields.

As they wrapped themselves for sleep, Caterin became aware that Colum Cille was on edge. He paced the floor and, each time he passed the window, he lifted the skin and peered outside. Not long after the monks had fallen into their first sleep, she was roused by him shaking Diormit's shoulder.

"Where's the boat?" he asked.

"In a boat-shed down on the loch-side. I wasn't going to leave it for the Cenel Gabrain to find. I wouldn't trust them to respect our monks' robes."

Colum Cille paced two more rounds of the hut floor.

"Go out now! Quickly! Bring our boat and hide it in the bushes at the back!" The monks rose, startled, none more so than Diormit, but ran to obey without question.

During the night, Caterin, finding sleep hard to come by, awoke to see Colum Cille gazing from the window again and she could have sworn that his face was reddened by the flicker of flames. The following morning, after they had recited their psalms, the monks again shouldered their boat. Down near the water, they came upon the burnt remains of the shed where their boat had been housed. Caterin stared at him, wondering. Could it be that he had the Sight? Was he a Wise One, after all?

Colum Cille, looking eastwards, paused in his stride and the agony returned to his eyes. The hamlet in the desolate fields was a smoking, blackened ruin. Had he been forewarned of raiders and left the villagers to their fate? The unspoken question was there in all their minds as they looked on the devastation. Colum Cille, himself, was the first to rush forward to search among the debris. But they found no bodies, no pots, no scraps of cloth. Diormit raised a beaming face to his master.

"These huts were deserted. The raiders fired the thatches out of frustration."

And the singing of the monks rang out as they paddled. Colum Cille's foreknowledge, if that was what it was, had not betrayed him.

When the curragh was halfway along the Loch of Ness, the rich voice of Colum Cille sounded over the gurgle and hiss of windswept water.

"We are nearing the border of your homeland, Princess Caterin." She twisted round to study him where he sat slightly behind her, one arm leaning on the padded framework. His grey eyes had lost their haunted look. Contact with the power of the All-Mother had brought him some form of healing. Or was it the confrontation ahead that had stirred him into animation?

"Do you still intend to barter me for our island of Io?"

The serene gaze showed no desire to avoid hers.

"Indeed, I do. And I'm asking for your royal word that you'll not attempt to escape while we negotiate a safe-conduct."

Caterin gave him a sardonic smile. "And if I don't give it?"

"In that case, when we land, I'll put you to the indignity of being tied up. I'd rather be able to trust to your word."

"I'm the Princess of the Pretani," she told him, "and I will not be bound."

It was a charming smile that Colum Cille gave her then. Not for the first time, she was aware of the vibrant power that radiated from him, that drew men to follow him and women to learn from his teachings. Curling brown hair sprang up from his lofty shaven brow to frame his face. The fresh air had brought back a healthy ruddiness to his skin. He was a handsome man who would have fitted the role of both warrior and lover and would have rivalled Diarmait for comeliness at the table of the High King of Tara. His hand, trailing lazily in the creamy wake was not that of a recluse like Liasrain who had pale, long-boned fingers, but was brown, firm and capable.

Her glance sped down the double line of men who fought with

their paddles against the mischievous, southerly breeze that teased at their frail craft. With each controlled stroke, their wide sleeves slid back to reveal strong, forceful arms and the weave of their habits stretched tight over the rippling muscles of their backs. She would never understand why the monks foreswore the love of women and the ultimate fulfilment of their healthy, virile bodies.

"There it is! The homestead at Airchartdan!" Drostan pointed and the boat swerved for the shore. "This is the last dwelling belonging to our kin-folk before the borders of Bridei's land. These people have suffered much at the hands of the Pretani." The grim note of warning in his voice was not lost on Caterin.

Leather-jerkined figures appeared on the shore, sending across the water repeated cries of welcome that hushed to an awed silence when they saw that no less a personage than the Bishop Colum Cille had answered their plea for a visiting priest to baptise and bless.

With Colum Cille going about his duties in the farmstead up on the hillside and the monks busily erecting a shelter on the grassy verge, Caterin scanned the view up Loch Ness for any sign that her own people were aware of her presence.

This was the great cleft that split Alba in two. In the grey, waning light, it was a scene of mystery as though the Ever-Living Ones hovered in the heavy air. The purple hills stared stolidly at their reflections in the loch, its pale surface furrowed here and there by waving lines that hinted at uncanny movement within its dark depths.

But there was no sign of habitation in the unruly, abandoned landscape. No newly ploughed earth broke the massed expanses of trees. No grey walls rose from among the rocks and crags. Yet, even if the farmers preferred the more fertile lands to the east, Bridei was sure to have outposts on the very water-way that had smoothed the journey of the monks from the west. Alert eyes hidden in heather would have followed their passage from the moment of landing. Lights would have flashed the signal from peak to outpost to Craig Phadric.

From now on, she was within her own boundaries. And it was the Bishop himself who was in enemy territory.

CHAPTER TWENTY EIGHT

In the pink light of dawn, Colum Cille chose three of his disciples as emissaries to the King, along with three armed men brought from the farmstead.

"In the name of the one true God, the Bishop Columba greets the King of the Pretani, Bridei Mac Maelgwn." The musical cadences rose and fell. In the grey, cloudless gaze and on the smooth brow there lay no shadow of doubt that his mission would be welcomed. "Columba brings greetings from the great Bishops of Eirean together with the commendations of Ceolfrid, Abbot of Monkwearmouth and Jarrow. Don't forget that last name for Bridei owes him a debt of honour. Bishop Columba waits on King Bridei's borders for a safe-conduct to his court at Craig Phadric. That will do. You needn't worry about an interpreter. Broichan, the Chief Druid, has enough of our Goidelic to translate." The skin over his shapely cheek-bones and strong jaw tightened. "Besides, Bridei will be well aware that we're here and that we have his daughter. God go with you."

For the rest of that long day, Caterin faced the fact that Io was the ancient resting-place of her ancestors. It was entirely possible that Broichan would consider it beyond price, too precious to be exchanged for a Vacomagie woman, however royal. A woman could be replaced. Io was unique.

Pacing the beach, she ground the pebbles under her restless feet and bit on a thumb-nail, forcing herself to wait with patience until the formalities were complete.

Colum Cille and Diormit walked westward to where the beach disappeared and the land rose steeply from the peat-brown water. Caterin turned in time to see a sudden swirl of foam and a revolving darkness that resolved into a waving head and a coiling body before it slid below the water. Diormit came running, his eyes a blaze of glory.

"A miracle!" he cried. "A monstrous beast was basking on the land when we turned the corner. Before I could escape it had my leg between its jaws. Then it met the eyes of my Bishop! And quailed before the power in them! And released me and slunk away!"

"A panic-stricken eel, I think." A brief smile pulled at Colum

Cille's mouth. But the monks would have none of it and Diormit had to retell the story again and again.

At last, when the sun had long past its zenith, a sail appeared far to the north, floating on the shining strip of the loch. Shading her eyes, Caterin saw the crimson Pretani pennant running fluid from the mast and knew it was a galley of the King's flotilla based on the Loch.

No flourish of ensigns decorated the yardarms, no gilded garlands swept the flanks, no trumpets sang a salute. In the prow of the ship, high above the lines of slow-sweeping oars, stood a figure with a score of warriors at his back. The blinding sun, her blowing hair and her leaping imagination combined to form a vision of Bridei until she drew her hand across her straining eyes. Neither was it the tall, half-desired presence of Gort. It was Uurad, pale and solemn, only his eyes moving, devouring her to make sure that she was unharmed. There was no message that she could read in his empty face. As the ship idled in the shallows and the rowers balanced it with their oars, Uurad shifted his gaze to counter that of the Bishop.

"Bridei mac Maelgwn, King of the Pretani, Overlord of Alba greets the Bishop Colum Cille. May your sojourn in his land be long and pleasant. I have the honour to escort your party to Craig Phadric." The flat, unemotional voice stopped but the air was filled with words unsaid.

"There is more?" prompted Colum Cille, grimly aware of the lack of welcome in the formal phrases.

"Not from the mouth of King Bridei. But I, myself, ask you to permit your hostage, the Princess, to enter her homeland in a ship of her kin, knowing that Bridei is an honourable man and will treat for her as though she was still in your hands."

It was a bold try and clever, because, when Colum Cille refused, as he must and did, he was implying a denial of Bridei's trustworthiness.

"It will be a pleasure to meet this wily King." Colum Cille, smiling ironically as though relishing the forthcoming clash of wills, motioned Caterin into the stern of the curragh. It took some determination to keep her haughty bearing in the rocking boat but she achieved it. Uurad's words persuaded her that Bridei was treading a careful path. He was not welcoming the monk with open arms as the saviour of his daughter. Nor was he treating

Colum Cille as the representative of the Kings and Bishops who now ruled supreme in north Eirean. Nevertheless, he was smoothing the way for the Bishop to enter his Kingdom. Bridei may have defeated the Dal Riatans and may be able to hold them firmly within the boundaries he had set. Yet, not surprisingly, he drew the line at tangling with the full might of the Ui Neill whose resources of men and materials far exceeded his own.

At the head of the Loch the monks disembarked and made camp while Uurad's soldiers formed a semi-circle around them. In the fading light, Caterin searched the landscape to the north until she could make out grey ramparts snaking round the flat summit that was Craig Phadric. It would be all of four miles away, she guessed. Easy enough now for Uurad to kill the monks and rescue her but both she and Bridei had given their word. One false move and the Pretani name would be blackened from here to Rome and beyond.

It was a strange procession that wound northwards on foot in the dewy dawn. The sight of a band of brown-habited men surrounded by soldiers should have drawn the countryfolk from miles around to stare. And Uurad could have commandeered horses for their journey. The fact that he did not and that he led them, not by the busy river bank, but by secluded woodland paths, meant that the visit was being conducted with the utmost secrecy.

At the foot of the crag, Uurad called a halt.

"My orders were to escort you to this point and no further. My soldiers will continue to guard you but you must make your own approach from now on." Smartly, so that he could not be questioned further, he arranged his men around the monks in such a way that their only exit was towards the roadway that wound upwards round the steep rock.

Presumably, the gateway to the fortress lay on the opposite side for, when the awed monks raised their eyes and arched their necks, the climbing rock-face rose towards the sky and was continued upwards by sheer, inward-sloping walls, unbroken and forbidding.

"A formidable fortress indeed," commented Drostan, rubbing his aching neck.

"You know what this means, don't you?" Diormit's sandals squeaked on the moist grass as he swirled angrily to face his Bishop. "It's a calculated insult by the King to your high rank both as a Prince of the Ui Neill and as a Bishop of the Church." Caterin looked on this small wiry man with new eyes. Until now, she had thought him a servant. Now, she saw him as a monk who had made it his duty to give service to his Bishop and, as such, he had the right to put forward his opinions.

Columba shook his head.

"It was to be expected. I come as a simple monk, not as an emissary of Kings."

"Ah, 'twill be a long weary climb up that cliff," put in a dry voice.

"Then we must lose no time." Colum Cille set out briskly, his habit flapping about his bare ankles. But Caterin was there climbing before him, her eyes alight with anticipation. The monks shouldered their burdens and followed. Diormit ran with a staff to his leader who refused it, laughing as he strode forward.

In the end, there was no meeting of leaders of men. When, panting and puffing, they reached the great double gates, the monks found them firmly shut before their faces. Diormit strode forward and pounded furiously on the thick timber planks. The hammering of his staff sounded pitifully weak in the silence.

Caterin, bewildered, heard the steady pacing of sentries on the wooden walkway and the grounding of their spears as they turned to retrace their steps. Not a helmeted head looked over the wall. Someone inside, was grinding metal with an insistent, inconsiderate rasp. Incredibly, the smell of frying pork hung in the air.

Caterin lingered in the shade of a clump of trees. On either side of the gateway, two immense square guard towers jutted out with a line of narrow apertures just an arms' length from the top. There was no movement within these dark shapes to catch her eye but she had no doubt that she had been seen and recognised. She gave the sign of Bride to let the watchers know that she was well and would wait patiently until the game was played out. For Bridei was playing with Colum Cille. Of that she was sure.

"Barbaric blackguards!" Diormit spat the words, his cheeks mottled with rage. "Ignorant heathens! Don't they know who they're dealing with?" demanded a monk with a face as knobbly as an oak tree branch. "My lord, let us inform them that you can command the armies of the four Kings of Eirean to avenge this humiliation."

How would the newly-humbled monk deal with this situation,

Caterin wondered. Could he put behind him the habitual authority of a man born into rank and wealth and yet meet this challenge with dignity?

Head thrown back, Colum Cille stood gazing upwards at the crimson gates where the Royal Bull was emblazoned across each one in black, outlined in silver. And not just outlined, for each powerful sinew was highlighted so that the huge animals lived and breathed, snorting and pawing the ground. A lesser man would have been diminished, overpowered by the very size and virility of the beasts. Instead, Colum Cille faced them with cool detachment, defying them with all the force of his noble personality.

"I have come to this land as a man of peace." The deep, melodious voice floated in the breeze to the top of the wall and beyond. "I have come to bring brotherly love and the sweet blessings of the angels. Never again shall I seek to gain power by the use of arms for this policy is a two-edged weapon, as I have found. Indeed, I have a deadlier weapon to use. The Princess Caterin is the Holy Sword that will split wide open the gates of the pagan King." The echoes of his plummy measured tones resounded off the walls and died in the air.

At that Caterin rose and walked to Colum Cille, her cloak billowing, her anger boiling.

"To the Devil with your Holy Sword," she cried, echoing an oath she had heard in Tara. "You fooled me with your tears and your humility! You care nothing for people, you only use them! You plot and scheme like any politician! And you'll use the Church to spread your own power across the land! You'll sacrifice us all for your ambition! Then, let me tell you, I'll wait here for ever if my father wills it. But your camp below is ringed with guards! And your time is short."

The face Colum Cille turned on her was as bland and innocent as it had been in Tara.

"Yet, my daughter, the decision is no longer in the King's hands. Bridei has kept his word but this is Broichan who bars our way. It is to be a confrontation between the pagan Druid and the White Christ. Come, brothers, let us pray for the souls of those within that they may find the true God and come to know the saints."

Which they did for the rest of the day, fasting, kneeling on the velvet grass. Only Caterin stood, her body numbed by disappointment, feeling that only her eyes were left alive as they searched for a sign, any infinitesimal sign from the fortress. At one point, she thought she saw the daylight reflect back from a pale face that could have belonged to her father within one of the long apertures but, in a blink of an eye, the shadows showed black once more. That night, around the fire at the foot of the crag, the monks were loud in their condemnation.

"If they saw their Princess lashed to a tree, they'd open the gates soon enough." It was the youngest of the monks, scratching secretly at a blister under his sandal strap.

"Hush, brother, we'll not win souls by holding a knife at a woman's throat."

"But Lasrian sent us to redeem the Picts from their wicked ways. And he would agree that the end justifies the means."

Colum Cille had sat silent. Now he unclasped his hands and lifted a branch to turn over a half-burnt peat.

"For the saving of souls, I'm ready to suffer in all things. But neither you nor I have the right to cause suffering to another for the advancement of our cause. If we but gain the island of Iona from which our mission to the pagans can begin, the greater will be our glory in the sight of the Lord."

Later, Caterin, seeking privacy in a clump of trees before she bedded down, heard a hoarse voice cry out. And she saw the shadow of Colum Cille kneeling, writhing with the anguish of his spirit. By his words, it was his own soul that he felt was in mortal danger.

"Sanctuary," the great man was pleading. "A soum of land where I can find my own salvation. You cannot send me to free others from the burden of their sins. Not until I have freed my own soul!"

And Caterin swept through the bushes past him caring nothing for his trouble.

"May the Lord smite the pagan Broichan," hissed Diormit the next day after they had again climbed the steep pathway and were drawn up before the implacable gateway. The doors remained fast, immovable.

"'Twill take a miracle to open these heathen gates."

"Even the great Water-Kelpie in Ness looked on our Bishop's face and turned tail before his power."

Caterin knew they were appealing to the Bishop for another

Cul Drebene, another prayer for victory, another glorious vision of Colum Cille in the form of a cross flaring across the sky.

Colum Cille stood before the towering structure, a patient presence, his feet sunk deep in the dew-spangled grass. Caterin thought she had never seen him look so splendid. Grace, intelligence and strength flowed through his bearing and played on his face. Fingers interlaced in front of his habit, his penetrating grey eyes scanned the walls. And then she saw where he was gazing.

The pale sun, sparkling on the crystals in the stonework, slanted on a fall of silver hair and beard in the shadows of an aperture far to the left. And Caterin rose to her feet. The Arch-Drui was taking the measure of his adversary. And it was as though some silent communication was flowing between the two men.

Broichan leaned his finger-tips on the cold sill of the window. From this high tower the still brown figure of Colum Cille stood out sharply against the sparkling green sward. There stood a younger and more virile version of the man he had once been. Broichan sighed. This man was indeed a danger, for integrity radiated from him. The old man had heard the story of Cul Drebene but he, more than most, knew that mysteries came about as much by foresight, good timing and luck as by supernatural means. Knowledge of the elements and the fears of the ignorant were tools he used himself. Not that the gods would have permitted him to become too powerful. But a suggestion of the supernatural often allowed the greatest good to prevail.

What exquisitely subtle plot had Colum Cille devised now, that he appeared here lacking his rich vestments and clad merely in a humble homespun habit, that differed only in colour from Broichan's own robes? It had been reported that the Bishop had repented of his prayer at Cul Drebene but repentance held no meaning for the Drui. Colum Cille had performed the correct ritual and spoken the incantation and his god had shown favour towards him.

Broichan became aware of the steady pacing of Bridei in the guard-room at his back and of the slight hesitations when it seemed the King might come through to speak to him. A powerful King, a gift from the Mighty Ones to the Pretani but a foreigner for all that. He did not feel the strength of the ties that bound the people to the Isle where the bones of their Kings lay under their cairns. The bones of an ancestor stamped the land as belonging to his descendents. When it came Bridei's time to die he had asked that his corpse would shine white in his father's land. Yet, Bridei had been astute enough to veil his eyes and press his lips together when Broichan had ordered the barring of the gate. For Bridei knew how the demands of the Bishops might multiply like flies in a bowl of yesterday's tripes if even this one request was granted.

When the first message had come from Eirean that the Princess could be exchanged for Io, Bridei had stormed at Broichan in a voice as brittle as glass. "What do I care for an island that lies in the centre of Dal Riata and cannot be defended? Let it remain a holy place that will attract whatever gods are called to it. Grant it to the Bishop on condition that he tends the mounds of the Kings and keeps them free from weeds and other despoilers. Broichan, I want my daughter back!"

"You want me to respect your love for your daughter," Broichan had replied. "Yet, you have no respect for the feelings of our people. It's unbearable to us to think of dirty Scots feet scrambling over our holy ground and urinating in our sacred soil. Io is the most beautiful burial ground in the world. The Ancestral Ones will take a devastating revenge if we allow it to be desecrated."

"Arch-Drui, if he wants the island for meditation, what better place?" Bridei's trained soldier's hands had gripped the thin arms of the old man cruelly, confronting him, but the Drui had allowed no spasm of pain to cross his face. "He's better there than creating a nuisance within our boundaries. Even if he uses it as a stepping-stone for launching monks into Alba, what harm is there? There have been missions before and a spate of public conversions but the same people are feasting at the next festival alongside the rest of the community. I'd stake my life on it that for every hundred people who kiss his dusty feet, ninety-nine will leap through the next Beltane fire."

"That's what the Druad of Eirean thought." Broichan's icy eyes had bored into Bridei's hot ones till he loosed his grip and turned away, opening and closing his fists. "And they were right! The people still protect their persons with iron and their homes with mistletoe. But now the Druad languish in their groves while the Bishops decorate the dwellings of their god with gold. Is that what you want? To welcome the Bishops with open arms? Then what will happen when they threaten to take over the state and bring about another Cul Drebene? May the Great Ones preserve the Pretani from such a fate!"

Bridei had drawn in his breath twice and let it out without speaking before turning on his heel and leaving the presence of his Drui.

And that night Broichan had slipped out of the fort and had gone to the well at Corrimony among the cairns of the Ancestors. And he had sat with an ash tree on one side and a hazel on the other. And he had looked into the black water and opened his mind. And while his head reeled and pounded he had seen a young girl feeding a flock of white doves. And the Mounds of the Kings were levelled and their shields had gone from the Tree. And he had cried out, "Pretani! Pretani!" and the girl had shaken her head at him, puzzled, and went on feeding the doves.

There had been a rain-storm during the night. As Caterin turned at the top of the slippery path, a refreshed and revitalised land stretched outward from under her feet and she was overcome with an unutterable sadness. With the bright morning sun drenching the colour from the landscape it was a world of light and shade, as if an artist had laid out a pale, gleaming calf-skin and sketched in ink with a bold, flowing quill. Sharp black shadows streaked across sparkling meadows. Curving contours incised themselves darkly against the bright sky. Dramatic charcoal lines scored the dazzling sweep of water. After the first impact, the sight of such beauty set up a clamour of yearning in her blood to be at peace in the land to which she belonged. Every swoop of bird-flight and wayward skein of cloud tugged at her heartstrings. Her longing for her father and her home overcame her. Tears began to trickle down her cheeks in a steady stream that would not stop.

At their third sight of the familiar, barred doors, the monks retreated into an uneasy, muttering cordon around Caterin, leaving Colum Cille to walk forward alone.

From his hidden eyrie at the top of the tower, Broichan saw the tears that left a trail down the dusty cloak of the Princess. Long ago, when he had been a young lusty Drui, the Ones had granted him the joy of loving a woman with all the depths of his spirit. Together they had made a daughter whose beauty and gentleness had been his delight. One day, when the girl had been almost grown, he had ridden over the flower-strewn hill to find two bloody lumps of flesh impaled upright on the stakes that edged their plot of ground.

247

It had been his faith that had saved him from going mad. If he had not believed that his two loved ones would live again on earth in another incarnation, he would have lost his reason. If he had not clutched that truth to his heart, he would have thrust into his breast the bloody stakes that held all that was left of his rosy-cheeked women.

In the days that followed, while he had gathered and washed their remaining pieces with tender care, he had called upon the Ones from the anguish of his spirit to give him a sign that his faith was justified. Half-crazed, he had looked in the face of every new-born babe, finding no likeness, no fleeting expression he could recognise; until his mind gradually took hold on his emotions and calmed him.

Since then the Ones had forced him to look upon death from war and plague, from drowning and burning. Until the day he had admitted that there was no sense to suffering, especially that of innocent children, unless life was a learning experience and an ever-repeating event. Bridei and the Princess would have to learn that lesson, too.

Yet, often when he lay, longing for sleep in some bleak dawn, he imagined the agony of his women. Repeated rape by drunken, bestial men, the torment of grinding, mutilating knife-thrusts, the exquisite torture of a slow, agonising death.

The snap of his ash-wand in his clenched fists brought him back to the present.

It was at that moment that Caterin found she could bear this mockery no longer. With a gesture that rose like a wordless cry to the cold grey stones, she threw off her cloak and launched herself forward before the monks could bar her way. Her yearning arms reaching for the entrance, she flung herself full length on the glittering lawn. Her pale robe, darkened with sweat and mud, swathed her despairing flesh. Like a long, shining sword-blade, pointing towards the great doors, she lay, her body racked with sobs. Colum Cille stayed the startled monks with a wide-flung arm. He raised his eyes to where the superb silver mane of Broichan poured over the sill.

The monks saw only Caterin, lying arrow-straight, aimed at the gates like an extension of Colum Cille's outflung arm. A dark line split the wood and widened. Without a sound, the massive doors swung open, slowly, magically. The Black Bulls retreated. A cheer broke from the disciples as they stored in their memories another miracle to be poured into the ears of his historian.

Only Colum Cille saw the compassion that blazed from Broichan's eyes as he gazed on the daughter of his King. Only Colum Cille had seen the white hand rise and signal to the keepers of the gate.

CHAPTER TWENTY NINE

Caterin was doing a fair imitation of Gustav Saw-Tooth making his praise-gift to the High King. Bridei chuckled as she lurched and lisped. Her women shrieked as she became Diarmait.

"Gods of my fathers! Get this cumal out of my Kingdom!"

And there, his eyes probing between the bobbing heads of her women, stood Gort. All at once the room blazed into radiance. And she knew her mouth, her skin, her heart had been waiting for this moment.

His name had not been spoken while Amis, snuffling like a mother rabbit had cleansed and perfumed every cranny of Caterin's body. Not once had Iogena babbled about him while she combed the short curls, a milky boy tied on her back. Devana, arriving with ravaged eyes in a pale thin face, brought only the news that Cennalath had been killed at Dun Durn. Even Bridei, filling her room with his presence, had given her no clue. She had assumed that Gort was still fighting the Angles.

But when her eyes sought for him again, he was gone. She stifled the cry of longing that sprang to her lips. She bit down on her overwhelming desire to run after him and throw her arms around him. Love must not weaken her resolve again. The Black Bull Queen had come home. The time for laughter was over. She cleared the room of all but her father.

The battle had taken its toll on him. She held the claw-like hands and when he winced she let him withdrew them. The planes of his cheeks and jaws had sagged into old age.

"I hear that Colum Cille is still camping down there at the foot of the crag."

"From all I'd heard of the man," Bridei told her, "I expected him to come storming up the Loch, towing you behind him by the hair, forcing a confrontation of magic that would turn our land into a bloody battleground. Instead he and Broichan go fishing, can you believe it? They've neatly side-stepped the fact that they have different gods, and they meditate side by side on the banks of the river."

"I thought Broichan, at least, would see through his false humility," Caterin cried.

"D'you know how they greeted one another? Broichan said, 'I

could have made the winds unfavourable to your voyage. I could have caused a great darkness to envelop you in its shade.' Colum Cille said, 'I heard that your weather-magic was powerful. Can you bring us the right weather for catching salmon?'" Bridei, sitting, when once he would have paced as he talked, chuckled and was clearly pleased with himself.

"Don't trust him! He's tricked us already and we've lost the Isle of Io for ever." There was something fatefully easy about the way it had ended.

"Not at all. The Pretani Kings will still be buried there. The Bishop has promised to maintain it as a holy Place. And, more important, it'll contain him and keep him out of our hair."

"Don't believe that! He'll send missions from there to found monasteries throughout Alba."

"That might have some advantages."

Before Caterin could reply she caught a glimpse of a half-wink and a tongue in his cheek.

"Listen, people don't throw out their hearth-gods with their ashes, despite all the laying on of hands. But there are some clever young men in Colum's Cille's train. We could use them."

"Broichan won't allow them to work within the Kingdom." Even as she spoke she was thinking that at last her father was treating her like an adult.

"He'll be forced to consider it! In my opinion the Pretani have been isolated for far too long. The North Sea has been filled with raiders. They've been a barrier to traders and travellers bringing in new ideas. Eirean, on the other hand, because of its position, has had access to the philosophies of other societies. It might be a good idea to open the gates to some of these monks, don't you think?"

"And the draught that comes in will sweep our heritage into the corners with the dust!"

"And blow the cobwebs away!"

"Cobwebs?" Caterin spoke quickly and eagerly. "One thing I've learned. That I don't want to live under the laws that prevail outside our land. Our Laws are just. They were made by the people for the people. No matter what you decide now, when I'm Queen I'll make sure these laws survive!"

"What about the law of a foreign Kingship?"

Caterin met his crafty twinkle with a laugh. But her eyes were on his pain-ridden hands.

"Now I realise that it can boost the power of the native Queenship. It all depends on the quality of the Queen."

Bridei paused with the words 'Good lass' unspoken on his lips. His daughter was no chit of a girl to be patronised now. She had become a young Queen, hedged with dignity, her brow ringed with purpose.

"Yet think on this! There's a young monk called Drostan who looks to have a lively turn of mind. A foster-son of Colum Cille, I believe. He's been in Kells writing the histories of the Kings of Eirean. That seems to me a very useful employment."

"And you want your praises told in a Book," Caterin teased. Once she had dreamed of her name in a bard-song. But during her efforts to survive she had grown wiser and found that fame mattered little. "The Druad keep a Calendar of Events."

"It's nothing but a list of Kings and their battles. Bones with no meat on them. The succulent stuff is kept in their memories. And in the Attecottie tongue at that. What if the plague came north and wiped out all the memories? Even the bards' heads are not immune from a raider's axe-blow."

"You have a point," she conceded.

Bridei stroked his beard. "There's a small plot of land at Kilrymont. The clan has moved and it's come into the Royal Holding. I have it in mind to let Drostan build a monastery there. You've seen the Room of Writs at Pitversie nearby. An influx of new ideas there would be no bad thing."

"And I've seen the monks at Durrow writing their books. Of course, there's much we can learn. Yet I think the Pretani have as much to contribute to other societies as to gain from them."

But Bridei's mind was springing ahead.

"There's also the question of a new kind of peace. The faith of the Christ-God is a growing bond between the kingdoms of the west and it works against us. If we allow the monks freedom to work here, that would weaken these alliances." He stroked his beard. "You know these hostages I'm holding, the two sons of the King of Orkney. They've been talking with the monks. Permission to build a monastery there might help to hold the allegiance of the Orcades."

"You're sailing in dangerous waters! I've seen what happened to the Druad in Eirean."

"There have been Bishops here in the past - Patrick and others. Most people listened politely, nodded their heads and went back to their hearth-gods." Bridei leaned back expansively in his seat. It was obvious from his bright eyes that the whole idea appealed to him immensely. "The way I see it, Drostan could work between the Calendar of Events and the List of Kings. He could add to that from the ancient Annals and the memories of the Historians. How does that sound to you? A Chronicle of the Pretani, in your own tongue at first, then later, copied in Latin. The whole world will hear of Bridei who united the clans, who strove for peace and who furthered the arts. Then there's his beautiful daughter, Caterin, who married the next King." His exultant laugh boomed round the room.

"The Wise Woman, Veleda, has foretold that I'll not be remembered in the bard-songs," Caterin put in lightly.

"Of course not. No need. For your name will be written in Annals that will stand the test of time."

"Unless they're burned in the next Scots raid."

Caterin could not share her father's optimism. Veleda's White Dove had come to roost. The Pigeon of the Church was quietly catching salmon with Broichan. And who knew what schemes would be hatched on the Island of Io.

As the days passed she thought carefully about Bridei's intentions. It was not the precepts of the new Faith that worried her. It was the whole powerful organisation of the Church. It rolled over age-old faiths like half-burned logs over tilled fields. The charcoal from the logs revived the earth as it crushed it. What would survive under the immense pressure of the Church? Yet seeds, buried for years, often sprang up into new life.

Colum Cille had renounced his wealth and power. Many monks were retreating from a world where politics had gone rotten and gold was a god. A Pretani Queen could foster a movement towards a simple life among the spirits of Earth and Air, if she had to.

There was another question that lay near her heart and hovered in the eyes of her women. The days passed and Gort made no move to share her bed as was his right. He and his men rode forth to visit far-flung strongholds in the north and arrived back only to report to the King. When Bridei announced that the Court would return to Dalgynch for the Marriage that would confirm Gort as the new King, she thought of summoning Gort. And found her pride would not allow her.

Then on the night before they were due to travel, Caterin heard his voice outside her room, sending her women rustling and laughing off to their beds. She met his eyes in her mirror and all her pent-up desire exploded inside her. Gort acknowledged her beauty to himself without a flicker of emotion. He saw that the proud tilt of her head was born of courage and determination and held none of her previous arrogance. Truly this Pretani woman had matured. But the bawdy jokes about Picti women still rang in his ears.

"This Artur mac Aedan, how did he use you?" She heard the creak of the chair set near the small brazier that Iogena had lit against the evening chill. She swung round, dislodging her dark-blue house-robe to reveal the sheen of creamy skin at breast and thigh.

He noted that she did not cover herself. It seemed she had gained in boldness since he had last left her in a fleece smeared with the blood of her maidenhead.

Her eyes took in his long flaxen nightrobe, woven with birds of prey, a tapestry of beaks and claws and hovering wings. Its wide sleeves, tied at the wrists gave his posture a lazy elegance. It lay open to his waist, showing the jet dragon lying amongst his chest-hairs. One leg was hooked over the arm of the chair and swung nonchalantly.

She had hoped she would feel nothing for him on her return. She should have known better. His presence started a familiar warmth flooding her limbs. His face showed that nothing about him had changed except for a new pink scar that puckered his cheek. Yet Caterin sensed a subtle change in herself. She had a task ahead of her. With a King who satisfied her body she would not be at the mercy of quicksilver emotions.

"Artur?" she queried, swivelling back to the mirror to hide her merriment.

"Artur. At Dun Add," he agreed firmly. He had seen the movement and his suspicions were aroused.

"You'll have some mead?" Her bare feet slipped through the silken fleece as she escaped into the shadows beyond the glow of the brazier. The code of honour of these foreigners was a tricky thing to deal with. They took an attempted rape of their women as a personal affront to their own dignity. They howled that their honour had been besmirched and used rape as a pretext to go blustering off to a war of vengeance. They used their women as a means of humiliating one another. That was how Artur had intended it, as the ultimate insult to his enemy, Gort. She sighed and poured mead into a cup. It was time Gort learned that Pretani women despised such weakness in their men. She smiled as she handed him the cup.

"Artur treated me as any soldier would," she answered, blithely. "I was the spoils of war, wasn't I? After you defeated him, he needed to prove that he was a hero again."

"You'd enjoy that then?" Gort grated.

"I did! It was the best laugh I'd had for a long time. I gave him a kick that sent him bellowing like a bull that's lost its balls!"

There was a shocked silence, broken at last by Gort who gave a great snort of laughter.

"And he was boasting from the ramparts of Dun Ollaig that he'd spawned a Scottie whelp in you! I warned him that one day I'd stretch his entrails till they reached from Tay to Forth. Then I burned his fort from under him."

Gort's amused eyes studied her over the rim of his cup. This woman was full of surprises. He might enjoy this business of making a new Princess after all. In the past few moons he had learned that this was a land where love was given freely, but not cheaply. These women treated it as a gift from the All-Mother, just as the blossom came before the fruit and the bud before the flower. It was good to be among women who enjoyed the act of love as he did himself, savouring it without guilt or remorse. But that was not the way in his country. Marriage was for the breeding of heirs and a woman had to be chaste. He feared that this woman would follow the custom of her people and love many men. Yet, their loving had been sweet in the past. Suddenly he could not wait to taste the freshness of her skin on his tongue.

His eyes resting on the line of her throat sent the blood singing along her veins. She was tempted to smooth the grim lines from his face, to trace the angry line of the scar. And why not? He had learned enough to wait for an invitation.

But before they were prepared for it, a fire flashed between them. They found themselves locked in a hard embrace. His body was hard and demanding but he put her from him and let his eyes rove over her loveliness until she led him to the couch and reached for him to come in to her. They moved together until their cries mingled and their spirits soared far into the dome of the sky and they discovered the joy of being at one with the Great Ones.

Yet, there was no word of love spoken between them. Though their bodies had known an exquisite fulfilment, their hearts were still divided. Caterin, watching the sleeping face on the pillow beside her, knew that while he had loved her body with practised skill he had allowed her no nearer his heart. But then she had not given fully of herself either. For if she did once, this man could use and hurt and betray her for evermore. A sharing relationship would have been good. It was one thing to know she would succeed on her own. But quite another to know she had her partner's love and support.

Once the Court had travelled back to the Citadel of Dalgynch, the preparations went ahead for the Royal Marriage.

Should be taking place at Samhain, the Clan Mothers agreed among themselves, when the weather was still mild enough for travel and families in the north could make a holiday out of it. Still, the start of the Growing season was as good a time as any. The rites of Imbolc were long past. The lambs and calves had been counted. There was an abundance of milk again. Just let the folk get their cattle cleansed through the Beltane fires and driven up to the shielings and they'd be free. With the seed sown and the Mother Earth placidly germinating it, they'd be ready for a grand old celebration. Just let the Wise Ones keep the war-chariots in their sheds until the new King and his Queen were feasted. And keep that traitor Artcois and his whelps in the Low Countries hiring themselves out to any ruler who needed three fine ships and would pay.

Meanwhile, Caterin found that her apartments belonged to her no longer. The long-awaited news of the Marriage had been borne on the wind and merchants' wagons blocked the four roads to the Citadel. King Bridei had released his store of silver coins to Devana for the foreign merchants would take nothing less. Furniture and floors were festooned with half-rolled bales, fold after fold of downy, sleek and feathery materials that invited a caress. Delicate shades of field and forest bloomed against flaring sunset colours. Glossy fleeces and petal-soft skins draped the walls.

Suddenly, Amis had come into her own. Long ago, when she had found she was barren, she had visited every Drui, every hermit, every Wise Woman. She had meditated, sacrificed, recited incantations. She had never conceived but she had found a certain fulfilment in the ritual. The appeasement of the Mighty Ones and the continuation of the tradition became her ideal. And now, the tradition had burst into life before her eyes. Her gaunt face shone with the zeal of a Drui in ecstacy as she took charge of the flock of traders that descended on the Capital. Clamouring pedlars who had been stamping their feet in neighbouring kingdoms now quailed under her fiery gaze. Gold-hungry traders who had been biting their finger-nails in ships in the two Firths formed a docile queue at the Palace door at a sweep of Amis's arm.

"This is too much," groaned Caterin one day. "There's far more stuff here than any one person would need in a lifetime. Far better to use the silver to found Healing Centres than to deck me out in all this finery."

"Not at all!" snapped Amis. "It's the tradition. Foreign Kings and Queens will be there. Your dresses and jewels must surpass anything they've ever seen. Now, how will this necklace go with the white robe?" She held a necklet of linked gold beads against a robe as dazzling white as mountain snow lit by the sun.

"Yes, and this cape on her shoulders." Iogena held up a silk cape newly embroidered, bright as a swarm of butterflies.

"Quick! Clear a place for this lot!" Devana came, balancing a pile of enamelled boxes. "Don't argue, Caterin! You must put up with this fuss unless you want to appear before the Kings and ambassadors with a ragged shift and a begging bowl."

They all ran to save the precious boxes before they fell. Devana took a twirling dance step about the room and snapped her fingers above her head.

"Come on now, Caterin! We need to say to the world, 'Look at us! No one can match us! See our new strong King whose sword is a whirlwind in the fire-reddened air? Feast your eyes on his Queen, radiant in beauty, swathed in jewels! Eat and drink from our silver bowls and gem-strewn cups. Join our revelries, marvel at our processions! This is our victory parade! This is the Feast of the proud Pretani who fought and defeated the Scots!'" Devana stood and let her hair fall over a face that she could no longer keep set at fair. "Caterin, let those who mourn feel that their sacrifice was not altogether in vain."

Before Caterin could enfold her aunt in her arms, Devana had caught hold of herself and was opening the boxes, the stiff set of her shoulders warning that any show of sympathy would make her pain more difficult to bear.

And Caterin put aside till later all thought of thin bairns with pinched faces whose homesteads had been ravished by raiders or decimated by illness and swiftly changed the subject.

"What on earth are we going to do with all these beads?"

"I've a room full of needle-women downstairs waiting for us to match beads to their designs."

This time Caterin set to work with a will. If the people wanted display they would have it.

Yet, she needed relief from the turmoil now and again. There was no escaping to the sportsground nowadays. The youths who had sported there had been replaced by shrill-voiced boys. Drust had been killed in a skirmish with a shore-party from Aedan's fleet in Catness. Moon-faced Prent, still incessantly smiling, had taken over the reins from Wise Cau who had grown suddenly frail. Fortrei had pursued his goal to be a warrior with such single-mindedness that his new-found confidence had won him promotion.

As soon as she had come back from Craig Phadric, Caterin had renewed her friendship with Crystal. The mare fondly displayed a foal whose coat was so red that Caterin promptly named him Jasper after the pebbles that made such pretty gaming-pieces. So she kept herself fit by riding out to visit communities in the neighbourhood.

One day, she rode north to Kilrymont to see what Colum Cille's disciple, Drostan, had made of his foothold in the land.

The slender young man in his brown habit came forward, smiling, his soulful eyes reminding her of a well-loved hound.

"Let me show you how our oratory is taking shape." The stones of the sloping walls were almost meeting and the long slabs for the ridge of the roof were being hoisted up and set in place. "And we've built our own cells already." He pointed to a scatter of round stone cells, domed like the hives of bees.

"King Bridei has been kind. He's supplied us with everything we need. Although we've been praying for another ox-cart to bring stones down from the quarry. The one we have breaks under the weight and work has to stop while we repair it."

Caterin nodded coolly, unwilling to be the answer to his prayer. She felt satisfied that this tiny building and its score of monks would never rival the great Druad School of Learning at Pitversie, just up-river. Her attendants made room for her on a sand-dune and passed round honey-cakes. A bracing wind blew across the wide estuary from the forest of Tentsmoor.

Not all the builders wore brown habits. One figure drew Caterin's attention time and again. His working clothes were grey and dusty. He was bent nearly double over a stone, so eager was he to chisel a true edge. Straightening, he looked out to sea for a moment, flexing his back muscles. Then he tossed back a rusty lock of hair that had fallen over his eye. He reminded her so much of Derelei that her heart twisted with pain. The same blunt fingers caressed the long stone as though it was the thigh of a woman. Was he a kinsman? Suddenly she had to find out.

As her shadow fell across the stone, the chipping stopped and he looked up. She gazed down into one eye that was half-blue, half-brown.

"Derelei!" she cried. A sob caught in her throat. But her heart filled with gladness that he was alive. Slowly he unbent until she was gazing up at him. "How could it happen? I thought you were dead."

"So did the Druad who found me. But the Healing Ones were with me and helped Veleda to cure me." He grinned in the old endearing way.

And suddenly she was back at Pitversie and young and free and there was no one in the world but this enchanting tender man. And all the love that he had awakened in her heart overflowed. For with him there had been no barriers. They had given and taken love freely. Their hands met and clasped tight and his delight in her was plain in his face.

"If you hadn't shielded me with your own body, I'd have been killed, too. You saved my life, Derelei."

"And will again, if need be," he said simply.

Derelei devoured her bright eager face with his eyes. News of her return from Eirean had sent him to a circle of stones beside a loch to lie for three nights. And he had cried her name to the stars and the wind had blown it from his mouth. And in the end his hands were bleeding from beating them against the harsh unyielding stone.

"And you're not a Drui now?"

"The break with the Druad was coming. You knew that. I had to

259

get back to working with stone."

She felt his roughened hands and saw grey dust in new lines at his mouth.

"But here with the monks? You haven't joined them, have you?"

"The Ancient Ones still speak to me through the stones. I'm back with my family, travelling to wherever there is a building to be raised or a stone to be decorated."

CHAPTER THIRTY

And Caterin felt young and carefree again with her long plait and her blue Drui robe and her longing to be loved and to give love in return.

There was such a depth of emotion in his eyes that she knew he still loved her. As she had never stopped loving him. With the first fine rapture of love in it. And all the wild beauty and passion of the Earth Mother mingled in it. And the unfettered joy of a shared companionship. There had never been any barriers of Queenship and duty between them. She had been his wayside companion and he had been the freedom she had never had. The freedom to love where she chose.

A silence stretched between them. With a sudden movement, he tossed away his hammer and chisel. They walked along the sand between the dunes and the sea, their hands swinging, as in the past. Gort meant nothing to her at that moment. She laughed up at Derelei and felt herself drowning in his love for her. Never, never had Gort looked at her as Derelei looked now, with such a painful longing in his eyes. Her gaze travelled to his warm urgent mouth and her senses stirred with a familiar arousal.

They climbed the cliff-path and came down to sea-level again in a tiny bay. Stranded by the erosion of the cliffs around it, a massive pillar reared out of the sand. High on its face, the slanting sun threw into relief a huge stone wheel-circle with a myriad of spokes radiating out from the centre.

"This is where the Great Ones spin the threads of our lives," he said.

Gripping her fiercely in his arms, he flooded her body with his heat. Unresisting, she melted into his embrace, feeling his strength flowing into her. She was ready when he moved his head and gave him her mouth in a kiss so deep that it engulfed her in rapture.

They sank down on the yielding sand at the foot of the Spinning Rock and she gave herself over to the honeyed sweetness of his tongue and the hardness of his body. His touch lit a fire in her breasts and her thighs. And they came together in a wild celebration of two lives that had almost been snuffed out in the first promise of youth.

Then as they lay together, fulfilled, his eyes closed, his face uplifted, his hands began to caress her hair, the curves of her neck and shoulders with a kind of reverence. She knew he was memorising the feel of her so that this moment might come alive again for him in his mind later. She did the same, drinking in the smell of his wind-scoured hair and the salt sweat on his skin.

Again she felt the tremor of his mounting desire. Before it could control them both, she broke away. He laid his arm on the stone pillar and hid his face in its fold. At once, she felt bereft, empty and aching.

"I'll never touch you again," he said. There was a raw huskiness in his voice. "But I had to hold you, just once more."

And Caterin knew that the days of dreaming were gone, that the girl who had loved Derelei with all her young heart was no more. And she was glad she had known that first rhapsody of love with him. And fiercely glad they had made love just once more. For she had thought that never again would she know a love that was carefree. It almost tore her heart out to have to leave him here.

She picked her way to the edge of the water. Wave after wave swelled and surged in, curled and frothed white and fell with a rush and a tumble at her feet.

Now she was a woman and a Queen and must marry Gort. And the woman who had taken the place of the young girl found to her surprise that she loved Gort too. Not in the way she loved Derelei. But with a love that held a challenge in it. There was an attraction between them if only they could overcome the barriers of suspicion. And if they could come together some day, sharing their thoughts and ambitions, it might happen to be a love that could embrace duty. Yet how could a woman love two men at once?

Derelei came to stand beside her.

"I didn't mean to distress you." He put out a finger and wiped a tear from her cheek. She had not been aware she was weeping. "But you have your King and a fine one. While I'm wedded to my stones. Although they're cold bed-fellows."

"Don't talk like that." She looked up at the huge stone spinning wheel above their heads. "For a span of time our life-skeins mingled. Then the All-Knowing Ones chose to break the pattern. You gave me moments of enchantment that I'll keep in my heart for ever. Some day, I hope to find a love that burns as fiercely as the love you gave me. I know now what I'm looking for. I even know how to deserve it."

His jaw tightened and a shadow crossed his face. Her eyes slid to his open shirt and the scar of the dagger-wound. And it had a queer wild beauty, the puckered pink lips against the golden skin. And she thought that the pain of a wound was nothing compared to the pain of a love that knifed into a heart.

"I want a promise from you," she said. "Don't let the love you bear for me go to waste."

"Oh, I'll marry a stone-mason's daughter and keep the craft secrets in the family." With a rueful grin, he thrust his hand through his hair.

"If you love me," she cried, "you won't freeze out another woman, one who could give you as much and more than I ever could. Love is a giving thing. If you can give it once, you can give it again. Don't bury it in a grave at the bottom of your heart."

He shook his head and turning, set himself to climb the path to the top of the cliffs.

"Maybe I'll join Drostan's monks," he said, turning, half-laughing at the top. "I like that man. He asked me to carve Christ symbols for his oratory and he understood when I said that I don't have the inspiration."

Suddenly he filled his chest with the clean sharp air.

"There's a different dream that simmers in my mind."

They stretched out side by side on the top of the cliff among the sea-pinks and looked down on the sea-bird colony that seethed below them.

"Our side of the family, my fathers and brothers and myself, we specialize in carving animal and bird symbols for the clan chiefs. My uncles and their sons work more closely with the Druad, cutting the magic signs and they use different techniques. But, because we're working from life, I feel we've developed an assurance and a delicacy in our work that has a merit of its own." He laughed shyly. "Some day I'll show you what I mean."

He plucked a blade of grass and chewed it between strong white teeth. A silence fell. They watched a kittiwake side-stepping on a ledge to keep herself between the grey chick and the sheer drop to the rocks below.

"How a kittiwake survives to adulthood is beyond my ken." He threw away the soggy stem. A passing shag snapped at it and bore it back to decorate his nest. "You see, Caterin, not only do we have the skill to cut a clear representation of the animal but we try to make of it a thing of beauty."

"That's taboo," she reminded him. "The only justification for decoration is its meaning." She twirled a black-tipped feather between her fingers. Yet, she knew what he meant. In her mind's eye she could see vitality in every curve and line of a horse or a deer.

"Why shouldn't a bird or a bull beauty as well as significance?" He raised his body on his elbows and gazed into her face. "Caterin, I want to take a further step. I'm going to insist that the chiefs have their symbols cut on properly dressed stones instead of on rough boulders and cave-walls."

"And what will the Master of the Symbols say to that?"

"Once it's done he'll find that the symbols have a greater impact when incised on stones that are shaped and smoothed. Drostan agrees with me that our designs deserve the respect of well-dressed stones. And Caterin, he's teaching me how to write in Eirean Ogam! It's just the script for inscribing on stone. It's like the calendar tallies on your dagger. But I'll carve the letters in our own tongue so that our people can read them." Unable to keep still in his excitement, he sprang to his feet and began to pound down the path to the sea-wracked sand. Caterin followed at his back. He was still fully aware of her as she was of him for he spoke again before she joined him.

"One day, I'll be using a different technique. Not yet, for I've not practised enough. After I've drawn the animal as we do now, I'll chip away the background." His arms went wild in the air. "Can you imagine it? With the Royal Bull standing out in relief! It'll stun you! You'll be able to see the strength flowing in it. Think of a horse with delicate high-stepping feet!" He jerked to a stop, swung round and grabbed her shoulders, forgetting he had vowed not to touch her again. "When you're Queen, will you help me to develop my craft. Not only that, but encourage the chiefs to understand what we're doing and appreciate it?" Intense eyes raked her face.

"And pay for it?"

His eyes lost their glow.

"I'd forgotten that part of it," he admitted.

"There's enough wealth in the Treasury," she assured him. "I'll back you to the hilt so long as you are working for the glory of the Ancestral Ones."

Before she rode for home, Drostan invited them to eat a simple meal with himself and his monks in their cow-hide shelter.

"I've never seen anything to equal the Pretani animals and birds in any art-form," Drostan told her. "When I come to illuminate my Pretani Chronicle, I'd like to use Derelei's designs."

Derelei shook his head.

"The sense of living movement won't transfer onto a flat page," he said.

"They'll be distorted," Caterin agreed. "In Eirean I saw the elongated shapes that result. Drostan, why can't you monks leave us something that's uniquely ours?"

"I like to experiment," replied Drostan smiling. "Colum Cille encourages the flowering of local art."

Caterin felt uneasy and could not say why. Was it because Colum Cille had taken a copy of the Godspell and called it his own? Was it because his every action was blown up into a miracle by his friends?

"I'm afraid," she told Derelei later. "These Churchmen seem to turn everything to their own use, to glorify themselves and their Church."

"Drostan's not like that." Derelei gave her a knee to help her mount. "Why shouldn't we share our designs with him?"

"Because they're original, unique to us. Through them we commune with the Learned Ones. They have meaning for us and that meaning runs in our life-blood. The Scots will play pat-a-cake with them and come up with something trivial and claim it for their own." She shook her reins. "Watch him, Derelei, don't let him steal our art."

Yet on her journey home, Caterin forgot her fears and went over in her mind the glorious days she had spent with Derelei. He had given her much and asked nothing in return. For that alone he held a special place in her heart. They had stood on the brink of everlasting rapture and had stepped back. Derelei had known that the time was near when Caterin needed to be Queen and Mother of the Royal Line. She had known that Derelei needed to be free to pursue his dream. Yet, some day, the skeins of their lives might interlock again under the Spinning Rock.

CHAPTER THIRTY ONE

Iogena clasped her hands in delight, as the metal-workers unrolled their calf-skin bundles and golden light flashed into shadowy corners. Devana darted among the leather-workers, towing a trail of belts and pouches in her wake. Exotic perfumes rose from the apothecaries' creams and oils and wafted out of the window to where the laundresses strained to catch the scent and the guards wrinkled their noses and grinned.

Caterin let the laughing crowd ebb and flow around her, feeling like an island in the middle of a loch. The goodwill, the banter, the purchases, none of these were connected with her. She chose a gold arm-band set with carnelians and gave it to Iogena.

"From one freed bond-woman to another," she told her.

Amis accepted an enamelled jar from Caterin and took a mighty sniff. Shrieking, the women dived for cover before the air was split open by a gigantic sneeze.

"Macha help me, that's done me a power of good," cried Amis.

"Will you come and look at this." Devana stood transfixed at the window, arrested in full flight.

The Master Steward had hoisted himself onto an inverted wash-tub before his kitchen door. Traders jostling for his attention thrust rare spices under his nose for him to pinch. He tasted crystallised fruits and licked his fingers. He sampled wines in strangely shaped vessels. At his back a line of servants staggered under sides of meat towards the cool earth store. The Master's arms waved wildly. He rose on his toes in a climax of well-being. And overbalanced! Slowly, one after the other, the row of servants toppled. The Master's head wearing a wicker basket poked out from under a side of meat. The mellow wines he had sampled kept his self-respect intact. Mounting his tub, he toasted his gleeful audience with a wine-jar.

Caterin, avoiding an olive-skinned pedlar, his arms covered in skeins of silken threads, escaped to the calm of her courtyard. Leaning her hands on the low stone wall, she took a deep breath of cool air. Let the women enjoy themselves. They deserved it, especially Devana. Let the people rejoice. They had earned it. And the Moon Maiden, the All-Knowing, send the Princess the strength to see it through with a smile. For her patience at the moment was not worth a basketful of rags.

From here she could look out to sea, where two headlands sheltered the sandy beach. The main Port to the Citadel lay further north but today trading ships, standing well out from the shallows, were sending smallboats in to a jetty that was already overflowing.

Near at hand, there was a coming and going at the house of Aeron, husband to Amis. As Guardian of the Treasure and Keeper of the Insignia, he had a comparatively easy task. In a walled passage underneath his house, the Royal Regalia and Ritual Vessels were stored. In the forthcoming ceremonies, all the Treasure in the Depository would be on display. A thin, dry stick of a man, Aeron hovered like a predatory spider. At regular intervals, a group of servants emerged from his doorway, weighed down by awkward, heavy bundles wrapped in leather. Guarded by double lines of soldiers, the servants weaved their way down to the cleaning and polishing shed, a large, gloomy chamber, partly built into the protective outer wall.

Caterin had never seen the whole Treasure at once. In all probability, she would not see it at the Marriage since she was one of the prize exhibits herself. A gleam of mischief brightened her eyes. Why not?

Glancing back into the room, she saw that the women were engrossed. Looking downwards, she saw a number of projecting stones that would provide footholds to the yard below. Tucking the hem of her skirt into her girdle she swung herself over. Somehow, her fingers and toes found niches to cling to, although when her feet finally touched the paving-stones, she wondered how she had done it. Hawker and Dagger set up a clamour and the boy who fed them poked his head briefly out of a window.

"We'll make up for lost time another day," she promised, cuffing them as she passed. Two weaving women looked up from their looms and waved her on her way.

Inside the door of the cleaning-shed, Caterin paused to let her eyes adjust to the gloom. Here again, guards lined the walls facing the tables that had been set about the room. The servants were being supervised by members of a travelling family of metal-workers who could work gold and silver with a breath-taking artistry. They were squat, dark men who spoke a gutteral language like a decimated Attecottie tongue.

Dustmotes danced like gilded fireflies in shafts of sunlight lancing through the windows. As each bundle arrived, a servant heaved it on to a table beside the pots of fine red ironstone for the first scouring. As the protective wrapping fell away, at once, the wavering flames in the fire-baskets sent a galaxy of sparks flashing from rim to curve.

On one table, great bronze garnet-studded shields, never meant to be used in war, were being polished. Their decorated scrolls ended in animal heads with eyes of topaz. On the other side, sat a pair of enormous golden bowls, with flying dragons and trumpet spirals encircling their rims. Caterin wandered entranced, her gaze caught by bronze cauldrons, swords and scabbards, hanging bowls, all decorated with the symbols of the great families of the Pretani - the crescents, the broken arrows, the double discs, or the deer, the eagle and the wolf.

One bowl boasted the spines and tusks of the Veniconie Boar. She touched it with her finger and it was as though the silver spikes had stung her. She sprang back, rubbing her hand and was afraid to send her thoughts to the Wise Ones to ask why.

On the last table, the heavy silver chains of office had been wiped clean of powder and polished with the skins of fawns. They lay in a shining tumble waiting to be wrapped and carried back to the House of the Guardian.

Caterin picked up a two-handled drinking cup, turning it this way and that so that the lights sparked off the silver and gold interlay. She found herself thinking of the wealth of Tara and how it had brought only a keening in the wind over an empty hill.

"Gloating?" The familiar sardonic voice came from a corner where a lean-hipped shadow leaned against the wall. That word bit deeply. She had hardly seen him since they had come back to Dalgynch, except at a distance in the Dining-Hall. Where then was he taking his pleasure?

"Do you think this wealth will be yours once you marry me?" she taunted him. "Well, you're wrong! It belongs to the People. You won't find our people taxed so hard that they die in the snow." Handing the cup to a startled guard, she turned to leave in a swirl of skirts.

"You surprise me." With a grunt, Gort pushed himself from his leaning-post and followed, dipping his head swiftly beneath the lintel at the last minute, much to Caterin's fleeting regret. "I would have thought that in a sharing community there would be no place for an idle, pleasure-seeking Princess."

Gort knew he was baiting her. What drove him to make love to her and then mock her, he wondered. He had been moved to admiration by the artistry of the Treasure. Daily these barbarians of the north surprised him.

How had they managed, in this day and age, to hold on to their robust love of beauty and their unique way of life? He had arrived in this land full of resentment but determined to fulfill the pledge he had given to his father. Yet, there was something about this kingdom and its customs that appealed to his sense of justice. They shared the wealth of the land and cared for their sick and aged with a kind of ingrained kindliness. And he had despised these brothers of the Clan Mothers as weaklings. Until after the first ferocious assault on the Scots forts.

And this Princess? She stirred his senses deeply despite his distrust of her. He had found it hard to respond to any other woman since the last time he had made love to her. Thundering Taranis, he must take hold of himself. He had his duty to perform and thoughts like these were weakness.

"It seems to me," Caterin said, her eyes snapping, "that since you cannot claim the Treasure and since the Princess is not to your liking, you ought to take yourself off to find richer pickings elsewhere."

"And leave all that lovely silver for the first raider who happens along?" His smile was slow and lazy. His next remark followed her along the narrow alley. "Not to mention a grubby Princess with a kilted skirt and skinned knees." She saw him no more, neither in the Hall nor the Citadel. But Eildon had come, slipping in quietly on a horse as lean and loose-jointed as himself. One afternoon, Caterin turned aside a blossom-laden bough and found him restringing his harp under an old cherry-tree that had been there so long the flag-stones had been laid around its roots.

"I've been in the Celidon Forest," he answered her question. "The southern half that extends below the Forth."

"Bridei's people are as welcome there as a basketful of rotten fish." Caterin sat at his feet. Eildon usually knew all there was to know.

"I slipped an axe in my belt and pretended I was a wood-cutter but never a sap-filled friend did I chop down."

"You're like Veleda. Shadows that disappear in the forest. And what secrets did you overhear? Or are they only for the King's ear?" A breeze, heavy with perfume, threw a scatter of pink blossom on them.

"You should know that there are some secrets I'd lose my tongue rather than tell." Eildon chewed at the end of a harp-string to wet it. "But some news is better to tell before the rumours grow wings and become fantasy. I went to stay with Myrddin, bard of King Gwendoleu. I'd heard on the wind that Gwendoleu had been killed by the Kings of York and the Pennines. And when they withdrew, guess who stepped in and took over his kingdom?" Eildon twisted the sinew through a hole in his harp. "None other than our illustrious neighbour, Riderch of Clyde. He frowns on bards so Myrddin and I lived very comfortably in a cave in the forest and watched events."

"Oh, come on, Eildon. Stop droning on like the bees in the blossom."

The Steward had his bee-skips lined up on the other side of the wall.

"A good bard always tells his sources first if he wishes to be believed." Calmly he knotted the sinew and pulled it tight. "But there's more. It concerns our late lamented Master of the Fleet, Artcois. And his two outlawed sons."

Caterin sat up, alert.

"I thought that would make you jump. Your future husband's ears grew longer, too." He tested the string softly against his ear and re-knotted it. But he gave her no indication of where he had met Gort. "Revenge was in the air. King Elidyr of Rheged backed by Artcois attacked Gort's brother Rhun and got himself killed. Nothing loth, Artcois collected allies, Riderch of Clyde, Nud of Dun Fries, Clytno of Dun Eidyn. No recruits from the Votadini, you'll note. The Kings keep the pot boiling in the Lothians between one king-claimant and the next. A united Votadini state would gobble up their small kingdoms." He stopped to bite at the string with his teeth.

"Go on!"

"Oh, Artcois didn't do much. Burnt Arvon and withdrew. Just enough to say 'See, we can do this anytime we want'. But they'll be sorry they twisted the Dragon's tail."

"The Dragon? Gort's brother?"

"Aye, he's gathering an infantry force now. No puny naval raids for him. These are men accustomed to fight in the narrow spaces between their native hills. If he marches that lot through the Spine country, there'll be few Kings will offer any resistance. Especially Elidyr's son, Llywarch Hen. He's famed as a poet, not a warrior. A rustic bard." The disgust in Eildon's last three words said it all and Caterin had to laugh.

"Tell me, what did my father say to this?" asked Caterin, watching Eildon pluck a note and tighten the gut again.

"Nothing for my ears. But his eyes locked with Gort's and they went into an inner room together."

"So Gort heard the news a few nights ago and now he's gone."

Why do I keep asking about him, she asked herself. He cares nothing for me. He's keeping our borders safe and that's what he's here for.

"What do you make of it all, Eildon?"

Eildon bent his head to listen again. "I just collect news. I don't interpret it."

"I don't believe you," cried Caterin. "You're one of the wiliest men in the Kingdom even though you pretend to be absorbed in the stanza and the note."

Suddenly, Eildon struck a chord.

"Eildon of Buckhinie Most liberal of bards.

Much news do you give To the kings of this world.

As you gather So you dispense

Happy the Pretani kings As long as you live.

Yet when I'm old and failing,

In the grim doom of death,

Who will remember my singing

Who will remember my song?"

"And I hope no one remembers that little ditty for it sounded worse than a tom-cat with the urge." Eildon laid the harp at his side. "You want to know what I think? I would be asking some questions myself. What made Elydir and Artcois attack Rhun in the first place? Rhun's a high-flying warrior with a huge body of men to draw on. Did Elydir feel threatened? And did Artcois sell himself to the highest bidder?"

A little silver pipe appeared in Eildon's fingers. He played a three-note melody over and over while he pondered.

"I doubt it," he said at last. "Would a mercenary have collected allies to avenge his pay-master's death? Never! So what was the real purpose when Artcois attacked Rhun." This time the melody had gained a couple of notes. Caterin waited. "You see, if Rhun marches north, he'll meet little resistance, and he'll be at the Forth before he can be stopped. Then the fat's in the fire. For centuries the Kings have been at pains to keep these two strong countries apart, Gwynedd and Pettaland. But with the Dragon-brothers ruling and their armies combined, the other kingdoms will be dancing to the tune of anyone who will protect them." Eildon broke into a merry hornpipe.

"You mean Artcois and Maelchon might offer protection and turn against their own land?" she cried, hardly able to believe it.

"Why not? There are so many small dynasties trying to keep their heads above water that anything is possible. Bernicia and Deira weaken themselves by constant bickering. With Traprain Law changing hands every other season and a young poet in charge in Rheged, who's to stop Artcois taking control? So, if your husband's missing on your Marriage Day, search for him down south."

"The thought of Gort in alliance with Rhun has worried me since the day he came. Yet if Artcois is still a danger ... !" Quickly Caterin sprang to her feet, her head disturbing the boughs so that blossoms fell like pale tears on the upturned face of the bard. "Did you tell Bridei?"

"Not yet. He's ridden out with his Guards."

She did not like this unpredictable situation that see-sawed in the south. Gort and Rhun, Artcois and Maelchon, fencing for power, all with their eyes ultimately on the Kingship of the Pretani. If she could only rid herself of this preoccupation with Gort she might be able to see the situation more clearly.

Eildon's blank eyes followed her as she paced the yard, tall and magnificent, impatient for the Queenship, intelligent and shrewd, fettered by tradition.

"The Council of Elders are fools!" she cried. "They've elected the very man who is plotting their downfall."

"Yet, who else is there?" he asked. And went back to his bleak three-note tune.

CHAPTER THIRTY TWO

The painted deer on her bedroom wall began a dainty dance around Caterin's head. As they gathered speed into a tipsy reel, Caterin knew there had been something more than warmed milk in her bedtime cup. Her cry for help strangled in her throat. She fought to rise and pitched into a swimming darkness.

Men were fighting, swearing, yelling above her head. How could that be? She must be dreaming! She dragged her mind back to reality. The clang of weapons ebbed and flowed in time to a rhythmic pounding in her brain. A whirling blackness still enveloped her. Yet her eyes were open!

Her hands found hard-packed soil beneath her. The tang of cattle-dung filled her nose and mouth until she retched. Her head was too heavy to lift. She pushed with her arms and fell back against a stone slab. It was a blind-fold! Of course! She should have known. Except that there was no blindfold. Only darkness. Above, below, in front, behind, blackness, deep and penetrating.

"Oh, Bride! Where am I?"

Men still battled somewhere near. She yelled. Her voice echoed as if round the walls of an empty chamber and lanced through her throbbing head.

"Back to the ships!"

She knew that voice! If her wits would stop lurching about she could put a name to it. She screamed again. The men's voices faded. A mindless, shattering fury possessed her and she staggered to her feet.

Shrieking, sobbing, she pounded the walls, tearing at them with her nails. Bride's pity, they could not leave her in this tomb!

That brought the first coherent thought flashing through her mind. Her women must have thought she was dead and had buried her! Alive!

No! Dead bodies were laid in a stone coffin. She was able to stand upright. Just! A wave of dizziness brought her to her knees. She rocked backwards and forwards, keening softly, trying to put one thought together with another.

This could not be happening! A Queen taken from her very Palace! Someone had been drinking the King's wine and eating his meat and plotting to abduct her! Someone who knew the habits of the sentries and her women. Maybe one of her own women had drugged the cup. But why? And why had she been left to rot in this filthy hole? The taste of sickness filled her mouth. She retched until she was exhausted and passed out again.

Her brain was clearer when she woke. Something had roused her. Feet padding somewhere above her head. Barking and grunting. A bear scenting its prey! Supporting herself by the slabs at her back, she rose.

Scratching and burrowing noises above her head. Where was her dagger? Bride help her, she was in her night-robe! If the creature dug its way in, she'd be eaten alive! No, Bride, no! No, she'd be out through the hole and away before it attacked. But not with these wobbly legs! With her fist she stifled a scream. A snort of disgust above her head. What now? Nothing. The beast had gone. Then, how in the name of Bride was she going to escape?

Her outstretched arms felt a stone wall on either side. An underground passage! She followed her dagger hand confidently. And fell all her length. Oh, Mighty Ones, never let me go blind! If I live to get out of here! A spasm of shivering shook her. Her flimsy night-robe could not keep the chill at bay. A blind fury attacked her.

"Whoever you are, you lily-livered scum, you won't destroy the Queen of the Pretani!"

Gritting her teeth she limped on into the darkness. The passage took a new direction. Now, her feet were sliding down a slope. The feeling of going deep into the very bowels of the Earth struck terror into her heart. Suddenly, the wall that guided her vanished! Her mind went blank. In a panic she began hitting out wildly with her arms, letting out a mounting series of cries like an animal caught in a trap, throwing herself this way and that. Sharp stones grazed her arms. She staggered. Lights exploded in her brain and she fell, half-stunned. She had found the wall with her head.

Yet, the shock had cleared her mind. The recurring smell of cattle-dung told her she was in the kind of underground shelter used in the past to protect cattle from cold and predators. They were strongly built to withstand the thrusting of heavy bodies. Now the beasts were kept above ground in sheds and the drains and passages below ground had been closed up. Of course! She was in the rounded chamber at the end where the animals had room to turn. At the other end she would come out above ground among the ruined dwellings. Unless they had closed the entrance. Then she would really have something to panic about!

She groped back along the way she had come, feeling along the sides of the tunnel. Once, there was a scurry and some little animal bounced off her foot. Rats! She stopped to calm her breathing, then moved on.

At last, the tunnel began to climb steeply. Relief flooded through her. Until she came up against a blank wall and an enormous slab at roof height. And that was that! She struggled to shift it but it was beyond her strength. A fresh draught of air, smelling of wet grass and earth, blew in around the stone, tantalising her, rousing her anger again.

Screaming her fury at the slab she pummeled it with her clenched fists. And her chilled blood began to flow warmer.

She stamped her bare feet, up and down, to the rhythm of her questions. Who would want to stop her Marriage? She swung her arms, wide and high. Who would gain by spiriting her away? She blew on her fingers and chafed her thighs. Who wanted to use her as a hostage? She found no answers but, by Dagda, she felt warmer.

Then the slab above her head jerked out of its resting-place. She gave a joyful cry. Slowly the slab rose and the pale gleam of the night sky appeared. Dirty claws scratched round the stone edges. A hairy head loomed in the space, jerked back and howled. The slab thudded back and there was a horrifying finality about the crash.

All reason left her. She pushed and pulled at the stone. If the beast had opened it once, it might do so again. Especially if it was hungry.

She forced herself to stop and listen, holding her breath. A low gutteral growling came from outside.

The slab rose again, stopped, and rose some more. Four dark tufted heads were silhouetted against a sky that showed the pale promise of the dawn. Rumbling, throaty exclamations came from their mouths. Eyes as black as berries studied her with interest. The fact that they were not wild beasts penetrated her mind gradually. Fingers pointed and they chattered among themselves. These were men! Small and hairy, but men! Growing bolder, she looked for handholds and began to clamber out. A foot caught her shoulder, pushing her back and the owner of the foot began to climb down into the tunnel beside her.

His bare feet were certainly human. They were wet and sandy and a strand of green seaweed was caught between two of his toes. She strained back from the smell of shell-fish that surged towards her and gagged at her throat as he landed beside her. When he straightened to his full height his curious flat-nosed face did not reach up to her chin. A stray gleam of light flowed over his thick mane of dark straggling hair and untrimmed beard and lighted up eyes that were narrowed and sharp as a cat's. His broad chest was matted with hair that seemed to grow as one with the pelt slung round his shoulders. But the impression of a powerful body lessened as Caterin looked downwards at meagre hips and spindly legs.

Under her gaze, he shifted restlessly from one foot to the other like an animal wondering whether to stay or flee. At last, head tilted, he hooked a finger-nail in the stuff of her robe. Eyes blazing, she slashed his hand away.

Short sharp grunts from above. Oh, Merciful Ones, they were laughing! The little man's eyes were twinkling. His face split into a wide grin, vivid with teeth that were as clean and sharp as daggers. He mouthed soothing words that held a faint echo of the Attecottie tongue. He belonged to the Little People that she had last seen, dressed in their finery, dancing their mimes under the brooding circle of stones. She found herself smiling back.

His long arms reached above his head and his companions lowered a large shell filled with a steaming soup that smelled of mussels. He nodded as she cupped its heat in her hands and began sipping, feeling its warmth circling through her veins.

Outside she heard the crackling of a fire. When she had finished drinking she made to climb out but a firm paw clamped on her shoulder. Another man clambered down carrying a couple of large furry skins. He fastened them on her shoulders and tucked them round her as if she was a bairn.

Now the men above lost interest in her and began to look at the brightening sky. A burning brand was passed down to light the shells of seal-fat in the wall-niches and rest of the tunnel sprang into view. Creels full of shell-fish and crabs were handed down and stacked on the floor. The fire above was stamped out and the last two men climbed down, replacing the slab neatly so that no sliver of light showed.

Nodding, smiling, they sat and began wedging open the shells as though they were at their home-hearth, gouging out the soft bodies and letting them fall into basins between their outstretched legs. Now and again, shy eyes slanted across at Caterin.

She could not believe it was happening. Were they not going to send for help? Were they going to keep her a prisoner? Suddenly one began to croon in his throat, a rhythmic sort of mouth-music and they worked in time to the beat.

"You must let me out!" she cried. They stared at her, not understanding. She tried the priestly tongue of the ritual.

"I'm the Princess, King Bridei's daughter."

They nodded and smiled and ignored her. There was a long silence, broken only by the scrape of bone tools and the plop of mussels in the basin. Caterin tried signing, pointing to herself and the roof-slab. They shook their heads. She gave up and sat down, staring at the roof-slab, knowing she could not move it without their help.

Suddenly a man nodded and chuckled as though his neighbour had said something funny. Again and again it happened. Their faces were alive with glances and grins as though they were chatting together. Then she knew. Thoughts were passing between them without the use of words. At one point, their leader held up his hand. They all inclined their heads as though listening to a voice in the air. Even their breathing stilled. Caterin, try as she might, could hear nothing. Huddled in her corner she watched them. And thought. Rude, primitive, barbaric and ignorant, folk called them. Because they were different they aroused fear that spilled over into name-calling. Who had the right to call them primitive because they chose to live simply within the Mother? Or ignorant, when they had minds that could span the world in a thought?

A chattering broke out and an odd burst of laughter. They nodded eagerly at Caterin as if to reassure her. Slowly her tensed muscles relaxed. Whoever they were talking with, would come.

"What's happening?" she asked. They stared and nudged one another. Their answer when it came was amazingly comforting but sheer gibberish. There was only one thing to do and that was to trust them. She curled round on the ground and fell asleep.

When she wakened and stretched her cramped limbs the men were refilling the lamps, clearing the empty shells into baskets, stacking their creels and dishes neatly against the wall. When they sat down again, cross-legged, it was clear they were waiting for something to happen.

Caterin was aware of the double beat of her heart growing louder as time passed. Who would come? Someone she knew and could trust? Or, Great God of the Sea, would she be given back into the hands of the very men who had abducted her?

When the sharp tap of metal on stone sounded above, her fingers closed round the broken mussel shell she had found and hidden. The odds would be against her but, she would damage a few eyes before she went to her death. Her other hand flew to grasp her amulets. There was an incantation that would protect her. If only she could remember it.

As the roof-slab began to lift, she drew backwards into the tunnel, ready to spring. Full daylight dazzled her. Then two green-and-scarlet-clad legs dangled from above and a familiar elongated figure dropped to the ground and straightened to face her.

"Eildon!" she cried, raising her arms. "You're a shaft of light from the Radiant Ones! How did you find me?"

Eildon's tawny eyes lit with relief.

"You're no ray of sunlight though. Have you seen yourself lately?"

For the first time she thought of how she must look with her tear-streaked face, bleeding knuckles and filthy night-robe. But Eildon had guessed right. If he had not made her laugh she would have cried.

"Oh, get me out of here, Eildon! I'm cold and starving."

"Wait, my bright-edged girl. There's a mystery here." Eildon began asking questions in the grunting language of the four men.

"Now, Caterin, what do you remember?"

"Nothing. There was a drug in my cup and I woke up here."

"Some blasted spy within the Citadel drugged you and your Guards and poisoned your dogs. Then your kidnappers came from outside the Palace." Eildon leant against the wall, his eyes distant. "Now, why would they throw you in here? Were they going to ransom you?"

"Eildon, just get me out of here!"

"And who surprised them and drove them off?" Eildon ignored her. "Hunnid here saw signs of a struggle outside - bloodstains and footmarks."

Caterin turned and began to climb the stone step to freedom

and fresh air.

Eildon's hand closed vice-like on her wrist.

"Not during daylight, Princess. Not while these murderers could come back at any moment. Here!" Eildon drew a folded docken leaf from his pouch and disclosed bread and cheese. "Sit down and eat. We've a few hours to wait yet."

Caterin obeyed. Her mind had suddenly gone blank. Murderers! Sweet Moon Maiden, had she not had enough? But Eildon was right. She could bring danger to her rescuers as well as herself.

"Thank Hunnid for saving my life. I'd have died of cold and hunger if they hadn't come. How did he know who I was?"

"He's seen you many times. From the shelter of a leaf or a petal. Believe me."

Hunnid produced a crude flask and poured an amber liquid into two shells. In the brighter light Caterin saw and admired the shy grace of his movements and wondered how she could ever have thought of them as beasts.

"They terrified me at first. But then, they were just as fearful when they found me in their tunnel."

"They're gentle folk," agreed Eildon. "And they belonged in this land before the Pretani. Don't forget that."

"Yet I can't speak to them."

"The Attecottie tongue the Druad taught you is no use. 'In the ritual language each word must be pronounced correctly and in the same order'," he mimicked. "But the Druad Attecottie is not a living language that grows with the needs of a people and sloughs off words that have lost their meaning. It's like comparing a sculpted eagle with a breathing one."

Above their heads his horse stamped and whinnied. Eildon paused to listen. "All's well. He's impatient, not startled."

"Look, Princess, some day I'll teach you their tongue for they're as much a part of your kingdom as any. Though I'm sure few Pretani have ever met a Hill-man face to face."

"No wonder if they hide underground half the time," said Caterin.

"Hunnid's people often steal down at night to harvest the shell-fish. They hole up in these old tunnels during daylight and hare off into the mountains with their baskets at nightfall. Their Protector is the Woman Thetil who drives her snow-white chariot through the mists of waterfall and corrie. Like all right-thinking people, I always pay my respects to her at the first stream before I venture into their land."

"How did you learn to talk without words?"

Eildon turned to look at the men and the planes of his long face seemed to lengthen in the shadows. The aura of mystery that always surrounded him was never more potent.

"You forget I live among them at times. Words are primitive tools compared to the power of thought," was all he said.

"Teach me how to do it, Eildon," she asked eagerly.

"It's not a skill you can learn. The power will come to you, if you ask for it. And it will grow as you use it."

That made sense to Caterin for she had shared thoughts with Veleda.

"I want to do something for them to show my gratitude."

"They want nothing more than to be left in peace."

"Some day they may need my help."

"It's more likely that you'll need theirs."

Dusk had come and the Mountain-men were moving. Saluting her with a clenched fist sign, they shouldered their creels and climbed out of the tunnel, leaving a faint tang of the sea overhanging the aroma of long-dead cattle.

"And now I can go home." Caterin put her hand on the ladder.

"You're not going back to the Palace."

Caterin whirled round.

"I must!" she cried. "I need to get ready for the Marriage."

"Look, my Princess, you're in danger in the Citadel. An insider betrayed you."

"What possible reason...?"

"There could be twenty good reasons why someone wanted you out of the way. It's always an unsettling time at the change-over of a Kingship. Sleeping ambitions awaken like dragons and take wing with fiery tongues and smoking nostrils. The Council want you in hiding, well away from the Palace."

"Dragons?" Caterin clenched her hands at her sides. "You mean Gort and his brother?"

"No, I meant nothing! That was my bard's tongue running away with me. You've been kidnapped once and it could happen again. Bridei wants you tucked away in a safe place."

But Caterin had jumped to the only conclusion possible.

"Ever since Gort arrived I've known he was working to betray us. Yet, he has the Kingship within his grasp. Am I wrong to be suspicious of him, Eildon?" She checked and her hand flew to her mouth. "Gort! It was his voice I heard outside, calling his men back to their ships. I was too dazed to recognise it then. Elldon, do you hear me? That's the truth! He meant to take me hostage. But he was attacked and beaten off!"

"Yet Bridei trusts him!"

Caterin's head went up in a gesture Eildon knew well. She was truly the daughter of his King.

"Bridei!" She snapped in disgust. "I'm going back to the Citadel! I am Queen in all but the Consecration!"

Eildon studied the sky.

"It's dark enough to move now. Listen! Bridei's arranged for you to be taken into a household at Pitmuies. You'll be a member of their kin and a lowly one at that. You've lost your family in the north from the coughing sickness. You've earned your keep before in Eirean. Can you forget you're Royal for a while?"

"I'll not go into hiding. This is all pure fantasy, Eildon!"

"Only Bridei, myself and Aortan will know where you are." Eildon was showing impatience now. "You must play your part."

"Who's Aortan?"

"The brother of the Clan Mother of the farm." Eildon gripped her shoulders under the fleeces. "Bridei must have your promise not to endanger yourself or this household by any reckless move. It's vitally important."

She had thought that Bridei would surely treat her as a responsible person now. How wrong she had been! He was going to tuck her away like a bairn in a cradle while the brothers of the Clan Mothers sold their land to the man with the sharpest sword.

"Who's in command at the Citadel? A King who's besotted by a substitute son? A parcel of old Councillors? An Heir whose loyalty is doubtful? Eildon, it's time the people had a true Pretani Queen to lead them."

She went up the ladder on wings and Eildon followed with a heavy heart. Bridei had told him he would need iron in his spirit to handle her. Outside she was stretching her arms to greet the starlit sky. He clenched his fist and swiftly hit her. She crumpled into his arms. He held her senseless body for a space, feeling Bridei's flesh and blood warm under his hands. Her time had not yet come but when it did, she would be worthy.

He bound her on a shaggy hill-pony that knew the lonely paths by heart and he ran at the side, straight as an arrow to the north-east, slackening speed only to circle round villages where people were moving outside settling their livestock down for the night.

CHAPTER THIRTY THREE

At a crossroads Eildon slowed, circling, glancing at the stars for direction.

"You traitor!" hissed the body on the pony.

"This is where you turn off for Pitmuies. There's a family awaiting your arrival. While you were on your way to visit them, you were set on by thieves and robbed of your mount and goods. A shepherd gave you a lift on your way."

"You'll have no praise-gift in my Royal Court, Eildon."

"Your name is Onid, after your grandmother." He saw the determined set of her face. "And you'll not attempt to escape. You're too intelligent, praise be, and you're aware I've eyes on every path and in every tree. Just remember, this is a time to lie low until the traitors' heads are on the parapet."

He raised a hand in farewell and smacked it down hard on the pony's rump. "When I ride back to Dalgynch tomorrow I'll have you whipped for this," she yelled after him

"If you can find me!" he cried as he vanished in the trees.

Back into slavery! Her mouth was bitter. A Queen, a Life-Giver, a Ruler and she had been felled and tied by a bard. What price her athletic training now? She should have sharpened her wits instead of her muscles.

Past the first clump of bushes, she found herself on the edge of a sizeable community. Timber-built houses clustered round a community green and more dwellings spread out into the darkness beyond. The smell of woodsmoke told of hearths still burning. One door alone stood open, its light spilling out across neat paving-stones. The pony, back on home-ground, bent to the water-trough and Caterin's bonds slackened. She slid off and went to stand in the open doorway, her night-eyes slowly adjusting.

"Oh, there you are, my poor bairn," came a deep, homely voice and she was clasped in warm arms against a soft plump bosom. "To be left without a mother and then to be robbed and beaten up! What a thing to happen! Come away in, Onid, and we'll have you bathed and fed in no time at all."

No one except Devana had embraced her so warmly before. Instinctively she recoiled. Then the smell of stream-washed linen and bread-baking enveloped her and she had a curious sense of home-coming. When the soft arms released her she looked into welcoming blue eyes. For a moment the eyes slid to Caterin's shortened hair. Then the woman was dragging a bath from an alcove.

"I'm Delys, sister to Aortan of Farg. We're your mother's kinsfolk." If Delys had been surprised at the sudden appearance of an unknown relative, she gave no sign. She upended the cauldron of water as if it was a feather. "I've told them all to keep away until you're presentable. Now, off with these filthy rags and in you go. My, my, how we'll ever get these stains out I don't know and such a bonny colour, too." Delys whisked the night-robe and fleeces into a bundle and tidied them away. From a chest she produced a tunic, shift and under-robe, shaking loose the dried herbs from the folds.

Caterin lay letting the warm water melt the chill from the marrow of her bones. Her eyes ranged over the large circular room with curtained archways leading to lesser rooms. Last year's corn-dollies hung from the rafters. Well-made chairs and stools lined the walls with patterned cushions here and there. On the table a sewing-box overflowed with coloured threads and a sky-blue tunic that Delys must have laid down when she heard her visitor. A half-carved toy horse lay beside it in a pile of wood-parings. From a hanging-bowl suspended over the fire-place came a savoury smell of cooking hare that brought the juices flowing in her mouth.

Soon she was at the table, pink-cheeked and wearing a green-and-white tunic, with her spoon poised over a bowl of thick stew.

Delys planked her wide hips on the seat opposite. Her round rosy cheeks shone like polished apples after her exertions. Her pure-white hair was parted in the middle and caught at the back by a blue braided ribbon before falling smooth and straight to her waist. Her clear eyes held no secrets. Few would be able to deceive her and few would want to, under the candour of her gaze.

"My brother says you've suffered and I've to ask no questions, so I won't." She looked down at her capable hands clasped on the table in front of her as though it would never enter her head to disobey her brother. There was a pause and Caterin's cheeks reddened.

Naturally, Delys was curious. A woman does not open her hearth and home easily to a stranger. But Delys would have her own ways of getting at the truth of things. Caterin laid down her spoon, intending to explain that she would be gone in the morning. But a mighty thump on the door interrupted her.

"That's Aortan's fist." Delys drew back the bar.

Aortan had a grim slit of a mouth that looked as though few words would pass it let alone a royal secret.

"Has she made you welcome under her thatch?" Dressed in a homespun tunic and leggings and as thickset and ruddy as a farmer should be, Aortan barked the question at Caterin.

"Och, man, you can see for yourself she's settled in. And she's a fine lass, so don't you be biting her nose off."

Caterin saw Aortan give her the sidelong look that people reserved for gods and royalty. She sensed by his gruffness that he was uneasy. It must have been a difficult decision to put his family in danger, however much he wanted to serve his King. And if she rode out tomorrow, he would feel he had failed in his duty.

Yet she must go. She had a duty also. Better to leave at first light and Aortan need not be troubled any longer. Yet how could she throw the kindness of their welcome back in their faces.

"Your sister bathed and fed me," she told Aortan. "What more could a body want? But it was the way she took me to her heart when I crossed the threshold that I'll always remember."

She knew she had pleased them. Delys laughed and nudged her brother. Aortan's eyes twinkled. And Caterin smiled, knowing she was accepted. Until tomorrow when she would beg their forgiveness. Yet as she bent to her stew she was aware that she had meant every word she had said.

Then the door burst open. A girl tumbled in, hair flying.

"Is she here yet?" she demanded.

"Monikie, shut that door before the Peskies creep in!"

"Wait! UUen and Tarain are at my back!" Monikie was all broad smiles and oustretched arms.

"I couldn't wait to meet you! And we're the same age! Just you wait and see! We're going to have rare times together." Monikie was a replica of her mother except that she was slimmer and the long smooth hair was pale yellow like sunlight after rain. She had her mother's apple-blossom cheeks and the same inability to stop chattering. "And here's my brother, Uuen. We're forced to have him here because he's so lazy about building his own house." She ducked away from Uuen's knuckles. "This is his wife, Tarain. She's the beauty of the family but she's all broody just now and no fun at all."

"Monikie! This poor lass is exhausted." Delys pointed to a low doorway. "There's the earth-house, Onid. For tonight you'll not be expected to refill the bucket of water. Now off to bed and don't chatter all night!"

Caterin hesitated at the doorway to the sleeping-room when she saw only one bed. The thought of sleeping beside another person troubled her more than she cared to admit.

"I hate sleeping alone, don't you?" All bare elbows now, Monikie rummaged in a chest. "It was awful when my sisters began to leave home." Her words were muffled as she delved deeper. "You suit that skirt better than I do with your green eyes and that lovely hair. There we are! Put this shift on and come to bed. This side's yours!"

Caterin lay stiffly on her back while Monikie blew out the lamp and slipped in beside her.

"Turn on your side, Onid," Monikie commanded. "Then we'll fit together like twin lambs in their dam."

As the soft body snuggled against hers, Caterin marvelled at the way this girl had accepted her into her home and her bed. An arm stole round her waist and she had a warm feeling of being cherished. She squeezed Monikie's hand against her heart and sighed drowsily. The chance of being close to a woman of her own age suddenly mattered a great deal to her. Life was full of surprises.

CHAPTER THIRTY FOUR

A baby's cry aroused Caterin next morning. She woke expecting Iogena to hold out Bran to be kissed. Instead, her eyes met a stuffed doll with a wide embroidered skirt and a flutter of hair ribbons hanging from the rafters.

Somewhere between her arrival and falling asleep, she had gained some insight and had made a decision. Bridei was not shielding a daughter, he was protecting a Queen. Whoever had abducted her still intended to use her. Whether it was the long forepaw of Artcois or the servants of the brothers Gwynedd, their plans had only been foiled for the present. Their next move would be bolder and deadlier. An appetising smell of hot barley cakes wafted in from the other room.

"Monikie, will you get that hen and her brood outside before I have shat under my feet and a chicken too many in the soup." Delys's rich voice was drowned in an outraged cackling.

"D'you have to rush around in the mornings like a scalded cat?" complained Monikie, yawning.

"And if I didn't, who would? Not you! You'd wait till the Flaming One herself appeared before you'd fetch the milk! And leave these cakes alone!"

Caterin got the message. She had been left to lie late on her first morning but it was a busy household. Monikie had laid washing water and a tunic handy on a table.

She hurried through to a room that was full of liveliness. Sleepy contented noises came from one corner where Tarain suckled her baby. Monikie, holding a milky bladder to the thrusting mouth of a lamb, made a face behind her mother's back. Caterin grinned. Her time as slave to the Northfolk was going to come in handy. She rolled up her sleeves.

"I'm a member of this mad clan now. So where's all this urgent work that's clamouring to be done?" She planted herself in front of Delys.

"H'm! You're going to be as cheeky as the rest of my litter." Delys skelped Caterin's bottom with her broom. "Sit and get some food into you. It looks like you're feeling better already."

If this was family life, Caterin knew she was going to enjoy it. It was all frothy banter on the surface with a steady stream of love underlying it.

After she had thrown her last crumbs to the spirit of the hearth, she lifted the lid of the brewing barrel and Monikie skimmed the froth off with a long wooden paddle. She guessed Monikie would splash her and hid behind the lid.

"Help!" wailed Delys. "Am I going to be deaved by witless laughter every time you two get together? Get into the cool room, the pair of you, and bend your backs to the churning. And for the sake of my temper, shut the door so that I can't hear you."

Monikie sang love-songs as she turned the handle, matching her churning to her own happy beat. After a self-conscious interval, Caterin joined in. Quietly at first and then louder with a surge of joy.

"You'll sour the milk with your skirling! And waken the bairn as well!" It was Tarain who poked her head in.

"Ach, I'm always in trouble," stated Monikie placidly. A calf with melting eyes had wandered in. Absently she let his rough tongue lick her milky fingers. After noon, Monikie took Caterin round the village. A woman, withdrew her head from a rain-barrel to wave. A couple stopped haggling over some horn spoons long enough to cry greetings. An old blind man, sitting outside the house with the potter's sign above it, tilted his head to listen as they passed. A scatter of boys, fighting a running battle with bows and arrows, shot a friendly warning across their path. A young man heaved a stone to the top of his dyke and leaned on it, whistling at them. A little girl dressed as Bride in a trailing white robe threw them a dandelion from her posy.

Engrossed in the hubbub of household and neighbours, Caterin had little time to wonder what was going on in the Citadel. There were a hundred things to see and do every day.

The first time they had a wash-day, Caterin and Monikie ran with their trailing bundles to the burn. Delys had given Caterin a block of clover-scented sheep-fat to rub on her stained night-robe but they threw the rest of the washing into the stream. Kilting up their skirts, they trampled and splashed and giggled. Their shrieks brought a bevy of young men from a nearby turnip field. Plunging into the burn beside them, they grabbed the girls, and began stamping out a merry dance to the rhythm of two old crones on the bank, clapping and showing their yellow teeth.

Breathless, Caterin waved away the arms of the men and waded to the shallows to watch for a moment. This beat any fun she had ever had on the sportsground. The biting cold of the water nipped her toes as it flowed past, straight from the mountains that still had snow in their high deep corries. Then the answer hit her. Here there was no competition and no barrier of royalty. Life and the sun were here to be enjoyed. For the cold season would return and war might come again. A brawny arm whirled her back into the dance.

The high spirits lessened as Beltane came near. After all it was the sacred oak wood they were gathering for fuel. Too much hilarity and the spirits of air and earth might repay that disrespect with a blight on the crop. The Beltane fires were built by the girls who were not in childbirth after Lugnasad nine months ago. On a grassy platform, half-way up the nearest hill, they erected two fires with enough of a passage for the cattle to move through. One day there was a strange young man helping Aortan to widen the trench around the fires. Caterin turned her face away. Any stranger might spell danger.

"Who's that with Aortan in the Sun-Circle?"

"Him? He's only my brother. Tomas the Bull."

"Because he's a bull with women?"

"No, he takes his bulls round the small crofts for the breeding. But he's easily roused by women, too. So, watch him. There, the fires are done. Let's get some rowan branches for the lintels."

"Hold on!" shouted Tomas. "I'll bring my axe."

"Ach, you just want to get your hands round Onid's buttocks, I know you."

"There! I was hoping to creep up on her unawares. Now, you've shot my last arrow." Tomas's dark eyes appraised Caterin's face and figure. He let out a low whistle.

"Wheesht or the Great Ones will make your bulls sterile."

The sly threat was enough to set him to work.

"Where did Tomas get his dark hair from?" asked Caterin later as they hung boughs laid with creamy blossom above the lintel of the stable.

"My mother had two or three handfast marriages in her youth. We're the proof that they were fertile but she always separated at later Festivals. Ask her why yourself. She'll just tell you she could never see a man in her road."

As they laid the last of their boughs round the dung-heap, Delys called from her doorway.

"Time to make the Beltane bannocks!"

Barley meal spread with a mixture of switched egg, oatmeal and milk was toasted before the fire. The Beltane cheese sat ready on a platter, made with the milk of ewes the day after the lambs had been weaned. "A churning past and a cheese made before sunrise on Beltane," chanted Delys. "Now, don't tell me you don't know how to make a caudle and you a farmer's daughter." She gave Caterin a long, appraising look.

Delys is making guesses, thought Caterin. But in Eirean she had never had to make a Beltane caudle.

"Make a custard of eggs and milk and add oatmeal," whispered Monikie.

On Beltane Eve, they let the fire die and raked out the year's ashes. Before dawn, the whole village was on the move, shadowy figures emerging from every doorway. Presently a long procession began to mount the steep hill-side, driving their animals before them. While the beasts grazed everyone, men, women and children stood silent within the Sun-Circle.

A bairn cried and was rocked to sleep again. All was still. A faint milky glow appeared in the east. A shy breeze shivered across the sky and the stars disappeared. Tomas, standing behind Caterin let his breath out in a shuddering sigh. The glow deepened to buttermilk and began to flush until, with a flash of blue light, the rim of the sun flared above the horizon. As if released from sleep by a wave of a willow-wand, finches all around burst into song. With a great exhultant shout, the people joined hands and swung into their praise-song.

"Greetings to you, Father of the seasons, gem of the morning as you travel on the wing of heights."

Now the Festival could begin. Already, Aortan had his feet planted on either side of an oak log, for no flint must light the need-fire. He twirled the drill between his palms at an astounding speed until the wood dust ignited the shavings. And the folk cheered again and ran with twigs to keep it going. Delys put two

290

lambs, freshly killed, on either side of the new fire to cook. Tomas grabbed Caterin's hand and they danced with the others, three times moon-wise round the need-fire.

Now it was the turn of the beasts. The two great bonfires roared into flame. Pillars of grey smoke rose into the pearly air and high above turned to flow north-east. And Caterin saw, in every direction, great pillars rising and billowing, carrying the tang of the Beltane fires to the nostrils of the Fertile Ones.

Tomas came leading his bulls and threw a pointed stick of juniper to Caterin to help prod them through between the purifying flames. A tall rangy Drui stood beyond, glowering at the capering bairns, sucking at the Beltane bannock and throwing every second bit over his left shoulder.

"This I give to you, O Fox, to spare our hens. This I give to you, O hooded crow ..." he intoned.

It was a dour pony that started it, planting his four feet on the ground and refusing to enter the burning passageway. Tomas poked Aortan's goat in the rump. It butted the pony clear through the passage but the goat came out the other end looking for trouble. Its horns found a cow who bellowed, raised her tail and deposited a steaming brown pancake on the ground. Everyone scattered except the Drui. His eyes had rolled skyward. He had reached the chant to the bear and had forgotten what came next.

The goat fixed his eye on the fluttering white robe. He took a run and overturned the Drui neatly into the pungent pile with a thud and a squelch. When everyone had dried their eyes, the goat was calmly eating the tail of the Drui's robe.

"You won't be needing to black your face with sacred ashes now!" roared Tomas. "For your buttocks are browned by the sacred dung."

Caterin and Monikie ran together, circling the fields and dwellings, whirling their torches of dried heather round their heads imitating the movement of the moon. Back in the village, the men put the beasts away while Delys took Caterin's torch and kindled the new-laid fire on the hearth. She dowsed the torch in water and broke off a lump of charcoal.

"Tomas, if you're staying here tonight, earn your keep. Crush these ashes in the mangers and don't forget the words."

"Come and help me, Onid," demanded Tomas.

"Not in a score of Beltanes, you vagabond," cried Delys, chasing him with her blackened hands.

"Emhad didn't get a need-fire," crowed Monikie. "Has he not paid his dues again?"

"Hold your tongue!" snapped Delys. She held up the caudle bowl and poured the last of the contents on the spitting hearth-stones. "May all the spirits of the air spare us from the storm. I don't think the Drui had time for that spell," she added without batting an eyelid.

But Beltane was not over yet. They feasted round a bonfire on the common green. Later, a melody picked out on a clarsach joined with the bass twang of a one-stringed fiddle and a rhythm from the blown-up bladder of a pig. Then old and young danced the stately traditional steps. But a barrel of ale later they were whirling around in the fast-flying reels of the Mountain-Folk.

The saining by fire and water was over. Next day came the Flitting. The young folk who were going to the shieling were up before dawn, busy as bees about to swarm.

Caterin stood with Monikie to cheer them on their way. Sheep with sad bewildered faces, barefoot shepherd boys carrying lambs and wolf-horns. Dogs, skelping and scurrying, knowing the way better than anyone. Patient cows, udders swaying, lowing at milkmaids who sang and swung along free and erect, on their backs, bedding and babies and milk pails. Goats, skimpy beards waggling and one, a young billy with a bad case of wind in his belly.

"Serve him right!" cried Monikie. "He left the Drui without enough tunic to cover whatever a Drui keeps between his legs."

Hill-ponies, offended by pots and cauldrons slung on their backs and fastened, clanging and chiming round their necks. Men, with ropes for collars and spades rearing high out of back-packs.

"And good riddance to their noise and smells!" cried Monikie suddenly, blinking her eyes.

"What's wrong? You wanted to go with them!" Caterin guessed. "And why aren't we going?" She had not thought to ask.

"We've to stay and weed the crops." Monikie's mouth was sulky. "It's all because I was going to meet my sweetheart up there. And when I yelled at Aortan, he shut his mouth as tight as a purse-string. He's a kill-joy, so he is."

Aortan was keeping the Princess here under his eye, Caterin thought. And Monikie had to suffer for it. She slipped an arm round Monikie's waist and hugged her. But Monikie could not be moody for very long.

"Let's go and see the Goose-Launching."

"I know I'm stupid," said Caterin slowly, "but why is Delys throwing a goose into the lochan?".

"It's our clan totem, silly! Because it feeds on plants and we grow plants. It brings good growing for another thirteen moons. How would you like to go looking for honey?"

They followed the flight of the bees to a hollow tree-trunk. They lit a fire and put an ember inside a pair of bellows. Caterin smoked the bees silly while Monikie scooped the contents of the hive into leaves. They walked back, laughing, with their arms round one another. In the dairy, they made a paste with combs, bees, grubs and pollen and all and ate it on bannocks, sharing it with three little girls who had followed them inside. Bairns, Caterin had discovered, wandered freely in and out of the houses, eating and sleeping wherever they chose.

As the days grew warmer and longer, and the girls worked side by side in the fields, a strong bond of friendship grew between them. When it rained, they worked in the weaving shed. It was the gatherings round the common bonfire in the evenings that Caterin enjoyed most when the chatter became storytelling and the singers broke into dance. And it seemed as though the Banqueting Hall had never existed.

Two moons came and went. Then one evening, Eildon was there in the circle, his hooded eyes warning her not to recognise him. Caterin, rocking Tarain's baby, found herself trembling. She handed the baby to Monikie with some silly excuse.

So, Bridei was checking up on her safety but had not summoned her back to the Citadel. The girl in her rejoiced. The woman felt a stab of guilt. What had happened to her high ambitions?

After Eildon had eaten Delys called for his news.

"What of Aedan and his rabble?"

"Does Bridei still have his foot on their necks?"

"Let's say that Colum Cille is keeping Aedan within his own boundaries." Eildon settled down with his cup of ale. News from the heart of things at court was not to be hurried. "Colum Cille's the Dove of Peace now. He's teaching Aedan how to rule a kingdom instead of rushing off to war like a stag in rut."

"When's the Marriage to be?"

"Where's the Princess?"

Caterin froze where she sat, her arm on Monikie's shoulders.

"If Bridei knows, he's telling no one. His eyes are trained south. Rhun of Gwynedd has marched north and was given free passage through Rheged. He's dallied so long around the courts of the Kings of York and the Pennines that his long march is becoming a legend. It's cried that the army has stayed away so long that their wives are sleeping with their bond-servants. It's true!" He had caught the laughter among his audience. "Rhun himself loitered long enough to catch the eye of a cousin of the King of York and marry her. No, Rhun's in no hurry. The fact that no one has faced up to him proves that he's as powerful as his father. Right now, he could weld them all into one large kingdom and be Overlord."

Aortan broke the hush that had fallen.

"From there it's an easy step over the Pettaland Hills to the Forth."

"Will he come to us in peace or war?"

Eildon extended his long legs.

"Only Rhun and his brother can answer that."

"And his brother is the man we elected as our next King." Uuen had put into words what was in every mind. Would the Pretani under Gort be allies or under-dogs? Caterin sensed the uncertainty in the hearts around her. It seemed she had been right to ask these very questions at the beginning.

"Where is he, this Prince of Gwynedd?" "He's not at Dalgynch."

"Does Bridei not know where his Heir is?"

"Now you don't expect Bridei to tell his secrets to a mere bard, do you?" Eildon's long features crinkled at Caterin. You liar, she mouthed.

But immediately, Eildon was serious again.

"Bridei will stay in Dalgynch as long as the Veniconie are hatching plots. It's the first break among the clans since Bridei united us. Think of it! The traitor sons of Artcois ruling the land down future ages. With no Elections! And no Abdications!"

"Yet whoever is King, he'll need the Queen to breed from." The eyes of Delys were large and innocent. "Poor lassie!" Caterin looked around swiftly. But there was no dawning of understanding on any face. She had been accepted as one of them. She felt a surge of quiet pride at that.

"Never fear," said Eildon. "That young women will survive, mark my words. She'll return to carry on the Royal Line, though whether it'll be with King Gort, I, for one, won't hazard a guess. Now, little Maidie, what song would your Highness like me to sing?"

The child at his feet rose to the occasion. She leapt up and held out a grubby hand in a commanding gesture.

"One I can dance to, my Lord Eildon, or I'll have your harpstrings to keep my leggings up."

There was a gale of laughter and Eildon launched into jolly rhymes that had the children all up and marching. When the alecups were refilled he changed to drinking songs so that soon they had to be refilled again. Then came heart-melting love-songs that heated the blood of lovers to liquid fire and sent them stealing into the shadows.

There seemed to be a special magic in the air that evening. Everyone lazed round the bonfire. The wondering eyes of sleepy children followed the drifting sparks in the still air. To the west, the sun was sinking in a glory of gold and red splashes against a background of amethyst. The smell of burning pine-wood, comforting in its sweet familiarity, mingled with the perfume of night-scented flowers that drugged the senses like wine. Yet, Caterin saw men with recent battle-scars and women whose scars went deeper and showed only in their eyes.

Then the women stirred and Eildon played a lullaby to tempt the little ones to bed. The men stretched their legs and gathered to discuss tomorrow's weather and the state of the crops.

Caterin slipped away, following the gurgle of flowing water, till she felt the land slope down to the stream. She sat on the bank, alert, listening. A sleepy cheeping in the branches overhead. That was all. Then a soft cascade of notes from Eildon's seven-stringed harp had her searching the clump of trees that leaned over the water. A long shadow was stretched on a branch, his face hidden in the leaves.

"Today I met a man with a nestling gos-hawk." His low words reached her before she could begin asking questions. His plucking fingers groped for a melody. "She came at his call to be fed. Cream and dusk-brown were the feathers on her breast. She glanced with a brilliant eye on the man who caressed her. And I thought of a girl-child at the knee of a father." His fingers still sought the notes that would clothe his song.

Above her head a lonely oyster-catcher wheeped plaintively as it crossed the darkening sky. Then the melody began to swoop and soar around Caterin again.

"And I thought of the hoods and tresses that would bind her," went on the bard. "Of the whistles and calls that would summon. Of the chains and bells that would tie her to the ground."

He paused, unsatisfied, and went over the lines again, changing a word here and there to fit the rhythm of his song. "In the sky birds wheel free above the mountain, envying not the little goshawk where she sleeps in a silken bed and eats meat that is washed in the stream. In the fields girls gather flowers, their laughter on the wind, caring naught for the other with the jewelled perch and the golden chain."

A soft sighing stirred the trees and rustled the leaves.

"Woman and gos-hawk, longing to be free, straining at the fetters. Remember the nets and snares of the bird-catcher, of cruel beaks and rending talons, and spies in a Citadel and raiders that come from the sea."

Sharp plaintive chords like the cry of a lost nestling shivered her heart-strings and died away into silence.

"That will be a good song I think," said Eildon, "once it's polished and has an ending."

Caterin dried her wet cheeks with her hand. Seeing Eildon had sent a stab of homesickness through her.

"Away with you and your pathetic little fledgling!" she chided Eildon. "Some day I'll give you an ending for your song that'll startle you out of your breeches."

"And why shouldn't I sing about a bonny milk-maid?" Eildon's mouth was just a hair's breadth from her ear and the warning was plain. "Have any strangers passed through?"

"None that I know of." She paused, a question trembling on her lips. "Eildon, is he a traitor?"

"Gort?" The name dropped like a pebble from Eildon's lips and sent out ripples of fear in the air. There was a moment's hesitation before he spoke and then it was only a ghostly whisper on the wind.

"Who knows?"

After he had gone, Caterin sat long into the night. If she had read his song right, Gort was the bird-catcher. Surely he would never be King now. This time last year she might have danced for joy at that prospect. Now she felt empty. Her body sang out to be loved. Life was a tasteless thing without loving.

When Tomas came to find her, she welcomed him into her arms. They made love with a lusty joy against a tree, rolled laughing down the slope into the shallows and made love again.

CHAPTER THIRTY FIVE

"Where have you been?" grunted Monikie as Caterin snuggled into beside her.

"Do you think I'd tell you, Blabber-mouth?"

Monikie swiped at Caterin's head with a pillow.

"I'd guess you were up at the Kissing Trees with a man," she laughed. "D'you know what? I'll find someone from Gair's village for you. We'll handfast at Lugnasad and have our bairns together."

"Put a gag in it, Monikie. I'm tired." "Oh, I forgot! What are you doing in the Harvest Competitions? The singing or the story-telling or the bull-baiting or what?"

Caterin thought she had not heard right but she was too tired too care.

"Bull-baiting," she said, pounding the goose-feathers in her pillow.

"Oh!" There was a long lovely silence and Caterin dozed off. "Then you'll have to start practising with Tomas's bulls, won't you?"

Caterin snored softly.

But it was true enough. Bull-baiting. Caterin had found an easy rhythm to the bending and binding of corn that toned up muscles she had not used for many moons and the thought of taking up a new sport excited her. At the end of the next day's work, they went to the bull-paddock.

"Tomas breeds good sturdy bulls for serving cows but he keeps the agile ones for the baiting." Monikie thumped on a solid gate.

"Oh, it's you, pest!" Tomas's voice complained. "I'm busy enough without unbarring gates for you."

But he opened the gate as she knew he would and pretended to box with her, confusing her mercilessly with his quick darting movements until she escaped to sit on a fence.

Tomas's bulls had been bred with a special skill. They were larger than the red shaggy cattle that grazed in the Royal Estates. Black and shining, with powerful chests and muscles that rippled in the sunlight. The living embodiment of the Royal Bull Symbol!

"Onid wants to start bull-baiting, Tomas!" Monikie cried.

Tomas gave Caterin a long measuring look and a swift grin at the end of it. "You've the body for it. D'you have the courage?"

Without waiting he whistled one of his hounds to detach a bull from the herd. Another whistle and all the stray hounds were back against the fence. Then he drew from his pouch a red-and-white sweat-cloth.

He circled the solitary bull once or twice, warily, drawing closer to it each time, flicking his cloth to confuse it. Then he began a series of lunging darts in towards the massive head. By now the bull was angry and tossing its horns. At the very moment when the bull began pawing the ground, ready to charge, Tomas ran at the lowered head. Missing the waving points by a hairsbreadth, he swerved, caught one of the horns and swung his body half-round the neck, to plant his colourful cloth expertly among the mass of black curls in the middle of its forehead.

"I want to do that, Tomas!" cried Caterin, clapping her hands as he ran up, leaving the hounds to snap at the heels of the bull and drive it back to the herd. "I'm used to balancing on moving horses. With a bit of practise I could bait a bull!"

Tomas's eyes lit up. He liked a woman who could take a challenge on board.

"We'll see once the harvest's in," was all he said.

"How about you, Monikie?"

"Oho, that's not for me!" cried Monikie, springing off the fence. "Besides, I've got myself a man."

"What do you mean?" Caterin's eyes still lingered on the sleek black bodies as they turned for home.

"Well, in the old days if a girl wanted a man, she planted her rosette on the bull's poll and the man who picked it off was hers to share the Festival nights with. You wouldn't dare, Onid, would you?"

"I'm going to try." Caterin flexed her arm muscles and laughed at Monikie's wide eyes.

"Oh, I couldn't bear to watch you!" But Monikie was caught up in the excitement too. "The men come down from the shielings for it. I've seen more than one bairn come from a bull-baiting."

"Wait! I'm not after a lover, just the sport."

The scything, stacking and gleaning went on with everyone in good spirits. It was a good crop and was drying nicely. There would be plenty in store for the Cold Season. Each evening, Caterin went to watch the bulls. And to be with Tomas. They made love with the rain bathing their faces, in the empty byre on the sweet hay and once, suddenly, in the paddock with the bulls. One day, Aortan brought his ale and bannocks and sat beside Caterin against a drying stack.

"This bull-baiting takes a lot of skill. Are you sure you have the nerve?" "I've done tricks on horses all my life."

"Horses don't have horns like our black giants. Would your father allow it?"

"I know enough not to be reckless."

"Well, Tomas can try you out. But if he thinks you might injure yourself the practice stops."

"People will start to wonder if you try to coddle me, Aortan," she warned.

It would be good to pit her wits and skills against an animal again. While the grain was drying, a few young men and women came to learn from Tomas in the bull-paddock. First, he showed them how to tease the bull before an experienced baiter stepped in and swung on the horns. At the same time, Tomas was selecting the bulls that he would use at the Festival. Caterin saw that he weeded out the most unpredictable ones but not the most fiery.

"Study each bull for yourself. See how he moves, whether he's fast to react or slow, how he usually swings his horns, to the right or to the left."

Then the day came when Tomas let them try on their own. Men with whips surrounded the bull while the hounds crouched, ready.

"Watch his eyes. They'll flicker the instant before he begins his charge. That's your moment," Tomas cautioned.

Caterin picked a spiky blue flower as she waited for her turn. The first man missed the horn completely, glanced off the solid side of the beast and scurried to safety, sucking skinned knuckles.

Next was a girl who hesitated at the fearsome sight of the lowered head. The bull began his charge and the hounds and the men went in quickly, heading the bull off while she sprinted to safety.

Caterin was next to go and, as she danced about, teasing the bull, she knew that her past training had made her ready. She concentrated all her mind on the bull, her nerves rock-steady. Now that she was near enough to see the moist black velvet muzzle at close quarters, he was even bigger than she had realised. The red-rimmed eyes flickered and she timed her swerve perfectly. Then she had a swinging horn in her hand and she slapped her flower firmly on its curly pow.

"Don't get too cocky," said Tomas drily as she passed him grinning. "Next time, he'll have a new trick to play on you."

"He's not the only one with new tricks," Caterin called back.

Tomas, Caterin found, had been with Gort's army at Dundurn along with most young men nearby.

"Once the harvest's in, I reckon Bridei will call us back into service," he told Caterin later as they lay on their backs under a tree. The harvest blush of the Moon Maiden, glowed through the branches. "Maybe we'll ride with the new King this time."

"Tomas will love you and leave you." Monikie said when she knew they were lovers. But that was all right with Caterin.

One day, Caterin was swinging her flail to the rhythm of the threshers' song when Aortan called her. She straightened her back and saw his strained face. Bridei? the Capital? The Veniconie? Gort? Bridei?

It was Bridei.

"It was a mere skirmish near Dun Troddan," he told her. "Not Aedan himself but that litter of sons of his. Two of them will never go home again - Eochaid and Find." He took a deep shaky breath. "Bridei took a spear in the throat."

She sat still and alone, seeing distinctly the knots in the wood of the table. And there was nothing else but to follow the grain with her eyes to another knot. And another. Someone was whispering.

"It's not true! It's not true!"

And a voice boomed out above her head.

"I'd give my spear-hand if it wasn't so."

And she stretched out her arm over the knots and saw the blood in the veins, living blood that flowed from Bridei.

Not the man that called her 'Kitten', in a voice that was soft and proud and pleased! And his skin warm and his breath on her cheek and his presence that brought a room to life. Not him!

"Not him!" She was up and screaming it out now at the face that loomed. And fighting against the hands that held her arms.

"Sit down!"

And she sat. And then she was up again.

"I must go! Where is he? I must see him!"

She would make him better! She would show them all that he was still warm and breathing! They were fools if they thought Bridei could die!

"There's nothing you can do. It's all been done."

"All been done? What do you mean? Never!"

She was not making sense! Nothing made sense! Nothing would ever make sense again!

"It was the spear of Artur that dealt him his death-blow."

Someone was moaning. Tell her to stop! I can't hear! Artur? Artur, he'd said. No, no, no!

Then she knew it was true. No one could have have thought up such a monstrous lie. And she clenched her fists and gave out a scream of rage that set the dogs barking and the hens fluttering for cover.

"And where was Gort? Away mopping and mowing Saxon heads. He should have been there. he should have been the one. He should be the dead one, staring at the sky."

And the words she said brought a black grinding pain and she gouged her palms into her eyes to destroy the image. She took a breath to scream again and a blow caught the side of her head. And she was down, her head ringing with the blow, staring at the floor where a lost bead lay half-buried in the close-packed earth.

"Stop that noise! They'll hear it in the fields. Get hold of yourself!"

She laughed at that, wildly, harshly, picturing herself pulling fragments of herself out of the air like a conjuror and glueing them together. And what if she stuck a bit in a wrong place?

"Life moves on. And you've got to go on with it."

And how could she go on if she had stuck a hand where a foot should be? Oh, Bride she was going mad! Think! What with? There was nothing there but a cold numbness.

"Who brought the news?" Her voice came out flat and dead.

"Eildon."

"Bring him. I must go back to Dalgynch."

"He's gone. And you'll not be leaving here."

"I must!" She pulled herself up by the table. "There are arrangements. A funeral, a new King." Any activity to keep her sane. To push the darkness away.

"Sit there and listen." Roughly Aortan thrust her into a seat and sat opposite. He had had to push aside his own grief for the King he had admired. His heart was sore for the daughter, but now was the time of greatest danger for his kin.

"There's more. Aedan has put his son into the Kingship,

Gartnait, a half-Pretani man to forestall rebellion."

Gartnait. Wholly Pretani. Acknowledged by Aedan but sired by a Pretani giant.

"Gartnait's there in Dalgynch in the midst of Veniconie country with Artcois and Maelchon sailing up and down his coast-line. Between them Gartnait and Maelchon would cut you in half to gain the Kingship."

"How can I stay here. Who else can rally the people to throw out these upstarts?"

"The time's not ripe. Let them kill one another off. Then you'll lead us, Lady."

Her grief exploded in fury.

"And where's Prince Gort? He was elected King to keep the Scots out of our land?"

"It was he who killed the two sons of Aedan. Then he took an arrow in his arm trying to rescue your father. Yet Eildon said it was strange he was not among the wounded who returned."

"So he's still around. Coward that he is!" She thumped the table. "Oh, it's infuriating to be in a backwater where the news takes for ever to filter through!"

"He might have been taken prisoner. More likely he's escaped to bring troops from Gwynedd. But you'll need him at your side before you make your move."

Caterin bit on her thumb. Aortan was right. She dare not leave for the Capital with so little information. Yet she must go soon. Someone would have to goudge out the canker the heart of Dalgynch. Bridei was gone but his blood ran in her veins. Bridei! Old Craggy-chin! How could she bear it?

The blackness returned and with it the echoes of voices as if through a fog. The workers were coming back from the fields. The door burst open and Delys stopped at the sight of the two still, shocked figures. Without a word, she turned and went out. Aortan gripped Caterin's shoulders.

"There's only one course for you!" His voice was rough. "You must carry on here as though nothing has happened. Otherwise someone will guess who you are."

"How can I?" she cried.

"Don't ask me!" Deliberately he hardened his tone. "You're the Queen! You're Bridei's daughter! Where's the strength and courage you'll need if you've to lead your people? Indeed you may be our last hope before we're completely overthrown by the Scots."

He talked on and on, repeating the same ideas until they sank into her mind. By the time the family came in, Caterin was sitting, pale but composed, a half-beaker of mead having taken the rough edge off her grief.

"You're the quiet one today." said Monikie, throwing a careless arm round Caterin's shoulders.

"And you're like a fly round a lump of dung." This from Delys as she banged a platter of stew on the table under Monikie's nose. "The lass is tired. I've always said that romping with bulls is too much after a day's work. Now eat that and stop your silly clashtrap."

"It's yourself that's tired out, I'm thinking," began Monikie, her eyes widening with hurt at her mother's tone. "Ach, you've had it too easy all your days, girl!" snapped Dilys. "Onid's had enough trouble this past while to last a lifetime. And now the King's dead. And only the Mighty Ones know where we'll all be next harvest." Delys stopped on a sob. Her ladle flew wildly scattering gravy across the board.

"It's nothing but Onid this and Onid that!" yelped Monikie. "I'd to stay home from the shieling because of Onid. And now look what you've done to my skirt! And Onid's got all my best ones!" She yelped again as a wooden spoon bounced off her ear.

"Don't!" cried Caterin. "Don't fall out over me. I love you both so much, I couldn't bear that!" Her voice broke. Tears were too near the surface on this dark day.

Instantly Monikie was hugging her.

"Och, never mind me. I'm a grump because I'm missing Gair." And she grabbed bread from the basket and began eating hungrily.

But Caterin knew that Delys had guessed who she was. Aortan would never have told her. With her generosity of spirit, Delys was grieving for her. She felt Delys's eyes resting on her and looked up to meet a look of love and concern that told her she need never go far to find understanding whenever she needed it.

After the meal, the bonfire was lit outside and the folk sat round it to mourn their King. They spoke of his courage, his defeated enemies, the prosperity and glory he had brought. They spoke of his young Queen who had died in childbirth and of his beautiful daughter, wherever she was, Bride save her.

The potter brought out his harp and they sang the songs of

Bridei's campaigns until the stars came out and the Moon Maiden slanted her long sad gaze on them.

From then on Caterin threw herself into every activity to try to forget the ache in her heart. Only once did she succumb to it. One day, she left the threshing shed and ran, climbing to the top of a hill. Throwing herself on the grass behind a rock she gave way to a bout of frenzied weeping, beating her hands wildly on the turf until her pent-up grief had streamed away with her tears.

Calmer, she lay on her back and looked at the sky, hating Gort in her heart. He had let her father take the brunt of the battles while he hosted with his brother. As a King he was worthless. Yet where would she find herself another warrior King? The Sons of Aedan were too close kin. The Lothian Kings were a weak-knead lot although there was a Prince at Dun Eidyn, that folk said had some merit. The young Saeson Princes had been decimated by Rhun. And who in their senses would invite a cruel barbarian giant into their land? Curses on Gort's head! He was still the best man for the job!

Yet he would betray her people time and again to further his ambitions. Of that she was sure. If she set up shrines of healing he would have them overflowing with wounded soldiers leaving no room for sick bairns. He would despise men like Derelei for seeing beauty in stone or metal. He might make his sons his Heirs or Bishops in the Church. Unless she could curb him. And Bride help her, she would!

She cooled her eyes with water from a stream. But Aortan knew she had been weeping and so, she was sure, did Delys. And when Tomas sat beside her at the hearth she shook her head absently and went back to wondering what could have happened to Gort.

CHAPTER THIRTY SIX

It was a time for the fruits and berries to be boiled up with honey, a time for the nets to be hauled home with the harvest of nuts. And a time for anyone who could pipe a tune or beat a drum to be spirited into a corner to play for the dancers practising for the Lugnasad Competitions. At night, Caterin fell asleep to the skirl of a bag-pipe on the hill or a sweet voice near at hand singing over and over the same tune.

On the morning of the Festival Caterin, leaning from the doorway to look at the sky found a whole village that had sprouted suddenly with bright waving banners and stooks of twisted straw. Monikie in green and gold took her arm. With proud shoulders and swaying hips they paraded with the rest to the nearest field, Caterin in a new robe she had made in white wool and embroidered with great sworls of dark blue and gold round the hem.

"Onid," said Delys,"you've been chosen as the Corn Maiden."

Caterin's breath caught. Only close kin were allowed that honour. Now she belonged.

Caterin took the ritual sickle from Aortan. For a moment she had to blink away the tears. Then firmly she cut the last swathe of upstanding corn-stalks. As though she had been doing it all her life she twisted and knotted it until she had a dollie to hang at her belt. A song came stealing into her heart flowing from the air around her, a song that Bridei used to sing, a song that let her know he was near her on this lovely day.

Suddenly the crowd parted and Veleda came forward. Shadowy eyes and green eyes met and locked and the air between them quivered with words. And Veleda lifted the jar and poured the libation at her feet.

"May Bride go with you and blend her power with your own."

And Caterin knew it was time to go. Onid ceased to exist as though she had never been. And as her mind filled with the knowledge of the destiny that called, her body straightened, her head lifted, her arms fell to her sides.

She felt herself withdrawing from those around her. From Monikie who had gone skimming over the stubble in a flurry of skirts and bare brown legs into the arms of a young man who had come over the hill with eager loping strides. From Delys who was flirting outrageously with a potter. Even, it seemed, from Veleda who had nodded and gone, stepping lightly among the poppies.

And Caterin went alone to watch the Hand-fasting, looking and waiting for the sign that she must leave. One couple asked to be freed from their union. They stood back to back in the centre, one facing north and one facing south. As they walked forward out of the circle, they were freed.

New handfasters lined up on either side of the Green. Monikie and Gair came together and held hands and promised before their kin to be Hand-fast for thirteen moons. Onid had made them goose-feather pillows and a blanket for their bed.

Onid had helped to spruce up the Playfield with its terraced slopes for spectators. She had decked the platform for the Competition judges with flowers.

It was Tarain who won the wafer-thin gold disc of merit to sew on her dress. Accompanying herself on a little harp, she had sung in a pure sweet voice a delightful little cradle-song to a baby called Dino telling how his father would go a-hunting with his dogs, Dig and Dag, to bring back grouse from the hills or salmon from the Falls of Rohastie.

Onid had promised to play the lute. Skilfully but without heart, Caterin played a simple tune that Eildon had taught her. A tall slim boy with nimble fingers and the spirit of music in his heart won the twisted silver ring for his arm.

And when Delys danced solo, her heavy body was weightless, her toes twinkled and her small hands were full of vitality and grace. And Onid wept and Caterin grieved. Never again would she be a daughter at the hearth of Delys.

"It's our turn to dance, Onid!"

Monikie, Tomas and Gair swept Caterin into the rousing reel they had practised. Three sweating musicians had the bairns clapping to the beat. As she lifted her skirts to twirl round Tomas, she saw a tall dark figure in the shadows. She turned on a stifled scream and stumbled. Tomas caught her by the elbows.

"Too much ale," he cried, laughing.

Next time round, the figure was gone.

It could not have been Gort. Yet she was sure the torches had shone on leather. After the dance Onid fastened the Corn-dollie to little Maidie's belt. The Corn Maiden must leave but her magic must stay in the village.

Monikie came running to dress her in the silver-grey tunic and trousers she had borrowed to wear for the bull-baiting.

"You're trembling, Onid!" she cried. "Oh, I'm beginning to wish you wouldn't do it. There's only one other girl trying it and she's been doing it for years. And look!" Monikie gave a sudden stifled cry. "You've lost your corn dollie! Oh, Spirits of the Herd and Flock, that's a bad omen, Onid. I'm going to tell Tomas you're not competing."

Caterin finished tying back her hair and set a tight little cap on her head.

"Fine sister you are! You should be keeping up my courage instead of bleating about bad omens. Look, give me your spray of poppies for a luck-charm in my cap."

Monikie unpinned from her breast the posy she had picked with a light heart earlier. Her anxious eyes cleared a little after she had made the sign of the crescent over her friend. In a sudden rush of affection Caterin held her closely. Even if her throat had not thickened and closed she dare not tell Monikie how much she loved her, how much she had to thank her for.

She dipped her kerchief in the trough so that it would not flutter in the breeze. Then picking up the crimson rosette she had made from an odd piece in Delys's work-bag, Caterin ran lightly down to the bull-ring. This would be her last carefree act. In later years the folk would know they had harboured a Queen and would remember how she had beaten Tomas's prize bull.

The first contestant placed his colours on his bull's forehead, almost before the bull knew he was behind him. Now he teased the bull to the ring-side. A squealing girl perched on the barrier and caught the flying streamer as the bull passed her. It had looked fatally easy.

A small but powerfully built lad swaggered into position. His scarf, as he waved it to his pals in the crowd, brought the bull's head round and it was charging before the lad was ready. The left horn caught him in the thigh and the black head tossed him in the air. The dogs and whips sprang into action and the lad was carried off bleeding and proudly nursing a broken bone in his arm.

The other girl contestant, Lydie, came next. Small and slight of build, she cavorted in front of the bull like a seed of thistledown.

The bull was angry now and quick, but she was quicker. She grasped the horn, planted her yellow token and sped away. No young man sprang forward to challenge the bull and take her token. Contemptuously the bull tossed it off, to the left, and stamped it into the ground.

Now he was hers. The black bull stood, swaying his massive head, his sinews highlighted in gold by the sun, the Royal Black Bull of the Queenship. And she was ready for the challenge.

Tomas called her forward.

"He's fiendishly angry," he warned.

Caterin strode to the centre and stood, poised, studying him. All her years of horsemanship coursed through her veins. All her hunter's skill was there in her rock-steady eyes. Evil red-rimmed eyes stared back at her. She began to tease him, showing him her kerchief at one side, then the other. He snorted and pawed the ground. But the flicker had not come in his eyes yet and a run that started too soon gave the bull the advantage.

Oh, but she would have him! And plant the crimson pennant of the Queen between those curving horns! Then, without warning, he bellowed and charged. And Caterin took one, two, three, four long, rhythmic strides, feinted to the left and grasped the high right horn. She used his up-thrust to launch herself high into the air and landed, legs astride on his massive shoulders. Grasping his heaving body between her knees, she planted her crimson pennant firmly into place.

A great gasp rose from the watchers as she pushed with her hands on his neck, brought her feet up lightly onto his back, and stood poised for a long moment before springing off. A mighty cheer went up as she skipped across the ring. Even Tomas saluted her with a grin as she went past.

The door at the far end of the barricade stood open for her escape. As she sped through, a black, leather-clad figure passed her, sprinting across the arena. She turned in time to see him vault onto the bull's back and bend to gather her rosette. Incensed, the bull arched his back and bucked. The man leapt off and ran, scooping up Caterin with his arm outside the palisade. It had all happened so quickly. No one had grasped what was happening.

"I knew it had to be you when I saw that act of bravado." She looked up into grey eyes, cold as sea-washed ice. With one hand he was pulling her towards the outhouses. With the other he was fixing her rosette in his cap.

"So you topped it with a piece of bravado of your own," she taunted, breaking from him. He caught her wrist again in a vice-like grip.

"Don't cry out," he warned her. "You won't be heard." The cheering from the Playfield was drowning out every other noise. "You're going to disappear. Aortan has been warned. He'll spread it about that you've gone to be with a sick kinswoman."

"How many more kinsfolk can you conjure up for Aortan without his own folk laughing in his face?" snapped Caterin.

"He'll concoct a story. I told him we may need to use this hiding-place again."

"You're wrong! I'll never go into hiding again!" She stopped and dug her feet into the earth. "And before I go with you I demand to know where I'm going and why!"

"You little fool! Be quiet! You'll ruin everything!"

"It's a trap," she cried. "You're forcing me against my will!"

"No trickery," he assured her. "Look, I was given this authority by your father before he died." He held out a hand and on his middle finger winked the gold ring with the engraved amethyst that had been her father's seal.

"A ring can be forced from a dead hand! And now that Gartnait is King, what authority do you have?"

She threw a swift glance over her shoulder. All she could see was the high palisade and every head on the other side would be trained on the spectacle below. She drew in a lungful of air to call for help but he forestalled her. His arm snaked round the back of her head and his hand clamped firmly over her mouth. She tried to bite him but his fingers bruised her cruelly.

"You didn't think I'd allow that puppet king to stand in my way did you? I've come here straight from the battlefield where Artur is lying dead and Bridei is avenged. Gartnait has gone whining back to Dal Riata. Now, either you return with dignity and take your rightful place as Queen or I throw you across the neck of my horse and you make your entry into the Capital like a sack of rotting turnips."

She knew he meant every word of it. Round the back of the outhouses, out of sight, stood a group of mounted warriors. Neither on their sleeves nor their shields was there any mark or insignia to show who was their master or where their loyalties lay.

310

Gort mounted and pulled her roughly up to sit behind him.

"Stirrups!" she scoffed as her legs fitted themselves to the round sides of the horse. "Only children need stirrups."

"If you'd ever tried to wield a heavy sword in battle you'd know how useful stirrups can be," he retorted.

As Gort put spurs to his horse she turned her attention to the other riders. Their faces were impassive and told her nothing. Yet they had no stirrups. They must be Pretani. But were they loyal men or traitors? Could she enlist them to her aid?

She had no time to find out for the speed set by Gort made speech impossible. They were travelling south towards Dalgynch. That, at least, she knew. But who knew what sort of chaos she would find there.

As she held on to Gort and the wind whistled past her face, little inconsequential thoughts took hold of her mind. Would Delys's bridies taste as good as they had smelled that morning? Who would Tomas love tonight beside the Lunan Water? Would Veleda tell a story beside the fire in the evening hush? Would Monikie lie with Gair under the Kissing Trees, intoxicated with the scent of the woodland? Would Onid ever find the love she longed for with all her heart.

Over the hunch of Gort's shoulder rose the Law of Largo with its cleft summit. Closing her eyes she summoned all her resources. When her eyes opened she was ready to face her destiny and a life shadowed by danger and suspicion.

The Capital was in darkness. The Commander of the Sentries shone his lantern briefly in Gort's face before letting them through. The passageways were empty and no heads looked from windows as they rode past. The doors of the Banqueting Hall were firmly closed. The traders had long since departed to find custom at less troubled courts.

At the doorway to her rooms stood two Guards. Their unsheathed swords lowered as she and Gort passed.

"On no account leave these rooms!"

She faced his flint-sharp face.

"So I'm a prisoner in my own Palace."

"Think of it as a gilded cage to keep the song-bird safe. Think what you like! The less you know the better for your peace of mind."

"Tomorrow I'll summon the Council of Elders!" They both

heard the heavy tread that came and halted beneath her window and the clink of weapons being eased before a spell of Guard duty. Gort raised his head, satisfied. It was then Caterin realised just how wary and on edge he was.

"You're using me as bait in a trap, aren't you?"

"Then think of it as a golden mouse-trap."

At that moment, Iogena came flying in through the doorway and hugged her joyfully. If Gort was surprised that the Princess and her servant were on such familiar terms, he gave no sign of it, apart from a mocking lift of one dark eyebrow before he left the room.

Once they had settled between them that little Bran and his father were fine, Iogena agreed that Gort had spoken the truth. Rhun had marched to show solidarity with the Pretani. Bridei and he had met at the Forth. Later, it had not been Aedan who had stirred up trouble but his bloodthirsty sons. Artcois had lent naval support to the Dal Riatans in the north while Maelchon had been with the Artur's army. Since Bridei was still a Pretani King when he died, his bones had gone to be set in a mound on the Island of Io close by the cell where Colum Cille meditated.

"It was while Gort and Uurad were taking Bridei on his last journey that it happened," Iogena told Caterin. "It was terrible! Everyone in the Citadel was watching his neighbour for treachery. Yet still, that night, the Guard were called out on a false alarm and ambushed. Artur and half his army crept in through an unlocked gate. They stood in the Courtyard defying us with the heads of the Guards still dripping on their spears. Artur set up his brother in the Palace here as King and went to meet Gort returning from Io. You must know the rest. Gort took Artur's head and Gartnait hared for home through the same bolt-hole as he'd come in by."

Caterin would have been a fool if she had not wondered whose hand had unlocked the gate. There was only one Scot who had free access in the Capital, who had married an Officer of the Guard and who knew the Palace secrets.

"What bolt-hole?" she asked.

Iogena answered the thoughts that had barely touched the surface of Caterin's mind.

"Know this, my lady Qurincess," said Iogena. "I come from Dal Riata but I'm from the Cenel Conaill. The Cenel Gabrain are our hated rivals. Besides, I wouldn't lay my own man and bairn open to their swords by the turn of a traitor's key. And I'll tell you how they entered the Capital. There's a wooden door in the outer wall, hidden by a hawthorn tree. The Veniconie used to use it as a short-cut for their wood-cutters to bring the timber through to their carpentry sheds."

"And I knew of it," agreed Caterin. Maelchon, Talorc, Prent, Drust, Fortrei and fifty other bairns had escaped through it until the Council had boarded it up. Who had reopened it to let Artur in?

That night, when Caterin pulled off her cap she found Monikie's posy of withered poppies still pinned there. The gods had smiled on her and on that Taezalie farmstead while the southern border lands were being devastated by battles.

And what for? Land-hunger? The gleam of gold or the joy of the kill? These were only part of it. In the end it was a power-hunger. And who hungered most for power? Aedan? Artcois? Maelchon? Or Gort?

CHAPTER THIRTY SEVEN

Trumpets sounded at noon from the Citadel Walls. Prent, beaming, slightly plumper, puffing a little, made the announcement to the world at large outside.

"The Mighty Ones have spoken to Broichan. After ten nights, when the sun has reached its zenith, Caterin, Princess of the Royal Blood, will join in Marriage with Gort, Prince of Gwynedd, Heir to our lamented King, Bridei, honoured champion of the fight before his death-day."

It was not lost on Caterin that the Great Ones showed a proper sense of the practicalities. Ten nights gave just enough time for messengers to be dispatched and for folk to gather from all corners of the Kingdom.

At once the curling smoke of a bonfire summoned the Guardians to speed the Royal messengers who were already galloping along the roads that splayed out from the Capital.

To make room for the expected crowds, the flocks and herds that supplied the Royal kitchens were set moving towards the hills herded by boys armed with wolf-bells and slings. Before night fell, tents had begun to sprout like toadstools outside the walls.

Daily then, by river, by road, by footpath through the forests, the folk came. Dusk brought the smell of woodsmoke and the sounds of merrymaking drifting upward to Caterin who looked on the shadow-crossed fires and torches and wondered if Delys and Monikie had come yet.

Soon the grass of the grazing meadow was hidden under a flood of cowhide spreading outwards from the Citadel. Whole communities arrived leaving the old men and boys to guard the granaries. It was a time for kin-folk to meet before the sleet-wind forced them to bar their doors. It was a time for lads and lasses from far-flung clans to meet, free from the taboo of close kinship.

The commotion inside the Capital increased tenfold as honoured guests arrived with their retinues. The paths between the buildings ran like rivers. The courtyards seethed like whirlpools. For the second time, the Treasure was brought out from below the Guardian's house. As the great silver bowls and cups were laid in the re-opened Banqueting Hall and the ritual vessels and symbolic weapons set in place in the Council Chamber, guards patrolled day and night. Then the entertainers began to arrive.

"Come and see this," Iogena cried to Caterin. Bran on Iogena's hip clapped his hands at the play of colour and the shimmer of movement. Flags and ribbons fluttering from tents, painted masks waving from poles, gaudy birds' feathers newly-dyed, drying in the sun. "Look, Bran, see the acrobats turning somersaults." Iogena took a deep gasping breath. "Oh, Qurincess, isn't it grand? The whole world has come to your wedding."

Small traders came, sniffing a profit. True, this was a celebration, not a market. Yet most families had a few extra chickens or fleeces. So, in the area farthest from the Citadel, plots had been hired out and booths erected. Now, bales of fine linen from the Low Countries were fingered by plump and merry matrons who had arrived earlier on litters and ponies. Younger women, bright as poppies, thronged around packmen who untied their bundles, letting the tumble of ribbons and laces, veils and trinkets, tell their own story. In and out, excited and shrill, ran children and dogs. Only the brewers had glum faces for free ale and wine in barrels had been sent down from the Palace.

Devana arrived from Aberlemno with two small versions of the tawny Cennalath. She was plumper than ever, with eyes that were not dead any more but full of liveliness.

"You're as brown as a nut! You look more like a Clan-Mother than a Queen!" she remarked.

"That's the title that pleases me most! How are you?"

"My heart still twists when I think of him and the boys miss him sorely. But the meadows are golden-yellow and the waterfall still sings. And there's a Mormaer up north with a coaxing mouth and kisses sweeter than dew."

"And there is fat on the breast of the grouse."

"It's my fate to be plump," agreed Devana, dimpling. "My, how you've changed."

Of course she had changed! And Devana had put her finger on it. She was ready and willing to be Clan Mother to all the clans who called themselves Pretani.

A cacophony of noise dragged Caterin awake on the morning of the Marriage. The laughter of men washing at the pump, the singing of children at a jumping-game and, somewhere, the sounding of one deep resonant note on a horn. It was her Marriage day and everyone was filled with joy.

Except the bride who felt little else but a quiet satisfaction that she had survived to begin her appointed task. And no sense of regret that the King had not yet had the courtesy to visit her. Today in public she would dedicate herself to her people.

"Where's that lazy lie-a-bed?" sang out Devana in the next room.

Caterin threw off the bed cover and submitted to the bathing and oiling, to the plucking of eyebrows and the tinting of nails. Then Amis came, banging down her dye-pots and brushes, her long nose burnished with excitement. Amis's one great talent was about to be displayed to the populace.

"Outside!" She shooed the other women away like bees from a jelly. "Now, lie still! And don't chatter! This is very important. I must have silence. I must concentrate. This is ..."

"I know, Amis. It's the tradition."

Starting with Caterin's bare feet, Amis drew outlines on her skin with a quill dipped in blue dye. She filled in the shapes with crimson, purple and green. It was a delightful sensation. Caterin watched her under half-shut lids. Amis's tongue followed every curve and flicked in and out when she began the rows of tiny gold dots. Soon she was bent over, working on Caterin's legs and thighs. Under her fingers the ritual shapes grew into designs of great beauty. As Caterin relaxed their magic power seemed to seep through her skin and mingle with her blood.

When Caterin's hips, breasts and arms were covered, Amis moved to her face. As she began to outline the eyes, she met Caterin's gaze and was momentarily startled out of her absorption. A shy smile softened the angular contours of her face.

"This is the greatest day of my life," she confided proudly. "I'll never forget that I adorned the Queen with the Bridal Embellishments." A flush of pleasure tinged the sallow skin of her cheekbones.

"You're setting the seal of my ancestors upon me. I feel more truly Pretani than ever before."

"How can a tree withstand the storm unless its roots are firm in the soil," agreed Amis. At last Caterin understood Amis's love for the tradition. The painted emblems of her Pretani roots were only skin-deep but she felt their virtue flow like sap in her veins. And from this power-base she knew she could conquer the world.

At last Amis arose, wiped her hands on her smock and called in the women to exclaim over the pure clear colours and the perfection of line and curve. While Amis added a last spiral, Iogena fanned Caterin until the dyes dried and powdered her before the robing began.

Her hair was left free to fall to her breast like twin waterfalls on either side of her face. From the ribbon of gold at her neck, fell the Mantle of Bride in the colour of the Maiden, the silver-green of the opening bud, transparent as the wing of a butterfly fresh from the cocoon. With every movement of her body, the panels clung and shifted, revealing the bright painted designs in all their glory and shrouding them again in mystery. Dress and designs were a master-piece.

The chatter of the sewing-women pressing in at the doorway fell silent. "She's beautiful, beautiful." came the whispers.

Caterin held out her colourful arms wanting to embrace them all. How could she explain to them that it was not her beauty but their artistry that would be admired on this day? Surely the Radiant Ones had inspired them all this bright day.

The sun had reached its highest point in the dome of the sky, when Devana came smiling to escort her kinswoman.

Caterin entered the Great Chamber, aware of a packed assembly of Kings, Lords, Mormaors and their ladies in a shifting array of brilliant colour and scintillating jewels. On the walls above their heads enormous shields shining like suns, were centre-pieces for designs wrought with ceremonial swords, spears and daggers, each one polished, engraved and encrusted with gems.

From the gallery above, a fanfare of trumpets announced her entry. Broichan waited for her on the raised platform, his imposing figure dwarfed by the Royal Bull Banner and the ten great ceremonial spears upright in their gold stands behind him. The enormity of the task before her struck a momentary blow at her heart and she paused. Then the mingled blood of Bridei and her Pretani mother flowed again and she moved confidently forward to take the oath.

Beside the Shaman, slightly topping him in height, stood Gort, resplendent in the robe she had embroidered years ago with pricked fingers and bored sighs. The dreams she had woven into these stitches came back to haunt her now. It was to have been worn by a prince as fair as a sunlit meadow and with a smile as gentle as the first snow on the mountain. Instead, here stood Gort, implacable, forbidding and contemptuous of her people. This ceremony was an affirmation of a commitment she had already given to her people. From his expressionless face she could only assume that the solemn oath he was about to take held no meaning for him. Although she could have sworn that his left eyebrow tilted a fraction at the sight of her painted body.

It had taken all the will-power that Gort possessed to conceal the tremor of shock that struck him as she took her place beside him. He had ridden in from days and nights spent in improving roads and repairing bridges so that his armies could move faster. He enjoyed working with the Pretani men, eager to repair the neglect of the war period. This day was an intrusion on the mountain of work he needed to achieve while the uneasy peace lasted.

Suddenly his senses burst into vivid life. Her beauty exploded in his eyes and filled his veins with fire. His eyes found joy in her body. The barbaric markings lent a wierd inhuman beauty to her face. There was no reason for the custom that he could see. It was another relic from savage times that stemmed from the matriarchs in the homesteads. He turned to face Broichan, willing him to begin, to end the war between his mind and his senses. At least the Druad gods of fire and water were familiar.

Broichan was never entirely at ease performing a ritual under a rooftree and enclosed by four walls. Ceremonies lost all significance for him unless they were shared with the indwelling spirits of tree, rock and plant. But this was the day ordained by the Great Ones for the Royal Joining. In his meditations he had been increasingly aware that the Mighty Ones were pleased with the Union. They had made their presence felt in his Grove at the right time and in the right place. But that time and place were not here in the Great Chamber, Broichan was sure. When peace was assured he would repeat this Joining in the Grove at Dunino. And instead of a Joining of the physical bodies, it would be a Merging of two spirits. He motioned the Law-Giver, to the front of the stage.

Prent, fighting valiantly to set the lineaments of his face into some sort of solemnity, recited the Charter that bound the Queen to her people and the people to their Queen for life. The King's Charter bound him only until the bond was severed by mutual agreement.

The scuff of feet on the floor disturbed the petals and herbs strewn freshly there that morning. A heady fragrance puffed into the air as the Druad brought forward the silver Mead-Cup, presented long ago by a King whose name Caterin had forgotten. When the Shaman held it aloft shafts of light lanced from the gold filigree interlacing and the amethyst rock crystals. And Broichan passed the Cup of the Golden Mead to Caterin.

"This is the Clear and Yellow Mead, the noblest prize of the champion. This is the Noble Mead earned by the greatest of heroes. This is the Praise-Mead, reward to the warrior for loyalty even unto death. This is the Golden Mead that must be paid for by service. Do you accept the Horn of Mead?"

Holding the two handles firmly, Caterin drank deeply. It was her place now, as Princess of the Royal Blood, to put the question to Gort. As her lips spoke the ritual words, her eyes mocked him across the rim of the Cup. 'You called our customs primitive, outdated relics of a society that would be forced to give way in time. Now I'm asking you if you will defend these same traditions.'

Gort felt himself drowning in the intensity of the shimmering green eyes. He knew she was taunting him. Yet he had earned his mead in the traditional way. Although he despised the tradition he had defended the right of the Pretani to hold to it. He took the Cup and drank off the remainder of the draught.

Again her eyes spoke. 'Either you have changed your opinion and that I cannot believe. Or you have sworn falsely. And if that, I will destroy you.'

His gaze met hers steadily now. There had been no oath to bind him to this Marriage and this Queen for his lifetime.

"By this Marriage to the Royal Blood, you become King of the clans known as the Pretani and you are oath-bound to abide by the traditions of the People." As Broichan's voice thundered out, Caterin again turned a wide-eyed, brilliant look on Gort that plainly said, 'Traitor'.

"Brude, Brude, Brude!" Throats opened joyfully, proclaiming the Pretani name chosen for their new King.

The ceremony broke up into a joyful medley of Druadic chants and humming responses from the assembly. Meanwhile the elected leaders of communities great and small, led by the Kings of the Northern Provinces, bowed their heads first to their Queen and then to Gort, accepting his overlordship.

Devana followed the couple outside into the sunlight. There the Royal Chariot waited, its glittering panels hidden under a profusion of flowers. Gort sprang up, balancing himself like a born charioteer. He unwound the reins of the two fine stallions who tossed their heads at his touch and the silver discs that hung from their bridles chimed and sang. Caterin joined him on his spearside and braced herself as he gentled the horses down the slope towards the sportsground. As the Chariot gathered speed to thunder through the gateway, Caterin threw up her head. Her hair flowed in the breeze like a banner. The drapes of her mantle moulded themselves against her body and streamed behind her. The people saw the familiar designs that covered her skin and their hearts overflowed in cheers and tears.

They were like a young Cruithne and Cruithna, thought Devana, comely and confident in their youth and beauty. If only there had been love between them how happy they might have been.

CHAPTER THIRTY EIGHT

When the Chariot appeared the sportsfield erupted. The Splendid Ones had smiled on the Royal Pair. Their good fortune would be mirrored in every homestead in the land. Gort slowed the horses to a walk as men who had fought with him reached to grasp his arm. His Queen? The women spoke from the sides of their mouths. You could tell from her hands she had been a slave right enough. She was no pale-faced ninny, this one. Those who knew her said she would stand firm for her people. Time would tell. But my, she was bonny, right enough.

From somewhere to the south, a bass voice broke into a grunting rhythm. Voices far and near took up the beat and added a melody. It was a song as ancient as the hills and told of loyalty to the kin of the mother. As the song swelled, Caterin joined in with the heart-stirring words. This was a pride and a glory she shared with her people.

Gort, the foreigner, with a rare sensitivity, stepped back, effacing himself, while the song soared around and within her. The Pretani saw the strength of her chin and the light of determination in her eyes and rejoiced. And as the chorus swelled, somewhere in the air that shivered between them, a promise was made and returned.

Steaming cauldrons of meat came down from the Citadel, baskets of bread and fruit and cheese, bowls of berries stewed in honey and thick with cream, barrels of ale, jars of wine. All set high on tables out of reach of the dogs. Strolling players erected their scenery and fought long-forgotten battles or clowned among the children. Bears danced, hounds leapt through hoops, little animals called monkeys found nuts and fruit in strange places among the clothes of children.

Caterin, alone for a few precious moments in her Courtyard, thanked Bride and stretched her arms to the sky in exultation. At last she was Queen! And now she would take a leaf from the Book of the Church. She would organise the teaching of the tradition so that it could withstand an influx of new ideas. She would open the doors of the Land to new philosophies and assess their worth. Music and poetry would flourish. She would gather like-minded people into her court. Kings and Princes would come to learn from the Pretani. She would send emissaries to spread knowledge of the Pretani far and wide.

Her arms dropped. And the Druad would eat mistletoe, the Moon Maiden throb with desire and Delys's goat would fly.

O Broichan, O Veleda, O Bride, my guides and mentors! she cried in her heart. It was one thing to set her feet on the golden path, quite another to fend off the powerful forces that threatened from the thickets! Then the curtains parted and the women arrived to dress her.

"Right! On with the Royal Regalia," said Devana, herself a sparkling vision of gauze and jewels. Amis was splendid in red and gold, colours that did nothing for her sallow complexion.

Iogena looped strings of pearls and rubies in Caterin's hair and crystals tied with gold wire.

Seven gold torcs on her upper arms. Seven twisted bracelets at her wrists. Seven gold lozenges hanging in tiers from each ear. Seven ropes of garnets girdling her waist. Seven strings of carnelians lying on her breast. Two great agate-encrusted brooches at each shoulder and seven rings on her fingers. "No more," groaned Caterin. "Or I'll be bent double like a crone with the craps."

Everything in the Banqueting Hall was brilliant from the thousand honey-wax tapers to the clothes and jewels of the guests. The food tempted the eyes as well as the palate for the Master Steward had at last come into his own. Every bird had been baked in its own gaudy feathers, every fish was laid garnished in platters, every beast had been roasted whole and laid bare from brains to trotters. Even the honeyed sweets had been fashioned into the symbols of each clan and tribe in the Hall. All except the Veniconie Boar.

The feast had been designed to impress. And it did. The guests ate, drank and made merry. Only the Queen had her own secret thoughts. She slipped away from the side of the King unnoticed and went to her bed-room. Of course it was an old wives' tale. But she loosened the knots and the clasps and the ties. For tonight she wanted to make a child, for herself, for her people. Tonight she would take his seed into that dark unknown place in her body.

For this day she had known that the Fateful Ones were there, just a thought away. And that they held in their hands a flame that was a spirit waiting for life. And the flame would spark into being in her womb. And its flesh would be her flesh and its blood would flow strong and sure, carrying the memory of the race within itself. For so it must be, now and forever.

But whoever he spent the night with, it was not with his bride. By the time dawn came she knew by the fiery rage in her heart that it had been Gort's body she had desired more than a child.

In the morning, she rode out and saw him on the practice-ground with the Mormaers from Catness. Great Dagda! Of course! He would have spent the night carousing with them, men whose loyalty was desperately needed with Artcois on the prowl.

Ribald cheers floated up to her. Gort had thrown off his stirrups and was competing, using his thighs and legs to control his mount as they did. It was a glorious display of manhood. His thrusting hips engulfed her in a wave of desire pulsing out from the inner places of her body. Yet she forced herself to watch, fighting her need, thinking like a Queen. Gort had only a few days to bind these chieftains to him by a personal bond of loyalty, to assess their strengths and weaknesses, to probe their ambitions.

Gort hurled his lance like a man with rage in his heart. She needed to vent her own aggression in action this morning. Yet she stayed, fidgeting with the reins, while Crystal rolled back an impatient eye.

This Capital was too far south. And hemmed in by the wayward Veniconie. Bridei had known the importance of a Court at Craig Phadric to keep the Northern Pretani united under the banner. Soon she and Gort must journey among the clans in the North among the Cornavie, the Smertaie and the Carinie, strengthening their strongholds, meting out justice and showing that they had the strength to enforce it.

Yet it was only from Dalgynch that they could make a stand against the enemies who pressed on their southern borders. And only within the Capital could they hope to weed out the traitors from their midst.

Like a swerving tempest Gort guided his horse in and out of a line of impaled spears. Women on the side-lines watched his every move with bold admiring eyes.

"Tcha!" Caterin cried and Crystal leapt for home.

"Look!" Amis called from the yard up to her rooms. "You have another gift. Prent sent them to replace your guard dogs."

Two hounds, tall and high-waisted, with thin curving legs strained at their chains.

"Prent was cheated! They're built for speed, not for attack!"

"They're fierce. No one's dared to go near them."

"No one feeds them but me, remember. And I'll leave it till tomorrow. Then they'll know who's their mistress. Where's my Cloak of Queenship?"

The Royal Remembrancer threw open the door of the Council Chamber and stopped. His mouth formed a perfect 'O'. The crimson Cloak of Queenship lay across the High Chair. The Master of the Hunt pushed him forward. And saw. His eyes bulged. From a window niche the Queen came and sat, flanked by Amis, wife of Aeron, and Iogena, wife of Uurad. The Remembrancer thought about protesting and changed his mind as the Queen's fingers began a tattoo on the arm of the Chair.

"Hrmph'm, yes," he muttered and threw a despairing look at the Councillors behind him.

"Come in, Clan Brothers," said the Queen.

Reduced to Clan Brotherhood were they? The Council of Elders moved towards her as one, supporting one another in this new turn of events.

Caterin saw their shocked surprise in a twitch of a beard and a flutter of pale fingers. She had guessed aright. Old men who live in the past, content to recite their stored knowledge when the King raised a finger. But the day-to-day business was done in the King's Council of War Chiefs and Stewards.

"It's been too long since a Queen sat here," she said. "Too long since the voice of the Clan Mothers was heard. Take your usual seats, please. Now, what's the business for today."

The business had been to arrange a hunting trip for the pleasure of the Northern Kings. The Master of the Hunt shot warning glances all round and shuffled into his place. Prent, the Law-Giver, alone stayed in the centre of the floor, white teeth gleaming in a crescent-moon smile.

"Since you've honoured us with your presence, my Lady Queen, we'll postpone our discussion. I speak for all here when I say how glad ... "

"I don't need a speech of welcome, Law-Giver." Caterin spoke firmly but kindly. "And I haven't honoured the Council. I have the right to preside. And the duty. Since you've no business worth mentioning, I'll proceed with mine."

Prent remained standing for a moment longer, his eyes seeking hers, sending a message of pleasure, of pride, of delight. The Councillors' heads pecked at the hard wooden benches she had ordered to keep their minds alert and promptly tucked their robes under their bottoms. Caterin gave them a moment to settle.

"I'm bringing in three new Guardians," she told them.

The Keeper of History rose, a long finger aloft.

"Not since ... "

"There's no limit to the number of Guardians, is there, Prent?" she asked.

"No, My Lady."

The Keeper of History subsided.

"First, a Guardian of Produce to organise the movement of food and building materials in time of famine or war."

The Remembrancer heaved his bulk and robes upright.

"That is a matter for the communities themselves, My Lady."

"And it's chaotic when the need arises. We'll have store-houses built and a method of quick efficient transport. And you need not stand, my dear old friends."

"But in your Ladyship's presence ... "

Caterin smiled.

"From now on this will be a daily meeting." Quickly she drew a breath and went on before she laughed out loud at the sick looks on their faces. "How can we work if you're bobbing up and down like ... " She swallowed that remark.

"Next a Guardian to encourage trade with other lands. Our folk have a wealth of furs and silver and the merchants cheat them. We'll build a central store. Then when the merchants come to sell, they'll not go away with empty holds."

The Remembrancer waved his hands in the air.

"My Lady, the merchants will stop coming."

"Not while we make the warmest caracallas and the finest silver cups."

"But our people are not used to the silver coins the merchants use," put in Amis's husband.

"I've thought about that, Aeron. Find out how this custom works and report to us. I remember I saw some inferior pieces among the People's Treasure on display."

Startled, the Keeper of the Treasure unfolded his arms.

"Have them melted down and made into ingots, ready to be exchanged for foreign goods."

"It may work at that." Aeron waggled his beard, wondering if these same sharp eyes had noticed that six silver bowls and spoons had been borrowed to entertain his kin from the north. His ears still rang from Amis's scolding.

"And lastly, an Adviser from the Druad to start Schools of Learning and Healing to combat the spread of the teaching of the new Church."

Broichan's representative, a Drui with a long pale nose who had always felt his talents went unrewarded, rose and bowed.

"And these two posts will be held by Clan Mothers of my choice," Caterin ended. Faces reddened, mouths worked as they looked at one another.

"There's nothing in the Law that says Councillors must be male, is there, Prent?"

"Indeed no, my Lady. The Druad at Pitversie taught you well."

"I found that fact out for myself. And a lot more beside. Who is the Keeper of the Royal Estates?"

He was a stout bluff man, the only man there in working garb.

"I see a big influx in slaves since the campaign against the Scots."

"Yes, my Lady."

"Those who wish to go home must be sent away with provision for their journey. Those who decide to stay must be freed."

"But how will I replace them?"

"How many of your work-force already come from homesteads with an abundance of labour?"

"About half."

"And more," said Caterin wryly. "I've worked for my keep as a slave. And willingly as a free woman. It's my privilege to free the slaves on the Royal Estates. Law-Giver, prepare to recite the Laws of Slavery tomorrow and we'll vote to amend them."

"The Mormaers who use slaves on their land will never agree, my Lady."

"First let's see how it works out in the Royal Estates. If it's successful we may persuade the Mormaers that free folk make willing workers. And no more land will be given from the Royal Estates to the new Church to build on, is that clear? Oh dear, am I going too fast for you?"

They would hum and haw for a bit, she knew. Under Bridei there had been few changes in the Law.

"I'll use this Chamber daily after noon to meet with the Clan Mothers. Have messengers dispatched. Tell the Clan Matriarchs from here to the Orcades that there's a Queen in the land again! Now I think we've finished the business for today, my friends."

She let them reach the doorway, shuffling a little and shaking their heads.

"Just one more thing!" she called. "It would displease me to find that there are still slaves serving in the households of the Capital."

She counted the heads as they filed out. She would need to promote more Clan Mothers in order to have more votes on her side. Unless Prent ...

He stood at the door facing her, the only young man in the Council of Elders. She could tell nothing of his state of mind from that rosy-cheeked face.

"The young are the stalks of corn who bend to the wind of change," he reminded her.

"And the old will snap and be carried like straw in the breeze," she finished for him. He was with her, her old playmate. "Tomorrow I'd like to hear the Law concerning the working of the Symbols on stone."

Gort, when he heard of it, was amused. He was deep in discussion with his War Chiefs over reports of a resurgence of power in Bernicia and Deira. He stroked the scar on his cheek to hide a smile and ended by feeling a grudging admiration for this Queen of his. Maybe he should find time to get to know her better.

But Caterin left no time to for thoughts of Gort that would distract her from her purpose. She summoned Eildon to the Receiving Hall.

"The Angles, Eildon. What's stirring in their lands? It's time you packed your travelling harp and found out."

"Why ask me? You've a parcel of Kings from down south here in your Court, my Lady."

"They're haunted by the thought of plots and usurpers back home. They're leaving fast."

"Gort and his brother send messengers to each other. The Flying Dragons we call them."

"I need a man who's a branch of a tree and a shadow in the night."

"And a man who scouts only for you, my Lady."

A late rosebud fell from his hand on her lap and when she looked up he was gone.

Devana bringing her two boys to take their leave, put her head on one side and considered. Now why should a new bride be as tense as a coiled spring?

"And what will you remember?" Caterin asked Cian, the eldest and boldest.

"The man with the long legs and his head in the sky."

"I liked the pretty lady that danced on horseback." Nerain still had his baby lisp. "She threw a flower at me and I caught it!"

"Ah, she fell in love with your big blue eyes." Caterin patted their tawny heads. "Now I think Iogena has some honey plums in a pastry poke next door." Iogena got the message and led the boys away.

"And does he bed like the Royal Bull then?" Devana was already distracted by a sweet barley cake alone on a nearby dish.

"A gelding more like." Caterin lifted a kid-skin and furiously polished her finger-nails. "He's had me before. He's in no hurry to repeat the experience."

"But he must!" Devana exploded, scattering crumbs in the air like pollen. "That's part of the pact. If I were you I'd keep him so busy in bed he has no time for other ploys."

"Good food and joy in bed is the answer to everything!" They laughed together.

Caterin hugged Devana and sent her home happy. She felt infinitely older and wiser than her little aunt who had never been involved in alliances and double-dealing and the naked ambition that motivated powerful men.

It did not take the Clan Mothers long to realise that they now had a Queen who would listen to their petitions. The brothers had had too much of their own way under Bridei. Now which Mother should own the fishing rights at the Crook of the Devon? And would the Queen order Fionna to return the swarm of bees she stole from the Mill of Pow. And the gathering of birds' eggs on the Isle of Maie. It would have to be controlled by one clan only or the population of birds would diminish.

Caterin did not summon Veleda, knowing she would come in her own time. And she did, to a garden where Caterin's mother had set up a dove-cote among the shrubs.

"The time has come," said Caterin, tall and queenly in a furlined robe that swept the grass, "to set up our Schools of Learning."

"There's a chief who'll lend me a pit of barren land in Oengus."

"Oh, we can do better than that. Broichan's Druad are ranging far and wide to find pits in good fertile land. The Treasurer is gathering materials and he can have a hundred workers on a site within a night. Your task is to provide teachers and appoint a Wise Woman as Mistress."

"There's one who could do it." Veleda's voice could barely be heard over the gentle cooing of the doves. "But few are willing to teach."

"Why?"

"Well, people are human." Veleda smiled at the absurdity of her remark. "Knowledge is a precious thing. It can mean a secure living." She leaned her head sideways to listen. "That blacksmith sounding on his anvil has had his son at the bellows since he's had muscles. The son will marry a blacksmith's daughter and the secrets are kept within the family. It takes a long time to learn a skill like that. It takes even longer to fashion your own tools for the task. It's the same with the craft of healing. The physicians want to guard their knowledge."

"Yet Schools will attract foreign healers bringing more knowledge with them." Thoughtfully Caterin took a handful of seed from her pouch, weighing the grains in her hand.

"I see another side to it," said Veleda. "Every year I tell the women of the inland villages to barter their corn for cod-oil so that the legs of their bairns don't curve like a hunter's bow. But they think it's the incantation that cures and they forget the oil. Next year there's a new crop of bairns stumbling over their own feet."

Caterin scattered her seed, bringing a white cloud whirring to her feet. She said more confidently than she felt.

"Think of our Schools as seeds that will take root and sprout, Veleda, long before the White Dove can peck them out of the ground." Caterin's hand delved in her pouch again.

"The servants of the Mother work best in humble ways, tending herbs and sick bairns. Schools are heartless places. There's no such thing as teaching, only willingness to learn. And True Knowledge comes in tranquillity, stealing through the soles of the feet and the pores of the skin. The Insight that comes from the Guardian Ones is only a thought away. And a thought has no words."

A flutter of wings and claws digging into Caterin's wrist and a beak, fierce and greedy, stabbing at the grain on her palm. And she stamped her feet and sent the white doves fanning into the air.

Derelei, was he just a thought away? As she had guessed, Derelei was announced one day as she sat in her courtyard, fingering a lute and brooding over a new statute she was about to suggest to the Council. He stopped at the entrance, his artist's eye admiring the picture she made, dressed in fine green wool, slashed on skirt and sleeves with scarlet and her hair trailing down one shoulder like a garland of primroses. He could not still the leap of his heart.

"I'm not ready to commission a Queen-house yet, Derelei." She lifted her eyes from the strings and caught the yearning in his eyes before he veiled them.

"Never fear, my Queen. Buildings don't excite me any more. I've come to wish you well before I go. I'm winging north with the pink-footed geese." He hung his cap on a rose-bush, brilliant saffron against the pale pink petals.

"Going north?" Caterin bent her head again. She would not let him see that a cloud had fallen across her day.

"You timed your decree about symbol stones nicely. Your Marriage has fanned the loyalty of the northern clans. Every chief wants a bigger and better one than his neighbour. They claim that the stones are to remind them of their origins. But who needs prompting when memories are long and pride in the mother's kin is in our life-blood?"

"Yet you must tell our story in stone, Derelei. Sometimes I'm afraid that little else will remain of this bonny Kingdom."

Derelei's incredulous laugh caught in his throat. He saw the shadows under each cheek-bone and knew that she looked beyond into the future with a certain distress. His mouth longed to kiss away the tiny wrinkle between her eyebrows.

"The race-memory will remain in the blood of the people, you'll see."

He heard a sigh and then her face became alive again.

"And the Queen's stone?"

"Just let me perfect my skills up north. I promised you a praise-song in stone and, by all the stars in the midnight-sky, you shall have it."

CHAPTER THIRTY NINE

Derelei sprang to sit on the wall, to allow himself the indulgence of a different angle on the slender lines of her proud head.

"Think of it! No more rough boulders, hurriedly cut and indifferently worked! Instead, monuments that will blazon our ancestry across the landscape."

"Devana in Aberlemno must have one. That will set the fashion." Derelei was delighted to see her so animated. It lit her face to an almost irresistible degree, and she was completely unconscious of it. "You'll have all the time in the world at my expense to bring a flowering of your art." She laid aside her lute.

In a whirl of splashing colour, he was on his knees before her, holding her hands in his, his cheeks glowing, his eyes alive with excitement. She bowed her head and saw his chisel-scarred hands curled round her own. She could not bear him to be so close and so dear at the same time. Gently, she removed her hands and took her trembling body to the wall to gaze seawards.

"Have you been to the Master of the Symbols for his permission?" she asked, once she had her voice firmly under control. "He must be assured that the designs will be exactly as laid down by the tradition."

"Indeed I have." He answered her more soberly, stifling his enthusiasm and the love that must not be allowed to flare. "I explained that we'll use the crescent moon and the broken arrow on each Mormaer's stone as a sign that the clans are united. He was actually quite impressed."

Caterin did not say that she had talked to the Master, long into the night, about the need to relax the rules so that the ongoing tradition of the Mother would continue to flower.

When she turned again to look at Derelei, the shine had left his eyes. And the yearning had returned. Yet not for one moment, dare they play at being two ordinary people in love sharing a dream that would never come true. But she knew how to make his eyes strike fire again.

"Tell me more, Derelei."

As she had guessed, he sprang up to pound the paving-stones

with his feet and thresh the air with his gestures.

"We'll take whatever stone is available, sandstone or granite, hard or soft, red or yellow. We'll shape them, rounding them at the top like the male organ. I've trained my brothers to dress the surface with pecks of a chisel, smoothing out the roughness where the stone is weathered or broken. Then the slabs will be set in place in the earth of the Mother and dedicated by music and dance. Next day when I come with my hammer and chisel the indwelling spirit will impart its magic into my hands and my eyes. My work will stand for ever to the glory of our people and the Great Guardian Ones."

"May they work with you," Caterin murmured.

He hardly heard her as he went, walking as though the earth bounced beneath his feet and his head touched the clouds. North, like a pink-footed goose, he had said. Did he remember the geese went north to mate and to breed?

Her fingers groped for her lute and then stilled. There was still one more thing that had to be begun. And she rose and called to Iogena to summon Gort to her bed-chamber that night.

And when he came, starting to talk of Councils and Statutes, she closed his mouth with her lips. And she received him into her body as the harvest-field welcomes the sower of the seed. Yet they kept their secrets hidden in their hearts and slept apart.

One morning, instead of the hum of the populace, Caterin awoke to a familiar lowing and the deep call of a shepherd's horn as the flocks returned to their home pastureland. From her courtyard she saw the sparkling bay empty at last of traders, the sportsground deserted, its tracks churned and trampled. Inland, the revellers had gone leaving pallid patches and blackened circles in the grass. A scatter of children and sea-gulls picked over the rubbish before the servants came with their cleaning-carts.

Caterin drew in a long breath of salty air and quietly enjoyed the peace. As she stretched lazily, letting her robe fall open to the caress of the breeze on her sleep-warm body, she saw a smudge on the horizon. A tardy trader who had mistaken the date and lost his chance of profit?

She leaned on the wall. The blurred image split into five ships breasting the waves. These were not white Pretani sails. These sheets were black. And menacing as they grew in size. And bore no insignia. Only three points of colour, three signal flags on the mast of the leader.

The alarm bell tore the stillness apart. The brassy summons of a trumpet from the East Gate cut across the frenzied clanging and the fear-sharpened barking of hounds. The Master of these ships had not mistaken the date. He had timed his raid nicely when the crowds had gone, when the Capital was exhausted and the sentries careless. And when the People's Treasure was still on display. And ripe for the taking!

The ships sailed nearer, cutting north before the Capital to catch the lively southerly wind.

Beasts bellowed at the boys who turned and beat them back to the hills. The sportsground filled with hand-carts of homesteaders gathering their offspring, whipping their ponies, frantic, before the gates of the Citadel thudded shut. Now the ships turned, veering in towards the headland. The sails plummeted. The oars stirred. At Caterin's back she heard the sharp voice of her Guard, ordering the packaging of the Treasure Jewels.

To the north and east, beacons took fire, summoning the Fleet from the Firth, warning the inland folk.

An uneasy hush fell on the Citadel. Every eye had a vantage point, a loop-hole to watch the passage of the ships. In the north, thunder-clouds mushroomed, swelling, angry, black and yellow.

Caterin felt Iogena's breath at her shoulder and the flutter of Amis's veil. And the ships passed from sight, round the headland, making for any one of the natural harbours on the coast. An outbreak of hammering began at once. Folk ran with planks, shelves, tables, to barricade windows and doors.

And the trumpets clamoured again as the King and his Guard thundered forth.

The women looked at one another.

"Pack the Jewels," said Caterin. "Bring my clothes. Something warm."

But she stayed, looking after the cloud of dust.

"He's leaving his Capital unprotected," she said aloud. "Why?"

What kind of raiders were these? A raider seeking gold and silver vaunted his insignia to strike fear in his victims. If this was Artcois landing on his own Veniconie shore, he would display his colours boldly. These black sails implied secrecy. A strong suspicion grew in her mind. Had Rhun sent an army to help Gort to impose the Gwynedd dynasty? That fitted.

She sent a cold and practised eye over the Capital. The hammering had almost ceased.

A figure, half-hidden round the corner of a lean-to shed, caught her eye. He was in the act of lowering a bow. It shouldn't be! But it was! Prent! "Prent! What are you ... ?"

Even the Law-Giver had to be ready to defend his Capital. He turned at her call. His shoulder hunched. His clown-face suddenly broke apart. His perpetual grin widened until it became a grimace of pain. A howl like that of a wounded animal broke from between his twisted lips. He snapped the bow and threw it from him and ran, covering his eyes with his hand.

Now the only swirl of activity was in the Courtyard. The People's Treasure must be saved!

"Strip the walls!"

"Clear a path to the Vaults!"

"Forget the wrappings, fool!"

The remaining sentries were strung out along the palisade with long aching spaces between them. Not enough to withstand a siege if Gort came back at the head of a Gwynedd army. And who would the sentries fight for? The foreign King whom they knew and trusted? Or their Pretani Queen whose only claim on them was in the flow of her blood?

"My lady, you must dress!" Iogena threw the tangled gold chains and their calf-skin pouches in a corner and whisked a rug over them.

Outside a clamour of voices rose and fell and rose again, crackling with fear.

"What is it?"

They hardly needed to hear the words. Filtering through the window came the dreaded smell of burning wood.

"Fire! Fire in the Barracks!"

CHAPTER FORTY

During an endless moment Caterin stood, her hands at her breast. Raiders on the coast! A fire in the Citadel! It might be a plot by Gort to cause confusion. Yet no man with a loyal army at his back would burn down the very Capital he needed as the base of his power.

She leaned from the window and saw a flickering point of flame and a thin drift of smoke above the rooftops. Already the Courtyard was alive with folk running with buckets.

"My lady!" Iogena, her voice stammering, strangling in her throat, her fingers digging into Caterin's arm. "Bran's with Uurad's mother! Her house is near the barracks!"

"Go on! And tell the other women to see to their families!"

Fortrei slammed through the door.

"I'll issue the orders. You women must stay to guard the Queen! I've not enough soldiers for that!"

"The women will go. The Almighty Ones will protect me!"

Somewhere below a child, screamed and screamed, "Mam! Mam! Mam!" Caterin swallowed and pushed past Fortrei. The paths seethed like a sea in torment. Bobbing heads lit bluish-white by lightning flashing in the hot air.

The barrack rooms were at the far end of the Citadel. Two were already alight.

"Leave them to burn! Drench the others!"

Like sprites set free, an explosion of sparks danced and swirled in a frenzy. Tongues of flame, lusting after dry timber, wooden palings and loose tunics.

A line formed, snaking back to the well. It took an agonizing time before a bucket came to Caterin. Hand to hand it passed to the firefighters high on the palisade.

"Go back!" Fortrei stopped the newcomers with his hand. "Bring water from your cisterns!"

And the world went dark. Faces lifted to the pall of black smoke that had cut off the light from the sullen sky.

A flame leapt from a doorway. A girl screaming, clawing at her hair. A man emptying his pail over her head.

Between buckets, Caterin dashed the sweat from her eyes.

"How did it start?" she shouted.

"Lightning!" a man grunted, saving his breath. "A strike on a leaning spear."

She doubted it.

Buckets came, hand over fist. Backs breaking, arms aching. It made no difference. The wind it was. It scattered sparks with abandon and fanned them into flames where they lay. If Gort had arranged this she would kill him!

Prent, like a windmill on the palisade, arms and robes sailing, swooping, pointing, directing the firefighters. Long grasping fingers of fire reaching over to a shed that leaned against the palisade. She would pass a law against sheds beside wooden stakes! Dear Bride, there was a law already!

The third barrack-room roared like a torch in a draught of wind. A woman ran forward, frantic, desperate, as though there was someone inside that was dear to her, a sick son or a lover.

A single crack above the roar and a falling beam, the woman pinned, engulfed. A shower of burning fragments and Fortrei's arm, sending her staggering, sweeping her aside and back to the Palace.

A ghastly cry, piercing the tumult. Folk stopped still, rigid as wood. It was Prent, high, high on the palisade, staring aghast at the fallen beam, frozen. And then the irrepressible grin was in place, the sad bulbous eyes looking out from the jester's mask. Like a clown inviting a child to watch a trick, he tilted his head and flicked his fingers. And he launched himself into the air like a swallow, his white-robed breast glowing red, swooping into the fiercest part of the blaze. The roof timbers split apart as he hit them. His body arced with the agony of it. A dark-like shadow where he had disappeared. And a surge of flame. A pillar of pure flame.

"Prent! Prent! Why, Prent?" Fortrei was crying, his throat raw with smoke.

"Why? Because he was a traitor!" Slowly Caterin forced the grim words out. The savage heat in the air brought tears streaming down her face. It was Prent who had fired a burning arrow into the empty barracks. His orders could only have come from the King. An order to cause confusion among the Elders and populace while the King and his brother entered to usurp their power. Prent had known she had seen him. He had betrayed his Queen and could not live with that knowledge.

Why, Prent? She echoed Fortrei's cry. She had thought they were working together, knew one another's hearts. Sick with sorrow at a friend corrupted and a life wasted by Gort, she turned her back on Prent's golden pyre.

"Which side are you on, the King's or the Queen's?" she asked Fortrei.

"What kind of question is that, my Lady? I'm sworn to both!"

Above the roarng and crackling a clamour of voices arose.

"The well's running dry!"

New orders rang out.

"Tell the line to spread out and move to the spring!"

Folk were stamping and beating at flames that sprang from nowhere.

"The palisade!"

Flames had leap-frogged along the tool-sheds. As the platform lurched and began to topple inwards, Iogena came running, a dark unknowing shadow against the orange flames, looking for her mistress.

The arc of fire sweeping overhead fell like a curtain over the girl. Fortrei's arm impaled Caterin to his body as she started forward. But his arm was too low. She bent at waist and knee, propelling herself forward, breaking his grip.

The smouldering beams of the sentries' platform had tumbled askew like jack straws. The heat was unbearable. Frantic, she pulled at the smaller debris. At last, in a kind of tunnel, she could make out Iogena's head and shoulders.

"Grip my hands!" she cried.

As Caterin took the strain, Iogena burst into sharp, piercing cries.

"Wait! Stop! My leg!"

"Kick! Try to free yourself!"

"I can't! I can't move!"

Caterin tried to heave the beams aside. Burning splinters rained down. The palisade above was ready to fall! She braced herself, exerting all her strength. But it was not enough. With every breath she choked on smoke. Coughing, she stumbled out from under the slanting beams and clutched at a passing tunic.

"Help me! There's someone trapped in here!" The crackle of burning timber drowned her words.

"Save yourself!" The man fled, staring over his shoulder.

The palisade creaked and swayed. Caterin glanced up and her terror mounted. A determination stronger than her instincts possessed her. The fire would not consume another friend. Not Iogena!

She snatched a water bucket from a passing hand and up-ended it over Iogena's head. Tearing off her soaking shift she bound it round the girl's hair. Once more she thrust at the beams. Splinters gouged her hands. Iogena's eyes had closed. Only her lips moved.

Stony faces flew past, eyes intent. Sprinting between them, Caterin made for the tool-sheds. In the smoke-filled air that lay like a pall of darkness over the Capital she blundered into a man carrying a lever and a saw and looked up into the grimy face of Fortrei.

The palisade still held, creaking and sagging as ripples of flame flowed along its stakes. At once, Fortrei began to lever the beams up while Caterin dragged them away. A youth appeared and took over her task. Caterin crept in to shelter Iogena.

The heat was intense. Smouldering slivers of wood fell like red-hot lances on her crouching back.

She wiped Iogena's glistening face. "They're going to have to saw through the last beam to cut you free."

Iogena nodded. Eyes streaming, they pressed their faces together when the sawing started, fighting to keep control.

Iogena cried out in pain as the beam cracked and broke. They caught her arms and pulled her through the hole. Fortrei swung the limp body up in his arms and they leapt to safety. The palisade lurched, held, then crashed down in a fountain of sparks. At that moment, incredibly, the clouds opened and a torrent of rain swept down.

Realisation came slowly. One by one the folk slowed and stopped, turning black faces to the sky. A few raised their arms thankfully. Most stood, letting the deluge cleanse their scorched bodies and singed clothes. There was enough water here to quench the fire by itself. The Capital was saved. Slowly the people roused themselves to beat out the last of the flames.

338

"That storm took its time about coming." Fortrei lowered Iogena to the ground and they helped her towards the Queen-House. At the corner of the deserted Courtyard, Fortrei's arm slammed them back against a smoke-blackened wall.

"I don't like the look of that!" The Queen-House doorway stood wide and unguarded.

"Everyone's fighting the fire!" Caterin's eyes searched the blank windows. Drifting smoke, falling ash, and a sense of menace still hovering in the air.

"Stay here!" Fortrei's sword sprang to his hand as he strode towards the doorway.

Caterin's thoughts sparked like flint.

"Where's the King? The Fleet must have arrived from the Tay by now. It can deal with the raiders."

"He must have seen the smoke," Iogena chimed in. "Why didn't he come back?"

"Because that fire was no accident! It was meant to distract us while the invaders landed. The question is, did Gort summon them?"

"The elected King?" breathed Iogena.

"It's happened before. I must find out!" She looked at the Queen-house. "Come on! I know a way in from the back!"

Prent's hounds lay, panting, alert. Almost as though an order had been given. Only their eyes shifted as Caterin helped Iogena over the low wall.

"Someone else has passed this way!" Slowly Caterin pushed open the kitchen door. Its hinges whined at the last. She drew back.

The passage inside was gloomy and deserted. Where were the servants? Still at the fire? She clasped Iogena's hand to keep them together and edged along the wall. A moan from an alcove stirred the silence. As they turned weapons clashed above their heads. A body hurtled down the stairs, toppled over on itself, spread its limbs at their feet. They sprang back into the shadows. Caterin stared into the lifeless eye of Fortrei. His head rolled over. The other side of his face, his young, pleasant face, was a bloody oozing pulp.

And Caterin's hair was caught and her head pulled back. A blackened face with white eyeballs glared into her face. A snarl of triumph and an unintelligible order. Iogena's hand was jerked out of her grasp. And a darkness fell over her head, a darkness that smelled and stifled her and blotted out all sight and sound. Her own screaming deafened her ears. Her hands were twisted from the heavy coarse sacking and tied.

She was thrown like a sack over a man's shoulder and the breath exploded from her body. Blind, deafened and half-suffocated, she wriggled and kicked. Her attacker held her tight as a snared rabbit.

Then he was running and she was bouncing up and down on his shoulder. Her breath jolted in and out, in and out. Scream again! The bag smelled of seaweed and oil. She retched instead. Only her scorched skin screamed as the fibres rasped against it.

Was this Gort's idea, to subdue the Queen as well as her people? Someone would sound the alarm! Where were they all! For Bride's sake! But there was no alarm, no noise, only the scuff of feet on flagged stones and the heavy breathing of her captor.

Then the world stopped. He heaved her off his shoulder onto a hard surface, that rattled every bone in her body.

"Iogena?" she called urgently. A muffled moan answered her.

"Quiet!" hissed a voice and a cruel foot kicked her in the ribs. She caught her lip between her teeth until the sharpness of the pain had passed. Beneath her she could feel hard planks of wood. A heavy object clanged on the boards beside her. More metallic bundles landed around and on top of her, pressing on her from all sides until she could no longer move.

A scream came from Iogena at one point and then nothing more.

"Let her faint, oh Kindly Ones," prayed Caterin. "But keep me alert, so that we can escape."

Suddenly the whole world began to heave and jolt. Wheels creaked. They were in a moving cart. And it took all her strength to keep the heavy bundles from knocking her senseless as the cart rolled and jerked and trundled. Iogena began to cry out again. Caterin joined in. Loudly. Someone must hear them!

No one did. Even their captors did not bother to silence them. It seemed that the cart was covered and their voices were muffled. Their cries died away into despairing silence.

Desperately, Caterin strained to hear any sound that would give a clue to their direction. No noise intruded above the incessant groaning and creaking of the overloaded cart.

After a while, the cart gathered speed and the ground became rougher. She guessed they were now outside the Capital walls. Objects began to slew around again. Once she was thrown violently against the side as a rock lifted a wheel, setting the cart on a slant, and jarring her when it thumped level again. Just when it seemed that the twisting and bumping would go on for ever the wheels crunched to a standstill.

Whispers and scuffles reached Caterin's ears. The heavy bundles were unloaded one by one. She was dragged out and dumped on a hard lumpy surface. Feet scrunched to and fro past her. Her mind began to form a picture to match the sounds.

They must be on a shingle beach. She was sure she could hear the steady swish of waves breaking on pebbles. Again she was hoisted onto a shoulder. This time she was aware of a jerkin of metal rings that dug into her ribs. The muted clank of a sword in its scabbard told her that this man was armed and ready for a fight.

The sea sounded nearer. And the grating of oars in row-locks. She was placed, with a little more care, in the bottom of a rocking boat that began to surge forward as soon as the oars bit into the waves. The rowers talked among themselves and gave the odd stifled laugh but their language was foreign to her. The swell of the ocean took them as they reached the open sea.

Without warning, a command was given. For a moment, she was paralysed with fear as hands touched her and she thought they were going to be thrown, bound and helpless, into the waves. Then the knots were loosened and the cover was pulled from her head. She drew in the sweet clear air, aware of how near she had been to suffocating. As Iogena was released their eyes and hands met for comfort. They were in a pool of water in the well of a small boat surrounded by a score of rowers. A vast number of bulky packages weighed down the boat till the choppy waves lapped over the sides.

The drifting pattern of vague cloud that had followed in the wake of the storm, was hazy over the Capital. A line of small-boats was strung out behind them.

"Look ahead," breathed Iogena.

The Island of Maie! The cliffs that gleamed with a startling whiteness in the sun were black and forbidding in close-up. Where better to hole up until the hue and cry wore off?

The rowers had stopped talking, saving their breath. Only the odd grunt issued from the hooded kagouls that hid their faces and gave them the sinister look of men who had no mercy.

As they drew nearer the uninhabited island, the sky lightened imperceptibly. Hundreds of birds, alarmed by their approach, glided out from the cliffs to come to rest on the surface of the sea. Huge gannets, their pale beaks and long necks gleaming, swished by on powerful wings. Plump puffins, with their sad colourful faces, careered out of their path, stubby wings whirring. Gulls screamed overhead. Kittiwakes thermalled lazily like white snowflakes caught in a breeze. Black shags skimmed towards the coastal feeding-grounds on purposeful scything wings. To them the isle was a refuge and they were free to take wing and leave. Yet for the Queen it seemed the isle was to be her prison. They rowed parallel to the shore seeking the landing-place. At last the look-out gave a shout. The boat veered in towards the land although no break showed in the rocky coast-line. A sudden swirling of waves caught the craft until it turned sharply round a jut of rock. In calm water they glided up a slanting inlet with the oars fending them off from the towering crags on either side. At the head of the inlet, a wooden jetty stuck out from a strip of sand.

The kagouls ignored the women and began lifting the cargo carefully onto the jetty and up to a ruined dwelling that lay almost hidden in a hollow. Not a hand was raised against them as they picked their own way ashore. The second boat rounded the point, its cargo glittering as the sun broke out from its escort of clouds.

"The King's Chariot." Stunned Caterin watched the men pass her and climb the path with the People's Treasure in its sea-stained wrappings.

"Halt!" She ordered. "In the Queen's name halt!" Not a step faltered. Not an eye blinked. One hand only stilled before hoisting a bundle. The Pretani command had not been understood. Not Veniconie then. And she could not speak the Gwynedd tongue.

CHAPTER FORTY ONE

"Well, that beats everything!" cried Iogena, as the last boat slid out between the black gritty rocks. "No food, no shelter, not a twig to make a fire. Do they mean us to starve?"

"And where's the fine crimson-crested fleet from the Tay?" Caterin could see to the bleak empty horizon now. "And the red-cloaked King and his noble Guard, tell me that?" She turned to scan the wind-torn island covered with swatches of soaking heather and harsh tangled roots.

Iogena was shivering. Caterin helped her up the path to the ruin. Sentinel gulls, stationed on crags, sent alarm calls into the air. Shags on nests opened angry yellow gapes and clacked aggressively till they were past.

"We'll warm ourselves first." Caterin unwrapped the great silver bowls and the jewelled shields. "I'll say this much. The Guardian of the Treasure spared no expense." The coverings were soft and woolly and made fine blankets. They hung their cloaks over the broken walls to dry and huddled together in a corner, sharing their warmth. Tears soaked Caterin's shoulder.

"Did you get Bran and your mother to safety?"

Iogena nodded and went on keening silently for her bairn and for his father out there under a leaden sky thrusting his body between the enemy and his loved ones. Caterin had no one she wanted to weep for.

"After all the King's fine vows at the Marriage, did you see him fighting in defence of his Capital?"

Caterin tried to make sense of the events that had turned her world grey. It felt as though she had drunk brackish water, expecting sweet mead. And her heart too, had supped from a bitter spring. Was the truth so bitter as it seemed?

"After all the glowing reports about his prowess, he's been a singularly unsuccessful King. And I think I know why."

It seemed a lifetime away, that carefree day when the Prince of Gwynedd had ridden into Dalgynch.

"Headstrong and inexperienced I may have been but I instinctively distrusted him. What goes on behind these icy eyes? Does he lust for power or does he hold his honour dear? Perhaps

343

Artcois, born and bred a Pretani, saw through to the truth of things. Now Artcois is an outcast, making allies wherever he can. Iogena, is Artcois trying to free his homeland from Gort's tyranny?"

The soft absorbed keening went on.

"I'm the lynch-pin in the centre again. I'm the magic symbol, they all want to possess. The pennant they want to flaunt from their masts."

Flying free at a masthead would be fine and grand right now. The waves slipping by beneath, the sweet air sailing past. Floating. Like a bird, clean-cut and contoured. Winging free as a bird. Free as a thought! A thought!

A thought winging its way to the Mountain Folk. To Veleda. To Eildon.

"It's a power we're all born with," she heard Eildon say. "Your Guardians are merely a thought-light away."

No sacrifice, no libation.

"They do not intrude. They wait to be asked. A thought is enough. They come and draw close."

No spell and no words.

"They will know what you need. In the hush of your mind, you will hear what they say. They do not impose. Yours is the choice."

"Thetil of the White Mists." The name sprang unbidden into Caterin's thoughts. Her mind shied away. She had never had any dealings with this Powerful One before. She tried to conjure up the face of Hunnid, of Eildon. Instead her mind raced and quivered and sank like an autumn leaf in the wind. The air in the ruin grew heavy and throbbed with some invisible force.

Images came and went. The blazing barracks. Fleeting glimpses of Iogena caught under the beams, of Prent flying into the flames, of Fortrei's staring eye, of dark hooded figures in kagouls. And each image spilled over and out of her mind like sand from a glass. She felt hollow and light. She was deep down in a place inside herself. And all was dark and peaceful. Until glorious bursts of colour welled up from nowhere and faded again into the shadows.

Now she let her thoughts reach out. Her whole being expanded. Her need overflowed. Of their own accord her eyes closed. A face took shape in the darkness behind her closed lids. It wavered, at first, almost disappeared and then sprang into focus. It was Hunnid, his eyes glittering, catching her thought and adding his power to hers. Then, magically, it was Eildon, smiling his long crooked smile.

She concentrated then, picturing the boats, then the island and the wheeling of birds. But, when she thought of the Treasure, the power faded till there was only a velvety blackness. And she was speeding along a dark timeless tunnel, a path leading from the past into the future, from what had been towards what was to come, from the unchangeable past into an ever-changing future where, far in the distance, a golden light beckoned. Then she came back inside her mind as if from a distant time and place. She did not want to open her eyes. But the skin of her face was cold. And the hands she lifted to her cheeks were burning hot.

"What's wrong?" Iogena, wide-eyed, was making magic signs over her head.

"I'm fine, fine." Her tongue slurred over the words. She squeezed her eyes shut, wishing she could return to that place where there was no beginning and no end, only peace. And knew in that instant that she could go back any time she wanted.

The worry in Iogena's eyes brought her surging back to the present. Yet she felt heavy, weighed down by the flesh of her body, her mind clogged by the effort of finding the right words to say.

"Help's coming. I'm sure." Through time and space her thoughts had sped like an arrow to Eildon. It seemed impossible. She had sent him south as her agent. Despite that, she was certain that he was nearby and that he would come.

Satisfied, Iogena tucked the wraps around them. Soon, warmed and at peace, they slept.

CHAPTER FORTY TWO

It was no more than a crunch of boot on shingle that roused them and brought them hurrying to the doorway.

"We're going to be rescued!" Throwing caution to the winds, Iogena plunged down the slope. And dropped like a felled bird out of sight behind a thicket.

Kagoul-huddled figures dragged their boats above the high-water mark on the sand. This time a warrior waded ashore, his face hidden by the smooth curve of a well-bruised helmet. Pale light gleamed on linked chain-mail and a hand lying idly on the hilt of a sword. As he climbed towards the ruin, there was a tantalising familiarity about him. He stopped, half-way up, legs astride, transferred hands to hips and the helmet tilted.

"Well, fair lady, is this how you greet a gallant rescuer?" The voice had deepened and matured since last it had taunted her. The body had thickened since the day it had forced itself on her and Nechtan had died with an aroow in his back. Maelchon tugged off his helmet so that his tawny thatch sprang up and his narrow colourless eyes were exposed. Loaded questions hung in the air. The Queen would not ask them. Let him now declare himself.

"Infamous outlaw or conquering hero?" There was merriment in his laugh but no warmth. "A villian or a noble? How will the Queen receive me?"

"As a traitor until you prove me wrong!" She stood arrow-straight, hiding her bitter disappointment that he was not Eildon. "And forbidden to land until purged of your blood-guilt."

"Who dares to forbid Maelchon, son of Gala of the Veniconie and Artcois the Bear? That arch-traitor from Gwynedd? Hah! He and I have battled half across the Pennines this last year in a passion of butchery. And yet you talk of blood-guilt. Yet, though I was cast out from my homeland, I didn't forswear my mother's kin. Shall I give the use of my sword to a Frankish nobleman while our Queen is violated and our Treasure plundered?"

His words held a ring of true valour, echoing the thoughts that had churned in her own mind, yet tinged with venom. Her eyes turned to follow the line of men reloading the Treasure onto the boats in the inlet.

"You're a soldier of fortune now. Your loyalty goes to the highest bidder. Who paid you to banish the Queen into the company of cormorants?"

"I've other incentives than wealth. Come, I'll show you a sight that will set your royal blood singing." His long cloak fluted out behind him as he climbed the hill. She hesitated till he passed her. Then, curious, she stepped after him over the tussocks. On the crest, powerful and assured, silhouetted against the dismal sky, he flung out his arm to the north.

"There, my noble lady, does that sight not give wings to your heartbeats?" Swanning in from the north-east came a fleet of warships, headed by the three ships of Artcois, white-sailed with the spine-backed Boar insignia and the crimson Pretani pennant streaming from their masts.

The narrative slotted swiftly into place in her mind. All this time, her father's Commander and loyal friend had kept vigilant eyes on the policies of the Court. Long ago, he had seen that Bridei's far-sighted wisdom had become blunted, that he was blinded by his love for his foster-brother into believing that the son was a man of honour. It was Gort who had drugged her and hidden her in the earth-house. And Artcois who had attempted to rescue her. Now he and his sons had brought the Queen and the Treasure into safe-keeping on the Island. Both would now be returned to the chastened Council of Elders. The sons would be redeemed by their valiant service in ridding the Pretani of their enemy, Gort of Gwynedd. Then, according to the law of the land, a new King would be elected.

It had all the ring of truth and valour but a bell tolled somewhere with a discordant crack in it. Maybe it was because the man at her side set her teeth on edge with a revulsion that was almost unbearable.

"And what reward do the Veniconie expect for this valiant act?" she asked with deceptive mildness.

His eyes turned on her, glassy and triumphant.

"The Kingship, my precious pearl. What else?"

Veniconie or Gwynedd? Maelchon or Gort? Both tyrants! Both seeking only to glorify themselves! One was kin, the other foreign! One self-confessed, the other's motives hidden! Which one would serve the Pretani best?

Maelchon smiled, a long, slippery smile.

"Talorc and I didn't run for the Low Countries after all. We made for our father's tower at Fif Ness. There we merely brought forward our plans. You see, we shared your suspicions of Gort." He was laughing at her, silently, secretly, revelling in the flush of anger that stained her cheeks. Yet, there was nothing to be gained by antagonising him, not while Iogena and she were at his mercy on this isolated island.

"Prent, too?" She had to know for sure though the knowledge would hurt.

"Prent always! Who better to change the Law than a Veniconie Law-Giver himself? Oh, he wavered in his loyalties, especially when your emerald eyes melted the marrow in his bones. But the call of his mother's blood was stronger."

Maelchon cared little for the fine proud face or the high-breasted body before him. He had consorted with Kings in the seats of their power. And he lusted to taste it for himself. He had learned that the force behind the arm that held the sword was the greatest leveller. And he had sweated blood to perfect his swordsmanship. Now he flexed his muscles and roared his contempt at this woman who dared to stand unafraid and uncowed.

"You fell nicely into Prent's little trap. Guard-dogs trained to squat at the cry of 'Veniconie'." He caught the expression of horror that she could not control. "Come, my Queen, Artcois will take us to the mainland where you and I shall enter the Citadel in triumph." He held out his arm to her in a parody of a courteous gesture.

Standing on the wind-blown hill, Caterin knew how heavy the burden of choice that lay upon her. Maelchon had ignored the will of the people. They would not forget the deeds of this day. Neither would she. But the Clans had elected Gort as their King. The Queen must uphold that decision.

Stepping forward, she drew her smoke-begrimed cloak around her, playing the Queen's role, warily, but not warily enough.

He threw his helmet high and his hand snaked out to fasten in her hair. Her breath tore at her throat as he arched her head backwards.

"Aha, you think you're going back to spend gold on the graceless poor and feed bannocks to your fancy horse-flesh? That's over for you and the clan of the Vacomagie! It's the turn of the

Veniconie to crack the whip and breathe the heady smell of power in the Halls." His cinnamon freckles stood out boldly in the white fury of his face.

A frenzied spitfire burst from the heather at his back. Clawing and threshing, Iogena launched herself at his head. As he twisted from her attack, she lunged under his shoulder. Fists locked together, she slammed at his arm to dislodge his grip on her mistress. One-handed he took her by the throat and shook her like a newborn cub until her face contorted and her eyes bulged. One woman in each hand he laughed down to his grinning men.

"Two squawking chickens hardly worth the cauldron," he crowed. "By all the Ones that sail the seas, I should wring their necks now and save myself a deal of trouble."

Fear had sharpened Caterin's senses. She caught the Brython words and knew the men to be mercenaries and merciless. A sudden thrust sent Iogena spinning in a whirl of skirts and exposed limbs on a bruising, sense-whirling journey down the slope. A ribald cheer rose as she came to rest, crouching, ready to tackle any man who made a move.

"Save that saucy slut for later!" Maelchon turned his attention back to Caterin. A malicious smile glittered and was gone. "But I have a long-standing account to settle with the Royal One. And I need her to hoist myself into the Kingship."

He wrenched Caterin's head round till she was facing out to sea. Artcois and his flotilla were spreading out to catch the freshening wind that would take them skimming round the southern cliffs of the island.

"There's the navy that will rescue you from the talons of the Cymry vulture." Even yet he could not resist vaunting his craftiness. Like his father. Fine poetic phrases that muddied the listener's mind.

She held herself limply as if defeated. There was a wide watery sea between here and the mainland and she had no desire to feel it closing over her head.

"A subtle plan, don't you think? We laid a trap by sending raiders to lure the King out of the Citadel. A long-maturing plan, that Prent exploded into action with his fiery arrow."

"A traitor's plot to end our independence!" The retort was out before she could bite it back.

She felt in his hand the surge of temper that was blind to his political need of her. Before he lost control, she kicked backwards onto the hard bone of his shin with the full force of her wooden-heeled boot. A grunt of pain exploded in her ear. But still he held her in a crab-like embrace.

"Oh, bravely whinnied, my fine brood-mare." His tongue wet his upper lip. "It was a pity the heat in my young loins was cooled by your bodyguard. Yet, it was a chance worth taking, wasn't it? And where's your hand-picked husband now, tell me? Prancing up and down the coast on his stallion, showing off his plump thighs, searching for his bride and his silver? But I have both. And I've yet to discover which I shall enjoy most."

He released her and she looked in his face, recognising the ruthless ambition in the white line of his lip. A great sadness overcame her. Here on this island in sight of her own Capital, she was alone, bereft of King, army, advisers. Where was Broichan working his magic today? What of Eildon and his thought-winging wonders?

The sun had shaken itself loose from the veiling clouds and was preparing a burst of brightness. For a moment, she thought that the sun had dazzled her. Or lack of food had crazed her brain. But there it came again! The glint of weapons on the decks of another fleet of ships, incredibly close and bearing in on the island from the west. Cliffs screened the ships from the men below. Maelchon half-turned to follow the line of her gaze but she forestalled him by laying her arms on his shoulders. In his arrogance, he had not even posted a look-out.

"It seems you win the Playfield prize, my lord," she said, her eyes melting, drawing his gaze. The longer she kept him there, the greater the chance of the flotilla catching his men by surprise. The leading sail she had glimpsed had been white with a red serpent emblazoned on it. Gort of the Winged Dragon! Swiftly she controlled the surge of happiness that blazed through her.

Maelchon's light eyes glittered strangely.

"What's this sudden change of face going to cost me?" he asked.

Her arms stole round his neck and fastened there strongly. She moulded her body to his length. Even through the mail she felt him quiver and respond while she looked beyond over his shoulder.

"You've won me fair and square." And make the most of it now, she added silently, for tomorrow you'll be yesterday's hero.

In the prow of the leading craft, among his warriors, stood a heart-stopping figure in black with streaming hair to match. Following in a line behind a full dozen ships, each with a distinctive broad yellow banner fluttering from the mast-head. And jauntily bringing up the rear, five black sails. She stifled her sharp intake of breath. Maelchon stirred and her arms tightened.

"Yet can you stand a whole night of it?" she asked, pressing harder against him. "Or will you fall off after an hour, gorged like a sheep-tick?"

Like a blow above the heart, she saw the truth. Gort had planned it all. The five black raiders had been under his command. He had known the intentions of Artcois all along. She saw again that hesitant hand among the kagouls when she had cried out in Pretani. That one had been Gort's man and she had almost made him give himself away. Prent had assumed the five black raiders belonged to Artcois and had set the plot in motion. And the traitor within the Citadel had revealed himself at last.

A shout of alarm carried up from below. Maelchon swirled and saw the fleet.

"You crafty bitch!" he cried and yelled an order to his men.

The men below were caught in utter confusion. Throwing down their burdens they ran for their weapons. At sea a hundred or more small boats flowered in the water around their mother ships.

Maelchon flung his cloak to the ground. He caught Caterin's arm, forcing her to keep pace with him as he leapt towards the cliff-edge. Gort's face and a thousand others tilted upwards as Maelchon held their Queen achingly near the brink of the precipice.

"Welcome, King Brude, into the jaws of our rocky trap! But be warned! The first boat ashore will ground on the bones of your Queen."

The wind had blown Maelchon's words unheard from his mouth but no one could doubt his intention to use the Queen to gain time while his men took up position. Pale upturned faces remained riveted on the two figures against the sky. A slight push from Maelchon would send Caterin cart-wheeling down the black cliff-face to be broken on the ledges below.

Laughter bubbled in his throat like the whimper of a half-crazed child. To emphasize her danger, he flourished his dagger and held it to a vein in her neck. She stared steadily out to sea, averting her eyes from the fang-like rocks and foaming waves that ground boulders to grit and pulverised pebbles to sand. With a quick gesture she loosed the tie that bound her hair. The wind caught it and lifted it like a banner.

She was no Colum Cille clothed in gold. Yet she knew the power of the dramatic image, how it put heart into a fighting man. How it would boost her own courage. Her cloak was drab, her face pale. Only her hair could blaze a signal to the army.

The Pretani men saw Bridei's daughter stand proud and unafraid, her hands clasped before her, her hair streaming in the wind, manifesting her defiance of the Clan of the Veniconie. Let Maelchon cast her down! But the Pretani must be free. Like her father before her, she trusted them to do what had to be done. She was laying a task on each man on each deck, in each boat, on each ladder. And every man of them understood.

As if Broichan had lifted his oak-wand and recited his weather magic, the updraft swirled her hair skywards, fanning it like wings from her head. And each man caught the wind in his teeth. And those with daggers beat them on their shields, and those with oars raised them and those with nothing stamped their feet and cheered.

She was magnificent! A Scathach, a Boudicca, a warrior Queen, fit to stride side by side with the King who had slain the sons of Aidan and whose brother walked tall in the land of the Angles!

Out of the corner of her eye Caterin saw Iogena on a crag, pointing, warning them of the fleet coming in from the east, making the shape of ships with her hands and signalling the numbers with her fingers. And this was the woman who, for one unguarded moment, she had suspected of being the spy.

She raked the flag-ship with her eyes for Gort. Instead Uurad stood stalwart in his place, looking at his woman, reading her signs, until a dark shape with an upraised dagger felled her. But already, helmsmen were leaning, oars biting and slowly the rearguard was turning southward, gathering speed to meet Artcois.

The small-boats clustered waiting for the sign from Uurad to cast off. He stood perfectly still, his eyes riveted on the spot where Iogena had fallen.

A spasm of grief threatened to destroy Caterin's outward calm. With an effort of will she withdrew into the fastness of her being and found a well of strength she could draw on. Her thoughts flew to Veleda's garden at Pitversie and the gentle spirits who lived there. Moments passed but time had no meaning for her. Uurad had no choice but to send his men in now. His sword rose and fell. The first of the small-boats broke away heading towards the shore.

Maelchon growled with satisfaction. The thought of sending a Queen to her death had aroused him. His loins jumped and hardened at the thought of it. But Caterin's spirit had found a place of peace.

CHAPTER FORTY THREE

Gulls screeching, cursing. Waves grinding boulders to sand. Sea-grass sprouting, waving out over the edge of the cliff.

Maelchon sucking in great gulping breaths, watching the small-boats draw near, judging when to make his last threat.

Caterin blinked. A line of black in the sea-grass. Not there before. Two icy pebbles among the stalks. Caterin's urge to survive came vividly to life.

Uurad's long long wait before giving the signal. Because Gort had been swimming through the boiling sea. Now Gort had climbed the cliff. And Gort's head would be severed neatly and cleanly once he lifted it over the edge.

She swallowed the lump of fear in her throat. The dagger bit deep. Blood oozed down her neck. She swung her body away from the seaward side forcing Maelchon to turn with her. At the same second, she jammed her foot between his legs. They swayed and toppled as one, Maelchon on top. His dagger sliced her shoulder with fire. Using his knee and elbow he sprang to his feet. But Gort was over the cliff, his sword scything from its scabbard. Maelchon swivelled, and planted his feet on the turf.

"Foreign scum!"

They faced one another, two men, ready to fight to the death for the Kingship. Their swords met, swung, thrust and parried.

Caterin rolled from under their feet and began wading through the heather to the hollow where Iogena had fallen. She found her, crouched, her hands held protectively round the hilt of the dagger that protruded from her side. Her eyes were closed. Her breath came in slow agonizing gasps that cut short each time in a moan as the pain caught her. Only a thin ring of blood round the entry of the dagger. The bleeding would come later when the dagger was pulled out. Caterin covered her in both cloaks. She wiped her forehead and kissed the waxy cheek and called on the Guardians to ease the pain.

"Uurad?" It was a breath of a whisper.

"He's safe."

"Tell me."

Caterin parted the heather. A full-blown battle raged on the beach. There was no sign of Uurad. Tears coursed down the back of her throat. She swallowed. Since she had to lie she would lie convincingly. A warship charged towards the opening of the inlet.

"He's there, bringing a ship into the inlet." The yellow pennant changed direction as the warship slewed round blocking the only place where Artcois could land men.

"That's strait's as tight as a virgin's slit," she heard Maelchon roar. "Chase that ship back out to sea and scuttle it!" He leapt downhill over the tussocks, Gort pursuing, the metal rings on their jackets bouncing as they went. The narrow inlet was jammed with small-boats coming in now from the blockading warship. Men jumped from boat to boat and splashed through the shallows to attack the mass of Maelchon's men. The two groups met with a clamour that sent a thousand birds spiralling and shrieking up into the air. The soldiers fought desperately, hacking, swinging, stabbing at one another. It was impossible to make out if any side was gaining the upper hand.

One of Iogena's hands fell from the dagger. Caterin clasped it. Dear Bride, Mistress of Healing, send your power through my flesh to keep her alive. She chanted the healing spell in her mind, over and over, endlessly.

A heart-stopping clang of shield on shield almost above their heads roused her. Iogena gave a long trembling sigh. Caterin, watching and willing her breast to rise again, changed her plea. Dear Bride, if her time has come, ease her passing into the life beyond. A gasp came and a flutter of an eyelid.

"Uurad?"

Caterin looked round and saw his helmet with its red plume, cutting a swathe through the kagouls towards them. Oh, let him come soon. But there were so many of the enemy in his way.

"He's coming for you. I promise he'll be here soon." Dear Bride, let it be so.

A gleam of pale sunlight lit up the combat. Maelchon erupted from a knot of men to take a stance on an over-hanging outcrop. His sword flashed as he turned to face his pursuer. It was Gort, lean and lithe, who sprinted after him. The two men sought for a firm foothold, eyes wary, measuring, challenging. Gort's sword swept downwards towards Maelchon's exposed neck. Maelchon parried with his shield and struck at the same instant. Then they were lunging at one another mercilessly. Gort's sword went clanging over the rocks. Shield held high above his head he scrambled crab-wise to reach for it. Then, deliberately, he threw away his shield and grasped his sword with both hands. Maelchon swung low at Gort's legs. Gort leapt. And almost before he had landed, perfectly balanced, he caught Maelchon a mighty blow on the shoulder that slewed him sideways. Turning, Maelchon caught the full force of the two-handed thrust of Gort's sword in his chest that sliced through between his iron discs.

Sword and shield fell from dead arms, rolled, hung, bounced and clanged, down the rock-face, sounding a death-knell to those who fought. Soldiers like images graven on a stone saw the body that followed, limbs spread, then folding, somersaulting over and over, from ledge to shelf to platform and hurtling at last into the sea. Almost before it had disappeared, Gort's men yelled and struck down the stunned enemy.

Suddenly Uurad was there, towering over Iogena, his face bloody, his eyes wild, lifting her, holding her to his breast. And Iogena gave a great shuddering moan that drew Caterin's heart from her body. So gently now he carried her and laid her on her cloak within a huge silver bowl from the Treasure. And they carried her down to where soldiers had prepared a place for her in a small-boat. And Uurad climbed beside her in the seat meant for the Queen.

Caterin helped to push the boat out and watched it go. Fight, Iogena, fight! Gort on a crag, directing the hunt for fugitives, stooped to wipe his sword on the grass and saw her. Matted hair, bloodstained clothing, still she stood with the waves lapping her feet, erect and stately, regal as a Queen waiting to accept the homage of her champion.

Caterin glanced upwards and their eyes locked. She thought she could detect relief, perhaps admiration, and another quickly concealed emotion that she could not fathom. She saw the tightening of his jaw as he turned and strode past the lines of dead and wounded and at last came towards her. Pain dulled his eyes as he looked towards the boat that carried Iogena's still form.

"A brave lass," he said. "But for her, Artcois would have sailed round the south end and caught us in a trap."

He saw the bruises of exhaustion under her eyes. And the trembling mouth that tried to smile. He sought for words to praise her courage. And in a flash knew that she would think him condescending. So he fell back upon his old mocking banter.

"Was that a new dance-step you were teaching Maelchon on the top of the cliff. Or was it a lucky ruse that just saved my life?"

Caterin's heart was too full to make a retort that would suit. Instead she turned and went to help the wounded down to the boats. For there was still Artcois, riding the ocean, waiting to pounce.

CHAPTER FORTY FOUR

A pair of long arms with supple-fingered hands reached over the gunwale and hauled the soldiers into the small-boat. Golden eyes raked Caterin's face.

"Thanks be to the All-Mother we came in time," said Eildon. "I caught your cry from the air, sweet Thetil be praised, just in time to alert ... that mad King of yours."

For Gort was racing to the top of the cliff. With hardly a pause in his stride, he launched himself outward, his sword high above his head. The warship he was aiming for bucked and heaved but he landed lightly in the well. The oarsmen bent and the ship leapt to meet Artcois.

Caterin's heart started up again, thudding fast and loud in her ears.

The gusting wind took their little craft surging and swinging out to the warship. Eildon caught the net that hurtled downwards. Above, the Master eyed his sail and leaned on the helm.

The sea heaved and crashed their frail vessel against the warship. Caterin guided the feet of the wounded men up the slippery rungs of a rope-ladder that hung over the hungry sea.

Aortan, a blood-stained bandage askew round his head, pulled her on board. Gair, his cheek laid open by a sword-cut, doggedly pulled up bundles of Treasure. There was no room on board for the small-boats. They were left to see-saw on the waves, spilling their oars, cracking and spreading their planks over the sea. All but one, half-full of Treasure, that overturned and sank.

Iogena lay, bandaged and drugged, curled in the bowl like a pearl in a shell, softly and sweetly asleep. Caterin followed the surgeon, holding men while he stitched their wounds, washing and cleaning, calming and cooling.

The ship staggered like a man full of mead as it met the force of the gale. And steadied as the wind caught the sail as a friend, not an enemy.

Eildon, bringing water in a jasper bowl, saw her fix Aortan's bandage where he sat and, kneeling, fold him in her arms. He gave the nearest men a drink, waiting while they talked, then sat beside them.

"The battle's over," he said. "It was decided as much by seamanship in this veering wind and rising sea as by force of arms."

"Artcois?" Caterin could hardly speak for exhaustion.

"When he rounded the south end of the island, he must have seen the ship blocking the inlet. It was the only place he could land to rescue Maelchon and his men. Whether he saw Maelchon fall, I don't know."

"But where were his allies?"

"With one eye on the weather growing dirtier by the minute and another on the strength of Gort's force they whipped their helms round and turned for the Forth. My guess is they decided they'd paid their debt to Artcois. It was his hard luck that it wasn't enough."

"Heave-to for a rescue!" sang out the look-out at the prow. There was a question in his voice as he looked towards the Master. Caterin ran to the side.

It was the flag-ship of Artcois, flying straight towards the spray-hidden reefs, seemingly out of control, for the helm swung free and the sail was in tatters. The same wave that carried her over one reef, opened and pulled her downwards to explode apart on another. Men and planks scythed through the air, hovered and dropped back into a sea that boiled and foamed like soup in a cauldron. The mast and a half-furled sail hung rakishly for the space of an in-drawn breath. The red pennant with the Boar and a flag with Talorc's trident sign gave a last defiant flutter.

"How could he make such a mistake, a master-mariner like Artcois?" breathed a young lad's voice.

"That was no mistake." Caterin strained her eyes for bobbing heads and waving arms, seeking help no ship dare offer. "His cause is finished. He had no will to fight on." Suddenly the world spun around her and she found her cheek resting on rough planks. Eildon held a flask to her mouth and a harsh raw spirit stung her throat.

"Here!" From his pouch he produced two soggy bannocks that tasted of sea-water.

Caterin spoke softly, sorrowfully. "Why didn't Gort tell me he was trying to tempt them into the open? Did he think I would fail in my duty?"

"No. He spoke highly of you to your father. He said that you'd a soaring courage that matched both your rank and your beauty."

"It's the insult to my intelligence that angers me."

"He told no one. But the suspicion grew on me as I went south. That's why I came back." Eildon sucked a broken finger-nail. "By the Ever-living Ones, I've a song floating in my head about a brave Queen and now I can't pluck my harp till this nail grows."

She did not tell him about Veleda's prophecy. The thought brought a wondering shadow of someone's death.

Night had fallen before they saw the guiding beacons on the beach and a crowd of folk surging forward for news of kin.

Caterin sat with Iogena, counting every breath she took, until Uurad came for her. Women led her away to have her own cuts and burns salved and bound. Later bathed and fed, she rested on her couch. A night-bird called loudly and insistently from the yard below. One of her women raised starry eyes to listen.

"Go to your men," Caterin told them. "And may you come together in joy."

Amis picked up a trail of amber beads spilled by the raiders and dowsed all the lamps but one before she left.

Caterin knew she would not sleep. Too many lifeless faces loomed in the darkness when her eyes closed. Too many betrayals cut at her heart. Yet Gort's

throw of the dice had paid off. The Veniconie chiefs were outcasts till the end of time and their clan would keep their heads down for generations. It was clear to her now that Gort had used all his powers of leadership to isolate the infection within one sept and prevent it from spreading.

One minute she was alone with the queer sweet sorrow of loneliness. The next he was there, leaning his elbow against the frame of the open door. At once the air in the room crackled with a subtle silken tension. The tiny bronze flame of the lamp glowed on his richly embroidered robe and gleaming girdle but folded his face in shadow, mysterious and remote.

Caterin lay, high and unmoving, in a froth of fur and feather pillows, her hair still damp and curling, her skin dusky pink and sweet-smelling. Only her honey-coloured robe and the fine gold strand of the chain lying between her breasts rose and fell with her breathing.

"Did you choose between the Boar and the Dragon or was the choice forced upon you?" he asked.

"At the time, a fire-breathing monster that takes wing seemed the more romantic of the two."

The wick spluttered, throwing out a spurt of flame that set the gold thread shimmering in the wall-tapestries. It lit his profile and showed the ravaged face of a man who had seen comrades die and who had fought beyond the limits of his endurance. She held out her hand, seeking to comfort him. He came forward and clasped it, looking deeply into her face. Two pairs of eyes, dazed with grief and exhaustion, met and clung.

"Yet, there was a choice to be made," she said gently. "I would have trusted my life to Prent. Artcois was a foster-uncle to me. Maelchon was a playmate. You were the one I had to doubt, the foreigner."

The blue-black of his hair deepened as he bent his head in acknowledgment of her admission. He drew a breath to speak, then swung to the window, drawing aside the drape. His rigid back told her nothing.

"Bridei knew there was a faction close to him who were preparing to bring down the whole fabric of the elected monarchy. He sent to Gwynedd for me, knowing that I would be under suspicion. But who better than an outsider to track down internal spies? It was inevitable that you should put the wrong interpretation on my actions as others did."

She sighed, moving gently so as not to disturb her stiff shoulder.

"I was the future Queen and Bridei should have told me."

His grasp tightened on the folds of the curtain and he half-turned towards her.

"You were an untried child then, flexing your wings against authority. But, I agree. You ought to have been told. In trying to shield you from some ugly truths, your father created greater problems for you."

"You went even further. You brought me from Pitmuies and put my life in danger to spring your trap."

His clenched fist beat once, twice on the woodwork. His chin sank on his breast. She let him suffer for a moment.

"You and Bridei! Foreigners! Pretani women bring their daughters up to face reality. But your reasons were sound. Your plot was successful. That's what matters. Only, I'd have been proud if you'd told me. Instead you classed me along with children and idiots."

Only his hand moved, frsctionally, as if he was at a loss for words.

"In future," she said distinctly. "I shall share in your decisions. Then I will have time to make peace with my gods before I face my fate."

When he answered, he groped into the past again as if trying to make a kind of bridge between them.

"I'd no intention of becoming King. It was Bridei who persuaded me that the situation was desperate. Whether he had a sign from the Fateful Ones that he was to die soon, I'll never know."

Caterin waited till the pain of her grief had eased and longer because she sensed he had not put all his thoughts into words.

"I didn't intend to saddle myself with a wayward bride. Nor to waste my father's proud seed, though it seems one of us is not as fruitful as we might be." There was no emotion in his voice, just a cold weary indifference. "But I've learned much since I've been here. For one, there's common-sense in an elected Kingship. The Pretani can boot me out if I fail them without the inconvenience of having to chop off my head."

That might be as near as he would ever come to an apology but his deeds today had spoken for him. The eyes he turned on her now were bleak, his brow and cheeks deeply engraved with lines of sorrow. With a great leap of her heart, she knew he needed comfort and had come to her for it. He had to be convinced that the wounding and maiming and killing had had a purpose so that he could go forth tomorrow, still the powerful warrior King. But he was not yet ready to rest.

He began to prowl about her room, sniffing her perfumes, fingering her jewels, sliding his hands up and down the wall hangings, his eyes unseeing.

"Those black-sailed raiders that alarmed the Citadel." His voice was tinged with irony. "Maelchon thought Artcois had sent them. Instead they came from Gwynedd with men from Dun Eidyn, from Clyde, from Rheged, from all the kings who owed an obligation to Rhun. I didn't know how many clans had been drawn into Artcois's net. So I had to be sure that the men under my command owed allegiance only to me and my brother."

Quietly she slid her feet to the fleece at her bedside and went to pour mead for him. He came to her side where she could feel the warmth of his body. Her grave, green eyes met his over the cup. The spark that flowed between them brought his dead eyes to life. The perfumes from her skin and her hair eddied about them. Her loose robe fell about her in straight folds to the floor. Yet after taking the cup he turned to pace the floor once more.

"My foray outside the walls was a pretence. But I left two loyal men, Uurad at the Gate and Fortrei guarding you."

"Fortrei, Prent and I were childhood companions. Prent's trained hounds fooled us all. Poor silly Prent. He was wise in the ancient laws but not in the ways of humans. Perhaps he hoped to prevent the wilder excesses of his clan in his position as Law-Giver."

"You can reason down many roads. The womb of the mother is where the man is formed. He suckles more from her than milk."

He was learning the value of the Clan Mother. Caterin smiled secretly. This time it was Gort who poured mead for her.

Gort was glad he had come. Always he walked alone, measuring the emotions that touched him. Too many sorrows, too much love, too much anger even, and his sword would falter, his resolution waver. Battles had been his birthright. In the aftermath he had fought his real battles. Alone, within himself, knowing there was another way out of the incessant chain of blood-baths, beating his fists and calling on the gods for strength. Strength to be the one who would stand out above the others and take the step towards peace. In this climate of greed and power-hunger, he would be tested. Maybe to the limit of his endurance. Yet some bright day, he would hold his sword high. And proclaim, 'You have tried force against me and you have failed. Now, let us talk of trade and the exchange of ideas.'

He was a fool to think it might come in his lifetime. It would take many men stronger than he. And maybe women. This woman, for instance. Her deep wide eyes mirrored the earth as it should be, green and tender. Eyes that had looked on the pain and death of this day. Eyes of compassion, eyes that told of battles as hard-fought as his own. She needed comfort as much as he. This was not a night for either of them to spend alone.

Once Caterin had thought those icy eyes could never glow with fire but she had been wrong. Twin points of light shimmered in his eyes. There was desire in the huskiness of his voice and a question in the hesitant way he cupped her cheek in his palm. Surely there was more to be said between them, words of love and commitment that would bring a new dimension to their love-making. Words of shared ambitions that would bring meaning to their life together.

There was a hunger in his gaze. She longed for him to make love to her with a longing that was sweetness in itself and mingled with the surging need of a woman who knows she has met with her mate. Led by that powerful and primitive urge she stroked his silky hair and the scar on his chin. He leaned his cheek against hers and the tension flowed from him in a great sigh. Her hands loosened the girdle of his robe and explored his warm flesh.

Lying in the warm quivering darkness, with exquisite tenderness she brought him the release he needed without thought for herself. And found in the act of giving a sense of fulfilment. Later she wakened to the slow pleasure of his caressing fingers that moved her from one pinnacle of ecstacy to another.

When the sounds of the morning roused her she stretched her arm to feel for his warm urgent body again. His place was empty and cold. The stamping of impatient hooves and the jingling of bits in the Courtyard took on a new meaning. She ran, pulling on a robe, to look through the slats into the cold dawn. He was in his riding leathers again with his Guard preparing their horses for a journey. How could he? He had said no word of this. He glanced up at her, threw an order over his shoulder and strode into the Palace. Eagerly, she waited to throw her arms around his neck and wish him well.

CHAPTER FORTY FIVE.

"I must breathe fresh life into the alliance of clans in the north," he started speaking as he came through the door. She drew back, her hand to her mouth, as though he had struck her. This after their intimacy of the night before! She had expected to be swept into his embrace. Instead the cold implacable warrior was back, arrogant and indifferent.

Gort saw her hurt movement and cursed himself for his roughness. But she surely understood the enormity of his task.

"You're named as my Deputy. Here's your seal of authority."

She watched him place Bridei's amethyst ring on the table. She let it lie.

He tried to soften his soldier's bark.

"I'm leaving a small garrison under Uurad and sending the bulk of the army back to their homesteads. The Citadel's in no danger with the cold season coming on."

He began to stride restlessly about the room, knowing there were other words he should be saying, eager to be back in a world he understood.

"The Dal Riatans are lying low. Too many of their sons have died. Only Mynyddog in Dun Eidyn is looking warlike, gathering stray mercenaries from all over Alba and housing them on his crag on Eidyn. Yet he assures me that his spears are pointing southwards."

He cocked an eye below at the horses and rubbed his gloved hands together.

"Messengers will travel between Uurad and myself if you have anything that needs my attention. Meanwhile the Council have orders to repair the fire damage. So there won't be much for you to trouble yourself with." His voice sounded bleak even in his own ears. "I cannot say when I'll return." Abruptly he gave the army salute of a clenched fist and turned to leave.

"King Brude!"

He checked at the cold fury in her voice. Slowly his face relaxed almost to a smile. She looked like a child with her hair flowing and her face puffy from sleep.

"Shall I repeat it more slowly?"

"Don't condescend to me! Take back Bridei's ring! You need it more than I do. I am my own authority. I am Queen and Deputy of no King!"

His eyes burned into hers. She knew that her eyes glowed with no less fierce a pride.

"One last thing! You'll report to me and not to Uurad!" She returned his salute. "The Guardians go with you."

She was testing him on two levels. First on his acceptance of the laws of the land. And, whether he guessed it or not, on his quality as a man. If he flared into anger, his arrogance stemmed from a sense of weakness within himself. She had to know. He seemed to grow in stature as he drew in a deep breath.

"Of course!" he said quietly. "I'm sorry. I'm not used to a Queen who thinks like a man!"

"And acts like a woman, armed with a deeper insight."

He bowed his head, acknowledging the rightness of it. He spoke on an impulse.

"I'll postpone my departure. You should be at my side on this journey."

"Not this time," she told him. "Peace brings its own set of responsibilities. There's more to ruling a land than defence."

"I leave the peace in your hands." In a rare tender gesture, he cupped her face in his hands, laid his lips upon her forehead and was gone.

She stood perfectly still with downcast eyes until the riders moved off. She took the ring he had left and cradled it in her palm.

Oh, Bridei, how I loved you! How I want to love this man! But now she must put on her mantle of Queenship. In the next room Amis was feeding broth to Iogena. Bran sitting on his grandmother's knee, raised his arms. Caterin hugged him, folding him to her heart, liking the trust in the arms that crept round her neck. And the strength that flowed, thinking of all the bairns in the land, blindly trusting inadequate folk like herself.

Before the days grew any shorter, she had the yard under her rooms spread with soil and sweetened with shell-sand to make a herb-garden with drying and distilling sheds over the wall. Under Veleda's guidance, she began studying again and gathering the last crop of the plants for a medecine chest of her own. As she had hoped, peace and her own interest encouraged an influx of students and visiting foreign medics.

On his next journey south, she commissioned Derelei to build a new Treasury. Apart from being secure, she wanted it to be as beautiful outside as the Treasure that it housed.

"I promised a praise-song," he reminded her when he came. "I've found a worthy stone at Cadboll. A massive slab, the height of two men. I see it in panels surrounded by decoration with the symbols at the top and yourself in a hunting scene below."

Surely it could never be, she thought after he left. Veleda had foretold no praise-song. A sadness came over her for Derelei and his empty dream. Yet maybe a praise-stone was different. She wanted it to happen, not for her own pride, but for his. As for herself, she had work to do.

A tiny Venicone sept had begun quarrelling over the bird-catching rights on Maie. She placed the island out of bounds until after the nesting season. For some time she had been concerned about the Miathie clan who had taken the brunt of the fighting and raiding in the past. Before the herds were separated for breeding or slaughter she chose a number of sturdy beasts to compensate them for their losses.

The snow came early that year. Caterin wondered if it might bring the King home. He was drawing up plans for new defences, he reported. He had settled a few long-standing disputes, two of them by the sword. Never a question was asked about herself.

Caterin's replies were equally brief, filled out by reports on the activities of Mynyddog. Uurad sent these, calling him 'Mynyddog the Wealthy' or 'the Luxurious' as the humour took him. For Mynyddog was feasting a vast war-band to some purpose in his great hall at Fort Eidyn.

Yet it seemed the Pretani need not fear the horsemen and their retinues that feasted and trained on the flood valley of the Forth.

Eildon had taken himself off to that very Dun to sing a lay and sample the lavish hospitality. The enemy Mynyddog feared, Eildon informed the Queen, was indeed in the south. The two kingdoms of Dewr and Brynaich who now called themselves Deira and Bernicia had gained a further influx of immigrants. Mynyddog had long been thinking of destroying them before they grew too powerful. The warriors he feasted were hand-picked for valour and came from many kingdoms, not only from among his own people of the Gododdin.

But Mynyddog himself was old and sick. It was obvious he could not lead his army. He was on the lookout for a warrior who stood head and shoulders above the rest for heroism. The messenger who recited it grinned at the end. Caterin, staring, thought ' Great goddess Thetil keep King Brude in the north, hidden in a mist!' The man's grin swung and steadied. Suddenly her face went icy and she knew she was going to be sick.

Later she lying on her bed, hands behind her head, she began to count the phases of the moon. The bairn would open its eyes during the long warm days of the Growing Months. She had been so busy she was taken by surprise. And by delight. And a sort of triumph.

She had taken a step into a new world. She was to be a mother among mothers. Her life would never be the same. What would it be like to be a mother? She would never be lonely or unloved again. There would always be a bond. Always someone.

She rose and went to her Courtyard, hugging herself, keeping the knowledge secret, close. But her feet felt light and her body swayed and her arms embraced the sky. Where the clouds sailed by, pompous, indifferent, unknowing. Never to know the soft burgeoning of new life. The daughter who would one day be Queen. The son who would one day be a warrior. But first the babe, milky as Bran, innocent and trusting.

She told no one at first, then Iogena and Amis, swearing them to secrecy. Then Uurad when she could hide it no longer, telling him that she must be the one to tell the news to the King.

But he did not return. And she judged he had found his woman with a star brilliant in her hair in the long-hall of a chieftain, serving wine at her father's feast.

The celebrations of Festivals came and went. At first Caterin spent long days with the Council of Elders planning new harbours to bring trade with the Low Countries.

But a new purpose grew in her heart alongside the babe. A House of Bride where babies would be born. And mothers could rest, free from their households for twenty-one nights. To be with the new bairn and learn to know it. The whole idea was new and exciting.

When it was ready it was a pleasant place to be, clean and sweet-smelling, filled with flowers and laughter. And more babies and mothers survived and thrived.

And one day, as she sat, contented as a milking cow, in the sun in her Courtyard the first pain came. A hot pain, searing her with fire. And went. And she knew there had been nothing like this before in her life. For this event made a woman a being apart. This event that was about to happen to her. For it was the whole story of the Creation in one fragile body. That might tear itself apart in the labour of it. Would it be more than she could bear? Would she die of it?

All to bring forth a new spirit to walk on the earth and be tested. Yet she would try. For what were all her hopes and ambitions for the future of her land, if there was no one in it of her own? Her own blood, her own flesh. And yet different.

And again her body surged with the need to bring forth. And she cried out for Iogena to make ready to go to the House of Bride.

It was a lusty, black-browed boy that sprang from between her legs, yelling, with a fine dusting of downy black hair on his back. She had Uurad send a brief message informing the King of the birth of a son. An even more curt reply came back. The King would arrive some days before Lugnasad.

The morning when the first reapers went out with their sickles started like any other day for Caterin. The sky promised that the harvest weather would hold. By mid-morning, Caterin was engrossed in plans for a visit from two physicians from Gaul, when a scout interrupted her. The King's retinue had been sighted and would arrive before noon. No sooner had the cooks and stewards been alerted than the crowds began to gather on the palisade to greet him.

When the cheers told her that the Guard were in sight, Caterin took her son in her arms and waited in her courtyard. Let the King come to her. As she waited, rocking gently she saw a troup of riders approaching with their backs against the southern sky. They were carrying the pennant of Mynyddog of Dun Eidyn.

They met Gort opposite the entrance. The exchange of words was lengthy and heated before the King turned and led them in through the Gate.

She laid him in his cradle and paused, wondering anew at the beauty of dark lashes, fanned on a fresh golden cheek. This was a miracle. What did Colum Cille know of miracles?

She dressed in the Robe of Queenship and went to the

Chamber.

"This envoy," he was saying to the Council of Elders when he saw her framed in the doorway. He strode swiftly across to her, his booted footsteps echoing in the high-roofed hall. The familiar grey eyes surveyed her gravely, satisfying himself that all was well.

"It was a summons from Mynyddog of Dun Eidyn," he said. "He calls upon me to repay my war-debt."

He led her to the High Chair and waited while she sat.

"When I asked for help to defeat the Veniconie, he sent warriors." The lack of enthusiasm was evident in his voice. "He says the Saeson Kings are growing in self-importance. He reminds us that if the Gododdin kingdoms crumble, our Kingdom is next in the line of their advance."

"When will you go?"

"As soon as we've eaten and changed horses. Our duty is plain and the commitment must be respected. Mynyddog dare not wait any longer. The sooner we march, the sooner we return."

She left him hearing reports from the Councillors and went to see to her bairn. It was not long before his boots sounded in the passage and the door-curtain scythed apart.

He went straight to the cot.

Sensing a new presence, the boy opened his eyes. A long identical, appraising look passed between them.

Caterin waited and watched, proud and yet wary, wondered what Gort would say and do. The bairn was hers by Law. Her joy in him overwhelmed her at times. It depended on Gort's attitude whether she would share him or not. Yet what was a joy if it was not shared? And by the man who had made the joy possible.

He did all the right baby things.

He burped, directed a leer at his visitor, punched the air with his fists and crowed.

Gort was startled at the flood of tenderness and pride that threatened to bring tears streaming down his cheeks.

"Have you named him?"

"His name is Kenet." Up till now he had been 'Little Blackpoll'.

"He'll not need a Pretani name. His name's Dafydd."

Caterin bowed her head to hide a smile.

"No King can claim the son of a Pretani Queen, not even by giving him his grandfather's name.

"Are you telling me that this is not my son? With that mane?"

"You planted the seed, there's no doubt. Broichan informed the clans that you had that privilege. Then Broichan named him Kenet before the gods."

Gort's eyes sparked. He had been so absorbed in his son he had forgotten the custom of the land. Despite herself Caterin was afraid. Not of his anger, but of the emptiness that would remain in her heart if he spurned the Pretani custom.

"Prince of Gwynedd, this Pretani son is a great honour for your people." She smiled, gravely. " But I hoped he might also be a love-bond between us."

There was a pause as he adjusted to this new relationship with his Queen. Then he threw back the covers and lifted his son out and up and peered in his face.

"Then Dafydd Kenet, you'll have two names, ten names, one for every day in the year!"

His eye caught the tremble of her lip before she could control it. His heart lifted and his stern features relaxed. He put his son back in the cradle.

"He's a fine boy," he said.

Now she felt she could show a little of her absurd happiness at his safe return and took him in her arms. He placed his hands at her waist and buried his face in her hair. The sweet moment did not last. His grip loosened. His eyes filled with longing as he looked from her to the cradle and back again.

"All this and I must leave!" He slammed his fist on the bed-table and the child cried out in fright. "The whole campaign stinks like a crow's dinner. I'm guessing Mynyddog will place me at the head of his army. That means my leadership will be disputed by every Gododdin prince that aspires to war-glory."

At last he was sharing his plans with her and there was no pleasure in it for either of them. Again he punched the table.

"There's no way out from this ill-conceived adventure. My honour's at stake." Pausing over the cot, he held out his hand for her to join him. "I had hoped ... "

It was a mere whisper. Then, giving his clenched fist sign that he used to put heart into his soldiers, he left her. The sigh of the curtain behind him set the gold discs above the cot sparkling and tinkling.

CHAPTER FORTY SIX

Caught in some unseen eddy, the golden discs above the baby's head continued to spin, faster and faster, flaring and sparking, lancing Caterin's eyes with pain. She flinched backwards, hiding her eyes. Fire still flashed in the darkness, straight from the eyes of Broichan. His voice roared in her ears. And she held her head, moaning, for it sounded like the bellow of a Bull.

When she came to herself the discs swung gently. The baby slept. The room was still. She went softly to find Iogena.

"I must go to Dunino."

"Why, mistress?"

"I don't know."

But every fibre of her being hummed with the knowledge that the march of Mynyddog was ill-omened. And that Gort was in danger.

She left her escort at the entrance to the oak-grove of Dunino where no birds sang. Where the trees stopped, the path led her into a gorge cut by a vanished river between rising cliffs.

High on top of a pillar of sandstone Broichan waited. His robes hung loose on a frame wasted of flesh. His eyes so sunken and his skin so bleached that it seemed impossible he still lived. In her blue Drui robe, she stood below and asked for the bones of the King-Bull to be thrown. Only a Chief Drui or a Queen of the Line could call on the name of the King-Bull.

Broichan's garland of tiny skulls rustled. He beckoned with his staff. She climbed the rough-hewn steps to join him. Here in the rock ancient hands had incised the shape of the Bull, massive, awesome, clean of moss and of lichen. Below, the gorge had filled and was white with the robes of the Druad. And they lifted their heads and sang. Of the Bull whose back is the strength of the herd, whose sinews are the ripples on the barley-field, whose seed is the prosperity of the people, whose muzzle is the velvet touch of love, whose hooves strike anger in the heart of the warrior.

The spirits of wind and water had hollowed a basin in the sandstone at her feet. From a ewer of silver she poured mead. For the Bull was a Champion.

There came the crack of bone upon bone. The rocky walls shimmered. The sense of a Presence filled and oppressed her.

Broichan stood, still as death amid a scatter of bones, bones burned by fire to a startling whiteness. His eyes stunned her with their brilliance. A great sough of wind swept through the gorge, as though it had been loosed from the very nostrils of the Bull himself.

Broichan gazed in sorrow on the sweet grave face of the Queen. This was the one who embodied his hopes for the continuance of the Tradition. Yet he had to send her into danger. In his meditations he had cried out in anguish to the Guardians. Please, there were others who could be sent, others who could save the life of the chosen King, the Royal Bull of the Pretani. But the Ones had blown clouds across his vision, clouds that crackled with their laughter and whirred with the wings of white doves. He had known then that the Splendid Ones had their own ways of keeping the Faith of the Mother alive. Not by the great dramatic gesture, nor by striking down those who opposed it. But by the creation of a legend that would live. Not in the minds but in the race-memory of the women.

"You must venture into the realms of darkness," he told her as though repeating a lesson learnt by rote. "There you will find the King. Your path will be made clear. Be sure you ask for protection every step of the way. The Might of the Bull goes with you. The Forces of Good are within you." His arms folded across his breast. His eyes closed.

His words had brought a new feeling within her. She felt strange and strong and dedicated. She floated down the steps, her feet on wings, her body, light as a spider's web, resiliant in the storm.

Her plan to go seeking the King went completely against the tradition.

"The duty has been placed upon me by the All-Knowing Ones," she said, sweeping aside the arguments of the Council of Elders."I'm the chosen one."

"It's impossible!" Iogena heard her decision with mounting disbelief. "With the King beyond the borders you're needed here."

"Out of the question!" Uurad was pale with fury. "And don't attempt it. For I'll have a hundred men watching you night and day."

"But the King must be warned! This is not just a battle. This is ... annihilation!"

The word in her mouth shook her, stunned her. For in that instant she had seen it. Devastation, a wasteland, empty footprints covering a vast wind-blown plain.

The word, forced out of her, had shocked Uurad. And the horror that turned her eyes black as a new grave-mound.

"I'll send another hundred men to warn the King!"

"And when Mynyddog gets wind of it he'll ambush them rather than endanger his last great project."

Their eyes locked together, hard and implacable. Then Caterin deliberately dropped her gaze.

"Then let your men escort us to Pitmuies, Iogena and I and the bairns. Your men can farm and breed bulls there, since Delys's sons have all gone with Gort."

As they rode to Pitmuies she knew in her heart the next move she must make. Not inspired by the random scatter of old bones. But prompted by love for a tall lean man whose mind and body had been honed to react to the harsh call of the trumpet, the brutal beat of the chariot. While his heart burst with compassion and the fear that the killing never would stop.

And now all around her she felt the protection of the Guardian Ones like a cloud that moved with her wherever she went.

At Pitmuies she told the women she was riding to visit Veleda. Their eyes accused her over Dafydd's cradle as she touched his soft cheek. The rough-maned hill-pony was over-eager but knew a firm hand on his rein.

Her journey took longer than usual through secret foresters' paths, circling back to see if she was being followed. Iogena would send word to Uurad. But maybe not until she was well away. Broichan had said her path would be cleared.

Veleda's cell was built into an earthen bank, thrown up to protect her first School of Learning. Inside the same bunches of drying herbs, dusting their hair. They smiled and clasped hands, the future, dark and unknowable, high in their thoughts. Two saddle-bags filled with salves and ointments and healing herbs lay open on the table.

"Your reason for travelling. You've as much skill as any practising healer." Cloths and bindings, knives and probes, tweezers and spoons were all there.

"I've marked each pouch and phial with a sign. You can't always depend on your nose in a hurry."

"No, Veleda, no food. I'll reach Dun Eidyn before nightfall and there's plenty of feasting there, I hear."

Caterin, absorbed in the journey before her, did not hear the shadow of Veleda's whisper.

"No, not a bard-song, but a legend."

She rode hard and fast, pausing only on the borders of her homeland to let her sweat-drenched pony drink at the Bannog Burn. Beyond rose the Pettaland Hills, where once the Pretani had ruled. The pony snickered a complaint as she mounted again and set his face eastward. Soon, rearing from the flat marshes, loomed the crag with its ramparts where King Mynyddog was securely entrenched on the Fort of Eidyn.

A pressure of knee and hand slowed the pony to a trot. Every dry patch of ground, sported its troop of cavalry, wheeling and charging, spears probing, swords weaving. Orders and oaths mingling on the wind. Foot-soldiers marching and forming lines, making ramparts with shields, hedges of death with spears. At the foot of the crag, smiths and farriers, sweating and hammering. Sparks flying in the air. Horsemen and soldiers, farriers and smiths, mere objects of war, puppets controlled by the sick hands of Mynyddog.

And she saw them as bairns once, eyes filled with wonder, tiny hands formed with beauty, reaching for love. Growing to lads, shamed into boasting, challenging, competing. Then men, coarsened by Kings, killing for gold, venting lust from their loins in a frenzy of passion. Only a few remained human in spite of it all. Deep down they were bairns still, reaching blindly for love, seeking words for the song of the All-Mother, too long suppressed in their breasts.

The road to the fort was clogged with horses and carts piled high with stores. The guard at the gatehouse eyed her thick warm clothing and her lack of weapons suspiciously.

"Dafydd, son of Onid," she told him.

"You're Pretani by the twist in your tongue?"

"I come to speak with King Brude."

"Then you'll have a fair road to travel, boy, to catch up with him. He's been gone since the first cock crowed from the dunghill this dawn."

"Gone? Already? Where?" This was the last thing she had expected.

"No business of yours, son of Onid. Tell me your message and if it's important I'll see that it gets to King Mynyddog."

This was the kind of situation she had feared if the Council had forced her to send messengers.

"My news is only of the begetting of sons," she lied. "It has no bearing on the plans of King Mynyddog. Tell me where King Brude has gone and I'll follow."

"Not so fast, boy. What do you know of the plans of King Mynyddog?" The gruff voice had an edge to it and the man laid a firm hand on the bridle of her pony. "Only what the rest of the country has known for the past year. That he means to stop the advance of the Angles. And the Great Ones be with him, say I."

He grunted, satisfied to the extent of dropping his hand from the bridle but not enough to let her pass. Yet, she had to get into the fortress. She had to find out where Gort had gone. Every soldier around her was bound to be as tight-lipped as the guard.

"You wouldn't turn away the personal physician of King Brude, would you? At least, give me a place at table tonight for I can't return home before sunset." She loosened the top of her bag, letting it fall open to give him a view of the instruments before handing him a jar. "Here, have a salve for those hacks on your hands and eat more pease brose in the mornings."

"Well, since your King's been judged fit to lead us in Mynyddog's place, we'll not grudge you a bite. Pass through, but you'll find little stabling for your beast in this cauldron of kale."

As he had forecast it was a maelstrom within the fortress. The smells of horse-dung and burning hooves from the smith's sheds mingled with male sweat and leather and the cooking of food. She found a half-empty trough of water and filched a bundle of hay from under the nose of an affronted mare. Tying the reins to an unused iron ring, she left her pony cooling off under his blanket.

How to find out where Gort had gone without being taken for a spy? That meant listening with a patience she could not contain. He must have gone south to scout out the terrain. And there was an air in the fort of readiness, of exhileration. She guessed the rest of the force would be marching soon to join him.

With the same enthusiasm they displayed in their exercises, the warriors set about the business of eating, drinking and boasting. Judging by the carousing of the soldiers in the tents below, they were as well supplied with food and drink as their leaders. Caterin ate among the lowliest artisans at the farthest end of the Hall from the King's High Table.

There were no women present except three, kin of the King who kept close by him. However colourful they looked, the men outshone them in richness of dress and adornment. That was as it should be. The fiercest of warriors proclaimed confidence in their prowess by the loudest checks and tartans, brightest gold and largest jewels.

Huge pine-log fires and a multitude of torches lit the scene. The haunches of meat and breasts of fowl were the finest, as men going into battle deserved.

He's been feasting this lot for a year now, thought Caterin. If he doesn't dispatch them soon, he'll have to support them throughout another cold season. Even Mynyddog, the Wealthy, couldn't afford that.

That King Mynyddog was ageing and sick was apparent by his pale glistening skin and the tremor of his hands. With his long thin nose, bent in an encounter with a shield in his youth and with his close-set ferrety eyes, Caterin thought she had never seen anyone she would trust less. She could well imagine he had smelled trouble within his restless ranks and placed a scape-goat to lead them so that his honour would remain unscathed.

Wines from Gaul and home-brewed ale were available but it was mead that was the favoured drink of the men reclining on couches. Not the full-bodied golden mead with flecks of honey-comb in it that was served at Dalgynch. This was a pale-yellow liquid, strained and pure, sweet on the tongue but with a faint bitter after-taste that lasted long and was good.

Huddled over her platter, Caterin ate and drank and listened. At once she was struck by the fact that their tales were not of past deeds of valour but of glory to be won soon, very soon. And the bard who joined in praised the courage of the warriors and their unrestrained longing for fame.

"He will slay the enemy with the sharpest of blades.

Like rushes, his enemies will fall under his hands.

In the day of wrath he will not shirk from the fight."

The bard who sang was an engaging fellow with a neat pointed beard, unusual in a land of bushy, virile thickets. His grooming and clothes told of a personal vanity that had been enhanced by travel. His harp was a good one with a little hawk-head of silver that tilted this way and that as he played. All the same, Caterin wished that his pleasant voice would cease so that she could fish out any hard facts that might swim in this pond of fantasy. "They will be like wild boars for fierceness,

They will give no quarter to the Angles,

They will slay a hundred princes wearing golden torcs."

But when? And where? Tomorrow she must go south after him but there were many roads she could take. And time was precious.

"They will be as stinging serpents to the mongrel hosts,

They will bear off the honoured portions in the palace,

They will be honoured as long as there is a minstrel."

There was a swirl of movement and a refilling of drinking horns. Another voice took up the lay.

"When he came to the borderlands his fame was renowned,

He deserved his mead, the man with the silver chain,

He marshalled a bright shining array, the bold one,

He is leader of three hundred chiefs and their men,

The noble warrior of renowned spirit, the foreign horseman,

Riding his white steed, from beyond Bannog Burn."

The voice praised Gort and the voice was Eildon's. She rose to her feet, not caring how much attention she attracted. Her eyes on Eildon, she held her carnelian pendant high in the air so that it swung and caught the light.

Eildon's long fingers paused. The rhythm stammered then sounded forth again, stronger than ever. His eyes flickered over his audience. The planes of his face lengthened. He launched into a Pretani marching-song that the men knew and sang with him. At the finish, his opaque eyes met hers in a long look. "Aneirin," he called and the other bard took up his melody. Then he slipped into the jostling crowd and left the Hall.

Caterin followed and found a space on a low wall. On one side a soldier buffed a battered shield that had weathered many blows. On the other, a boy was hurriedly mending a tattered pennant with unskilled stabs of a needle, before the light finally faded from the sky. A man came and squeezed in at her back. She knew it was Eildon because of the clean earthy smell of him in the smoke and sweat-drenched air.

"What in the name of Dagda are you doing in this fox's lair with no Bodyguard?" It was a dreadful oath to name such a One. But he was using the pure Attecottie so maybe he would not be felled by a lightning bolt.

In the same language, she told him, wasting no words. He bent to slide his harp into its case of soft leather and lay it underneath his legs. This was no time to be called upon to entertain the drunken louts who reeled about the yard. "Then you can go home now," he told her. "At first light you can leave this stinking hole and its burden of toad-spawn. Tomorrow I'll ride to Gort myself with the warning of the Bull. It would look suspicious tonight, a lone horseman leaving for the south."

"No, the Wise Ones have sent me. There's more than just a warning to be given. The vision was clouded but the command was clear. Just tell me in which direction I must point my horse's head."

Light from a bundle of flaring rush-lights flared on their faces as servants ran to kindle the cruisies in the walls. Eildon hunched his knee up on the wall and turned his dark hooded eyes towards her.

"A darkness would overwhelm your spirit if you didn't do the bidding of the Powerful Ones," he agreed. "I'll go with you."

"Then tell me all you know," Caterin urged him.

"When Gort arrived, Mynyddog greeted him with a horn of mead and an abundance of bard-praises he'd picked up from Aneirin. You'll gather that bards are in demand on the crag of Dun Eidyn. Here are the bare bones of the story he told Gort. Ida of Bernicia was fortifying Bamburgh. Aelle of Deira took it as a direct threat. Mynyddog's been waiting for a year for such an excuse to separate these two allies. So he sent word to Aelle to meet his Gododdin force at Catraeth and together they would annihilate Ida. Aelle agreed but whether he'll turn against his own Saeson kind will depend on which King wields the heaviest stick, I'd say."

The boy hoisted his pennant, not much improved, on its pole and went off whistling.

"Full well Mynyddog knew he couldn't hold this lot together much longer, despite his hospitality. They say Gwlyged, the steward, has a marvellous drinking horn that never runs dry. There are full three hundred lords gathered here. Too many little jumped-up chieftains and their retinues that are sword-happy and plunder-hungry. Especially when they're pumped full of mead and praises every night. Aedan of Dal Riata sent nine Mormaers, twelve came from Eirean, the same from Aeron and Elfed. A contingent led by Cydywall even came by ship from south Gwynedd. They went south with Gort. They're not so bad. It's the ones from the Lothians, the Gododdin themselves, I wouldn't trust with my spare catgut." Eildon's thumbnail rasped on his chin, grating on her nerves, as he paused to think.

"Morcant's the one I doubt most. Dark and moody. Not unlike Gort in some ways but young and unseasoned. Envious of anyone who's ever spitted a sword through an enemy's gut. 'This is my battle and I should lead this expedition' he told Mynyddog. His voice is high-pitched like a bull-frog on a lily leaf. 'My lands extend as far as Bamburgh and east to Lindisfarne. With Lothian, Deira and Eidyn in it together we can destroy Bernicia without the help of the Pretani. I demand that you place me at the head of the army.'" Eildon broke off to draw in breath for a huge fearful sigh. "And that's the man who'll be at the back of Gort in the battle."

"He had the ear of some of the other chieftains. That was clear by the scraping of bootnails on the floor. But Mynyddog was ready for them. 'And next, no doubt we'll have a long line of princes putting forward their claim,' he said. 'Stop rattling like spoons in an empty cup and listen to me. You're all kin to one another. Half of you were got on kitchen wenches if the truth were told. You've bickered amongst yourselves since you were cubs in a pack. My eyes have not been blind this past year. There's not one of you has the stature to command this ragbag of conflicting loyalties. But this King of the Pretani is different. He'll take you all by the scruffs of your unwashed necks and make men of you.' It would have done your heart good to hear him, my lady, if it had not been for the fact that he was building a wall of resentment around Gort that not even an eagle could soar over."

There was nothing Gort could have said or done to take the bitter taste from that pill and they both knew it.

"By now Mynyddog had hold of the heifer's tail and wouldn't let go. 'If the Prince of Gwynedd can beckon Rhun to march over the Spine of the Country to join him so much the better' he said. 'How many allies can you call on to send a contingent, Morcant?' The men round the King were hiding smiles behind their hands. Morcant's well-known for picking fights with his allies so that the bards can sing of his prowess. Gort stood and listened to it all, as stiff as a spear in the ground. He left at dawn with the vanguard. Prince Cynon, son of Clydno of Eidyn was at his side, a frank and true-hearted youth, unlike his uncle Mynyddog. Small in size but whippy as a hunting hound." Eildon picked up his harp-case by its leather band and settled it comfortably on his back. "The rest of the army and the baggage train follow tomorrow. We'll ride with them. Come and sleep by me in the Hall for safety tonight."

Cynrain from Aer in the west was not averse to adding a bard and a physician to his train. Morcant rode out first down the steep road at the head of his young nobles in their burnished mail and plumed helmets, picking up his foot-soldiers on the way. Other leaders followed with their life-guards and troops. By the time the baggage mules and wagons fell in behind, the mud was churned under hundreds of hooves and marching feet. Caterin and Eildon merged with the physicians and bards, just one place in front of the rabble of cooks and servants.

The army cut westwards across the Pettaland uplands towards Crawford and down to Carlisle rather than venture down Morcant's Lothians where they would be exposing themselves to a whole line of Bernician coastal settlements. They took one of the old trading routes that led straight through a disused mile-castle on the Roman Wall. Passing through Penrith and Appleby, they were protected from the Angles by miles of hilly country all the way until they crossed Stanemoor and came down almost at Caetreth, plumb at the joining of the lands of Bernicia and Deira.

The baggage train and the foot-soldiers halted on raised ground. Far ahead they could see another encampment, its pennants flying. Caterin did not need to search for the Black Bull to know that Gort was there.

Morcant and the chiefs rode forward to consult with their Commander. There was no need to set up guards because the arrival of Mynyddog's army would not have taken the Bernicians by surprise. After all, he had trumpeted his intentions abroad for a whole year.

The journey had been long and weary, keeping to the slow pace of the mules and the foot-soldiers, with the cavalry strung out wide on either side of them. Nights of lying sleepless, frustrated by inactivity had persuaded Caterin that she had little chance of meeting up with Gort until part of his obligation had been fulfilled at least.

Eildon and she had made friends with Aneirin, the bard, riding daily with him, hearing tales of his journeys in foreign parts. In camp, Eildon tended to stay close to Caterin but Aneirin was always on the move. He divided his time among the various groups of men from different parts of the land, entertaining them and keeping their spirits high. In return, he demanded details about their chieftains that he could turn into praise-poetry when the battle was over.

There was nothing Aneirin could do to keep Caterin's spirits high. She had already seen one army go out from Tara seeking immortal glory to be crushed and it had left a scar on her memory. When Aneirin announced he was going into the forward camp to earn his mead, Caterin was faced with a difficult decision.

"Do we go with Aneirin to warn Gort?" she asked Eildon.

"The warning from the Wise Ones came to you," he replied. "What does your spirit tell you to do."

"That it's not right to send a man into battle with his head looking over his shoulder."

As it happened, the decision was taken completely out of their hands.

CHAPTER FORTY SEVEN

Caterin would not leave her pony and its precious panniers. So Eildon went scouting and came back, pulling at his long ears, shaking his head.

"The Bernician army's there all right, making camp already. And guess who are marching from the east to link up with them?"

"The Deirans! Blood called to blood in the end."

"Mynyddog's gamble's been lost before the battle's even started."

That night round the camp-fires, the boasting flowed as freely as the mead and Eildon and Aneiran excelled themselves in flattery. The empty words sang over and over in Caterin's brain. They had sounded brave and heart-stirring on the Hill of Tara. They had rung out with confidence in Dun Eidyn. Now, the echoes of the mead-merry voices were caught up by the chill damp wind to fade and die in the black oblivion of the night.

Next morning, the sun rose between cumulus clouds building into a promise of rain to come. Apart from the jangle of mail and the stamp of hooves, the men were silent as they prepared. Yet, when the chieftains swept forward they looked fair and gallant as though the sky would forever rain victories upon them. The foot-soldiers sang as they went, swinging their weapons in time with their marching feet. No Drui poured a libation nor carried a pennant before them. No Bishop spread his arms and prayed over this army. Only a gathering of crows wheeled silent overhead.

"I've always hedged round a battle," said Eildon, mounting, his harp aslant on his back. "But there's a King out there needs men with more than a song at the ready." He drew back his cloak and patted a short-sword. With a stiff-lipped smile he was off.

Cooks and servants, to a man, deserted the camp and took to the high ground to watch with the chariot-lads. Caterin wondered if they knew how vulnerable they were, with bare, flat ground all around them. Some memory of Tara led her to pack her belongings and to hide her pony in a clump of trees that had grown over an ancient barrow. Then she went forward to where the healers and doctors had set up a tending-station for the wounded, siting it on a grassy knoll where their flag could be clearly seen.

Once the instruments and salves had been laid out there was nothing else to do. Caterin and the others gathered to gaze on the enemy in the distance, covering the plain, a vast concourse of men, spreading like a flood from a burst dam. The army of the two Saeson Kings who had shelved their differences in the face of attack, now far outnumbered Mynyddog's matchless army.

Silence. Then the beating of chariots, low at first and then swelling, until the very air was a massive heartbeat and the heart-strings quivered. Then the slow advance to the beat of the chariots, quickening, and the high fierce yelling of war-cries, three hundred, all different. And over it all the long slow moan of the Saeson horns.

It was ghastly and predictable. First the crash of the meeting of shields and a rising cloud of dust. And only the sounds, resounding, rasping, splintering the air.

Then rolling back across the plain to the watchers, the first broken bodies. And the need to save life was upon them.

Gaping flesh and spouting blood. An arrow to be gouged, an axe-slash to be stitched. A body to be held, a leg to be sawn away. Mynyddog, the Wealthy, Mynyddog the Murderer!

They were broken dolls from her childhood, bits and pieces to be patched and sewn up and bandaged. To be cleared from the pallet for the next to be dragged in. And some reeled and staggered, back to their playground, to do Mynyddog's bidding, to follow his command. If she thought about it she would run. If she stopped working she would be sick. If she did not stop and think she would become less than human.

Outside a carrier laid a boy at her feet. He was dead, thrown away, like a used toy, discarded.

"What's happening?"

The carrier stood, spent, panting.

"We're being scattered like mice, slaughtered like hares."

She pressed a pad to the bleeding gash on his cheek.

"The bastards won't obey him. That King Brude. He signals to go forward, together, to attack. They hang back. Look for their own lord and mass round him."

He followed her under the shelter. Held a head while she gave a man poppy juice.

"Stands to reason, I suppose. If he'd had time at Dun Eidyn to break a few heads and flay a few backs, they'd follow him more readily. As it is, each ass-headed group is being hacked to pieces."

The man's head fell to the side.

"Aye, King Brude. What a man! Spitted one through the gut. Used his boot to pull his sword out, turned and took off the head of the one creeping up behind. He's a champion, that one, a god among warriors."

Caterin's breath caught. To liken him to a god was a bad omen.

"Here, hold his arms." She had found a needle and sinew. The flesh was slippery as she pressed the pieces together. The man was coming round again and juice was running short. She worked fast. It was all happening as Gort had feared, she thought, while she stabbed and pulled sinew through flesh. Mynyddog should have known. Men followed the leader they knew. She spread ointment and bound up the shoulder.

They lay on the ground, under her feet. Old men, staring at their boots, knowing they had fought their last battle. Young men, the ones who had sung of the fine free flow of the river of blood, watching their gut spill out on the ground. And the pain and the stench that drowned all thoughts of glory.

She was splinting a broken arm when the doctor in charge gave the order to move.

"The army's retreating. Fall back nearer the camp. Crawl if you have to, you men. And for pity's sake, bring the medecines."

As Caterin left the tent, supporting two wounded man, she saw the slaughter for herself in the distance. Each man of the Gododdin army was surrounded by three of the enemy, yet, not one turned to flee. And one by one, they fell.

For one incredible moment she saw Gort. From among a press of men and a forest of flying axes, his horse reared skyward. His sword was a blur as it flashed and bit. A body of huge fair giants rushed upon him from the rear. He whirled and attacked, cutting forward, forcing them back. He swung his sword in a bright arc and shouted for the army to follow him through. But the Gododdin men wavered. A pennant broke from out of the turmoil to the right. It was Morcant and the remains of his contingent as they turned to flee. The sky darkened as a shower of arrows flew from a thicket. A band of men had been stationed there for just such a break. Axes cleaving the air. Morcant would boast in his cups no more.

Pain seared her arm. The two men she carried, half-crazed by pain stumbled and fell, pulling her down. An explosion of light inside her head and nothing.

She opened her eyes on a dusk-filled landscape and a pale fitful moon, low on the horizon. She moved and a fiery pain stunned her into stillness.

A weight, a man who had fallen on top of her. A lifeless arm lay across his body. It was her own arm! She had been supporting him! An arrow sprouted from his back. But first it had pierced her flesh! They were impaled together!

Her horror mounted! Her mouth opened and twisted in a scream that was silent because if she took breath the pain would be more than she could bear.

She would have to remove the arrow that bound them together! No, she could never do it! Sickness gagged at her throat. She would lie until help came!

A rush of wings above, the cruel yellow beak and claws of a buzzard landing. The shock had her setting her teeth and twisting her body until she could grasp the handle of the dagger in her belt. Inching it out was painful enough but sawing, desperately, one-handed, at the shaft of the arrow was agony. That went on and on. Until the shaft split and the corpse fell away. Some of her flesh had gone with it but that was all. She was not bleeding badly. She would live. She had a task to perform.

Once the sting of the wound had settled into a dull ache, she cradled her wounded arm to her body and pulled herself up. The victors had done a good job of despatching the wounded. The man on her other side had a new gash in his neck. Weapons, belts and boots had gone. But the soldiers had not considered it worth stripping them of their clothes or they would have taken the blood-stained cloak that had hidden her.

The throbbing in her head sent her fingers probing to the back of her skull. There was a lump and a suspicious wetness. She dared not stay here. Once the blanket of darkness fell on the plain, other looters would come, to strip the corpses bare of everything the soldiers had left and not averse to finishing off anyone still alive. After them would come the wolves. The carrion crows were here already.

With an effort she dislodged the body on top of her. She bound docken leaves round her arm with stalks of grass. Anything was better than the filthy rags that littered the ground where the medical station had been. She staggered, shook her head and tried to collect her thoughts.

Her pony! He might just have been missed by the Saesons. And Gort! There was a chance he might have been taken prisoner by the Saesons thinking to ransom him. At least, if she found his body, she would know what word to take home. She shook her head, again and again and again to clear it. No, this was not right! This was not why the Bull had sent her! To crawl home defeated!

Muttering, whispering, nagging, forcing her body by words and will, she plunged forward into the horror of the battlefield, half-crazed by a burning obsession to find Gort.

Her feet squelched on ghastly unnameable things, as she turned over the death-distorted limbs of the lads who had danced at Dun Eydin.

Moaning Gort's name, scurrying, half-stooping, she peered into the grimacing masks of the lads who had toasted in mead.

A splintered harp-frame tore at her foot and she cried "Eildon! Eildon!" Hushed for ever the boasting and the proud dreams of glory.

They had chosen their pathway, those who had feasted and sung. Tonight they were food for the gory muzzles that snarled as she blundered past.

An arm waving, there to the left. A remnant of cloth in the wind. Again something writhed. Warily, warily, a step at a time. A pile of bodies, three or four deep. All was still. Then a moan! And she was among them, heaving, pushing the carcases out of the way letting them flop to the ground, grabbing the body by the rings of his mail-coat, her injured arm raging, ravens opening their beaks and cawing in fury. The tangled fair hair told her that this was not Gort. He was not bleeding and no bones were broken. There was nothing she could do except leave him to come to himself and tell her where he was wounded. She picked out a tree, stunted like the rest but whose dwarfish outline she would recognise again and laid him at its base.

A mist kept clouding her eyes. She tried to brush it away. It was weariness. She must find Gort before her strength gave out. And under her feet a dark figure reared and she screamed in her terror. A white waxy face floated before her. She recognised Aneirin, blood trickling down the side of his face and dripping from the point of his beard. With little mercy, she pulled him to his feet, guiding him through the tussocks and pointed him towards the other wounded man.

"The tree, Aneirin! Make for the tree and wait there!" With a last push she sent him on his way, hoping her words had penetrated his shocked brain.

By now it was quite dark. A bleak moon sheened the eerie scene with silver. On the far side of the plain, dark human shadows moved furtively. Fearsome skirmishes broke out at her side between scavenging birds and beasts. She knew that, in her forlorn quest, she was going over the same ground again and again.

A horse screamed as a crow tore at its flesh. She picked up a fallen dagger but the horse thrashed and died before she could reach it. She could not go on. A great wave of exhaustion came and her strength flowed from her. She wanted to sink to the ground. She swayed. The dagger in her hand was the only way out. With one thrust of her arm, she could free herself from pain, from ugliness, from this thankless quest.

A fatalistic calm came upon her. She took the dagger between her two hands and raised it above her head, directing the gleaming point straight at her breast. Escape. Above all else a dark place of peace. She took in a deep breath. It would be her last.

Then her spirit cried out in shame and in anger. And she longed for the plunge of the dagger. But her arms would not bend and the hilt would not move. Like the pin-point of a star the hilt suddenly gleamed as she grasped it again. Engraved on the hilt was a dragon with wings! With a cry she flung it from her.

Peace, have done with me! Let me be! I've done enough! There were other men from Gwynedd with dragons on their hilts! But her feet moved. In a circle. And she saw them. A heap of corpses. And if she pushed it the pile would topple. And their mouths opened and their eyes stared and their black hair swung as they fell. And not one had hair so silk and dear as the body that lay underneath them.

His beloved face was ashen. His sweet skin as chill as death. His side gaped. His sweet blood had flowed and dried on the grass. His fine hands lay lifeless, cold to her touch. Except for a pulse, faint but fluttering under her finger.

Throwing back her head and arms she howled her triumph to the sky. She was sure she heard the bellow of a bull in reply.

388

CHAPTER FORTY EIGHT

Caterin could not have told how long it took to drag Gort's body over the tufted grass. Incredibly, her pony had not been stolen. He was by the tree, up to his neck in the thicket, rolling his eyes at the two men who lay near him. Her breath tore at her lungs, her muscles screamed at every movement. Still she dared not rest. The lives of all three men now lay in her hands. She had to get them away from this ill-fated place before dawn.

Two broken spears tied with her own blanket made a carrier that would trail at the back of her pony.

"Help me, Aneiran, you're not wounded!"

His beard went up. He shuffled forward and helped her to tie the two men into the rough-and-ready litter. Then he mounted the pony and looked down his nose as she took the bridle. She lead them north towards the base-camp, the cloying stench of spilled blood following them all the way.

Staggering and falling, her head swimming dangerously, she knew that the past few hours had drained her of strength. She would have given anything for the flagon of mead she had left back at the camp. Surely she would find other survivors there for she desperately needed help.

She was almost through the camp before she recognised it. She stopped and stared for there was little left. Scattered tent-poles stood stark out of the ground between burnt-out fires. Even the very coverings had been ripped off. It was a desolate scene, empty of stores, mules and men. In grim silence, she threaded her way through the wreckage, noting by the traces in the mud that a party of horsemen had passed through at a gallop. The bodies of two young grooms lay, struck down as they had turned to escape. Afterwards the local inhabitants had crept in, descending on the tents like a column of ants, systematically emptying them of their contents and driving off the wagons. Even the remains of the morning meal had vanished.

Tying the pony to a forlorn tent-pole, she left Aneirin still dozing on its back. Their first need was food if they were to have any chance of survival. She found a trail of bannocks, dropped by some scavenger clutching more than he could carry. Some were trodden into the ground but she gathered the rest. A vixen erupted from under a tent, dragging the skinned body of a hare that some luckless soldier had hoped to enjoy on his return. She burrowed under the collapsed canvas and found another.

"Come on, Aneirin," she urged. "Help me to rig up a shelter."

Aneirin raised heavy lids from red-rimmed eyes and dropped to the ground. Between them they made a make-shift tent and laid the men in it. Picking her way among the debris, she found more treasures, tucked into dark corners, a battered pot, some flints and a water container. She pounced on them as though they were gold. Taking one simple task at a time, she kindled some dry twigs in the ashes of an old cooking fire and set the hare on to stew. Only then could she start thinking about the men. Gort was the most seriously hurt and she had no compunction about attending to him first.

Lying on his back, his lips tinged blue, he looked as though he had gone. Her own cloak covered him but his body was chill to the touch.

"Heat flat stones in the fire and lay them around the men," she told Aneirin. "Move, you lazy luckless poet!" She had to bully the bard into moving to keep the blood pounding in his veins or he would sink back into that shocked apathy that frightened her. It was a sword that had opened his side but its impetus had been deflected by his lower ribs. She eased away his jacket and slit his trousers from waist to thigh. The oozing wound gaped, red and angry, white fleshy lumps protruding from it. It took all her strength to pull Gort's boots off and lay the warmed stones at his feet.

Her medecine pouches were still safe and dry against the flanks of the pony. She pulled the flesh together and stitched it, tying one stitch at a time as she had been taught and smeared on unguent of nettle.

"Right, bard," she said, padded it firmly. And he lifted the long heavy body as she bandaged it.

The movement must have sent pain lancing through Gort's wound for she saw his lips clench. When she placed a smooth stone under his head for a pillow, the hollow eyes opened. Whether he knew her she cared not. He left her again whether into sleep or unconsciousness she could not tell. He had lost a great deal of blood and there was a fearsome lump on his temple. She set Aneirin to hold a damp pad on the swelling and went to examine the other man. By this time a savoury smell from the pot was beginning to waft around them.

The eyes of the young man opened at once as soon as she smoothed back the fair tumbled curls from his forehead. His flesh felt softer and warmer than Gort's. He lay back, yielding to her touch as she cut the sleeve at the shoulder where his blood stained the fine leather. An axe-blow had made this wound and it may have sliced sinews that would mean he would never hold a sword again. Working quickly she padded and bound his wound. Judging by the tattered remnants of his clothing, he was a young man of wealth and standing. Pale bands on his fingers and bleeding knuckles showed where rings had been forced off his fingers by looters. She returned to Aneurin and felt gently over his skull where the brown hair was matted with blood.

"Your brains aren't spilling out," she told him, trying to make him smile. Slightly unfocused eyes squinted at her. "You'll have a head-ache for a few days, that's all." It was the best she could do.

The hare broth with its floating slivers of meat and sprinkling of herbs put heart into them all. Even Gort managed to swallow a few mouthfuls.

As she rose from his side, she saw that a grey dawn had arrived. Yet, there was still the pony to tend. At long last she threw herself down and slept. Curled on the hard earth, one bloody arm outflung, she did not hear the baying of wolves, the groans of the men. Nor yet the cheeping of sparrows hopping among the carnage that man wrought upon man.

It was Aneirin who shook her awake and held her mouth so that she would not cry out. There was an insistent tearing sound that she recognised but could not place. When Aneirin raised his head above their shelter, a bleating broke out and small hooves pattered away, panic-stricken.

"That was a shepherd boy ferreting around." Aneirin squatted beside her. His eyes were clearer but he winced when he moved his head. "When he goes back to his village the word will go round that there are survivors here." She saw he had tied a dirty rag round a wound on his leg and automatically sat up to examine it. He pushed her hands away. "Don't you understand? We have to get out of here fast or the Deirans will be after us."

She sat back and considered.

"Where do we go? If we go straight north we're in Lothian and that's worse. The dynasties will have heard of Morcant's death and be at one another's throats again." She thought for a minute. "Westwards we'll come to Rheged where we might find shelter. Let me look at the men first."

"The Prince is awake but weak."

"Prince?" Caterin's eyes had flown automatically to Gort where he lay still, breathing heavily.

"Prince Cynon of Eidyn, Mynyddog's nephew." Aneirin gestured at the fair-haired man. Sure enough, his cheeks had a faint tinge of colour.

"Get the pony and the litter ready then. You'll have to walk today. We can't burden the pony more than necessary." Aneirin twitched a sulky shoulder. It was plain he disliked being ordered by a woman. No matter. He could make his own way home if that was how he felt.

Gort's skin had a deathly pallor that worried her. The lips of his wound were pressed together but around the stitches, the skin had an ugly look as though it might fester. If she had had more time and water she could have brewed him an infusion to fight the poison. As it was she could only squeeze the last of the water between his lips before hoisting him onto the litter. Prince Cynon was there already but the effort had sapped his strength. Aneirin twisted his fingers in the mane of the pony to keep himself from stumbling as they moved off.

Caterin's mind blanked out the details of that journey for ever after. She laboured only to put one foot in front of the other as they climbed narrow sheep-tracks in the foot-hills or deer-trails through the forests. Her grinding tiredness kept her going for she knew if she stopped she would be unable to start again.

She seemed to have walked for ever in a half-dream when she saw in front of her a lonely steading with a low turf-roofed dwelling and a wooden barn at the back. A woman was milking a white goat in a wattled enclosure. She looked up as the goat shied and gave warning of their approach. Wiping her hands on her apron, she stood up to face them.

"May the Radiant Ones shine on your hearth," said Caterin, searching for the right language.

"God bless you, strangers," said the woman. She had the new Faith but the age-old wariness of any traveller until he had declared himself. Her narrowed eyes moved over the three wounded men and the weary boy who led them.

"Who's the King in these parts?" asked Caterin.

"Urien's our over-lord, and protects us well though we're on the borders of his land." It was a warning. Her tone said she would have to know more about a traveller from the land of the Saesons who spoke with a barely intelligible accent.

"I bring three men wounded in the battle with the Saesons. Can I buy some goat's milk and a night's shelter in the barn?" She dug deeply in her pouch, coming up with a pair of silver earrings, worth much more than she had asked for. The woman's face closed.

"We came by this silver honestly for these are Princes who lie wounded here." "And likely to have a pack of Saeson horsemen after them in that case." She came and stood at the gate, her stolid body barring their way.

"One of them is Prince Gort of Gwynedd, brother of Rhun." Her voice was cracking with desperation.

The deep dark eyes studied the wan faces.

"My son fought with Rhun last year. He was wounded and died, trying to flee across the moor. Not a body there opened a door to him." Her voice was flat and unemotional as though her griefs had left her empty. Then she opened the gate and led them round to the barn, even helping to bundle straw together for beds before she disappeared. Later, she brought a crock of milk, warm from the udder but refused the earrings.

"I've no use for them. They'd only bring suspicion on my goodman if he tried to sell them," she said.

Later, her husband came to look them over, setting his thickset bulk foursquare in the doorway.

"Aye, we heard there'd been a battle. The talk in the steadings is that the Saesons left no survivors."

The suspicion was plain in his voice but Caterin had no answer for him. She had too much to do to renew dressings and try to feed the milk to Gort. Aneirin's leg was swelling now after walking so far.

The farmer rubbed his chin and left. To ride to the nearest village and carry news of the strangers, thought Caterin. But he came back with warm water and cloths, his wife at his back bearing a chicken stew.

Later, when the three men had fallen asleep, Caterin sat beside Gort to eat. He was tossing and turning and opening his wound.

His skin had the look of lard and glistened with sweat. She made a strong brew of dried crottle from her pouch, forcing him to drink it and bathed his inflamed sores with what remained. Afterwards she took his head on her breast and he seemed to fall into a more restful sleep. The black winged dragon, gleamed with his sweat as it lay on his breast, rising and falling with each tortured breath.

It was time, she judged, to put herself and her burden in the hands of Bride otherwise the men might die of exposure. She took Gort's dragon amulet and eased herself away.

Outside in the yard, the farmer and his wife were doing the last chores of the day, shutting the hens in their shed and fetching water from the well.

"I told you that one of the men is the Prince of Gwynedd," said Caterin. The couple stared at her owlishly. "I want someone to take this token to King Rhun and tell him that his brother's here and grievously wounded."

"Would that today was yesterday and there was a son in the house to send on such an errand," the man muttered. He turned to go back to the house.

"Then tell me where to go!" cried Caterin. "That's my husband in there, dying of fever!"

The man paused and his mouth gaped.

"I'm Queen of the Pretani. Mynyddog forced Rhun's brother to lead his army." She waited proud and tall while they stared at her dirty face and boy's clothes.

"Right enough, there were Pretani marks on the earrings," said the woman. "Rhun's brother? Get on the nag, man, and get to Blackford fast. The chief there will send word to Rhun." Tears fell from Caterin's eyes as she went back to the barn to wait.

And while they waited, Aneirin began to mourn. His fingers stretched unthinkingly for a harp that was not there. He hid his face in his hands.

"Rali, Rali, my precious one, tuned to my golden voice, lying shattered now in your soft needlework case."

Suddenly, he threw back his head and sent his light voice ringing out with force, piercingly sweet and high-toned as only he could sing.

"This is the 'Gododdin'; Aneirin sings it.

"The men went to Catraeth, fierce in their laughter, the pale mead was their feast.

Bitter with spears in battle, with red blades in dark-blue sockets, their metal shortened their lives.

I have lost a friend to whom I was loyal, one swift in the struggle, ever foremost."

His voice rose and fell like a woman keening. Each verse praised a man Aneirin had known and loved.

"The son of Bogodad, the deeds of his hand wrought vengeance.

Rheithfyw, the pillar of battle, delighted in giving gifts.

The young son of Cian, his was the bravest station in combat."

He sang in the Votadini tongue. Prince Cynon stirred, groaning, and turned over on his side to listen. Aneirin tried a different opening for his verses.

"The men went to Catreath with the dawn.

They drank sweet, yellow ensnaring mead.

May their spears never be cleansed, the retinue of Mynyddog the Luxurious.

When Tudfwlch the Tall arrived, the strengthener of his people, there was a slaughtering in that place of spears.

Before Erthgi, armies groaned, he was a fence of shields.

Blaen reclined on his cushions, delighting in gold and purple and well-fed horses, he was a bear in the pathway.

Long biers carried off bloodstained men. It was a pitiful fate that was doomed for them.

Though we drank bright mead by the light of tapers, though its taste was good, its bitterness was long-lasting."

Caterin could hardly bear to listen to the heart-breaking cadences. Like the mead they brought a bitter after-taste. She rose and went to the doorway. The night was black and still, so still that she could hear the beating of her heart. Feathery fingers touched her face and she knew it was the first snow of the cold season. Her heart grieved for Eildon who had vanished without trace. Was he even now making his way home? Or would his name one day be heard in the dirge of Aneirin. She thought of Little Blackpoll and wondered if she would ever hold him close again. Her eyes were drawn to his father. She could just see him through the doorway in the dimly lit barn. A dark stubble hid the white hollowed cheeks. A long strand of hair lay across his forehead. He looked utterly defenceless. She caught her breath, loving him so much, it was a pain at her heart. Along with the surge of her love, there came a tingling of the Life-Force in her palms and her fingers. She laid one hand on his breast and one on his forehead and asked that the healing of the All-Mother should flow through her.

Aneirin had begun a new set of verses. The pauses between the phrases were longer as though at times his sadness was too heavy to bear.

"You drank mead and wine in the palace Your drinking horns were handsome in the Hall of Eidyn,

You were a winged stallion in battle. Three battle-horsemen of Eidyn of the many goldsmiths, three hosts wearing mail-coats, three lords wearing gold torques, three battle-peers bounding forwards together, three in hardship like gold in the close-packed battle, three lords of the people who sprang from the Britons.

Breichior the Fierce was world-famed. The son of Sywno sold his life that his glory might be told forth. Their frenzy was appeased before the grave of Cydywal had a green surface."

It was fleeting impressions of people that he portrayed, appealing to the ear and emotions rather than to the understanding.

As Caterin, too, grieved for Eildon, her tears fell on Gort's face. He opened his eyes and he smiled. His lips moved. She leaned over him and caught the words on his breath.

"Some day I will fill my embrace with you again."

It was as though a doorway had opened in her heart and the sun had poured in. This was the man who had awakened her to love. There was nothing she would not do now to keep him alive so that they might share the years ahead.

It was evening of the next day when they heard the hoofbeats. Caterin ran to open the door.

"Stay hidden!" warned Aneirin. "It's too soon for it to be Rhun." But he was wrong.

A troop of horsemen milled around the wattle gate. Their rangy, dark-browed leader was alighting from his horse and following the pointing finger of the woman. He strode towards the barn, throwing back his cloak, and went past Caterin straight to where Gort lay asleep. With a gentle hand for such a big man, he felt the heat of Gort's forehead. He folded back the cover and studied the clean bandages on his side.

These were the two men she had feared for so long. Now she loved one and sought help from the other.

Straightening, Rhun turned to Caterin and put his hands on her cheeks. Eyes, bluer than Gort's, searched her face. Before he spoke, he had to clear his throat.

"My dear sister," he said. It was unexpected and infinitely more welcome than the formal phrases of greeting.

"He needs help." Her voice was a mere croak.

"We'll not move him tonight. You've done more than was humanly possible. Leave him to the All-Mother for a few hours more."

Meanwhile, Rhun's men were busy. They had borrowed an axe and felled trees to make a proper litter for the wounded men. They went hunting into the forest and brought back wildfowl to cook over their fire. Rhun sat on a log, talking to Caterin.

"I must have heard the call of the Ever-Living Ones," he said. "I was checking my borders to make sure that no plundering Saesons had spilled over into my lands chasing the remnants of Mynyddog's army. We're kin to the Gododdin through our ancestor Cunnedda. I sent to Urien of Rheged to warn him what I was about. It was he who told me there had been no survivors. Tell me, how did my brother come to be mixed up in this?"

Caterin told him how Gort had had to fulfill his duty, how she had been warned by the Royal Bull, how she had found him among the dead.

That night, Aneirin was in a mood for rejoicing, thinking that he would soon be back in Dun Eidyn. He sang for the ear of the young Prince who was able to sit beside him. It brought a brightness to his sad, shadowed eyes to hear the bard praise him.

"Never was hall built so durable.

Cynon of the generous heart, the bejewelled prince, he sat at the end of the couch.

Very sharp were his spears; with lime-white shield hacked small, he burst through armies;

Breathless in the presence of a girl, he earned his mead."

Everyone knew Prince Cynon's sweetheart was the daughter of Urien. Shyly he hid his blushing cheeks in his hands.

"Never was hall built so faultless;

How bountiful, in fury like a lion, most widely travelled was Cynon, the noble and most fair;

His war-cry on the farthest wings was like a fortress;

He slew the enemy with the sharpest blade, like rushes they fell before his hand;

Son of Clydno of enduring fame, to you, lord, I sing; fame without bounds; without limits."

Aneirin knew he would have a brooch for his praise-song but it was no matter. It was the resonance of the syllables that he listened to and relished.

CHAPTER FORTY NINE

The next day they crossed southern Rheged to Rhun's castle at Dynas on the coast. Caterin was received by Rhun's wife, Angharad and saw Gort handed into the care of the best doctors that Rhun could summon. As soon as the healers had left, Caterin slipped quietly into his room, unwilling to leave the caring of his daily needs to servants.

He lay in a great bed-chamber with a wide window facing southward towards snow-capped mountains, purpled with shadows. Painted walls carried the landscape around the walls and out again. The bed was of blackwood, carved with leaping deer and running hounds. He leaned against white herb-pillows. Silver fox skins lined with purple covered him. She had only ever seen him asleep in her own cosy childhood room at home. This was a chamber fit for a King. They would have one as grand as this when they returned.

Fever still stained his cheek-bones but that was better than a deathly pallor. She drew a stool to his bedside. Without opening his eyes, he held out his hand, in the most natural way in the world. His skin was warm to her touch but healthy. His grip was firm. His lashes lay in dark curves on his cheeks. Shout for joy, little Blackpoll, your father's coming home.

"Is it true?" he whispered.

"Is what true?"

"That only three came back?" Deira and Bernicia had boasted that Mynyddog's army had been wiped out to a man.

"Yes."

He sighed. "I warned him." His hand fell limp. But he was sleeping, peacefully.

Later he stirred and murmured. She leaned forward.

"We must go home soon. We have a Kingdom waiting. And a boy growing up. And you and I. We have some living to do."

She laid her hand on his heart feeling the steady throb of it. All the love that she bore for this man came welling up into her breast. They had years before them that would be richer and more fulfilling than any that had gone before. She urged the health and strength that sang in her blood to pass into his body to make him whole again.

Two nights later, he was strong enough to have Aneirin and the Prince in his room for an hour. They were leaving the next day for Dun Eidyn, riding overland with a party of monks going north to join Abbot Kentigern on the Clyde. They would never have a safer escort to go through Riderch's land. So, Caterin heard Aneirin's poem all through in the language of his listeners while he played on a borrowed harp. The ending amused her.

"Never was hall built so famous.

When Cydywal hastened out he raised the battle-cry with the green dawn:

He showered ash spears from his hand, from his slender chestnut horse;

Because of his pledge, he charged forwards in the forefront of the men from Gwynedd.

The men who went to Catraeth they were famous;

Wine and mead from golden vessels was their drink for a year;

Three men and three-score and three hundred chieftains wearing golden torques;

Of those that hastened forth after the choice drink, none escaped but three, through feats of combat;

The battle-hound of Gwynedd and Cynon the well-born and I, with my blood streaming down, for the sake of my brilliant poetry.

Gododdin, I claim your support in the valleys beyond the ridges, a youth desirous of silver without reproach.

Thus Aneirin, the son of Dwywai, the gentle one, the courteous one, the rampart of battle -

Aneirin and his poetry were not to be parted.

When Aneirin is killed, all poetry in Gododdin will come to an end but his poetry will live on and his fame with it."

Gort smiled with his eyes at Caterin. The lamps in the bed-chamber were burning low. Aneirin and Prince Cynon made their farewells and they were alone again, holding hands.

"His vanity would not let him tell how a woman bullied him back to life and music," said Gort.

"Veleda foretold it." Caterin smiled at him. "Bard-songs are shooting stars. Life is having your feet on the Mother and your loved ones around you."

A strange peace came to Gort. Now he could tell her. Now he could open the door of his heart and let his feelings come through.

"Bard-songs came between us. Oh, my dear, how I misjudged you."

"Love is stronger when it's freely given."

"You saved my life. My house is honoured, wife of my heart."

"And the woman with the perfumed breast. And the star brilliant in her hair?"

"A dream woman." His voice was fading. "I've a real one. One who braves the wolves to rescue her man. One who sews his wounds and cleans his filth. Her breast is sweetest to my lips." He was asleep. She blew out the lamps and sat by him in the darkness, content.

They were back at Dalgynch before Gort declared his love for her. And he made a public offering of it for all the people to hear.

It was in the Banqueting Hall where he sat in the King-seat. Tonight he wore the King-robe although there were no guests to honour. The silver chain of Kingship girdled his waist. Rubies flashed as he signalled. A flagon cut from a solid piece of polished jasper was brought. It lay on the table beside the silver and gold Loving Cup. The King stood and poured golden mead from the flagon into the Cup. A snap of his fingers and a harp played softly in the hush that had fallen in the Hall. Gort raised the Cup and spoke across the music in a voice resonant with deep emotion.

"When I first met you, Queen of my heart, you strode proud and tall through my dreams. Your hair sprang golden like mead flowing from the flagon. The glitter of the yellow mead that I drank among the tapers in Dun Eidyn was dimmed by the brightness of your glance."

Caterin hid her surprise better than the others in the Hall. Their eyebrows shot up and their eyes glanced sideways. The bards told how Princes wooed and won their ladies. No lover sang of the beauty of love itself.

"Since we came together, no wild honey tastes sweeter than the touch of your lips. Even the after-taste is full-bodied and satisfying. You quench my thirst like a cool draught after the battle."

He did not speak with the measured beat of the harpist. Yet it was poetry and came straight from his heart.

"Like the ensnaring mead you were stronger than wine. Your body was taut from the hunt like the grip of mead on the tongue. Your eyes met mine straight and cool like the clasp of mead on the throat."

The harper hushed. Gort's own voice was all the music that Caterin needed.

"No champion has been deserving of a greater portion of mead. No warrior has earned the horn of mead with greater honour. No liegeman paid better for the sweet mead of life."

"May your sons and daughters honour their mother as I honour her now."

His eyes met hers with a secret smile above the rim of the Loving Cup as he raised it to his lips.

HISTORICAL NOTE

Since most Pictish records have been either destroyed or altered, I have had to work from the histories written by their enemies. These records were invariably biased. Still I enjoyed reading behind the lines to gain insight into the Picts themselves.

My main resource has been the Pictish Symbol Stones themselves, many of which are to be found in the Dark Age Sculpture Collection in the Museum of Antiquities, Queen Street, Edinburgh.

Since the word 'Pit' is Pictish for a piece of land I have used farm-names with this prefix as the places in my novel.

The name 'Dalgynch' was given in an old book as the Southern Capital. When I visited the local farm of this name I found myself on a ridge from which I could view the Pentland Hills, the estuary of the Forth and the Grampians. What better place for monitoring movements of ships or troops and for spying beacons?

I had to telescope the timescale in order to fit the historical events into the life-span of my heroine. The probable dates of the events are as follows*-

550 Kingdom of united by Bridei
560 Feis of Tara and Battle of Cul Drebene
565 Columba visited Bridei
584 Bridei killed
605 Raid by Mynyddog and the Gododdin
Note that 'dd' is pronounced 'th'.

SOURCES

A History of the English Church; Bede
The Picts; Isabel Henderson
The Symbol Stones of Scotland; Antony Jackson
The Archaeological Guide to Scotland; Euan W. Mackie
The Age of Arthur; John Morris
A Celtic Miscellany; Ed. Betty Radice
Picts; Anna Ritchie
The Pictish Nation, Its People and its Church; A.B.Scott
The Orkneyinga Saga; Snorri Sturbison
The Problem of the Picts; Ed. F.T. Wainwright